NIGHT SWIMMING

NIGHT SWIMMING

ROBIN SCHWARZ

WARNER BOOKS

NEW YORK   BOSTON

Song lyrics on page 162 are from "Smile," music by Charles Chaplin. Words by John Turner and Geoffrey Parsons, copyright © 1954 by Bourne Co. Copyright renewed. All rights reserved. International copyright secured.

Warner Books

Time Warner Book Group
1271 Avenue of the Americas, New York, NY 10020
Visit our Web site at www.twbookmark.com.

Printed in the United States of America
First Printing: June 2004
10 9 8 7 6 5 4 3 2 1

Library of Congress Cataloging-in-Publication Data

Schwarz, Robin.
    Night swimming / Robin Schwarz.
        p. cm.
    ISBN 0-446-53253-3
    1. Overweight women—Fiction. 2. Los Angeles (Calif.)—Fiction. 3. Women swimmers—Fiction.
4. Bank robberies—Fiction. 5. Terminally ill—Fiction. 6. Swimming pools—Fiction. 7. Weight
loss—Fiction. I. Title.
    PS3619.C488N54 2004
    813'.6—dc22   2003021176

Book design by Giorgetta Bell McRee

To my father, who gave me my love for words,
and to my mother, who told me to take typing as a backup.
I love you both, dearly.

ACKNOWLEDGMENTS

*F*IRST AND FOREMOST, I would like to thank Jim Patterson for his unending support. He not only offered his invaluable advice and encouragement, he took me under his wing as well. His immeasurable generosities included an invitation to join him on his book tour. A simple thank-you seems greatly insufficient. Suffice it to say that I will be forever grateful.

I would also like to thank my dear and closest friend Laurie Garnier, who unfailingly read every draft (and there were several) and who provided countless ideas and insights that enriched the story in so many, many ways. I wish to thank attorney Millie Wayland for her legal expertise and continual magnanimity and Richard Viets, a U.S. Marshall, who patiently explained the workings of our criminal justice system. Thanks to Irene Markocki, who never lost faith; Janet Wollman, Shana Kelly, Fran Marzano, Tanya Gunther, Joe Smookler, Rob Snyder, Linda Kaplan. Thanks to Flag Tonuzi for his beautiful cover; Michael Carr for his copyediting extraordinaire; Penina Sacks, my production editor, who is a pearl of a girl; Le Biarritz for the countless hours I sat in there writing, rewriting, drinking, rewriting; David Schneiderman; Carter Campbell; Megan Rickman; Christine Price; Scott Mills; Stuart Pittman; Emily Nurkin; Dr. Tom Pearce and Dr. Charles Hatem (to whom I owe a long-overdue thank-you and who in no way represent the doctor portrayed in this book). To my dear friend Sally Chapdelaine, who offered excellent suggestions in making *Night Swimming* an even better swim. A special thanks to Dick Duane who championed my efforts well before *Night Swimming* was even a trickle. And to my wonderful agent, Suzanne Gluck, who took me on, believed in me, and made all the hard work worth every word. Finally, a big, big thank-you to my fabulous editor, Caryn Karmatz Rudy, whose sharp mind and tender counsel was vital in guiding me through. Her suggestions always and only made this book better and better and better. And I promise you, Caryn, I will not make any more changes to *Night Swimming*. And when they are on the shelves in bookstores, I will not take them down one by one, rewriting sentences I think would be better if only there had been an "a" instead of a "the" or that the sky should have had more stars or less stars or no stars at all. Let the stars fall where they may, and thank you all.

NIGHT SWIMMING

There came a time when the risk to remain tight in the bud was more painful than the risk it took to blossom.

—ANAÏS NIN

CHAPTER 1

*C*HARLOTTE CLAPP hated going to the doctor. All 253 pounds of her hated going to the doctor. Especially Dr. Jennings. Handsome, young, single Dr. Jennings—the most successful and eligible bachelor in town. Of course, in a town as small as Gorham (population fifteen hundred, including newborns) the competition was slim.

Charlotte considered why Dr. Jennings chose to settle in Gorham. He wasn't born here, and most people who are, set their sights on getting out. There must be something wrong with him under all that perfection. Why else would he be here in Gorham—in other words, nowhere? Gorham boasted one tiny two-man police station, a post office, a 7-Eleven, a fish plant, a church, a Bickfords restaurant, a bowling alley, a beauty parlor, a bank, one school, one doctor, one gas station, and an upside-down stop sign that had been swinging from its hinge for months. Summer or winter, most of Charlotte's neighbors found their entertainment by staying home and watching TV. Living in Gorham was like watching paint dry.

Charlotte Clapp had lived in Gorham her whole life, all of it in a small house on Middle Street. Middle Street—even the name was neither here nor there. It wasn't the beginning of anything or the end. It was simply and unremarkably the middle. And this middle was where she lived, floating in what felt like a long and everlasting in-betweenness.

Charlotte looked around Dr. Jennings's waiting room. Two other people waited there as well. A woman was knitting a scarf that was so long, she could throw it out of a window during a fire to save herself. Next to her sat a man with an utterly nondescript face, notable only for its extreme thinness. Charlotte held up her wrists and squinted to compare them to the man's scrawny pipe-cleaner neck. Was it possible her wrists were wider?

This depressing thought reminded her that she would soon have to disrobe for the fantastically fit Dr. Jennings. She shuddered. If only there were another way to have a physical. Virtual physicals. Yes, why hadn't someone thought of that yet? They probably had. It was likely they existed everywhere except in Gorham. *But how would I know, having never left the zip code?* And then he appeared, Sir Doctor Jennings, white coat and all, looking like a Nobel Prize winner or, worse yet for Charlotte, Dr. Kildare. She stood up to enter the examining room. *I don't care what anyone says; I'm not going to get on the scale. That's for damn sure.*

"Good morning, Charlotte," he said, motioning her in. Charlotte paused, aware of just how much room was left in the doorway in order for her to pass. None. He moved.

"Take a seat and relax," he said, motioning to the chair. "I'll be back in a minute."

The nurse handed her a paper nightgown. "Change into this, honey, and leave the opening at the back." Charlotte stared at the flimsy garment before her. It was a joke. She could use it as a handkerchief or a handy wipe or something to line the inside of a gift box with, but certainly not as a cover up. Calista Flockhart? Maybe. Charlotte? No. The armholes in the gown were no bigger than the holes you'd find in Swiss cheese. She tore them open, leaving her backside exposed like the state of Texas. Now all that was left to feel sick about was the reemergence of Dr. Jennings. Handsome, single Dr. Jennings. It would be an awful visit: He'd come in and ask her to sit up, when she was already sitting up. He was probably outside that door right now, dreading the prospect of having to touch any part of her. Why else would he be taking so long to return? Charlotte sat as straight as she could but still had more folds than a blanket stuffed in a trunk. She wondered if Dr. Jennings talked about how fat she was to other people.

I have this patient who is incredibly obese. I was thinking of suggesting that she get her stomach stapled.

And then he'd be off to an office supply store to get the necessary equipment. Hammers, nails, sump pumps. *Oh, Charlotte, stop thinking like this. He's a professional. Act normal.*

Finally, there was a knock at the door, and Dr. Jennings entered. Charlotte's resolve to act normal evaporated like steam disappearing from a teacup.

Oh, God, don't look at me. If the blind can read braille, surely you can just close your eyes and figure it out.

"Why are you in a gown?" he asked, to Charlotte's surprise.

"The nurse told me to change."

"I don't need to examine you; I only need to talk to you about the tests we took last week. They just came in today."

Thank you, God.

"But, since you've already changed, we can talk like this."

"Maybe I should just change anyway."

"No, that's not necessary. I have some things to go over with you. Please, why don't you sit over here," he said, pointing to a chair.

"No, I'm fine." *If I move off this table, this thing will rip open like the Grand Canyon. Jennings will try to hide his eyes, but he won't be able to, because everywhere he looks, there I'll be, filling the whole room with mountains of flesh. My cleavage alone could be a danger to him. He could fall into it like a crevasse and never be heard from again. And then the room will go dark while my behind blocks the sun like an eclipse.*

"No, really, I'm fine up here on the table. It's comfortable, in fact."

"Okay. Well, Charlotte, I have some rather upsetting news. We got the results from the blood tests you took, and they weren't exactly what I'd call good."

Dr. Jennings's voice delivered these words as if he were placing a dinner order. It sounded as matter-of-fact as "Oh, and no butter on the scrod . . . I like it dry." Charlotte stared at him, watching his mouth move but only heard the slow, syrupy sound of bass notes pull his lips apart like taffy.

"Charlotte, we checked and rechecked the lab results, but I'm afraid it looks unquestionably like cancer."

Dr. Jennings continued, but Charlotte's brain was stuck on one word. The *C* word, the unmentionable disease she had feared since the first time her mother sat her down eight years ago and softly, ever so softly, told her the terrible news that Charlotte had already known but simply could not face. The *C* word only meant one thing, and that was death.

". . . and so, Charlotte, I am in the unfortunate position to have to tell you that, as I see it, you have a year."

She had gone in last week for a routine physical. No big deal, just a tune-up really, as if she were having her car inspected. Then this morning she had received a call from Dr. Jennings's nurse.

"Can you come in today, Miss Clapp? Dr. Jennings needs to do a follow-up with you."

A follow-up? Of course, this made sense. An efficient doctor, must be routine. Nothing to worry about. Certainly nothing to prepare her for the news she'd just received.

No, this couldn't be right. This had to be someone else's news, not hers, not thirty-four-year-old Charlotte Clapp's. Her life might be boring, but it was predictable. And this . . . this had not been predicted. And yet here was Dr. Jennings, cool, self-assured, twenty-nine-year-old Dr. Jennings, doling out fates like a postal worker tossing letters into the correct address bins.

"One year, Charlotte . . . one year," Jennings repeated. Or maybe he hadn't. Maybe she only thought she'd heard it again, as the words were irrevocably lodged in her brain, echoing over and over like a distant drum of doom.

For the first time in months she forgot about how fat she was. Weight seemed gigantically unimportant now, like losing a button or missing a bus.

"I know how difficult this is to hear, Charlotte, particularly after your mother's own passing."

You don't know anything. You have no idea how I feel. You with your sixteen-inch neck and penny loafers.

"Is there anything that can be done?"

"Unfortunately, it's exactly what your mother had."

"What does that mean?"

"There's nothing to be done. Medicine just hasn't advanced as quickly as it needs to."

Charlotte stared at the clip on his tie. A stupid thermometer. Probably rectal.

Up until now her life had been as tedious as water dripping from a faucet, drop after drop, day after day, year after year. It was as steady and monotonous as the white noise coming from the freezers of the fish plant at the end of her street—the endless hum of refrigeration to keep the dead fish fresh. This is exactly how she felt. She was going to die—and she hadn't yet lived.

The years rolled over her like a dark intractable wave that suddenly made her feel like she had to swim for her life. So on that very same day, without the hint of hesitation, she walked into the bank where she had worked for fifteen years, and quit.

CHAPTER 2

*C*HARLOTTE LAY IN BED, staring at the ceiling, recalling the dark canopy of gloom hovering over her mother's final hours. Even in death, Charlotte thought of her mother as lucky, at least luckier than she was. Her mother had found love, borne a child, and accepted the life she was given as a happy one, in spite of the fact that it seemed to Charlotte that her mother's happiness had been doled out in tiny teaspoons. Teaspoons so inconsequential it was as if a single packet of sugar had been poured into a lake. Yet her mother could still taste the sweetness of it.

And her mother had grace to accept the things she could not change. And within that tiny circle she found her happiness. But Charlotte did not share her mother's stoic grace at facing death. Her mother was still young then, young enough to enjoy life and maybe even see Charlotte marry and give her a grandchild.

But her mother became ever weaker, slowly succumbing to the

invisible worm crawling through her body. Charlotte had tried to make her as comfortable as possible in the end, and her mother responded by telling Charlotte more about herself in those last few months than she had in all their years together. She thought now of their last real conversation.

"Mama, take a little water before you sleep," Charlotte had coaxed.

Her mother waved the glass away, instead making a request of her own. "Charlotte, reach in my jewelry box. There's something I'd like you to have."

Charlotte opened the small mahogany music box and saw a single delicate diamond suspended on a simple chain.

"Where did you get this, Mama? I've never seen it before."

"It belonged to your great-great-grandma on my mother's side. It's old . . . older than me, and I'd like you to have it."

"Thank you, Mama." She closed her palm around it as if it were the Hope diamond.

"Charlotte . . ."

"Yes, Mama?"

"I am going to die soon."

"Mama!" Charlotte protested, as if by denying it she could make it untrue.

"It's true, Charlotte, and we both need to face it. But first I want to talk to you about something. Something that's been troubling me."

Oh God. She's going to bring up marriage, my pathetic lack of suitors, my weight.

"I've lived in Gorham my whole life." Her mother paused, seeming to consider the weight of the words she was about to utter. "I loved your father, of course, and there was never a day that I was sorry I married him. And then we had you, which was the best part of us."

Charlotte smiled and nodded tentatively. Where was this going?

"However, Charlotte, I do have regrets."

"Regrets? What kind of regrets, Mama?" She had never heard her mother express anything like this. The glass was always half full;

there was always a silver lining, a pot of gold, a ray of hope. God always provided. Regrets were counter to everything she knew to be true about her mother.

"My one regret is that I never did anything special with my own life. Something important in a personal way."

"But Mama, you *are* special. You are loved, and you mean so much to so many people."

"I am blessed in that way, but what I'm saying is something different, Charlotte. I wanted to travel in my life, see Paris or Italy. Once I even wanted to see the pyramids."

This struck Charlotte like an epiphany, a cymbal crash at the end of a movement. She believed her mother thought what lay beyond Middle Street was simply and only the moon.

"I never knew," Charlotte whispered.

"I'm telling you this, my angel, because I don't want you to wake up one day and say 'if only.' I want you to live your life, see things beyond Gorham, experience it all. Life is like a tasting plate. You have to try everything . . . at least once."

Charlotte continued to be stunned by her mother's confession. If she had wanted to do these things, why hadn't she done them? But Charlotte knew, deep down, that it was a rhetorical question. People just got stuck in life. All she needed to do was look at her own life for proof.

"Don't be afraid, Charlotte. Don't let life slip through your fingers as it did with me. Don't let it get away. In the end all we have are our memories. So have wonderful memories, Charlotte. If you don't have wonderful memories to look back on, then you'll have your regrets. Do you understand, my sweet daughter?"

"Yes, Mama."

"Good. That's all I wanted to tell you."

Charlotte wanted to go on talking, to find out down to the last detail what else her mother had wished for herself, but she was looking away, exhausted and lost again in her regrets.

Charlotte slipped the necklace on in front of the mirror and turned around to show her mother. "Look, Mama, look how beautiful . . ." But her mother had already closed her eyes. Charlotte stared down at her, one shade paler than snow and cool to the touch. At that moment, she looked like Snow White. Eggshell frail, old and powdery, but still beautiful.

"Mama," Charlotte whispered. "Mama, take some water before you sleep. You have to stay hydrated."

Charlotte helped lift her up a bit, and her mother's knotty arthritic fingers, knuckles thick and twisted like the branches of an apple tree in winter, reached out tenuously for the glass of water. Charlotte raised the cool, clear liquid to her mother's lips. But she could not take any of it in. Not one drop. And yet she looked up at Charlotte and said, "That's better, that's much better. Thank you, honey. Now you should go rest."

Charlotte clutched the necklace resting against her chest: a single diamond on the thinnest chain. It was all her mother had to give her. But no, there was more. It was that last conversation they ever had together that became the greatest gift of all. Less than an hour later her mother was gone, leaving behind words that would linger for years at the back of Charlotte's mind.

But now her mother's words pulled at her like an undertow. Charlotte had a year left to live. Dr. Jennings had been quite clear about that. He said she should go about living her life as she normally would, that it might be several months before she would begin to notice symptoms. Hadn't that been true for her mother, too? One day she seemed fine, and the next, well . . . Charlotte knew how that went.

And now it seemed that there wasn't enough time left for the one and only thing she had ever truly wanted: to love and to be loved in return. A happy, pleasant existence complete with a garden, lace curtains, and conjugal visits.

But perhaps her moment had finally come to be brave. Brave enough simply to go up to handsome strangers and engage them in conversation, ask them to dinner and inquire if they would be amenable to a brief but affable affair, no strings attached, of course— just for the night, perhaps, or an hour, or less. Charlotte would take anything. She was dying—what was to stop her from asking such candid questions of strangers now?

But who on earth could love me? I'm fat, boring, and dying. Not a great calling card, by my own admission.

Maybe if Charlotte were rich, none of this would feel quite so oppressive, so thoroughly depressing. She could stuff herself with buttered lobster and twice-baked potatoes until she burst. She could say whatever she wanted, to whomever she wanted, and sound amusing, as only the rich do. But Charlotte couldn't afford fancy meals that came with toast points. And she couldn't say whatever she felt. She would come off as rude and inappropriate. No, she wasn't rich or rude. She was just Charlotte Clapp, living on Middle Street, with middle-class savings and middle-class dreams.

Nobody in particular.

Someone simply passing through.

Simply Charlotte.

What could she possibly do now? Eat. Yes, she could eat. She rushed to the cupboard and opened every door, pulling down chips and dip, Oreos, Cheez Doodles, Pinwheels, cashews, Pringles, peanut butter cookies, trail mix, chocolate-covered cherries, and frosted cupcakes.

She'd been trying to limit her consumption lately, but the thought of dieting disappeared with her diagnosis. She dove into this smorgasbord like a last supper. She cracked open a bottle of wine, brought down one of her mother's fine and fancy crystal glasses that hadn't been used in years, and, after rinsing the dust off, filled the wineglass to the top, finishing it off in one swallow. She was almost dangerous in her consumption. No one would have dared put their hand in for a cookie—not if they wanted to see it again. One Krispy Kreme after another, until she resembled a cardboard clown with a ring of white powder around its mouth, begging to have a ball thrown into it—or at least more food. She moved on to the freezer, microwaving pizzas, blintzes, cheese ravioli. Soon it was back to the wine, opening a second bottle. She was on her way to drunkenness; that much became clear when she decided to forego the glass and drink directly from the bottle.

She tried to hold back the tears of lost time and lost chances. But a terrible grief grabbed her by the throat. She struggled to remember every moment of meaning floating somewhere in the alcoholic blur of her brain. *Memories.* That's what her mother had said, Have your memories. So in a haze of Muscatel she began sorting all the sad and silly incidentals of her life. Memories stored away in the inner recesses of what was still good and what had made this little town meaningful. Benny Sanaswaso claiming that Ernie Pinkwater got a big part in *Hamlet.*

"Oh, really, Benny? Which part is he playing?"

"Macbeth."

She almost couldn't breathe for the laughter he caused.

Then there was Jimmy Swenson, who, on a bet, stuck his tongue out against a frozen bike rack, forcing the fire department to come and get him unglued. There was her mother forever poised at the sewing machine, making all of Charlotte's school dresses. The heavy Singer sat in the sunroom, its peddle worn from wear. She could hear the *rat-tat-tat* of the needle repeating itself along the hems of her cotton skirts, silver thimbles clinking like castanets, and scissors that sang like a song through the cloth. When her mother sewed, the house was filled with music. She could smell the sweet color of crayons, the nostalgic musk of store-bought Halloween costumes, the subtle Scotch tape from distant Christmases. Oh yes, these were the good memories, the sweet used-to-be memories before she was fat and dying.

Dying. Just the thought brought her crashing back to earth like a rocket reentering the atmosphere. And there she sat, shaking, short of breath, trying to regroup. Dying. What did that mean? Unbidden, a scene long forgotten lodged itself into her consciousness.

It was a Saturday afternoon and overcast; the day seemed to have a certain sadness built into it. Charlotte was at the vet's with her hamster. Everyone else sat in the waiting room with their giant Labrador retrievers, Great Danes, Clydesdales. Charlotte sat with a little shoe box, holes punched at the top so that poor Jasper could breathe. Jasper, the center of the universe, her first pet, who was unceremoniously bathed by the veterinarian in some antiseptic grease and died the next day despite her efforts to keep him alive.

Charlotte could barely contain her grief, positive it was the vet who killed him by lathering poor Jasper in brilliantine. A proper burial and service was prepared the following day, and Charlotte was comforted by MaryAnn, who reminded her that two years was a long time for a hamster to live and that Jasper was two and a half.

But that first introduction to death did nothing to prepare her for the next. Timmy LeBlanc sat in front of her in first grade and had a disease she couldn't pronounce. "C.F." was what he called it for short. They would pass notes and draw funny pictures of Mrs. Kleem, the meanest teacher this side of hoosierdom. And then one day Timmy didn't come in, and a day stretched to a week, then two. No one was talking, so Charlotte finally asked Mrs. Kleem where Timmy was.

"He transferred," was all she said, avoiding Charlotte's eyes like an accident you try to look away from. That's when Charlotte knew Mrs. Kleem was lying. Mrs. Kleem always looked directly at Charlotte. It was her own unique way of driving daggers into the hearts and souls of ill-behaved children. She couldn't hit them but she could stare them down into submission, or so she thought. And so Charlotte called Timmy's house and learned that he had died.

Charlotte was shocked. Hamsters died. Ants died when you stepped on them. But children didn't die. She wept for weeks. There was nothing sadder than this, not even Jasper's passing. And from that moment on, her perspective regarding life took on a different view forever.

And now Charlotte would find out for herself what it was like to die. She would finally meet up with Jasper—that was if animals didn't have their own separate heaven. A special heaven. However, she would certainly see her mother and Timmy LeBlanc again . . . and maybe even some people she preferred not to bump into. What could she do? If the Catholics were right, this was inevitable.

Charlotte puzzled over Heaven, hell, and holy ghosts for a minute before falling into a complete stupor on the sofa.

It was dark when she woke, and she felt around for the light. Her head pounded like a toy drum as she lay anchored to her seat, amazed. Somewhere between sobriety and sleep, a plan had formed. Had she

dreamed it? She believed in destiny, and this seemed so serendipi-
tous, like a vision a saint might have. However, there was nothing
saintly about her plan. On the contrary, it bordered on blasphemy.

She had one year to live and two thousand dollars in savings. She
certainly couldn't make up for all the time she'd lost on two thousand dollars. How could she seize the day and throw caution to the
wind on funds so meager they could be stuffed into a cookie jar? No,
she needed more money, but how? The plan came to her as simply
as bending down and finding cash at a carnival, fallen from the
pocket of some unlucky fair-goer. She would rob the bank.

CHAPTER 3

THE FIRST SAVINGS AND LOAN of New Hampshire was located in
the center of Gorham. Low brown brick buildings that once signi-
fied industry now meant depression. Gorham was a town of hard-
working middle- and lower-middle-class people. *Middle*—there it
was again.

Charlotte spent her last morning there going through her file
cabinets and desk drawers, much the way one would rifle through
the crevices of a couch searching for loose change. Reaching back
into the deep cubbyhole she discovered discarded candy wrappers
and Gummi Bears covered in lint, a buffalo head nickel, rubber
bands, paper clips, nail polish that had hardened to a solid mass, and
a stick of gum, so old now it could be snapped in two like a tongue
depressor. Going through her things felt no less than an archaeolog-
ical dig of a life utterly disposable, of no importance at all, a life that
had been buried in the back of a cabinet for fifteen years.

A hastily arranged going-away party was planned for Charlotte
and would occupy much of her lunch break. Finally, a party that

would signify closure and put a period at the end of this unmercifully long sentence.

"So why are you leaving, Charlotte?" Happy Turner inquired. Happy worked at the bank with Charlotte and lived on Middle Street as well.

"I've been doing this for so long, I just need a break," Charlotte lied, nervous in her own story.

"Maybe this is a wonderful opportunity, Charlotte," Sara Cabot added. "After all, one never knows what's around the corner."

"And Gorham isn't getting any bigger," Dottie Spencer concluded, suddenly embarrassed by the implications of the word "bigger." She moved away as quickly as her clumsy legs could take her. It didn't matter. Charlotte could hear the hushed buzzing coming from a hive of coworkers in the corner:

"Oh, Charlotte, if she only lost that weight. She has such a pretty face."

"You know, if you can see past all that chubbiness, she's actually very attractive."

And "Charlotte? I knew her when she was thin, and she was beautiful."

Charlotte was tired, tired of overhearing the judgments passed upon her, and she wanted out. She wanted to be some other person in some other place. She could not hear, taste, touch, feel, or see anything anymore. She was removed from the world, removed from the living. If she felt any hesitation up to this point, it was gone now.

Everyone was at Bickfords by noon, so they could safely return to work by one. Charlotte hated Bickfords, a dull, antiseptic restaurant chain whose greatest business came from its 25-percent-off special for senior citizens who ate dinner at three o'clock. It seemed somehow appropriate, though, that cheese rollups and weak punch be her send-off.

Charlotte desperately wanted to make a speech. If she were ever to have her fifteen minutes, this was it. But a rush of fear ran through her. She hated public speaking. She had even tried hypnotism to overcome her anxiety at speaking in front of groups. She'd asked MaryAnn to come with her and simply sit in the room, worried she'd be raped under the doctor's spell. She'd read in the tabloids about things like that happening.

Halfway through, the hypnotist had asked Charlotte to raise her hand if she felt it was working. Charlotte squinted, opening her eyes ever so slightly to see if MaryAnn was still there. She was indeed, lifting her arm so high in the air it looked as if she were hailing a taxi. MaryAnn became an exceptional public speaker after that.

Yet, on this particular afternoon, she was determined: By hook or by crook she would make her speech. What did she have to lose? Absolutely nothing.

Today the room was filled with the usual suspects. She looked around at them recalling some anecdote they'd each shared with her. Bittersweet moments flashed like photographs against the walls of her heart. And she remembered.

She remembered the time she insisted that a bunch of the girls go on a skiing weekend. "We live in New Hampshire, for God's sake. People come from all over to ski here, and we don't let our feet touch snow." And so Dottie, Happy, MaryAnn, and Charlotte all headed to North Conway for their big ski outing.

When they arrived at the top of the hill, MaryAnn had to go to the bathroom. But seeing there was no bathroom up there, she contented herself by hiding behind a tree.

She undid her pants until they rested around her ankles, and squatted down as low as she could. Unfortunately, her skis were pointed downhill, and they lost their grip on the snow. There she was, screaming at the top of her lungs as she headed bare-assed toward the lodge.

The ski patrol picked her up, no worse for wear, just painfully embarrassed by the whole episode. On their way down the hill, they stopped to pick up an injured skier. He looked as if he'd been attacked by a dozen angry trees, and they brought him into the vehicle on a stretcher.

"What happened to you?" MaryAnn inquired, eyeing the twigs caught on his coat.

"You're not going to believe this, but I was skiing away when I spotted this woman, buck naked from the waist down, flying toward the lodge. Watching her, I skied smack into a tree. Never saw it coming. And you? What happened to you?"

MaryAnn went red with the question. "Exposure," she said, and then, realizing what this implied, quickly added, "to the cold—exposure to the cold." But it was too late. The man recognized her, and even his pain couldn't dampen his laughter.

Afterward, MaryAnn failed to see the humor of the situation.

"What's so damn funny, Charlotte?" she demanded.

"No denying it—you skied your ass off."

"Are you done yet?"

"Done?" Charlotte asked, perplexed.

"Laughing *your* ass off," MaryAnn fumed. It would be months before she could laugh about it herself, and some even wondered if it was that incident that had served to sever Charlotte and MaryAnn's friendship.

Charlotte continued conjuring the slow, backward curve of her past.

Cal Vincent Clay's daughter was there, poor thing, endlessly forced to endure the stigma her father had created by shooting at her mother. Fortunately, he missed, though no one could figure out how. The kitchen wasn't that big.

Edgar Halfpenny was there, the only self-made millionaire in Gorham. No one could ever figure out why he settled in the town, but he showed up at every local event, whether he was invited or not. Halfpenny held a special place in Charlotte's heart, for he had come to her aid when Charlotte was trying to raise some money for children with cystic fibrosis—a cause she adopted soon after Timmy LeBlanc's death.

When Halfpenny heard about the shortage of funds to complete a neighboring medical center three towns over, he anonymously donated the deficit. He never uttered a word about it, but because Charlotte handled the day-to-day operations of his funds, she knew damn well it was Halfpenny who made the wing possible. She respected his wish to remain anonymous, so she never mentioned it. But a simple glance between them at the ribbon-cutting ceremony had said it all.

And then there was Al, Charlotte's assistant. Al was so tall and skinny that when he walked next to Charlotte, people whispered that they looked like the number *10*. Another hurt she would work hard to forget.

Charlotte watched Al in the corner, being chastised by Kelly, the bank president, for God knows what. Sadly, this exchange was nothing new; Charlotte had seen it at the bank all too many times. The abuse had become routine for Kelly. He was a bully when it came to the meek, the fearful . . . Al. And still, Charlotte didn't understand why Al put up with it. "Just kick him where the sun doesn't shine, Al," she advised under her breath. Her muttering drew MaryAnn's attention. "One swift kick, then just walk away," Charlotte continued. MaryAnn sidled closer to Charlotte and surprised her from the rear like an enemy plane flying below the radar. Charlotte immediately pretended she had been chewing on a cheese roll-up. *Wouldn't MaryAnn just love it if I were now reduced to talking to myself? Hell, one thing's for sure—it would be more interesting than the conversation I'm about to have.*

"Well, good luck, Charlotte," MaryAnn said, lifting her cup of watery punch up toward the fluorescent lighting that sibilated like an incessant insect.

"Was Bickfords"—*the most depressing place on earth*—"your choice, MaryAnn?" Charlotte asked, knowing the answer.

"It most certainly was."

"So I hear you're going to visit Florida," MaryAnn continued. "What draws you there?"

"Palm trees, good vacation packages, Disney World."

"Yes, Florida is nice," MaryAnn said with mayoral authority. "Tom and I went to Water World for our second anniversary." She paused before continuing, but she always continued. "And then? Are you staying on there?"

Charlotte hadn't thought much past that lie. She figured that people wouldn't care what she was going to do with her life after the weekend in Epcot. Not that MaryAnn actually cared; she was just nosy. Nonetheless, it was a reasonable question. She wasn't going to spend the rest of her life in theme parks.

"No, after Florida I'm off to . . . to . . ."

Charlotte's eyes darted desperately around the room. That's when she saw the calendar hanging above the cash register. It was exactly the same calendar Charlotte had hanging above her own desk back at the bank: a states calendar that had come free with a gas purchase. The coincidence depressed Charlotte; her accessories were as banal as Bickfords's. The calendar's pages hung open to August, revealing the old capitol of Louisiana, a boring brick building against a boring blue sky.

"I'm headed for Louisiana," Charlotte lied smoothly. "I have an aunt there. She asked me to come. Louisiana, now, that's an exciting place, MaryAnn. Ever been there?"

She knew damn well MaryAnn hadn't been there. The bullet train to Florida and the Mall of America were the extent of her worldly travels. She never stopped talking about that mall. An old conversation came crashing back like a rogue wave: the mall. *The damn mall.*

"And do you know how big it is, Charlotte?"

"No."

"Acres and acres. And did you know it has a Ferris wheel and a roller coaster and a shark tank?"

"No."

"And a chapel. People can get married right at the mall. Isn't that fantastic?"

Fantastic? Hell on earth was the only thing Charlotte could liken it to. It was everything she wanted to leave behind.

"And if you plan it right, I suppose you can have your honeymoon right there in the Mall of America. All under one roof. You never have to go outside."

Or breathe air, or see trees growing in nature, or witness an actual sunrise. Hey, if you play your cards right, you can die and be buried right under the food court between Blimpie and Chuck E. Cheese. That's, of course, if you're lucky enough to get a spot.

The shop-till-you-drop motto had become dangerously close to possible as Charlotte saw it. MaryAnn could collapse in front of the video arcades and be whisked away in a shopping cart, just as if she were heading to sportswear or lingerie. There was no place on earth like the Mall of America, and Charlotte honestly believed that if there were the remotest chance of being buried there, MaryAnn would have probably secured a plot. Charlotte could just imagine the epitaph:

> *HERE LIES MARYANN*
> *IN PAYLESS SHOES AND SOCKS*
> *BURIED IN HER TARGET DRESS*
> *AND CRATE AND BARREL BOX*

But MaryAnn was still breathing, which was all that was needed to ensure that she would ask her next question: "Louisiana? I didn't know you had any relatives in Louisiana, Charlotte. You never said a word."

"Yes, several, as a matter of fact." In all the years they'd known each other, Charlotte had certainly never mentioned family in the South. She saw MaryAnn give her a sideways look.

Stick to your story, Charlotte. Stick to your story. "Anyway, I've always dreamed of living in New Orleans. This is a dream come true."

"Be careful what you wish for, Charlotte. I've never known any dreams to come true without some price to be paid. But maybe it will be different for you."

Charlotte was surprised; she thought MaryAnn's dreams had come true. What secret lay behind this cryptic admission? *Who cares? It doesn't matter anymore,* Charlotte reminded herself, turning away, leaving MaryAnn alone with her hateful little jealousies. There was no reason for MaryAnn to be so snippy. The rivalry was long over, and MaryAnn had won.

MaryAnn's husband, Tom Barzini, had been Charlotte's boyfriend first. The months she'd been with him had been the best in memory. During this period her mother was still doing okay and Charlotte was her old self, "thin and beautiful," as the reports went. But best of all, she was in love.

Meeting Tom had lifted her out of the humdrum existence that life had dished out and ultimately buried her beneath. She was in love, and suddenly nothing was ordinary anymore. The fish plant, the bank, the brown bags she hauled her groceries home in, the carports covered in their green corrugated canopies, the blue plastic pools gathering up bugs behind every house, the short, stingy driveways lined with trailers that were bought to pull motorboats down to the lake once a year, the depressing ornaments of dwarfs or ducklings and the shiny silver balls that reflected back the dull monotonous condition of life in Gorham, and even Middle Street itself were no longer boring. All the tiny deaths she suffered in the everyday wasteland of cups and saucers, snack tables, and laundry lines disappeared. She was filled with the promise that there was life after death in a small town, and his name was Tom.

At the six-month mark in their romance, Charlotte's mother had become gravely ill and needed constant care. Charlotte was unable to see Tom as regularly during this time, and one night when he came to pick her up at the bank, he found that Charlotte had left. Her mother had called her home earlier that day. But MaryAnn was still at the bank, and she and Tom went out that night for drinks. Gossip spread like a rash, and before Charlotte knew it, Tom and MaryAnn were a couple.

That's when it started: the terrible weight gain that steadily began filling in Charlotte's waistline and other fine curves with heavy creams, puddings, and cookie dough dense as clay. Slowly but surely, a perfectly proportioned person was transformed into something round and enormous, like a bowl too big for the potter's wheel.

Her mother hung in there for several months, and for several months Charlotte fed her fury with flapjacks, cream puffs, and rich, buttery brownies. The longer her mother lived, the larger Charlotte got. Finally, after eight months, she had to take a leave of absence from the bank to care for her mother around the clock. It was during these final three and a half months that Charlotte's weight tipped the scales. Her poor mother watched as her only daughter became the size of a small third world country. But she was incapable of doing anything about it, trapped as she was in her own dying body. And so she prayed.

When Charlotte went back to work after her mother's passing, shock reverberated throughout the bank. The old Charlotte had virtually disappeared; she had become almost featureless beneath the layers of her own flesh. Everyone stared while her sausage fingers hoarded the candy bowl left out for customers. And she seemed genuinely unabashed. Perhaps everything that had happened made her numb.

The worst of it was that Charlotte knew she had only herself to blame. MaryAnn had a reason for her betrayal; she was getting even for the improbable night that happened long ago. A night that happened well before Tom Barzini ever came into the picture—an awful, irreversible night that changed everything.

Charlotte tried to content herself by saying that losing Tom to MaryAnn was destiny. She hoped that this would finally heal things between them and make things equal. But she knew they would never be friends again, not the way they had been best friends since the first grade. It pained her to lose Tom, pained her more than anything in life. But it also pained her to lose MaryAnn. Yet one irrevocable hour in their lives had changed everything.

Charlotte liked to think that wearing that god-awful purple chiffon bridesmaid's dress that made her look like an Italian ice at Tom and MaryAnn's inevitable wedding was penance. And yet this still didn't soften MaryAnn. She continued to harbor resentment, which puzzled Charlotte. Wasn't it Charlotte who should have held the grudge? After all, the man she loved was stolen away from her. But she had let it go, managing to eat her way through it, slowly and steadily gaining 138 pounds over the next several years. So much sadness, so much regret. And while her heart could not hold all that grief, her body expanded to accept it.

This gave Charlotte one more reason to be happy to say good-bye to Gorham, New Hampshire, good-bye to MaryAnn and that unmercifully endless wedding. And most of all, the terrible night she would rewrite in her head a hundred times, the night she would work hard to consign to oblivion and dismiss from her thoughts forever.

And in remembering all this, and the sad regrets her mother had confided to her on the day she died, Charlotte finally had the nerve to break away from the crowd and move to the back of the room. All eyes began to turn her way. There was something single-minded in her walk. Everyone saw it. *You can do this. You can do this. You can do this.*

She repeated these words like a mantra. Like a drum growing ever louder. Like the sound of a train gaining speed, leaving the station by way of her brain. Faster. Faster. Her adrenaline pounded. *You can do this. You can do this. You can . . . chug-a-chug-a-chug-a-chug-a . . .*

Suddenly, her brain screeched to a stop. And with that, she turned to the waiting many.

"Just look at you all. Can our parties be as boring as our lives? Is there anyone actually having a good time? This is like a wake. A word of advice to all of you: Live. Live like there's no tomorrow."

And with that, she moved toward the front of the room, parting the crowd like the Red Sea, and walked out of Bickfords with the biblical impact of Charlton Heston.

CHAPTER 4

$\mathscr{S}$HE RETURNED TO THE BANK that afternoon with a dozen plastic garbage bags, ostensibly for gathering up all the mementos she'd collected over the years: a dog whose head bounced up and down in nauseating agreement, a windup flower that danced to the tune of "April Showers," a dead Chia Pet, a ceramic donkey pulling a cart, a chipped coffee cup that read *Employee of the Month,* a scented candle that was a present from . . . Who could even remember now? It was as gone as the scent itself. And then it was five o'clock, as it had been five o'clock every day for the past thousand years when Charlotte closed the bank.

"Want me to close tonight, Charlotte?" the assistant manager asked.

"No, let me . . . for the last time, Al. I'll drop the keys by after I clean out my desk."

"You sure?"

"Yeah, for old times' sake. I just want to take it all in before I leave."

And so it went. The last few obligatory hugs and kisses.

"That was some speech," Happy said, getting her things together. "Very unexpected."

"Yeah, for me, too."

"Was it rehearsed?"

"For fifteen years."

"Did you mean it to come out that way?"

"No, it was much better than I imagined."

"Well, Lordy me," Happy said, "who'da thought you had it in you?"

Nothing else was said about Charlotte's speech. In fact, it was glaringly avoided.

Happy and Al were the last to leave the bank, offering up their parting well-wishes.

Finally, gratefully, Charlotte was alone. She turned the combination to the vault just as she had for the past fifteen years. But this time, when she entered, she filled her Hefty bags with piles of cool, crisp, cumbersome cash. A million dollars in twenties weighs 125 pounds. It was a fact she had looked up on the Internet that very day—preparation was key. But this mother lode was a mishmash of fives, tens, twenties, and fifties. And it wasn't one million; it was two million. She persevered like an exhausted mule, lugging each bag, one by one, through the back door to her car. It was Friday night, so it would be at least two days before anyone realized the money was missing.

The upside to Gorham (if there was one) was that the Savings and Loan was too small a bank, in too small a town, to have any sort of security guard. But the downside was that there would not be very much cash in the vault. So why did Gorham's Savings and Loan have this money? Charlotte knew why.

Every so often the bank president would allow his brother-in-law to temporarily store inordinate amounts of cash for several days before he took it out again. No one in the bank said a word, though everyone knew about these goings-on. Jobs were scarce in Gorham, and it was better to turn a blind eye than risk unemployment.

According to her count, this was the sixth time such excessive amounts of money had sat in the vault without explanation. Charlotte chalked it up to gambling wins and tax evasion, though she wasn't really sure what the story was. She didn't care, either.

All that mattered was that the gods had conspired to make this cash available to her. And while Charlotte knew it wasn't legal for her to help herself, she was comforted by the knowledge that the president's brother-in-law and, in all probability, the president himself were as corrupt as the day was long. Besides, if he'd done it six times already, he certainly would have no trouble replacing it. Charlotte was meant to have this money—why else would the timing have been so perfect? She just wished she could see the president's face when he discovered it was gone.

Charlotte dropped the bank keys safely off with Al. Al, who had been assigned the ponderous title of assistant bank manager and who would be immediately promoted upon Charlotte's departure. Al, who now faced the awesome responsibility of opening the doors at nine and closing the vault by five. Al, who would have to deal with Kelly even more than he did now. Poor Al.

Little did Kelly know that Al would get even. He was simply waiting for his moment. And that moment would come. It would most definitely and triumphantly come.

CHAPTER 5

*I*T WAS DARK WHEN SHE ARRIVED HOME. Dark enough to drag the bags into the house without causing suspicion. She felt as if she were dragging bodies, an eerie feeling for Charlotte, who had never ever done anything remotely unethical.

Her life felt as though it had become another person's, a pantomime, an accidental trip into someone else's reality. It was as if she were waking up out of a long anesthesia induced state. And she was.

At around two in the morning Charlotte drove her '89 Toyota over to the Point of Pines Bridge at Gorham Pass. Leaving her car running and the driver's door wide open, she heaved her enormous body against the back of the car. It moved, but not enough to break the fence and topple into the dark waters below. She pushed again. One thing became clear in the exasperated push and pull, the grinding determination of iron weight against iron will: She would need a new strategy.

Standing outside the driver's door, she stretched her right foot into the car and onto the gas pedal. It jerked forward, and she grabbed the roof to keep her balance. She tried again, this time advancing the pedal slowly, steadily: The car finally began to push the fence out like a tight metal parenthesis bending in the middle, enough so that she could push again on her own. And she did. Inch by inch, her car nosed ever closer to the edge, and finally let go into the tumbling darkness of the Gorham River.

She stared down into the featureless water, and a small sadness washed over her. She had owned that car for fifteen years. Now it was alone at the bottom of the Gorham River. How lonely it would be by itself in this cold, murkish underworld, slipped from its devotion like a loved ring off the knuckle of a swimmer. "Good-bye, old car," she said. And as she turned to walk away she felt the sadness of the car at the bottom of the Gorham River, grieving inside its own dumb heart.

She trudged the two miles home, like a tugboat caught in fog. Nothing stirred: no cars, no rabbits, no branches. This was Gorham, after all, where nothing happened . . . where nothing was ever going to happen.

At three a.m. she called a cab from a town sixty miles away and waited for an hour among the objects that she would leave behind: faded floral curtains, a beanbag ashtray, a worn-out ottoman, and several small, dusty glass figurines because her mother could not afford Hummels. Yes, she would pay for the time and mileage; yes, she knew it would be extra. Closing the door to the paneled living room one last time, she left the front door unlocked. Why lock it? Her life was over in that house. She struggled with her four large suitcases—suitcases that had been collecting dust in her cellar for years. They'd been used for storage. Her mother had bought them years ago, perhaps hoping one day she would really and truly take that trip to the pyramids, but the suitcases remained in the cellar, collecting dust instead of memories. Now, as she wrestled to lift them into the taxi, the cab driver did not budge to help her. Why? *Because I'm fat,* she thought. Watching her trying to hoist the bags into his trunk was like watching Dumbo trying to flap his ears fast enough to fly. But there would be no liftoff here. By the time the task was over, she sank like a boulder into the backseat, all 253 pounds. The seat was wide and comfortable and able to accommodate her bountiful behind, a behind softly dented like an old couch she'd been sitting on for years.

"Going far?" the cab driver asked.

"Yes. Florida."

"You got a lot of bags."

"Well, I'll be gone for a while." *Forever.*

"Where to now, lady?"

"The Whitestone train station."

When he dropped her off, she asked to be left just before the platform.

"You sure? These bags look heavy, lady."

Like you might help. "I have friends meeting me."

"Whatever."

She paid him his money, and he drove off, leaving Charlotte to drag the bags into the high grass along the side of the lot. There wasn't a soul in sight. Nor would there be. There was no train till morning. She walked three blocks until she finally reached Tally's used-car lot. She found the '86 Jaguar she had purchased with two thousand dollars in cash the day before.

The old inspection sticker was still on the front window, and it would stay there. She only needed license plates and the good luck of not being pulled over by a state trooper. If she were pulled over, it would reveal that the sticker and plates did not match.

The keys were exactly where she had asked for them to be: under the passenger's floor mat. She drove back to the train station and found her luggage untouched in the weeds. She had no clothes or shoes or soap or snacks, just a medallion she rescued from her mother's jewelry box, and every CD Tony Bennett had ever recorded. Charlotte loved Tony Bennett.

And of course, she had money. Lots of it. Two million dollars, in fact. And then she drove off. But not to Florida. *Who would go there?* she thought. *It's so humid.*

There was, however, one place she had wanted to see before she died: Hollywood, California. Both she and MaryAnn had girlhood dreams of going to Hollywood and would muse endlessly about all the romance they were sure to find there.

"Imagine us in Hollywood!" MaryAnn would exclaim. "I would be quite famous and have a chauffeur drive me wherever I wanted to go."

"And where would you go?" Charlotte would inquire.

"Disneyland, of course."

"Yes, of course. And I will be famous, too," Charlotte vowed. "I will be a famous actress and sign autographs when I have time."

"Me, too," MaryAnn chimed in. "And go to the Oscars."

"And win."

"And make a speech thanking all the little people who helped me become so successful."

"And go back to my seat and kiss my husband, Tom Selleck."

"No, I want Tom Selleck; you take someone else."

"No, I want him; I said him first. You can have Warren Beatty or Robert Redford. I'm taking Tom Selleck."

"No way."

And then a big fight would ensue, and an hour would go by until someone would break the ice by making the supreme sacrifice of giving up Tom Selleck, and the day would return to normal.

Charlotte and MaryAnn knew more about Hollywood than Rex Reed. They read the tabloids, *People,* and *Us,* and watched every TV show that gave them the inside scoop on every piece of Hollywood trivia known to man. Ask them anything, and they knew it. They knew all about John Barrymore, including the loss of his virginity to his stepmother. They knew that Valentino's wife locked him out of the bedroom on their wedding night and that their marriage was never consummated, that the tabloids declared Tom Selleck had the head of a Viking and that each of his dimples could hold a split of champagne. They were always astounded by Gig Young's story. So many attested to his warmth and stability, so many insisted he was the sweetest, kindest human being they'd ever met in spite of the fact that he blew his wife's brains out and then his own. Their encyclopedic inventory of every star and event known to Hollywood was recorded and stashed away in Charlotte's and MaryAnn's memories. To them it was all magic and all possibility. The more they knew, the closer they were to their dream.

And when they were old enough, they promised they would go there together and step into this wonder world, which up until now they had only envisioned from the confines of their finished basements. They were certain they'd both end up in Hollywood, the land where dreams come true.

Charlotte imagined herself in Hollywood, mingling with movie stars while waiting in the same grocery line to get milk. Maybe even Tom Selleck would be there, standing in the *under 10 items* express lane with his orangeade and Krispy Kremes. Mmmmm. *Wouldn't it just be so, so perfect if we loved all the same snacks?*

Yes, she would drive to Hollywood in her brand-new secondhand Jaguar. An airplane was out of the question. Charlotte had never been on a plane and could not fathom how so much tonnage was capable of leaving the ground. She could only compare the concept to her own tonnage. And so she would drive and, at long last, see all the unexplored country that now lay between Hollywood and herself.

The first stop she made was just beyond the driveway of a dark house inside the New Hampshire border. She wanted to steal plates as far away from Gorham as possible, but needed to obtain them from New Hampshire so they would match the inspection sticker. There, with the lumbering agility of a refrigerator repairman, Charlotte stole quietly into some anonymous driveway and, with a screwdriver in one hand and her pocketbook in the other, knelt down in the half-light of a street lamp and began unscrewing plates on a blue Pontiac.

When both plates were finally removed, she drove the car to an empty lot in back of a 7-Eleven and put on her new plates. Her mission complete, she took off like a thief in the night. Which was, suddenly, who she was.

Her only tenuous connection to her old life now was the phone ringing madly back in her empty house on Middle Street. But the person calling would never reach Charlotte to tell her the news that would have changed the course of her life, news that would profoundly affect the journey she was about to embark on: An awful mistake had been made. There had been another Charlotte Clapp from Durham, New Hampshire, who'd gone to Doctor Jennings that very same day. With no one home to get the phone, Charlotte would have no way of knowing that her chart had gotten mixed up somehow and that she, Charlotte Clapp, from Gorham, was going to live, and while it might be short of forever, she would live a long, long time.

But the call came too late, like the punch line of an ill-timed joke. For Charlotte was gone now, driving as far away from her old life as possible while her phone rang on to no one and nothing at all.

CHAPTER 6

New York City. Charlotte had never been there, but then again, she'd never been anywhere. She had decided to find her way cross-country slow and easy; no one was waiting for her in California—no one even knew her in California—so she could take her time. She contented herself in thinking that such freedom was the upside of being completely alone.

She knew about New York City from gossip and movies and books. She also knew about it because MaryAnn had relatives living on Staten Island. They made annual visits to Gorham, and Charlotte was once invited over to meet these exotic family members. All the way from Staten Island. Imagine. She was only six at the time, but Charlotte still recalled the visit. She didn't know what she expected. Accents? Uniforms? Crowns? But they were just ordinary people. Nonetheless, MaryAnn insisted they were quite special, and they both sneaked into the guest room to forage through the suitcases and look for any signs of royalty. A Norelco shaver, an electric toothbrush, and lacy red see-through underwear were as close to something special that they would find. Armed only with these memories, Charlotte entered New York City.

She arrived midafternoon on Monday, having first been lost in Queens and then in the Bronx. Before finally wending her way out of what Dante might have described as a bad section of the underworld, she witnessed the most extraordinary scene. Amid the tossed tires, boarded windows, and general rust and ruin, situated right under the El, appeared an ice-cream truck, merrily painted with cups and cones, sherbets and ices, slushies and Slurpees. An ice-cream truck sat incongruously like a calliope of color under the crush of a neighborhood that looked as if it had had its teeth knocked out. The truck had broken down, and now the refrigeration unit was failing, melting all the ice cream inside.

The driver opened the back doors and called out to every soul within shouting distance to "come and get it." There was free ice cream for all. Dozens of children dashed out from every dark corner and dived into the pure deliciousness of it. Cherry vanilla and orange Creamsicles, push-ups and Popsicles that left their tongues purple, blue, red, and green. And there were root beer Popsicles, too, that left gold wet kisses on their lips. This was truly an unexpected gift from the ice-cream gods. Charlotte had a theory that there were gods for everything: quick-pick gods, love-at-first-sight gods, outlet gods, and even gods that made bricks fall on your head every once in a while. And today, in the middle of litter and lament, the ice-cream gods had blessed the Bronx.

Charlotte pulled over and disappeared into a vat of caramel creme. It was such an odd sight to see this flock of ragtag kids covered in smiles, indifferent to the broken glass underfoot. Where on earth had they come from? They looked like flowers that had fought their way up through the cement and declared life in spite of the odds. Tiny scoops of children and chocolate, sloshing and swashing their way among the irrepressible mayweeds and nettles.

There's good to be found everywhere. The gods never cease to amaze me. Just when you think you're lost, something wonderful finds you. Just when you think it's over, it's all just begun.

At last she found her way into Manhattan. No wonder the world spoke of Manhattan the way they did. Life was everywhere, and it had a current all its own, an energy that rose from the belly of the beast and spread over the avenues like magic.

But what she truly came to see was Lincoln Center, for that was a place Tony Bennett had sung. Maybe he would be there tonight. She could go and see him and wait outside and get his autograph and tell him that she knew every song he ever sang and that she thought he was even better than Frank Sinatra, and . . . and . . . and . . . But he wasn't in town, so that was that.

Lincoln Center was a square of buildings surrounding a large circular fountain, where Charlotte was sure wives met their husbands on warm moonlit nights—expectant husbands who were holding tickets for that evening's performance, probably to celebrate something romantic like an anniversary.

She walked around the circle. *I bet the three tenors sat here. Pavarotti, Placido Domingo, and . . . and . . .* Charlotte could not remember the third tenor. Who was he? How come no one could ever remember the third tenor? The parallelism to her own presence did not go unnoticed. She had shown up in this life; she had been here, but no one could recall her. She suddenly felt bad for . . . for . . . for whatever his name was.

With no Tony Bennett performance before her, Charlotte scanned her possibilities, and, never having been to an opera, she was inspired to buy a ticket to *La Boheme*. Why not? This was a new time in her life, and everything was open to yes.

The curtain rose to tragic backdrops and moody lighting, but it was the singing that electrified the theater: The perfect silvery notes that hovered like breakable angels over the audience. And they sang, and they sang, and they sang. And Charlotte sat frozen in her seat, transported to that cold, wintry garret in Paris, dying alongside the young girl whose last breath, full of snow and grief, was lifted toward heaven in that final and heartbreaking aria.

And then Charlotte wept. She wept for the girl; she wept for herself; she wept for everything that had been created in this world that had this much terrible beauty. For the first time in years she was feeling something other than the deadening numbness that life in Gorham, New Hampshire, had served up.

The next morning Charlotte felt somehow cleansed, new. She settled her bill, leaving New York City under a sky as gray as gunmetal. She hoped it would rain. Rain always made her happy. It smelled like hope to her.

She was somewhere in New Jersey when she heard a siren grinding closer and closer toward her. She looked down at her speedometer. Christ, she was twenty miles an hour over the speed limit. But maybe it wasn't her. Maybe they'd pass her on their way to something really important. A fire—no, a murder if she was really lucky. She balanced the two in her mind. Speeding ticket, murder, speeding ticket, murder. *They'd skip right over me if it were a murder.* As she slowed, she watched them come up behind her like a hound dog on a fox's tail. With a sticker that didn't match her plates, she was doomed before she even began. It was over, all over.

A trooper got out of his car just as they do in the movies: slowly, with Gestapo boots and a bulletproof swagger.

Charlotte rolled down her window.

"You know how fast you were going?"

"Yes, sir."

"Twenty miles over the speed limit."

She could see her fat, pitiable body in his mirrored sunglasses and knew there would be no mercy here.

"Can I see your registration, please?" he asked, looking around, hands on hips, feet spread apart, clearly the king of Route 4.

Charlotte reached over into the glove compartment and fumbled around for the paper that was about to seal her fate.

Suddenly, Herr Schtopenglopper's walkie-talkie crackled. There had been a shooting in Shorthills, a domestic brawl on a well-known estate. All hell was breaking loose, and the husband was holding the wife's boyfriend hostage.

The cop looked at Charlotte. "You're lucky this time. But if I catch you going eighty again, I'll have your license."

"Yes, sir," was all that Charlotte was able to utter. The speeding-ticket gods had looked down on her, and just like that she was free.

She sat there for a moment, contemplating her fate as the car sped off. If that woman had stayed faithful, or met her boyfriend at a hotel instead of her own bedroom . . . How unpredictable life was: Simply turning a corner could make the difference between living and dying, finding love and not finding love, incarceration and escape.

Her heart was still beating hard as she started up the car—beating much faster than fifty miles per hour, the pace at which she now resolutely set herself. And as she pulled onto the highway, she remembered what a famous actor had said about himself: "If they ever find me out, I'm a goner."

Meanwhile, back in Gorham, Al had opened the bank just as he was supposed to on his first day as assistant manager and discovered that the vault was open. And it was clearly less full than it had been before the weekend. He notified the Gorham police immediately, exclaiming, actually panicking to Chief Makley that the bank had been robbed.

When President Kelly got in and learned of the news, he nearly had an aneurysm. Everyone assumed this reaction was because the bank had been robbed. Normal reaction. It would have been strange if he weren't upset. He paced back and forth, drinking Pepto Bismol straight from the bottle and yelling at Al through the pink chalky circle that enveloped his lips. His face was beet-red and his ridiculously large distorted pink mouth made him look clownish, like one of those drive throughs that you yell your food order into, "A cheeseburger, a Coke, and a large fries."

The ranting continued, Kelly pointing at Al as if Al had robbed the bank when the only thing he did was report it. Poor Al, all he could think of was this was his first day on the job as assistant manager and somehow he had already screwed up. The finger waving continued until Al was backed up against the water cooler, Kelly's finger practically up his nose.

How could reporting a robbery become a criminal act? Al suddenly felt so ill, he thought that perhaps he was not cut out for his new job. But to his credit, he stood his ground (he had to, he couldn't be pushed back any farther, as the wall stood in his way). And so he bit the bullet that had just been fired at him and tried to be philosophical. Hell, it was only his first day. How much worse could it get? Much worse.

CHAPTER 7

*W*EDNESDAY AFTERNOON found Charlotte somewhere near Ohio, eating a whole cherry pie and drinking gallons of hot coffee at a truck stop. She thumbed through a newspaper a patron had left behind. But it wasn't a local paper. Someone from Louisiana had come through earlier and left it. *Louisiana.* Surely this was a sign. If there had been a NASA calendar hanging over the register at Bickfords, would she have told MaryAnn she was going to the moon? Again she thought about how funny it was—the little coincidences that make up your destiny. Charlotte continued looking through the paper for nothing in particular when her attention was drawn to the obituaries.

Maybe it was because in the minds of the good people of Gorham, New Hampshire, Charlotte Clapp was newly dead. And as she'd never been dead before, she was curious about those who were newly dead, too. The obit that caught her eye was that of an old woman whose wake was extended for two extra days at the Germaine Devoe Funeral Home so that the whole community could get a chance to say good-bye.

It read:

> Blossom McBeal 1916–2004
>
> Beloved wife of Henry McBeal, mother of Sara Hutchkins, grandmother of Sam, Tara, and Billy Hutchkins, sister of Danny Peck.
>
> For those who knew her well, she was nothing short of extraordinary. By the time she was twenty-five, she'd been married three times. She was quoted as saying, "Better to be alone than with some jerk. He's gonna take it out of you, and then there's nothing left over for the world."
>
> Courageous to a fault, she did some volunteer work in Bechuanaland, where she walked from village to village. There were nights she slept in trees to stay clear of the lions. Unfortunately, she did not know that leopards slept in trees, too, and lost her middle finger one night trying to escape one of the beasts. Despite the jokes that were spun from that, Blossom showed great bravery.
>
> As beautiful as she was bright, she returned to Louisiana and enrolled at the state college. It was there she was nominated and won the title of Miss Louisiana. Her striking good looks did not go unnoticed by Dr. McBeal, who became her fourth husband, a fine proctologist from Baton Rouge. She became his nurse practitioner, often trudging out in the middle of the night to bring medicine to the elderly. She raised fifty thousand dollars single-handedly for St. Paul Charity by selling potholders to hospital cafeterias all over the South, an endeavor that took her ten years to complete.
>
> When Baton Rouge made a calendar of its more mature beauties, Blossom graced the cover. In 1984, she and her husband

moved to New Orleans. It was there she helped open a school for the mentally challenged and spent every Saturday teaching the children palettes and macramé. At fifty she went back to Africa to teach again, but fell ill with malaria and had to return home. But even malaria couldn't keep Blossom down. From her bed she wrote low-fat recipes so her husband could hand them out to high-cholesterol patients. This was such a success, a book followed and some even thought it could be a movie, if done right. At sixty, Blossom created Deaf-Awareness Day and raised money by booking the local band at the church. This created a political brouhaha because the point was raised that the deaf couldn't actually hear the music. But Blossom prevailed and named her campaign "The Feel-the-Music Extravaganza." She also named it something else to flag her annoyance at the people who had a problem with it, but we can't print that here. *Modern Maturity* did a lead article on her, and enjoying immediate success from the fund-raiser, she got to do a milk ad shortly after that. While she was in her seventies, the hospital erected a plaque of one of her low-fat recipes.

Blossom was the pride and joy of our community, and she will always be remembered for the final words she uttered: "I'll be back, you sons of bitches, and next time I'll really knock your socks off." Blossom will be waked at the Germaine Devoe Funeral Home through Monday. Services will be held at Our Lady of Precious Blood Church.

Wow, Charlotte thought, *now, that's a woman. Beautiful, smart, brave, of average weight, and married. . . . Now, that's someone I'd like to be.* Even if Charlotte were only married for a short time, that counted. Hell, Dennis Hopper and Michelle Phillips were only married for eight days. Charlotte's thoughts rolled back to Blossom.

If she left the truck stop now, she could take her time and still get to Louisiana to pay her last respects. Life was too short not to make important stops along the way. This was an important stop. She knew this because she had been given the sign, and it spoke to her in a way that only she could hear. She pulled out her map. Everything was possible. A whole world lay before her, and getting to each far-flung place was as easy as following the long blue highways with her finger.

CHAPTER 8

CHARLOTTE FLEW SOUTH like a bird clapping each county behind her. She finally crossed the invisible boundary from Tennessee, and entered the damp, mossy back roads of Mississippi. The air was warmer here. Ash, oak, and gum trees stood like Southern soldiers along the Natchez Trace. Rivers and oxbows and bayous watered the land—so much so, it seemed as if the delta would never have to take another drink.

It was late when Charlotte pulled into an old motel, lost in time on Moon Lake Road. It took her less than ten minutes to check in and find her way to bed, fatigued as she was from hours of driving and dust.

She was tired, so tired that she could barely smell the perfume of the crepe myrtle and magnolias rising into the drowsy night air. Every breath drew Charlotte deeper and deeper into sleep, until she was tenderly released into her first dream that had something to do with milk and honey.

The sun came up over the delta as it had for the past thousand years, except this time Charlotte Clapp was there to greet it. She stood at her window, gazing past the cattails and willows to the tall, lazy cypresses. Their Spanish moss blew out over the brown riverbanks like young girls in hoopskirts. Charlotte looked beyond the banks and saw the dark indomitable Mississippi River exploding forward in the swarming heat. She knew right then and there she had arrived at a place that demanded its due. Clearly, the strict southern gods were out in force. She would never say or even allow herself to think of the word f-u-c-k. But if she were to think it, only for a moment, a moment so quick no one could possibly know that she'd ever conceived such an unspeakable word, then, without a doubt, these would be the "gods not to be fucked with."

She looked away from the river and went outside, relieved to see the morning sky shining bright as an amethyst. Spreading her map out like a quilt on her lap, she noticed an old woman in a sleeveless shift sweeping the walk.

"Excuse me," Charlotte interrupted. "Could you tell me the fastest way to get to New Orleans from here?"

The old woman paused, rested on her broom, and considered the question as if she'd been asked if God exists.

"The fastest way or the most colorful way?"

"Good question. I say the most colorful way."

"Highway sixty-one."

"A highway is the most colorful way?" Charlotte asked skeptically.

"Why, Highway sixty-one ain't like no other highway. It's Blues Alley. And Clarksdale is the place to start. Blues men, that's who traveled it, back in the twenties and thirties. My husband was a blues man, played a mean guitar. It's how I fell for him. He used that guitar to woo me like a box of chocolates. But he's been gone now many years." She became wistful. "Yeah, he played the delta up and down, up and down. If there was a juke joint within a stone's throw, then you can bet that's where my Johnny would be. Jumpin' Johnny Jackson."

Charlotte's curiosity was pedaling at top speed. "What exactly are these juke joints?"

"Shacks. You'll find them all along Route sixty-one. You know 'em when you see 'em. Tin roofs, broken porches. But that don't matter—it's what's comin' out of 'em that matter. And that's all the music your ears can hold."

This appealed to Charlotte's romantic side, and it was just the sort of experience she was hoping for when she bade her boredom good-bye.

"I like the sound of this," Charlotte said. "I don't really know blues, but I do know a thing or two about feeling blue."

"Then you know the blues if you know that, child. Now, don't get the jukes mixed up with those low-class lounges you'll see along the road. Best they can offer is clean toilets, and they're not all that clean, if you ask me. The music is the thing. The music can set your soul free."

Set my soul free? There was no longer any question as to where Charlotte was going that day. She was going to find music that would set her soul free.

Now, a fat white lady in a Jaguar is bound to get some attention in the middle of poor, black rural Mississippi. Clarksdale, Mississippi, to be exact. It was there she pulled over to a farm stand glistening with fruit and vegetables. Several children rushed out to see what Charlotte was all about.

"Can I help ya, ma'am?" The question came from the old black man coming out of the house with a flock of little girls in tow. They looked like half a dozen brown-eyed Susans.

Placed perfectly in proper rows along worn wooden benches were boxes of berries and beatroot, okra, and onions. Turnips, tomatoes, and sugarcane stalks. There were sweet peas and sweet pies from just-picked potatoes. There was sun tea and cider and hot pepper jelly, corn bread, and honey still caught in its comb. There were pecans and fruit jams and blueberry butter, all set out like a long Southern Sunday picnic.

"Weez got possum an' fish out back, ma'am. Fresh fish. Weez got some bream, crappie, and catfish out back if ya want fish, ma'am."

"I think I'll take two sweet potato pies, a piece of honey, and handful of pecans, please."

A pickup truck was hiccupping its way down the long, dusty corridor toward the group. It stopped at the stand as Charlotte collected her pies.

"Nice car, lady," the man said as he slipped like an adder out of his pickup. His face was thin, and his eyes were slit so that only the narrowest gleam could escape them. His friend stood behind him, not saying a word.

"What can I getcha?" the old man asked, leaning over to bring up more bags from under the table.

"Nothing I want from you, but I'd like to see what's in that poke of yours." He was talking to Charlotte now and wielding a long, sharp hunting knife. It took her a moment to figure out what was going on. Suddenly, she got it. She was getting mugged in the middle of a beautiful road in the middle of a beautiful day. The old man told the little kids to get back into the house, and they ran like a rush of rabbits tumbling down their hole. Charlotte opened her purse.

"Five hundred dollars! Wow, Earle, we hit a goddamn jackpot. We got ourselves a rich lady from . . . from . . . where you say you from?"

"New Hampshire," Charlotte said softly, barely above a whisper. All she could think of was that she was going to die buying sweet potato pies.

"What's your name?"

"Charlotte."

"Well, Charrrrrlotte, what else you got in that fancy car of yours? Why don't you just open the trunk so we can take a look, like a big girl? Get it, Earle? Big girl?" he laughed. His broken front teeth showed like a junkyard dog's growling at an intruder.

Charlotte stared at his mouth. She couldn't even hear the snorting coming out of it. It filled her screen like a silent bark pushing ever closer toward her face. It was the ugliest face she'd ever seen.

"Well? I ain't got all day, lady. Open the fuckin' trunk!"

She had stolen two million dollars, and for what? To be robbed on some godforsaken road in Mississippi and to never get to Hollywood? How cruel was this? She contemplated jumping into the driver's seat even at the risk of getting knifed. What difference would it make now? If they took the money, she'd have nothing to live for anyway. She'd never get to California. She'd never hear Tony Bennett sing. She'd never meet Tom Selleck.

She walked over to the car, fumbling for her trunk key. She slid it slowly into the lock and opened it. There they were: her four suit-cases. Her future. The man with the knife leaned in to lift them out when he was interrupted by the old man behind the fruit stand.

"Excuse me, boys, but y'all is on my property, and I don't like these kinda of goin's-on here . . . if ya gets my gist."

The old man pointed a fat-barreled shotgun at the gut of the man with the knife.

"It's been at least a week since I kilt somebody, and I hate to have to end my streak. So why don't y'all back off, get inta dat truck of yours, and drive on back ta whatever sewer you dun drove out of. I don't want no problems here, and I don't wanna ruin my afternoon buryin' two big cracker boys like yourselves. That takes a heapa lot of energy, an' I had plans to go fishin' for some crappie later." The old man pulled back the hammer.

The two white boys started to move away from the trunk. The old man's calm was disconcerting. He was way too quiet—quiet enough to be scared of. Even these backwoods boys could tell that with the least amount of provocation, *bang!* and it would be over. Where they were all bravado, he was all business.

"Hey, we don't want no trouble. We were just havin' some fun, is all."

"Well, get your butts back inta dat truck an' go have your fun elsewhere. Fun's over here."

They moved cautiously, quickly, sliding into their old beat-up Ford.

"Hey, wait a second, son."

The mean one stopped. The old man grabbed the five hundred dollars out of his hand and gave it back to Charlotte.

And with that, they were off, eating the same dust they'd kicked up when they arrived. Charlotte was still frozen and hadn't found her voice yet even to thank the man. All she could think was this must be where all the extras in *Deliverance* ended up.

"You okay?" he asked. She jumped.

"I don't know what to say. You saved my life."

"They wasn't gonna kill you. They was just after some extra beer money."

She couldn't tell the old man her life was in that car. That all the money she had to live on was stashed in small bills in the trunk.

"Take this," she said, handing him the five hundred dollars. He looked at it and shook his head.

"Dat's a right lot of money for two sweet potato pies, a bit o' honey, and a coupla pecans."

"It's the pecans. When they're out of season, it's a seller's market."

CHAPTER 9

IT WAS CLEAR. Mississippi was a force to be reckoned with. Charlotte was no longer in the mood to find music that would save her soul or set her soul free or whatever the hell it was, and she wasn't of a mind to do any more driving. She just wanted to stop somewhere, so she decided to find another place to hang her hat for the night. She'd leave Mississippi with the morning light in time to make it to Blossom's wake.

Otis's Place wasn't much to look at. It was a small weather-beaten house with a weather-beaten sign that boasted clean rooms, but it was good enough. Charlotte just wanted a roof, a bath, and a bed. She laid her head on the pillow at around eight and fell fast asleep. At about midnight she woke up. She could hear music coming from the porch. Banjo, guitar, mouth harp, fiddle, mandolin. It sounded so perfectly perfect, she couldn't help but open her window as wide as it would go and lean out to hear some more. Every chord, every note, cried a river. It reached right down into the soil of the land they were playing on. Charlotte was sure that if they played long enough, the flowers would be teased right out of the earth.

"You sing it, Mazy. You sing it loud, Miss Mazy Watts," the banjo player yelped. And then Mazy Watts began to sing. One song after another, so absolutely beautiful, Charlotte wondered if she had sold her soul to be able to sing like that. She'd heard such stories about a man who, one hot summer night, sold his soul to the devil to be able to sing the blues. A summer night as hot as this one. Charlotte closed her eyes and inhaled every sweet scent, every sweet sound surrounding her. She'd never heard anything like it, and she simply couldn't contain herself. She was suddenly clapping and singing from her window like a big-bellied warbler.

"You sing it, girl," the fiddle player yelled up to Charlotte.

And she did, calling to Jesus and polishing those pearly gates with her hands that were waving wildly in the warm midnight air.

"Praise Jesus!" someone cried.

And they did: Mazy Watts, Charlotte, and a chorus of others who slowly gathered to the porch that night and sang until the sun came up. Maybe thirty people showed, maybe more, from who knows where, to sing, to praise, to give thanks, to ask for forgiveness, to ask for salvation, to lament, to exalt, to grieve, to accept, to weep, to live, to die, to sing the gospel. It was as if church were open all night under the stars. And for a moment, Charlotte felt okay. Okay about her life and okay about the prospect of dying. Somehow, she thought, dying is what we have to do to complete the circle. The music was telling her so. It had been so many years since Charlotte had experienced the sensation of being held in someone's arms. But tonight, between the music and the moon and the unaccountable black magic of the Southern air, she was embraced in the spirit of everything that was good in this world. And she felt free.

Every part of Charlotte felt free by the grace of the great gospel gods: her arms, her legs, her hips, her feet, but especially, most especially, her soul.

The following afternoon, she woke to the harsh clarity of late light spilling off the walls while the sun sluggishly climbed down the backside of another day. However, one thing was clear, clearest of all, and that was she did not want to die. The music had made the dying seem okay last night, caught in its current and carried to the "shores of milk and honey," but today was today, and she wanted to live and hear a lifetime of it now. However, time was short, and with only a year she had no time to ruminate about how much time she did not have left. So she hurried off in search of Mazy to say good-bye. There she was, raking the flattened grass in front of her porch as if bent on giving a straight road back its curves.

"Good-by, Mazy Watts," Charlotte said, pulling her close, nearly suffocating the poor woman in her full, generous bosom. "I have to tell you, Mazy, I've never heard a voice like yours in all my life."

"And you, too, sister Charlotte, you got yourself your own beautiful voice."

"Thank you, Mazy Watts. Thank you. One night in Mississippi. I saw more in one night than I ever thought I could, because of you."

"What'd you see, Charlotte?" Mazy asked as they walked toward Charlotte's car.

"I saw . . . I saw . . ." Charlotte was trying to put her finger on the feeling. And then it struck her. ". . . a glimpse of paradise, a passing glimpse, but a glimpse nonetheless."

"Ahhhh," Mazy said, "that can happen in the delta."

"You take care, Mazy," Charlotte said. She wanted to say that she'd be back one day, and that they would meet again, that perhaps if all was right with the world they'd have another incredible evening like the one last night. But Charlotte knew she wouldn't be back. She knew that life was taking her to other places now. And besides, she knew there could never be another night like that.

"Bye, Miss Charlotte," Mazy said.

"Bye, Miss Mazy." And Charlotte drove off, looking in her rearview mirror at the closest thing to an angel she'd ever seen.

The roads leaving town were long and flat. She passed general stores that were hammered up with old tin signs, signs that looked as if they'd been hanging there since 1920: *Coca-Cola, Lake Celery, Cold Barq's Root Beer, White Flyer Laundry Soap, Wood-Coal,* and *Ice.*

But the thing that struck her the most were the kingdoms of cotton stretching out before her like a field of clouds—white froth spilling over the open fields like cold beer or soda that had been poured too high over the lip of its glass. It fell everywhere along the roads and looked like swatches of Battenberg lace. There were cotton fields in front of Charlotte, in back of her, cotton growing out of old riverbeds and across abandoned plantations. If Mississippi was known to have ghosts, then they were all right here, blowing down Highway 61.

And then, suddenly, in the middle of nowhere, breaking like a brown god out of the ground, stood a strong, solid oak tree. But this was no ordinary oak tree. The cotton had blown right up into its branches, and it looked as if a hundred hankerchiefs were waving Charlotte good-bye as only proper southern ladies can. She got out to look at the tree. It had to be a hundred degrees, maybe more, and yet this big old oak, which looked as if its bark were blistering from the heat, hung full of snow under the southern sun.

Charlotte felt certain that this place held a magnetism all its own. It was where time slowed down, where afternoons slouched toward evening, and evenings seemed suspended in the opium shades of sleep.

Maybe because it was so hot here, or maybe it was something else. Charlotte pondered the notion of time slowing to a crawl, of air so still, the wind dare not exhale a single sigh. So still you could hear the breath of a butterfly a mile down the road. Charlotte only had a year left to live, but if she stayed in Mississippi, maybe, just maybe, she could live forever.

CHAPTER 10

THE RIVER HAD BEEN DREDGED, and the Gorham police stood nearby as Charlotte's car was lifted out of the water, the driver's door swinging open on its rusted hinges. The entire front had been crushed like a tin can. It dangled from the crane, a final tribute to its sad ending.

Having recovered the gray Toyota a day after the "incident," they spent the following week looking for Charlotte's body. The search had been going on for almost two weeks. It was odd that she hadn't been found in the car or close to it. Thus, the commitment to finding her was ever-increasing, and Gorham could not close the chapter until they did. Without a body, there was talk of foul play, and a separate, growing suspicion that perhaps Charlotte had something to do with the missing money. Those who knew her best ridiculed the idea:

"Charlotte? Our Charlotte? Charlotte Clapp?"

"No. Never."

The police asked everyone who knew her to come forward and tell them anything Charlotte might have said to them the day she disappeared.

It was MaryAnn Barzini who volunteered the entire contents of the conversation she'd had with Charlotte the afternoon of her going-away party.

Chief Makley had held his position for over twenty years in Gorham. He was a somewhat portly man with unsuspicious eyes and a kind smile. It seemed as if he had stepped out of *Father Knows Best* and directly into the modern world. But while his demeanor was somewhat unobtrusive, he did have a nose for police work. His dad had been a cop and had instilled in him the ethic of "always get your man." So while tough investigating tactics seemed out of character, *cop* was in his blood.

"Well," MaryAnn began with a dramatic flourish, relishing her fifteen minutes of fame, "we talked about how she was all excited with regards to visiting Florida and about how she was going to visit Disney World. I, of course, told her about SeaWorld. I went there with Tom for my second anniversary, and I think she was completely taken with my description."

"Go on," Chief Makley said. MaryAnn was obviously taken by her own descriptions.

"Well," she continued, "then she said she was heading to Louisiana . . . to visit relatives down there."

"Relatives?" asked Hobbs, Makley's second in command. Looking through his Coke-bottle glasses, he was barely able to discern MaryAnn, let alone evidence.

Hobbs was somewhat clownish, and some townsfolk wondered if he had taken the job because he got to wear the uniform. But having grown up in Gorham, he knew everyone and was well liked, although never taken too seriously. Charlotte and MaryAnn used to laugh that Hobbs was Billy Bob Thornton to Makley's Brian Dennehey.

"So tell us about these relatives," Makley continued. "You sure it was Louisiana?"

"Yes, in or near New Orleans, I believe she said. I found that odd since she had never mentioned to me any family living in Louisiana. I mean, it seems like something I would have known. And Charlotte being such a dyed-in the-wool Yankee, too, it was just so strange she had family from the South. Maybe she was embarrassed. I would be."

"Were you particularly close with Charlotte that she would have mentioned that?"

"We were close once . . . but we drifted apart. We still worked together, and we had plenty of conversations at the water cooler and such. We didn't really socialize after my wedding. She was a bridesmaid."

"She was a bridesmaid at your wedding, and you didn't socialize with her?"

"Not really. I think she took it too much to heart when I went off and married Tom. Tom and Charlotte had been dating first, and I don't think Charlotte ever got over that."

"So, to your knowledge, no one has even contacted her relatives in Louisiana to tell them what's happened?"

"No, not to my knowledge."

"Well, Jesus H. Christ, somebody better."

And with that, an all-out search began for Charlotte's aunts, uncles, and cousins living somewhere in Louisiana. Makley picked up the phone and called New Orleans information. So far, none of the Clapps living either there or in the surrounding areas seemed to know her. It was all a big mystery at this point, the biggest Gorham had ever experienced. And where the river didn't give up its secrets, Hobbs, Makley, and the good people of Gorham hoped the Big Easy would.

It was evident to Makley that before going anywhere, he needed to bring in the FBI. The possibility of Charlotte Clapp's having robbed the bank seemed ever more likely. And if she had indeed robbed the bank, she had committed a federal crime.

He made the call to the feds to officially start the investigation. If she wasn't in the river, then she was, in the eyes of the law, a suspected criminal. In only a matter of a minute, Charlotte went from missing person to alleged felon.

"There's one other thing that continues to bother me, Hobbs," Makley said when the two were alone. "The money. Where does the First Savings and Loan of Gorham get two million dollars? And the president of the bank doesn't seem . . . I don't know, very forthcoming. I asked him for records, and he keeps telling me he's getting them together. I think we should have a chat, President Kelly and me. Don't you think, Hobbs?"

"Well, when you put it that way, I'd say a chat is in order. Mind if I come? I just love mysteries, like the ones you see in the movies where the bad guy gets cornered and has no place to run. Then he grabs for his gun, but it's too late—John Wayne has already done him in."

"Well, when you put it that way, Hobbs, yes, I totally mind if you come."

CHAPTER 11

*T*HE GERMAINE DEVOE FUNERAL HOME was located just off Bourbon Street in the French Quarter. Nothing less than sensory overload blasted Charlotte as she made her way over to the wake.

Wreaths shaped like horseshoes spread their luck around Blossom's casket. She rested on a bed of forget-me-nots, while a garland of white gardenias crowned her head. Even in death Blossom looked as if she were coming into bloom.

Candles lit the room with a dusty, operatic softness. Charlotte half expected a phantom to step out from behind the cheerless purple curtain hanging heavy against the wall.

She stared at Blossom long and hard, as if she could will her awake. And then she did the oddest thing. Scrambling through her purse, she found the medallion she had discovered in her mother's jewelry box and had carried with her since her mother's death. She wanted to give Blossom something, a token to take with her into the next life, and she wanted Blossom to know it was something very special that meant a lot to her.

It didn't matter that she didn't know who the saint was or what the saint stood for. It was just a small silver-plated medallion with *Cadoc of Llancarfan* written on one side, dated *c 580,* and with a simple cross etched on the other.

Her mother had always prayed for Charlotte's happiness, prayed that she would meet someone, prayed that she would have no regrets, and prayed that Charlotte would lose all that fat. That was where the medallion came in: Unbeknownst to Charlotte, Cadoc of Llancarfan was the saint of cramps, deafness, and glandular disorders. There were saints for everything you could imagine: headaches, gallstones, eye disease, hernias, even gout—but not for fat people. Glandular disorders was as close as Charlotte's mother could come to obesity, so she prayed to Cadoc of Llancarfan.

Charlotte took the medal from her purse and slipped it into the pocket of Blossom's blue suit. Blossom McBeal would now be protected from cramps, deafness, and glandular disorders for all of eternity.

Finally, kneeling down, Charlotte whispered something that only the dead could hear. And Charlotte knew with all certainty that Blossom heard it. She even thought she saw the hint of a smile cross her lips.

Why shouldn't she be happy? Blossom was so loved, Charlotte could not think of anyone luckier.

She sat there for two hours until someone finally came over and put her arms around her.

"It must be hard," this total stranger said, trying to comfort Charlotte.

"Oh, it is," Charlotte said, with unfeigned sincerity.

"Did you know her long?" the woman asked.

"All my life. And you?"

"Only recently, but I sure did like her. Wasn't a soul that didn't."

"Well," Charlotte said, getting up to leave, "it's nice to know at the end of her life she had the one thing that no one and nothing can take away. Not even death. She had love, and I envy that." She looked one last time at Blossom, patted the stranger on the shoulder, and walked back out into life.

CHAPTER 12

*N*EW ORLEANS IN OCTOBER—Charlotte had never seen anything like it. It was a Tilt-A-Whirl of wonder and whiskey, smoke and seduction, of food, music, saints, sex, devils, and desires. China masks shrouded in hard colors peered out from everywhere; hundreds of porcelain heads culminating in distorted jester hats, an ironic contrast to the silver tear painted on their cold white cheeks. Above their large, clownish collars, sewn from sequins or lace or gold taffeta, loomed a sad, blank stare. It was a simple face with small lips and dead eyes, looking forever inward and outward at nothing at all. It chilled Charlotte. There was something oddly familiar in its lifeless gaze. How was it that glass and fabric and paint could conjure up such a feeling of isolation in her?

"Do you want to buy one, my dear?" the clerk inquired. "They're very popular." The clerk looked exactly like one of her dolls, with tight red lips and blank eyes. She lifted the figure up and shook it so that Charlotte could hear the tiny gold bell ring on the top of its hat.

"No," Charlotte said, "no, thank you," and she walked on as if she were turning her back on an accident.

Voodoo tours, tarot readings, and visits to Marie Laveau's grave were posted everywhere. It was as if she had just entered the under-world. Jugglers, street clowns, and mimes insinuated themselves on every corner. Musicians, ladies of the night, and their patrons were just rolling home at nine in the morning. And yet, in spite of its dark underbelly and questionable gods, it was wondrous and bewitching to Charlotte.

The houses resembled cakes trimmed with sugary white icing, while intricate iron braiding encircled the porches like charm bracelets and wedding ribbons. Balcony apartments boasted so many flowers, they looked as if they were defying gravity: lingering in midair, not quite falling down, not quite staying up.

Charlotte decided to stay at the Cornstalk Hotel on Royal Street. A cast-iron fence, known as the cornstalk fence, enclosed the prop-erty, and morning glories climbed over it like a chain stitch.

She entered and rang the silver bell on the welcome desk. A middle-aged man came out from the back.

"Do you by chance have any rooms available?" Charlotte inquired.

The man looked her over but avoided eye contact, as though the less he looked into her eyes, the less he knew about her. And that was just fine with Charlotte.

"Yup, got the back room available. It's very large."

Large? Was that a slight? Jesus, Charlotte, let it go. "I'll take it."

He simply handed Charlotte the key and pointed the way. "Last room on your left."

She stayed in New Orleans for two weeks, gorging herself on Creole and pastry, po'boys and oysters, blackened catfish, and powdered beignets. She'd wander into seedy establishments to enjoy unknown drinks that had their own swampy aftertastes and left her feeling sluggish and happy and forgetful that she was dying.

Mrs. Sippi was a bar on Tulane Avenue. In Charlotte's brief visit she took to going there on a regular basis. She'd never been a "regular" anywhere before, let alone at a bar, but she liked the idea of going to a place where they recognized her, where they said, "Good to see you." Maybe it was because the bartender spoke to everyone equally: the millionaire with his spats and Panama hat, the call girl with the extreme cleavage, the dwarf with his bad jokes. And then, of course, there was Charlotte herself. She wore a proper paisley dress with flats and took up nearly two stools. But he talked to her, too.

One night Charlotte dared to exceed her personal limit. Everything that had been a rule in Gorham, New Hampshire, was broken here in New Orleans. She allowed herself to laugh too loud, live too large, and drink too much. She had chosen to drink mint juleps that night, and they tasted so damn good, she had another, and another.

"Henri, why do you call your bar Mrs. Sippi when you're in Louisiana?"

"'Cause dats wheres I'm from, darlin'."

Charlotte paused. "You happy, Henri?"

"Happy enough."

"What makes you happy?"

"I gots my wife, my chillun, my gran'babies. I gots weekends off, a good fishin' hole, a friend or two."

"Is that enough?"

"Plenty for me."

"What if someone told you you were dying? What would you do then?"

"Then? Well, den I guess I'd take stock."

"How?"

"I come to 'preciate what I gots more den I do."

That's reasonable, Charlotte thought. "Anything else?" she asked.

"Well, I guess I'd smoke my ganja a little mo den I do." Henri laughed.

"Ganja?"

"Yeah, you knows . . . marijuana."

"Oh," Charlotte said. She'd never smoked marijuana before.

"You wouldn't do anything extravagant? Maybe visit a place you'd never been? Buy something expensive?"

"Well, darlin', seein' as I don't have so much money, I think I'd have to content myself with lovin' up my wife a little mo den usual, spendin' mo time wit doze gran'babies of mine, an' sittin' unda dat big ol' oak tree I gots an' enjoyin' dat sweet, happy ganja of mine."

"But what if you did have money, Henri? Say two million dollars. Then what would you do?"

The old black man put an ice cube to his forehead. It was hot in the bar. Only a single fan turned around, and reluctantly at that.

"Well, den, pretty lady, after I buy my wife da lovliest dress dis side of da Mississippi, I'd go and sit under dat oak tree wit all my friends and spread da joy an' good feelin' around we all gets from dat ganja."

"That's all?"

"Actually," he said, "dere is one mo thing I been wantin'. A brand-new fishin' pole. I just seen one da other day down at Tyrone's Fish an' Bait Shop, an' it's a beauty. I'd get dat rod fo sure, Charlotte, an' go fishin' dat afternoon."

"That's what would make you happy?"

"As I sees it, life is hard, sweet Charlotte. But if you gots dat special thing dat makes you happy, den you gots youself everythin'."

"Never thought about it that way, Henri, but you're right about one thing—life is hard. Why does it have to be so damn hard?"

"Da Lord do dat for a reason. If'n it come too easy, den ya don't know what you gots. You takes it for granted. You might have youself a diamond, but if'n you comes by it just by luck, how you gonna know its value? No, I thinks da good things gots to come to ya a little harda den dat. Dats da part dat gives 'em dere significants. It's all about da honey, Charlotte; it's all about gettin' dat honey out of da rock."

"So, Henri, do you think that sadness is good, too?"

"Hell, yes. A little sadness is good for everyone. It's da only way ya gets to happiness. If you happy all da time, you gots nuttin' to compare it wit. No, sorrow is a gift, Charlotte. You takes it, you tip your hat to it, an' den ya moves on. But ya gots to acknowledge it or else it will have ya fo breakfast. Give sadness its due and move on."

Honey from a rock. That's what he said. That's what she'd remember.

He poured Charlotte another drink and one for himself as well.

"Here's to you, little lady, wherever life's fixin' to take ya." He lifted his glass. "Gots to click, Charlotte; clickin' keeps the devil away." So with both glasses held high, they clicked. He leaned toward her and whispered, "Remember, pain is just the messenger dat happiness is comin', Miss Charlotte. So beez happy." He raised his glass again. "One fo da sorrow an' two fo da road." And they clicked again. "You can never click too much!" he exclaimed, then threw his bourbon back in one shot and smiled. Charlotte lifted her glass and followed with a toast of her own. "Here's to getting that honey out of the rock, Henri." And then she drank her bourbon down as if she were drinking water from a tap, and nearly choked to death.

Henri made sense. She was looking at a happy person, a person who had everything. All he needed was the time to enjoy it. And he would. Charlotte slipped Henri's tip next to her empty glass. She would be well out of the bar when he cleared it. Five thousand dollars lay folded unassumingly in a napkin. Five thousand dollars because Charlotte believed that sometimes good things *could* just come someone's way. At least that's what she wanted to believe: that once in a while, maybe life didn't have to be that hard. And that was still okay with the Lord, and if not the Lord then at least with Charlotte. She had scrawled something on the napkin just before leaving the bar. Moments later Henri discovered the note hiding all that honey: *Here's a little something toward that fishing pole.*

CHAPTER 13

*A*ND SO CHARLOTTE CONTINUED to enjoy New Orleans. She had her tarot cards read, and they promised her a long and healthy life, which she knew, of course, was not true. And when she told the old man that he must be wrong, that she'd had a checkup, he hushed her, indignantly saying that the cards don't lie and she should get another checkup.

She set her big hips free and rocked to the rhythms of zydeco. She rode a paddleboat up and down the Mississippi, letting the Louisiana sun warm her northern blood. She glutted herself with crawfish until nothing was left but the empty shells of an insatiable hunger.

There was no doubt about it. Charlotte had fallen for the Big Easy and might even have stayed, but the world was waiting. California was waiting. Tom Selleck was waiting. Tony Bennett was waiting. Blossom might be on her way to heaven, but Charlotte was on her way to Hollywood.

Charlotte felt free, going down the highway, her fat cheeks pulling back like a bulldog's in the wind. She felt inordinately good for someone who was dying. *Attitude,* she thought to herself, *it's all about attitude.*

Who cared if she was fat? She felt good. Hell, Jackie Gleason never worried about it. And wasn't it Tom Hanks who once fessed up that he thought he had a big ass and fat thighs. *See, nobody's perfect. The thing is to feel good, and I do. I'm a quarter of the way to Hollywood. So there, MaryAnn.*

Her thick, dark ponytail flew back, and facts floated in and out of her head as she wound her way to her final stop.

She and MaryAnn had studied game shows religiously. No one was better at *Jeopardy* or *Wheel of Fortune* than they were. No one could guess as accurately the cost of a dinette set or a Maytag washer or an RV equipped with all the modern conveniences on *The Price Is Right*. And *Hollywood Squares*? Forget it. Both MaryAnn and Charlotte were unstoppable. This, after all, was how they were going to make their first fortunes, as game-show contestants.

"Charlotte, it's your turn."

"Famous Hollywood insults for four hundred, Alex."

"Ding, ding, ding. Charlotte, it's the Daily Double. Are you ready for this?"

"Yes, Alex."

"How much are you willing to wager?"

"Everything, Alex. Thirty thousand dollars."

"Did you hear that? Thirty thousand dollars. Okay, Charlotte . . . Who said, 'Not since Attila the Hun swept across Europe, leaving five hundred years of total blackness, has there been a man like Lee Marvin'?"

"Who is Josh Logan? He directed Lee Marvin in *Paint Your Wagon* in 1969."

"You are right. And you walk away a very rich lady once again."

Charlotte imagined the prizes she'd win as she sped down the highway toward her new life. But her fantasies ended abruptly with the realization that she couldn't risk being recognized on TV now. To her surprise, she wasn't really disappointed. Come to think of it, she didn't even want to watch game shows anymore. Or soaps. Just overhearing the TV from another room drained her and made her feel lonely, like a light left on in the afternoon. There were just some things, she decided, she would never do again.

She drove as night settled over the lifeless landscape until she eventually found herself at the King of Hearts Motel. It looked like an oasis blinking on the distant right. It struck Charlotte as somewhat odd that in the middle of a red-dirt road, beneath a flat, starless sky, stood this tacky tribute to neon. There was a naked woman curled up inside a martini glass, her legs wrapped around a flashing cherry. And lastly, there was the king of hearts himself, rocking back and forth in a light southern wind. Except for one other car, Charlotte seemed to be the only guest.

"Got a room?" she asked. A middle-aged man with teeth like a broken fence, and tattoos climbing out of his blue collar, studied his log. Every room was empty. What the hell was there to figure out? Yet he studied his book as if he were stuck on a word in a crossword puzzle.

"We got room thirteen available," he finally said as if he remembered that Charlotte was still standing there waiting for an answer.

"Thirteen? There's no twelve or eleven or nine or six . . . just thirteen?"

"What's wrong with thirteen?"

"Well, it's not the luckiest number in the world, is it? I mean, it doesn't look like anyone else is here. . . . I'd think you could give me another room."

"Superstitious?" the manager asked, scanning his book again with a grin that was so tightly locked it was as if a key had been turned one too many times and thrown away. He waited a minute or two before looking up.

"Nope, thirteen's the only room we got available, lady."

"Well, shit," Charlotte said, "just give me the damn keys." And then she began to laugh, and laughed louder.

"What?" the manager asked, and at that moment the power in the room shifted. "What?" he asked again. Whatever control he'd had seconds before was lost in her laughter, lost in a flurry of giggles so effervescent that bubbles might burst right out of her mouth. Why was she laughing? What did she know? Was she laughing at him? He could not know that she was laughing at herself—because for the first time in her life she had said the word "shit" out loud, and for the first time in her life she was beginning to feel good.

This simple expletive made her feel giddy. Oddly, as if by saying it, she had located a little undiscovered pleasure center inside herself that had gone untapped for a very long time. Charlotte turned and headed out the door.

"Hey, lady," the manager yelled to Charlotte as the screen door slammed behind her, "I gotta sign you in. What's your name?"

Charlotte paused. "Blossom," she said, "Blossom McBeal."

And so Blossom McBeal was reborn and Charlotte Clapp was officially laid to rest. The new Blossom knew she had a lot to grow into. The dead Blossom was spirited, unsinkable, and most of all, a survivor. Yes, the new Blossom would do everything to live up to the dead Blossom. Now there was even more reason to live, and there was something to live up to. Charlotte had a legacy. It wasn't exactly her legacy, but it was something nonetheless. She may be dying, but she had been given a year to live, and live she would. This Blossom was about to bloom.

The open highway and the flat plains made it seem as if 120 miles per hour were a leisurely stroll. Tony Bennett sang out "The Best Is Yet to Come." Perfect traveling music. She thought, *If I could ever get my behind on the back of a horse, I'd gallop to this song.*

Blossom laughed out loud. That was twice in two days. In fact, her whole body had been smiling for miles, as if some sweet elixir had a slow drip into her entire being. Had she been fake-laughing all those years in Gorham? The kind of "yuk, yuk, yuk" you're forced to produce when your boss bores you with a bad joke or MaryAnn Barzini tells you something adorable about her only daughter? Yuk, yuk, yuk—awful. Blossom resolved then and there never to fake-laugh again. If it wasn't funny, screw it.

Up through the northern panhandle to Amarillo, where the soil burned yellow and you could smell the dark, rich perfume of mesquite in places named Sweetwater and Rosebud. Blossom breathed deeply. As she passed the dusty hills rumored to be jammed with turquoise and tales, she felt the wind play against her cheeks like butterfly kisses. Layers were beginning to peel back. Her senses were returning.

She blew through towns like a tumbleweed, crossing the rest of Texas into the muted tones of the New Mexican desert. She drove past ghost towns and mining towns, where so many lost dreams wandered in search of the gold that never was. But Blossom would find *her* gold, for Hollywood glittered like a promise somewhere just beyond the horizon.

CHAPTER 14

 HE CHARLOTTE CLAPP CASE had become big news in Gorham. Everyone knew about it, including the doctor who had made the grievous error in sealing Charlotte's fate. Makley ordered Jennings down to the station upon learning this new and shocking information.

The trail to Jennings was paved by Happy Turner, who was to have had lunch with Charlotte the day before she quit the bank. Charlotte had canceled because she had an appointment with Dr. Jennings, and Happy remembered Charlotte coming back to work "a bit out of sorts. Then two hours later, she up and quit."

Happy was sorry she hadn't remembered this sooner, but in going through her own calendar, it came back to her. That's when she called Makley. She didn't know if it was important, but everyone was told to come forward with any and all information they had. So she did. And that's when Jennings was invited down to the precinct to tell all—"all" being the bizarre confession that felled not only Charlotte's fate with an axe, but Dr. Jennings's as well.

"You told her she was dying?" Makley asked Jennings incredulously.

"Yes. It was an innocent enough mistake, though. She had the same exact name as the other woman who had come in on the same day," Dr. Jennings explained.

"Jesus," Makley said, scratching his head: "What happened to the other woman? You tell her she was fine?"

"At the time."

"And then?"

"Well, it seems she didn't have a year left, after all."

"Jesus H. Christ," Makley said again.

"Short of amputating the wrong leg, it doesn't get much worse than this," Hobbs chimed in. "Maybe taking out the wrong organ or—"

"All right, all right," Jennings interrupted indignantly. Clearly, this wouldn't be good for his career. He sat there pondering a new practice in Guantanamo Bay.

"So if Charlotte Clapp is indeed alive, then she thinks she's dying? Is that it?"

"Yes."

"That's if she's not in the river," Hobbs said. "But face it, this kind of news could make anyone jump in the river."

Everyone just stared at each other, and Makley said "Jesus H. Christ" one or two more times.

At this point it was decided the divers would continue to comb the river, but both Makley and the FBI knew it was time to pursue that uncertain tip that would take one or all of them down south to Louisiana. All eyes were on Makley.

"Jesus H. Christ," he said one last time, and was on his way by morning.

Makley, a small-town cop from a small-time town, was not of any particular consequence to the New Orleans police. Upon arrival at the local precinct, he was essentially ignored for hours. He was like a flounder in catfish waters. He sat alone in the back room of the department, looking at a wall of wanted posters. Same culprits, different zip code.

Because Makley was not in his own jurisdiction, all he could do was show the New Orleans police photographs and offer hunches. A cop finally came in and sat down to hear the story, but a missing person with alleged felony charges was not a big deal in Louisiana— it was your kin. But to the Gorham police (who thought it was a big enough story to follow all the way down to Louisiana), it was as big as big got, and Makley had no intention of just shaking it off.

Meanwhile, back in Gorham, the president of the First Savings and Loan was behaving as if he were as confused as everyone else. He claimed that the records he had regarding the money had been stolen with the cash. He acted concerned, worried. He should have been—it was clear he had fallen into quicksand, and the harder he tried to get out, the faster he sank.

However, his complicity was swiftly revealed when an anonymous employee called Hobbs and said he urgently needed to talk to someone in charge. Hobbs was thrilled Makley was out of town—he was so rarely in charge. The employee came in that very afternoon and revealed his considerable suspicions regarding his boss. He said in no uncertain terms that Kelly was "full of bullshit." The place to look was with the brother-in-law, who stored large sums of money in the vault from time to time and then moved it out of there. The employee said he'd been doing it for years.

"Kelly's brother-in-law?" Hobbs asked.

"Yeah," said the disgruntled employee, "it's a close-knit family like the Sopranos, except with Izod shirts. The Yankee version."

"Why are you telling me all this?"

"Why? You want to know why? I'll tell you why. Because Kelly is so goddamn cheap, and whatever happens, well, it serves him right. You know what we got for Christmas? He wouldn't put his hand in his pocket for Tiny Tim. Oh, but he makes sure to give himself a big bonus every year. The rest of us? We get hams. Honeyed hams. I've worked for this bank for twenty-two years, broke my back for this bank, and you know what it got me? A goddamn honeyed ham. And I don't even like ham. In fact, I hate ham. So there's your answer. The ham did him in."

Hobbs took the ham story very seriously. He promised the weary worker that as soon as he spoke to his chief (who, in the end, was always in charge), he would check out the president and the brother-in-law thoroughly. Hobbs was a ham hater, too.

Back in New Orleans, Makley sat with the old sergeant, who stared at his northern counterpart as if he were some alien import. "We'll have our boys post these pictures," he said in a slow southern drawl.

"That's it?" Makley asked.

"It is for now," the sergeant added, annoyed that this interloper was questioning his tactics. Makley wondered if he was still holding a grudge about the War Between the States. The Confederate flag hung in the sergeant's office.

Makley got up. "Let me know if you get a lead on anything. I'm staying at the Howard Johnson's just out of town."

"No problem, friend," the sergeant said, gathering up Charlotte's photos as if the next place he was about to put them was the garbage.

Makley left, but he wasn't finished. He decided to hang around the quarter himself for a while and do a little investigating on his own, jurisdiction or not. The sergeant really ticked him off and he damn sure wouldn't take the word of a cop who looked like the poster boy for kickbacks. Makley kept a few copies of Charlotte's picture and headed out to take in some of the local color. There was a lot to see in New Orleans. And maybe, just maybe, someone in this strange and carnival-like place had seen Charlotte. A bartender, hotel clerk, a tarot card reader.

CHAPTER 15

$\mathscr{B}$LOSSOM DROVE RELENTLESSLY on toward Arizona while thoughts of her past life moved like shadow dancers at the edge of her memory. This was the trip that she and MaryAnn were supposed to take together. This was their shared dream, and even though events had made them go their separate ways, Blossom still felt a twinge of loss in making this trip without her.

What had happened to their friendship, a friendship that was supposed to stand the test of time and turmoil? What happened to those days of laughing on seesaws that would rocket them up into the blue air and bring them gently back to earth? And those rainy days when the two girls would arrive at school together in their wet hats and coats and pull off their rubber boots while Mrs. Kleem hovered over them, exuding an overwhelming sweet-and-sour smell that was always mixed with some form of admonishment. Who could ever forget the potent wave of perfume that caught the girls in its undertow every morning. My Sin. An aroma that always confirmed Mrs. Kleem was still in the building, albeit lost in a cloud, somewhere in the 1950s.

That perfume was the impetus for Charlotte and MaryAnn's first and most memorable prank: stealing Mrs. Kleem's treasured bottle of My Sin and replacing it with a clear cleaning fluid. How were Charlotte and MaryAnn supposed to know that this cleaning liquid could lift the stripes off linoleum? (It only left the slightest rash on Mrs. Kleem's neck—she really didn't have to make that big a deal out of it.) It was only one tiny dab. It was as if she had drunk the stuff, the way she carried on. Did she really have to have their parents come in for a parent-teacher conference?

They had to stay after school for the rest of the year, clapping erasers, washing blackboards, and writing, *I know what I did was wrong and I am very, very sorry,* until their fingers ached.

Charlotte and MaryAnn stuck it out together surviving the wrath of Mrs. Kleem through first, second, and third grade. In other words, an eternity. How could a friendship like that falter or, worse, end?

And now what had that once unbreakable bond become? MaryAnn always tried to make Charlotte's life a little more boring than it already was. She had worked at the bank a week longer than Charlotte, and in MaryAnn's mind this seemed to give her seniority. If Charlotte wanted to have the Christmas party at Church Hills, the only fine dining establishment anywhere near Gorham, MaryAnn would make sure it was where it had always been. Bickfords. If Charlotte wanted to bring someone into the bank to talk about new packages they could offer their customers, MaryAnn would nix it, claiming the First Savings and Loan didn't need strangers peddling newfangled ideas. When Charlotte wanted to do a trick grab bag on April Fool's Day for the bank employees, MaryAnn vetoed the idea, saying gag presents were in bad taste. Charlotte remembered how fond MaryAnn was of saying, "Why do people waste their time dreaming? Dreams very rarely come true. And then they've wasted all that time just pissing up a rope." *Pissing up a rope.* MaryAnn actually said the word "piss." But how could MaryAnn feel this way? She got what she wanted. She got Tom.

At that moment she felt enormous relief being gone from Gorham. Gone from MaryAnn, who was probably saying "no" to someone at that very moment. Gone from the memory of Charlotte. Blossom shivered. The old weight of her past life was still upon her, heavy as a wool shawl hanging over her shoulders on a hot day. She wondered if she would ever be completely free of her past, or would she feel that shawl becoming heavier, holding her in the heat of unhappiness while she tirelessly tried to shed it?

CHAPTER 16

*B*LOSSOM'S FIRST CALIFORNIA palm trees were an epiphany. They waved above her like graceful Japanese fans offered only to royalty on the highest of holy days. They flattened out against the blue sky like exotic umbrellas, rocking slowly on their tall, narrow stalks. Palm trees. She had only seen pictures of them, and here hundreds lined the streets like sacred icons, welcoming her to a place where all was possible. She got out of her car immediately and took her first roll of pictures.

Somewhere Tom Selleck was sitting with a martini, discussing a big upcoming project with some big Hollywood mogul. *Maybe even Sydney Pollack. God, Sydney Pollack. Imagine!* Somewhere Sydney Pollack and Tom Selleck were sipping Asti Spumante at an outdoor café while other stars were rushing into their waiting limousines.

But as she got closer to her destination, all she saw were low-slung stucco buildings, car washes, Fat Burgers, and advertisements. Where was that grand threshold she would have to cross, making her feel she had entered Hollywood, the Land of Dreams? *Oh, calm down. Stop acting all upset. You've just arrived. Remember, it's all about good stuff now. Positive thoughts. But, God, why does this look so much like Queens with palm trees?*

She pulled into a gas station and bought a new Los Angeles guide. Her first guide book had gotten lost somewhere in her travels, but she couldn't for the life of her remember where. She fanned the pages, searching for a place to stay. Blossom hadn't heard of any of the hotels. The Beverly Hills Hotel was the same as the Sunset Vista, complete with kitchen efficiency units and color TVs. The Four Seasons Hotel sounded the most glamorous in its description, so she headed over there.

"Checking in?"

"Uh, yes . . . yes, I'm checking in."

"May I take your luggage?"

Luggage? Blossom's luggage was loaded with stolen money. But no one here was carrying their own luggage into the hotel. How could she carry hers without appearing suspicious? Especially four large suitcases. Reluctantly she acquiesced.

What struck Blossom as she entered the hotel was the abundance of flowers. She didn't know what they were, had never seen some of them before, but they were everywhere. Trumpet vines, morning glories, and maidenhair poured over braided branches of fat, ripe oranges. Bittersweet and honeysuckle wrapped themselves around hundreds of lilies of the valley, and roses exploded like fireworks. This rivaled even MaryAnn's wedding.

She wondered if people ever lived in hotels, because she knew on sight, this was one place she could live. Never had she seen floors shine as bright as polished ice, a bar with couches more comfortable than the ones in Jordan's, or people who were so accommodating that it made you want to hold the door open for *them*.

She was completely baffled by the bronze statue in the entryway: a man posed on a bench, reading a paper he would read today, tomorrow, and for the rest of eternity.

And then there were the guests, who looked as if they were coming in from somewhere important and going off to someplace wonderful. Blossom felt self-conscious. Here she was in a plain brown dress that looked more like a wrapper, nylons with runs, sensible flat shoes, and a rhinestone butterfly pin that drooped from her collar and looked as if it would fly away if it only had the power. Shame. That's what she felt, and she hated it. So with her head down, she slipped into the elevator as though it were a closet she could hide in.

"Hold it," the approaching voice called out, hurrying toward the closing doors. Blossom fumbled for the buttons.

"Just made it," he said, pressing six. "Thank you."

She looked up. "You're . . ." was all she could manage. There, standing next to her, close enough to touch, stood Gene Hackman. GENE HACKMAN! Blossom's first star. She was paralyzed with disbelief. Gene Hackman. She had seen every movie he ever made. She even owned two of his videos back in Gorham. Should she say anything? Should she get his autograph? She should stop staring at him. But she couldn't. She couldn't take her eyes off him. *Say something, Blossom. Tell him you loved* Crimson Tide, *or that* The French Connection *was the best movie he ever made, or how good he was in* Terms of Endearment. Terms of Endearment? *Wait a second . . . Was that him or Jack Nicholson? Oh, God, I'm all confused.* But the sixth floor had arrived, and Gene Hackman was getting out.

"*Crimson Tide*," was all she was able to finally say.

"Excuse me?" he asked.

The door closed, leaving him with a puzzled look on his face.

What an idiot! Crimson Tide. *How could I have blurted out* Crimson

Tide? He must think I'm mad. Crazy. Celebrity challenged. Oh, who cares? I saw Gene Hackman. It doesn't matter. French Connection, Crimson Tide, The Poseidon Adventure. *Who cares? I wish I were on the sixth floor. Right next to Gene Hackman's room.*

She just knew Hollywood would be like this. Stars on elevators. Gene Hackman sleeping just below her. The shock of it had even made her forget about her attire for the moment. She wished she could tell someone. She wished she could tell MaryAnn.

The last event of the evening called for nothing less than the Lord's thanks. It was the discovery of the minibar. A bedside refrigerator and drawer jammed with cashews and candy bars and cute little individual bags of Famous Amos chocolate-chip cookies. Midnight snacks, just an arm's length away. And the final blessing that made her truly realize she had indeed entered heaven by way of Hollywood? The mints on her pillow.

There was a knock at the door. Blossom opened it like someone who had a bounty on her head.

"Can I make up the room?" the maid asked.

"No . . . thank you. That won't be necessary," Charlotte said from the closed door.

"Do you want fresh towels?"

Fresh towels? Well, Lordy Lord. "Yes, fresh towels—that would be nice. Just leave them outside, if you don't mind."

Blossom got on the phone and pressed *Housekeeping.*

"I don't want anyone coming in and out of my room. If you could mention that to your staff, I'd be much obliged." She then asked to be connected to information and got the names of several real estate agents. She would have to buy outright, because no bank would take more than ten thousand in cash without checking her out. Her own bank experience had taught her this. Her dream was a fancy furnished Hollywood apartment with a kidney-shaped in-ground pool on a street lined with palm trees. Could she pull it off, an offer in all cash? *Stop it,* she admonished herself. *Stop thinking like Charlotte. You are Blossom and, this is the start of your new life. Blossom would have made it happen, and so will I.*

She shoved the suitcases under her bed and headed out for her first appointment by way of Rodeo Drive. Blossom's shopping experience thus far had amounted to no more than B. J.'s Wholesale Club and an occasional pilgrimage up to Harriet's Large Size Outlet for Ladies in Portsmouth. She hated buying new clothes. It somehow reinforced the irrefutable fact that she was still a size eighteen-plus and would be a size eighteen-plus forever. Shopping avoidance helped her deny the obvious: She was fat. But Rodeo Drive dazzled her. Even the tall, lanky mannequins sporting size-four statements dazzled her, despite the grim realization that to look like that at her weight, she'd have to be thirty-seven feet tall.

Versace, Gucci, and Escada; Chanel, Valentino, and Dolce Gabbana; Cartier, Armani, and Rolex; Tiffany, Harry Winston, and Baccarat—it was all there. Even if she'd only seen them in fancy magazines at the Gorham beauty parlor. There were shops devoted only to sunglasses or chocolate or water. There were luxury cars everywhere. Cars two blocks long, with swimming pools on the back. Cars she'd only seen on *Lifestyles of the Rich and Famous.* But most of all there was an air. The smell of money pervaded everything. It gave Blossom a feeling that no matter how hard she tried, she would never fit in.

She entered the air-conditioned office of Sandra Lockley Fine Homes Realty and was immediately struck by the pictures of palatial estates on every wall. Some of them were so grand, they looked like consulates. Were these the homes of the stars? Had Sandra Lockley personally found all these mansions for the rich and famous? Could Blossom ever live in a place like that? *Oh, Blossom, these are the houses of the upper-upper. This is where Babs and Sly and Ophrah live. Madonna and Zsa Zsa and Cher. Ivana, Fergie, and J.Lo. Perhaps even Elvis lived here once.*

It suddenly occurred to Blossom that maybe people who were able to assume one name lived here. For didn't people with only one name have either money or fame or the "it" factor? Yes! Sting, Prince, SpongeBob. With this philosophy, even Shamu could live here with a swimming pool the size of Cleveland. Or Kato. He could still be lurking about, residing in yet another guest house. If the one-name rule applied, and the truth be told, Blossom preferred Lassie over Kato. And Bozo over J.Lo.

At that moment Sandra Lockley emerged from the inner sanctum of her office. Blossom could tell immediately the agent was repulsed by her appearance. In a city where no one weighs more than a bowl of Grape-Nuts, Blossom McBeal knew she looked like the World's Largest Woman. Sandra Lockley, on the other hand, was Modigliani-thin and angular, as if she'd just been put through a pencil sharpener. Where Sandra Lockley flit, Blossom lumbered like a loaded wheelbarrow, her dress looking more like a tablecloth for a seating of eight.

Nonetheless, Blossom did have money—and money, after all, was money. The pointy-faced woman tried to hide her judgments as she showed Blossom her first apartment. But Blossom could feel the sting of her glances like darts on the back of her neck and knew she was thinking, *She's so unsophisticated, so overweight, so Gomer Pyle-ish. It must be family money. Perhaps the heir to the Dunkin' Donuts fortune. And clearly brand-loyal.*

"As I was saying, Miss McBeal, I think you might like this choice. It's really quite lovely, with expansive views of the valley. The living room has a sunken conversation pit, and the master bathroom has a bidet and a Jacuzzi. Marble, marble, marble . . . Would you just look at this foyer! I know it comes furnished, but if you had a grand piano, it would work beautifully right here in the entry."

Blossom surveyed the apartment. It was beautiful. In fact, aside from the Four Seasons, it was the most beautiful place she'd ever seen.

"You share the pool with fourteen other apartments, Miss McBeal, but rest assured, the people at Beckman Gardens are top-drawer. The only people here are people who can afford to be here. No riffraff." The agent bit her lip and looked up and down at her client, trying to assess exactly which category she fell into. Eccentric? Trashy? New money? Old money? Donut money? Was it an accident claim she was able to collect on? "So let's go down to the pool and take a look, shall we?"

They descended a circular staircase, passing flowering balconies, and entered the manicured gardens. A huge kidney-shaped pool with decorative fountains and lush shrubbery spread out before Blossom like an invitation. Marble sculptures dotted the property, and a lovely blue-and-white-striped cabana rose up from a knot of lemon trees like a French mirage, in the southern corner. Pink and lavender fuchsia hung over a reflecting pool near a cherry swing nestled under a weeping willow. The whole thing resembeled an embellished stage set, in an extravagant musical that could only end happily ever after. But Blossom could barely concentrate on all this beauty. The only thing she could see was the six-foot-two pool man who was skimming leaves off the water. Blond, built, and absolutely gorgeous, he was better than Brad Pitt. Better than Robert Redford in *The Way We Were*. Well, maybe not better than Robert Redford, but just as good. Blossom could not take her eyes off him.

"What do you think?" The agent's voice was as faraway as an echo. "Miss McBeal?"

"Oh, I'm sorry, yes . . . yes, it's very nice, beautiful."

"So with everything, you're looking at a million two. But I think they'd be willing to let it go for a million. They want out because the husband has to relocate. As a matter of fact, I think he went on ahead, so the wife is really anxious to sell."

The man lifted the leaves softly out of the water, as if he were laying porcelain and fine silver down on a dining room table. His features were perfect, separately and together, and his torso looked like someone had carved it out of alabaster. He looked exactly like the picture on the cover of every romance novel she'd ever read: *Marcello Brigatino and His Secret Amours*.

"Miss McBeal? Does this seem like something you're looking for?"

"Yes, it's exactly what I'm looking for," she said with a longing that was almost painful.

"And it's within range of what you were planning to spend?"

"I'm sorry, how much is it again?"

"A million two. Utilities are included in an up-front fee of thirty-five thousand dollars, to be paid on a yearly basis. Maintenance is part of that fee. But as I said, I think we can get it for a million."

Blossom figured she would have to pay for her phone in person, in cash. But that was not what occupied her mind at the moment: She was in a garden, and it could have been Eden as far as she was concerned.

Was she imagining things? Had he looked up at her just then? Was that the sun in his eyes, or did he smile at her? *I think he smiled at me just now. I think that was a smile.* She sighed, slowly and expectantly, before turning back toward Sandra Lockley.

"Do you take cash?" Blossom asked nonchalantly, as if she had just asked the grocer to add a chicken to her order. The agent laughed—that fake laugh that Blossom hated.

"No, really," Blossom repeated, "do you take cash?"

The agent stopped laughing. "Cash?"

"Yes."

"Well, ahhh . . . I'm sure something can be arranged." She fumbled for her phone in her bag. Blossom could tell that the agent was blindsided. It was as if she had hit a jackpot, the daily double, and Publishers Clearing House Sweepstakes. She got on the phone with the seller immediately and began chattering away, nodding her head like a happy woodpecker. But Blossom couldn't see or hear her. She was miles away again.

Yes, that is a smile. A beautiful Marcello Brigatino smile.

And then, from the most inaccessible part of Blossom's being, she reached down, deep down, and did something she had never done before. Something she thought she'd never do come heaven, hell, or high water. She smiled back.

CHAPTER 17

*B*LOSSOM BOUGHT THE FURNISHED apartment for a million dollars that day. To say the transaction was the strangest that Sandra Lockley had ever experienced would be an understatement.

Blossom brought two large suitcases to the office later that afternoon, stuffed with cash. It took them eight hours to count out the money in fives, tens, twenties, and fifties.

"I know it's none of my business, Miss McBeal, but I can't help but wonder why you're paying like this."

"Well, you can blame it all on Mr. Dow and Mr. Jones."

"Excuse me?"

"I lost a fortune in stocks when the market fell, and at that moment decided to save my money the old-fashioned way. I would not be talked into too-good-to-believe investments after my first million was lost to a stockbroker's bad judgment. Not me. So I began saving my money where I knew it would be safe. At home."

"But why didn't you put it into a bank?"

"A bank! Absolutely not. Those bankers are robbers. They'll take you for every penny you've got." Blossom couldn't help but be amused by her own mockery. Between MaryAnn and herself, she was always the better storyteller, always the one to get them out of a pinch, but she was still surprised by the tall tales tripping off her tongue.

"They want you to put your money into CDs, they say, so it will grow. Baloney. You can't get your money out for six months when you do that. And sometimes it's a year. No, the mattress was good enough for me."

"Clearly!" Sandra Lockley said, her eyes wide with amazement.

Any thought of Blossom's coming by this money illegally had been dispelled; her customer was clearly just eccentric. But how she had actually made the money was still a mystery.

"If you don't mind my asking, Miss McBeal, what did you do for work before you moved to California?"

"Oh, I didn't work. I played the horses."

Blossom didn't know a lot about horses, but she knew something. Two towns away from Gorham stretched the Wonderland Racetrack, which she had visited with Tom Barzini, her intended. Tom loved the races. As a matter of fact, Tom enjoyed many things that he didn't share with Blossom. He had often ignored many of her questions about what he did or where he would go.

There was a part of Tom that felt like a black hole to Blossom, a density of secrets and stories yet untold. But she chalked this up to someone who was simply private, and figured that when the time was right, Tom would open up to her. She wondered if he revealed his secrets to MaryAnn, but she forced herself to stop thinking about this. It could ruin what was so far a good day. All that mattered now was that Tom had taken her to the track enough times so that she could bluff her way through with Sandra Lockley.

"Yup. The track. Sometimes I was just lucky. I won more than a couple of trifectas in my day. There were some races I'd just take chances on when the odds were stacked against me. And on those occasions . . . well, I'd come out smelling like a rose." *Wow. I'm good. I especially like that "smelling like a rose" part. It's like I'm Faye Dunaway in* Chinatown *or Jackie Gleason in* The Color of Money. *No, wait, not Jackie Gleason. Too much of a resemblance. Paul Newman—yeah, that's better. I'll be Paul Newman. And I love his buttered popcorn. Perfect.*

Sandra Lockley looked horrified, no doubt envisioning Blossom at the track, flapping her fat hands in the air with a wad of sweaty hundreds.

"Isn't that something!" was all Sandra Lockley could manage to get out.

By nine the money had been counted up, and Blossom was the proud owner of a fancy, furnished Hollywood apartment with an in-ground kidney-shaped pool on a street lined with palm trees. *There, so you see, MaryAnn, dreams can come true.*

And so Blossom moved in with her four suitcases, two of them empty now, and two of them still bulging with their secret contents. She walked from room to room, trying to get accustomed to her new surroundings, but every room drew her to the windows that over-looked the pool. Where was he? She could feel her curiosity creeping into a mild obsession. Catching a glimpse of herself in the mirrored entryway, she wondered if she had a snowball's chance in hell that he would ever find her remotely attractive. She pulled her belly in and lifted up her breasts, trying to reduce the property size of what felt like no less than an acre of flesh. *There's just too much of me.* She lay down right there in the foyer and threw her arms over her head, trying to look longer and leaner. *Better—still horrible, but a tad better . . . it'll be tough to go through life in this position.*

She rose and walked back to the window and looked one last time before closing the drapes. She hoped closed curtains might help break the spell she now found herself under. But just as she was about to pull the tie, she saw him. There he was: shirtless, strong, and sexy, a vision among the roses, a virtual homage to the glory of love. Her eyes fixed on his back with a laser precision.

Turn around, just a little so I can see your face.

He leaned in Blossom's direction, ever so slightly, but enough for her to see him.

Oh, my God, you're beautiful.

She could not turn away, but at the same time, she wanted desperately to get down to the pool before he went off to do something else.

Blossom was greedy, greedy to see more of him. She took a chance and left the window, hurrying down to the pool. She entered Eden by way of the flowering hydrangeas leading into the courtyard. But where was he? *Damn.*

"Morning." The voice came from just behind her. Blossom

turned, much like the slow-motion turn that happens only in the movies, the deliberate turn that suspends life for just a few seconds before the dramatic crescendo. . . . *This* was *that* moment. Suddenly, she found herself face to face with her Adonis, her Romeo, her Marcello Brigatino. She scarcely knew what to say. "Good morning" would have been fine, but she couldn't even find those words. It was as if English weren't her first language. She opened her mouth, but the only thing that came out was a flutter of invisible butterflies. By the time she was able to form something that resembled a human sound, he was gone.

How could I have let him walk away? I stood here like a mute. He must think I'm rude or slow or deaf. I'm so humiliated. "Good morning" was all you had to say, Blossom. Is that so hard? "Good morning"? You've been saying it since you were six.

And as if Blossom were trying to right her missed opportunity, she kept saying "Good morning" over and over again. Marcello Brigatino must have heard her, because he stood up from behind the shrub he was clipping and, in playful imitation, uttered back to her, "good morning, good morning, good morning."

Astonished for the second time within a minute, Blossom simply, straightforwardly, and unabashedly laughed. And the best part? The part she couldn't have written any better? He laughed, too. Loud and euphonious laughter, without judgment. And laughed and laughed and laughed. *Yes, sweet Jesus . . . yes, yes, yes!*

Blossom grabbed her bag and some cash and headed out the door to the fine shops she'd passed on the way to the Realtor. She would buy herself nice clothes, jewelry, perfume, but most important, she would buy herself some big, floppy frocks to wear poolside. She'd definitely be spending some time there.

"May I help you?"

"Oh yes . . . Where are your cover-ups?" Blossom asked.

"Cover-ups?"

"Yes, you know, the little shifts you wear around the pool."
Blossom bit her tongue. How could she have said "little"?

"What I mean is, a smock, a housecoat, a toga of some sort."

"I understand, madam, but you won't find them here. We sell
only bags. Perhaps you want to go over to the Beverly Center. They
have several floors. I'm sure you'll find what you need there."

But the woman said it with such disdain that Blossom wished she
could respond with something. All she heard was, *Yes, I understand,
madam; what you need are tarps, tents, and horse blankets.*

Heat rose in Blossom's cheeks. *You arrogant b.i.t.c.h.* But she could
only spell it. One day she would have the nerve to say it, but not
today.

When she was done shopping for her muumuus, Blossom reluctantly wandered into the bathing-suit area. The last thing she
wanted to do was try on a bathing suit, but it seemed ridiculous not
to have just one. Especially if she were going to spend the remaining
days of her life at a pool. But she was far too self-conscious to wear
it in front of anyone, particularly that gorgeous pool guy. If she were
to swim at all, it would be at night, long after he'd gone home.

She looked at herself from every possible angle in the mirror, but
every single angle was unforgiving. There were black suits, red suits,
striped suits, flowered suits, leopard suits, suits with sequins, suits
with skirts, suits with matching tops, suits of every imaginable cut
and color. Thank God she had decided to swim at night. Only the
moon would judge her.

She tried on no less than thirty-three suits before painfully
deciding on one. She had better luck choosing her saris and purchased no less than two dozen, most of them in dark colors, which
she had heard were slimming. What would he think of all these
pretty things? she wondered. *He? I don't even know his name!* And so
that became her next mission.

When she got home, she called the managing company of the
complex immediately. "No, not the maintenance man, the gen-

tleman who does the pool." She waited, feeling as if some tele-tarot reader was about to reveal the name of the man she was going to spend the rest of her life with.

"Really?" she said, as if surprised by the answer. "No . . . thank you very much . . . That's all I needed to know." Then she hung up. She felt like someone who had just been told a secret that would change the world as she knew it—as if his name alone was the password to eternal happiness. "Skip," she said out loud. "Skip Loggins." *Isn't that beautiful? Isn't it lovely? It sings; it exults; Lord, it downright jubilates. Skip Loggins . . . It's perfect.*

And like a mantra, Blossom repeated it the rest of the day. And most of the next.

Life is different when you think you are dying. Ordinary things carry a different meaning, a different significance. The mind plays tricks on you: A cold is the precursor to pneumonia, and a headache is the forewarning of a brain tumor.

Blossom simply had a stomachache, but this put her to bed for two days. She realized, as she trembled under the covers, just how precious life was. And maybe the doctor had made a mistake. Maybe she had less than a year left; maybe she had only twenty minutes left. What a waste. And she didn't even have the chance to tell Skip Loggins she loved him.

Of course, she didn't love him. She knew that. But she wanted so much to love before she died.

When her stomachache finally subsided, so did Blossom's anxiety, and she was ready once again to take on the world . . . or at least the immediate pool area. She slipped into one of her abundantly dark yet cheerful shifts and went downstairs.

Should I say, "Hi, Skip"? Should I let on that I know his name? He'll wonder how I found out. Then he'll think I'm stalking him. No . . . When I see him, I'll simply say, "Good morning." Let's see if I can finally manage to get that out of my mouth.

And at that moment she saw him from the far right corner of the garden. It was Blossom's opportunity.

"Hi, Skip," she said, without thinking. *Skip! Skip! Why did I say Skip? What's wrong with me? I might as well have gone up and kissed him. Oh, Blossom . . . just . . . just . . .*

But before she could finish, Skip had waved and yelled "Hi" back. "How are you today?"

"Oh . . . fine, just fine," Blossom said, blushing like a sixteen-year-old.

"I don't think I know your name," Skip continued. "You just moved in, didn't you?"

This was more than Blossom had ever expected. This was a conversation.

"Yes, I just moved in a few days ago. Blossom McBeal," she said, extending her hand. A warm current ran through her when he took it. It had been so long since a man had touched her, even just to shake her hand. It was as if a tiny light had been turned on at the end of a lonely road that had been dark for years.

"Like it here so far?" Skip asked. He was cordial and nice, and Blossom's heart pounded like the hooves of horses.

"Oh, very much." She couldn't think of anything to say next, and when he simply said, "Well, enjoy the day," she was both upset and relieved. Upset because she couldn't come up with intelligent words around him, but relieved because her heart was beating so hard, she was sure that if he stood there for another moment, she'd have a heart attack.

But the ice had been broken, and now she could go down to the pool and make small talk as a normal person would . . . even though she felt anything but normal.

Blossom sat out there the whole day. It was not so much that she was waiting for another chance to chat, though that would have been nice . . . very nice. She just liked being in his presence. However, when it was five o'clock, the working people in the complex began to come home. It seemed odd to sit there as the sun was going down, so Blossom rose to leave. When she did, she felt a sting as her shift brushed against the bottom of her leg. She had sat out too long, and whatever exposed areas there were had turned brick red. It was painful to look at.

She didn't see Skip when she left the pool and went upstairs. She tried to ease the damage by smoothing on all kinds of lotions. But she still looked rubbery and nuclear, like Ronald McDonald. The worst part for Blossom was that she would not be able to sit by the pool for at least two days. Two days. It might as well have been forever.

⤳

CHAPTER 18

*M*AKLEY HAD RETURNED HOME from New Orleans. Nothing had turned up yet but he needed to address the business of the bank president; he'd return to New Orleans once he'd sussed out exactly what Kelly was hiding.

An irritated Kelly entered the police station dressed in hunting gear, the rifle slung across his shoulder leading Makley to wonder if the ammunition was intended for the ducks or for him.

"Sit down, Kelly. Thanks for coming in. Can I get you a cup of coffee?" Makley asked.

"No, thank you. Anyway, what's this all about?"

A fine line of perspiration formed on Kelly's forehead. "Warm in here," he observed nervously. Makley smiled.

"Now, Kelly," the chief began nonchalantly, as if he were asking Kelly about the new Camry in his driveway, "I have to ask you what you were doing with two million dollars in the vault."

Kelly had rehearsed the answer to this question a thousand times.

"Okay, okay. I knew you'd come around to asking me that. Fact is, my brother-in-law had some assets from a portion of a strip mall he sold in Columbus. He had to put the money somewhere while he was deciding where to invest it again."

"What about his own bank?"

Kelly paused. "Good question. Never even thought to ask."

"But my understanding is that it's not the first time this kind of cash has turned up in your vault."

"Who told you that?"

"Seems to me I'm the one asking the questions here," Makley said evenly.

"Well, my brother-in-law is always turning over some deal or another. So I offered him a place to put his money. I didn't think I was breaking some big federal law. Or that it was anyone's business particularly. I mean, what's the big deal?"

Makley could think of several reasons that this was a big deal, but he didn't want to discuss them with Kelly. The less Kelly knew what was going on in Makley's head, the closer Makley was to nailing Kelly. "I think I need to talk to your brother-in-law."

"Why?"

"Because I still have some questions that are troubling me a bit."

"Like what?"

"I'd like to ask him, if you don't mind."

"Jesus, Makley, don't you think you're overreacting here a bit? Calling my brother-in-law in is like impounding Chitty Chitty Bang Bang for overdue parking fines."

Makley laughed. "The only reason I can see for not talking to him would be that you don't want me to. And if you don't want me to, then I have to wonder why that is."

"Christ, Makley, I don't care if you talk to him. I mean, he's a busy guy and he has to come up from Boston. But I'll call him. Hell, what do I have to hide?"

Plenty, Makley thought as he walked Kelly to the door. Plenty.

CHAPTER 19

$\mathcal{B}$LOSSOM'S BURN took a few days to heal, but as soon as she could move without wincing, she returned to the pool; this time she took up her vigil under a tree. She watched Skip move around the grounds like a cloud, softly and gently. She waited for him to approach. She was determined to talk to him beyond the general courtesies of weather and salutations. And she had to find out if he was married.

However, the whole day went by before he wandered into her tiny circle of surveillance.

"You keeping cool?" he asked, disentangling the green hose from its own embrace.

"Oh, yes. I learned my lesson two days ago," she said.

"Why? What happened?"

Hasn't he noticed that I wasn't at the pool . . . or that I got this terrible burn? Blossom's face fell.

"Nothing really. I just got myself too much sun, is all."

"Oooo, watch out. Burns can be nasty out here. Been there myself."

She glanced over covertly to see if he had a ring on, but his hand was in his pocket.

"Do you live around here, Skip?" Blossom was getting bolder. Questions began coming that she hadn't even planned on.

"I live in Venice."

She waited for him to offer something more, but he didn't, so she persevered.

"Isn't that the place near the beach with all the canals?"

"Yes, it is," Skip laughed. "You aren't from California, are you? Where are you from, Blossom?"

She hadn't been prepared for that question. Further, she was flabbergasted when he said her name. The combination rendered her speechless once again.

"I'm . . . I'm from . . . Well, originally, I was born in New Hampshire." *Oh, Jesus, Blossom don't tell him that; it's way too close to the truth. Think, where can I be from? How can I not know where I'm from?*

"And then?" Skip asked.

"Then my family moved to . . . to . . ."

"To?"

"To Louisiana." *Yeah, that's right, Louisiana. That state does seem to come up a lot.*

"Whereabouts?"

"Near New Orleans." *Please don't have any relatives there. Don't tell me you know it well and ask me if I know the Lafittes or if I'd ever gone shrimping as a kid.*

"Louisiana?" he said. "Never been there, but I've heard it's nice." *Thank God.*

"Oh, it's beautiful," Blossom gushed like an expert. "It's wonderfully exotic. A perfect place to live."

"Then why did you move here?"

Another trick question. "When the last of my family died, I just didn't see any sense in staying. I wanted a new beginning and thought that California might give me that. I was left a nice inheritance, so I didn't have to worry about my future in terms of income. I could settle wherever I wanted to." *Not bad, Blossom. And, after all, California* is *a new beginning, so that's not really a lie. And you don't have to worry about money. All in all, a good cover.*

"Oh, I'm sorry," Skip offered apologetically.

"About what?"

"Your family and all."

"Oh," she said, mindful again of the fictions she was recklessly inventing. "Yeah, it was sad, but that's all water under the bridge." *The Point of Pines Bridge, to be exact.* "Thank you anyway."

Skip took his hand out of his pocket to give Blossom a sympathetic tap on her shoulder before moving off to spray the sun-parched peonies.

In the blur of that gesture she saw that he was not wearing a ring.

"Skip," she said, watching him drag the hose across the grass, "I have a picture I need hung, and I was wondering if you might be able to help me with it at some point or another." *Now, that's brave, Blossom . . . in fact, it's beyond brave. It's downright plucky.* "I'll pay you, of course."

"Sure, no problem. You don't have to pay me, Blossom. Happy to do it. Would tomorrow be okay?"

"Absolutely. Tomorrow would be perfect." And he disappeared behind a crush of shrubs. Now all Blossom had to do was go out and buy a picture.

That very night Blossom hurried over to the Beverly Center to find a painting. Any painting would do except for velvet paintings of cats with big eyes, or those that you could plug into electrical sockets. She once saw a painting that had street lamps that actually lit up, and she swore she'd never be brought down to that level of taste no matter how long she lived in Gorham. MaryAnn would make a pilgrimage to a nearby Sheraton where they would have their yearly sale of "famous paintings." Van Goghs, Picassos, Monets—MaryAnn always acted as if she were getting a masterpiece.

"But, MaryAnn, masterpieces are not nineteen dollars."

"They say right on the TV commercial that all paintings are at a fraction of their retail price, Charlotte."

"Their retail price? That would be somewhere in the neighborhood of ten million dollars."

"I know they're not the real thing, Charlotte, but who can tell the difference? You have to be some kind of art expert."

"I just think you'd want a painting that doesn't have a sign at the door of the exhibit hall that says prices are being slashed, everything must go. I would think you'd want an original."

"But then no one would recognize it."

Charlotte cringed just remembering, and settled on a signed print. Yes, it was from the Beverly Center, but at least it was a limited edition.

The next day, she did not go down to the pool. She waited expectantly for a knock on her door. For Skip to be standing there, happily waiting to hang her picture. When five o' clock rolled around, he still had not appeared, so she ventured out.

"Hello, Blossom," he said as she entered the garden. "How are you?"

"Fine." *No, not fine. Hurt.* He had obviously forgotten. She had planned her whole day around his coming to her door to hang the print, and he didn't even remember. She decided to mention it.

"Think you can get to that picture today, Skip?"

"Damn, I forgot all about that, Blossom."

Obviously. "No problem."

"Could I do it tomorrow? I'm running late and have to be somewhere by six."

"Tomorrow's fine," she said, smiling graciously, although the exact opposite was simmering in her brain.

She was dying to know what plans he had at six, but felt funny asking him. After all, she didn't know him well enough. A question like that could be construed as invasiveness instead of mere idle chatter. And she had zero interest in idle chatter.

She wondered if he was taking a beautiful woman out for dinner, followed by a long romantic ride up Highway 1 to watch the sun go down over the water. She was jealous of all that she didn't know about him, and all possible combinations of love that were his to be had.

Later that evening she sat by the window, staring blankly out at the gardens, listening to the quiet. The insect zapper with its purple fluorescent glow was silent; the gardens were silent; even the Japanese maples stood elegantly hushed without a whisper of wind.

The calm seduction of the night lured Blossom down to the pool. She gazed at the flat blue water. It seemed like a seal that begged to be broken. And so she obliged by lifting a large stone from the garden and hurling it down into the waiting water. It was as if the rock had smashed a pane of glass, shattering the night. A flock of sleeping birds nestled in the bushes rushed out like applause.

Blossom had made life change its course simply by throwing a rock into the water. Just that simple motion and suddenly everything was different. She shook her head in wonderment, then slowly submerged her own endlessly buoyant body into the dark water and, like the stone, settled into a place of peace. Yes, the pool became her solitude, like an anchor at the bottom of the bay, like that stone.

The first night, all she did was float like a whale that had surfaced after its demise and involuntarily undulated its way onto a beach.

The next day she decided not to wait for Skip to knock on her door. Instead, she headed straight down to the pool. Life was too short to wish for hopeful encounters that would change the course of the world. Even her tiny world.

Skip would have to take a lunch break. Everyone had to have lunch, so lunch became her opportunity. And at noon, throwing caution to the wind, she asked him if it was a good time to hang the print, and he said yes. All he had to do was remove a rock some nincompoop had thrown into the pool. Blossom blushed.

"Of all the nerve!" she said. But her guilt was quickly assuaged by her excitement at having him in her apartment. In anticipation, she had prepared an extravagant spread of smoked salmon, caviar, and champagne. She had read about such gourmet repasts in *Los Angeles* magazine. It named famous stars who took food like this on picnics, and while Tom Selleck was not one of them, it still seemed like a good idea.

"You eat this for lunch, Blossom?" asked Skip.

"Oh, only two, three times a week," she lied. "Sit down before it gets cold." *Dumb, Blossom, dumb. It is cold. Laugh, like you made a joke.*

"What about the picture?" he asked.

"Oh, that? That can wait. We can hang it after," she said, pulling her chair as close to Skips as was appropriate. "So what do you do for fun, Skip?" she asked nonchalantly.

"What do I do for fun?" he repeated. "Well, I'm on a committee in Venice to improve and restore the town's architectural antiquities.

Not that Venice has that many old buildings. But architecture has always been a sort of a hobby with me."

It's wonderful that you like buildings. I know nothing about buildings. I don't even care about buildings. I gotta get this chitchat going in another direction.

"Oh, that's nice. I like buildings—the leaning tower of Pisa, Buckingham Palace . . ."

Skip laughed.

"So, got a cat or a bird . . . or a girlfriend?" she continued, as if that were the next likely question.

"Let's see," he said. He was as unsuspecting as prey leaning over to get a drink at the river while a lion, feline and treacherous, hid in the bushes, making ready for her pounce.

"No cat, no bird . . . no girlfriend."

Relief.

"Do have a wife, though."

Blossom was paralyzed with grief.

"You do?"

"Yup. We've been married for seven years. No kids yet."

"What does she do?"

"She's an actress. Of course."

Blossom had visions of a tall, gorgeous blond with cheekbones that could support books. She imagined a perfect Barbie doll running in slow motion toward Skip when he came home at night.

"We're sort of separated right now."

Separated?

"She says she needs time to figure stuff out. I tried to get her to do it in the relationship, but she said she just needed some space for a while. She moved in with a girlfriend a couple of blocks from where we lived."

If a whole chorus of Bible-toting Baptists had risen in one great heavenly voice and sung hallelujah to the Lord Jesus Christ at that moment, it wouldn't have approached the joy and glorious cries of exultation going on in Blossom's head.

"Separated—oh, that's a shame," she said. *A crying shame.*

"I know. But I haven't given up on us. We have a lot of good things going. I like to think of this period as a sort of time-out, like in football. Sometimes you need that to get your focus back. Teams have come from behind taking that kind of breather. I like to think that Jeannie and I are at half-time."

Hearing Jeannie's name and all those meaningless football metaphors confounded Blossom. She didn't know what to say, so she said something irrelevant.

"Does Jeannie like football?" *Who cares? Who cares what she likes?*

"No, but that's okay. We have to work on things we can both like together."

"I love football," Blossom lied.

"You do?"

"Yup. All my life."

"You root for the Saints, then, I guess." Blossom didn't have a clue what Skip was talking about.

"Yeah . . . love those Saints. Go, Saints."

Skip looked at his watch. An hour had passed. "Uh-oh, Blossom, I better get going. I lost complete track of time. Get me talking about myself and I don't shut up. One of Jeannie's complaints, I must admit." As he made his way to the door, it occurred to him that he hadn't even gotten around to hanging the picture.

"Oh, don't worry about that. It'll be here. You can do it when you've got more time."

"If that's okay. Thanks for lunch, Blossom. It was good. Got a little buzz on from the champagne."

And as she escorted him to the door, she thought, *yes*—it had been a perfect lunch. She had gotten to know him more than she had hoped that afternoon, and relished every greedy moment. Maybe he would come back tomorrow to hang the picture. No matter, Blossom thought, he would come back. That was the most important thing. He would come back.

That next night, without exactly meaning to, she found herself wandering down to the pool after dark, taking comfort in how it cradled her, how it rocked her into a feeling of reassurance. And the next night. And the next. Something was happening, something magical. Each time she lowered herself into the water, her body felt welcomed, as if it were entering a place it hadn't been in years, a space of ultimate exoneration from all that had weighed so heavily on her for so long. Here in the waters she was weightless. And so she began swimming every night, late enough so no one knew she was there. No one except that old man in the moon, smiling down at her from his silver porthole.

CHAPTER 20

A WEEK HAD PASSED, and Blossom had not seen Skip. Every morning she would dress in one of her boundlessly blessed kimonos and head down to the pool, but he did not show up. Anxiety rose in her like bad weather. She was distracted beyond hope, wondering where he was. Did he quit? Did he go back to Jeannie? Did he move away? She couldn't bear the questions repeating like rain in her head. She had to find out.

Blossom waited until well after dark, and instead of taking her nightly constitutional in the pool, she decided to try to find Skip's house. She took the long way, down Santa Monica Boulevard, because she was so nervous. At least this gave her time to change her mind. His address sat next to her in the front seat, scrawled only moments ago, after getting the information from an operator.

"Are you sure that's the only Loggins in Venice?"

"Yes, ma'am."

"Jeannie Loggins, no Skip."

"That's right."

"Well, it seems strange that it would only be under his wife's name."

"Do you want the number or not?"

"Actually, if you could give me the address, I'd appreciate that."

And so the operator spelled out the address, and Blossom had it memorized before it could hit the paper.

Am I crazy? What if he's outside with his wife, enjoying a barbecue? What if the whole family is there, celebrating a wonderful and unexpected reconciliation. No, they wouldn't be out now. It's midnight. Jeannie and Skip will be inside. I'll see their silhouettes on the shade. Oh, Jesus, Blossom, you sound like a bad AM radio show.

She wound her way through the watery avenues, looking for a number 9 Rose Street. Number 9 . . . number 9 . . . 16, 15, 11, 10 . . . 9. There it was. A sweet little cottage, trimmed in flowers and awnings and shutters. But the shades were drawn, and it was dark inside.

Maybe he's gone to bed. Maybe he's inside, curled up under his covers, all alone.

How she wished she could go inside and slip in next to him. Be as close to him as two spoons in a drawer. But she couldn't. *Ever, ever, ever.* There was no more use in sitting in front of the dark house. It only made her feel lonely. And so she put her car into drive and silently rolled away like a lost marble.

As she was driving home, she noticed several large white trucks lining the street in front of Venice Beach. They were movie trucks with *Miami, New York,* and *Los Angeles* written on the side. Orange cones cordoned off the area. But it was what was between the trucks that grabbed Blossom's attention.

A forest of pine trees had been erected on the beach. A vast swath of green, its unmistakable aroma wafting over Blossom. Pine. She hadn't smelled pine like this in so long, it made her eyes water. Screened-in porches, lemonade, children laughing with the lyrical lightness of distant wind chimes. It was the smell of home. Not Gorham per se, but New England, Robert Frost's New England. And the rich, warm drowsiness of pine sleepily cast its spell on her.

Blossom couldn't help herself. She parked the car and walked toward this unexpected oasis.

What she saw inside the pine forest was even more extraordinary than the forest itself. There, standing like a memorial to a time long gone, was a 1930s roller-skating rink. It was as bizarre as if she'd found a grand piano standing all alone on an empty beach, or a lit chandelier hanging deep in the woods from high in an aspen tree. The whole scenario was straight out of a Fellini film.

Curiosity drove her in. A sign hung above the doorway read, *Lake Arrowhead Roller Skating Rink.* Trophies gleamed in the dark, and the pipes on the ancient Wurlitzer looked like a bell tree. There was an ice-cream stand, and a clutch of skates hanging like a tease in the corner.

Blossom wanted to roller-skate. She hadn't been on skates since she was a little girl, and the urge, mixed with the perfume of the pine, brought her back to a time of unadulterated happiness. There, hanging on a hook, was a pair of red skates with silver laces. They were the ones that caught her eye. She made her way over to the clanging collection and lifted the red ones off their peg. Slowly, she wedged her pudgy feet into the openings. They were tight, but not tight enough to dissuade her. Wobbling up and onto the worn-out, unpolished wooden floor, she began to skate.

She imagined how ludicrous she must look, a large balloonish shape making its way around the rink, like a low-floating dirigible. *This must be a present from the roller-skating gods.*

Suddenly, a light went on and flooded the entire room. A young boy, no more than twenty, covered in tattoos and piercings, glowered at Blossom.

"What the fuck are you doing in here?"

Blossom was too startled to say anything at first.

"Well?"

"I was passing by, and I smelled the pine, and I walked over to see what was hiding in the grove, and I saw that it was a roller rink, so I came in and went roller-skating."

This was all true, albeit a little bizarre.

"This is a closed set, lady. They're making a film here. If they knew you got in, my ass would be fired. I just went to get some coffee and all hell breaks loose."

Blossom started to cry. She didn't know why, exactly—all she had to do was take the skates off and go home—but some untapped sadness, some sense of not belonging made her sad.

"Hey, lady," the boy said, "what's the matter?"

But Blossom just wobbled over to the side, her tears falling on the uneven wooden floor.

"Hey, look . . . it's not me that doesn't want you here. I'm just a hired gun. I mean, if it were up to me, I'd let you skate."

"I understand," she said, her eyes large as lakes.

She began to take off her skates.

"Wait, wait a second," the boy said. "You want to skate that badly? Go ahead. I mean, if it means that much to you. What, were you some kind of roller-skating queen once?"

"No, I just wanted to skate among the pine trees like I did as a little girl. Stupid, right?"

"Hey, I've wanted to do some pretty wacky things in my day. See if my motorcycle could reach a hundred and twenty, make it across the rails on a bridge before the train came."

It wasn't exactly the same, but the kid got it, understood that crazy ideas pop into everyone's head from God knows where and God knows why, but they just do, and these desires must be granted.

"Okay, you ready for the whole thing?"

Suddenly, the ceiling opened, exposing the dark dome of heaven above their heads. The silvery planets painted on the ceiling were eclipsed by the actual nighttime sky, awash in constellations.

"Now you can really see the sky," he said, as though he had invented heaven himself.

"It's beautiful, truly beautiful."

"Did you know all those planets were named after gods?" he asked. He didn't wait for an answer. "There's Mercury, the winged messenger, and Venus, the goddess of love, and Mars, the god of war," he proclaimed, proudly exposing the extent of his education.

Blossom thought for a moment, trying to bring up the sketchy memories of what she'd learned in sixth grade. "Then there's Jupiter, who was the main god, the big-cheese god, sort of like the president of the gods; there's Pluto, the god of the underworld, and let's see, there's Neptune, god of the sea . . . but wait, I'm leaving two out . . . they'll come to me in a second. Oh, yes, there's Saturn, but I can't remember what he was the god of."

"Maybe cars," the boy said in all seriousness.

Blossom giggled. "Yes, maybe. But there's one more. Oh, yes, Uranus. And I must admit I have no idea what he was the god of."

"Oh, that's easy," the boy said. "He's the god of assholes."

This struck Blossom as so funny, she nearly fell off her skates. "Yes, of course," she agreed, "Uranus is the god of assholes. So in all likelihood, he's the busiest."

Now the boy laughed, while "Moonglow" and "Pennies From Heaven" played from the ancient Wurlitzer, and the ocean clapped along the shore in absolute approval. And Blossom skated. Her cumbersome body rolled easily to the tunes coughing out of the old organ, and the millions of mirrors surrounding the hall made it seem as if the rink were blessed with infinite fields of Blossoms.

"Falling in Love Again" played under the starry canopy while the Wurlitzer gods bestowed one last gift upon her. And three more times she glided around and around to the tune of "Moonlight Serenade." That was the best note to end it on.

"Thank you," she said to the boy, who was smoking a cigarette upstairs.

"No problem, lady. Just don't come back with your friends, if you know what I mean."

"I know what you mean," she said as she was untying her laces. "By the way, what's the movie about?"

"I don't really know too much about it. It takes place on Lake Arrowhead in the thirties. There's some old brothel upstairs here, and someone gets shot."

"Who's in it?"

"Nobody you would know, except for maybe Gene Hackman. I guess he's the only star."

Blossom smiled: her old friend, Gene Hackman. She stood and turned to leave.

"Well, thank you . . ." she said, and was about to say the boy's name until she realized she didn't even know it.

"That's okay. Best left unsaid, if you know what I mean."

"More than you can imagine." And Blossom left, stepping out of the thirties and back into this decade, feeling as if she were the only person in the world to have truly time-traveled. She drove home thinking about what had once been said of Hollywood. "Holly-wood? It's rather like living on the moon, isn't it?" Yes, it was.

The next morning Blossom decided to call the management com-pany and try to find out exactly where Skip was.

"I was wondering," she asked, "I was wondering about the pool. When will it be attended to?"

"We've been sending a guy down there every night to do the work. Is there a problem?"

"No, not at all . . . I was just wondering when the usual guy would be back."

"Not for another week."

"Another week?" Well, at least he wasn't dead. But who knew? Maybe in another week she would be. "I guess we all need a little R and R," she said feebly.

"Yup."

"Okay, thanks for your time."

"Okay." The anonymous voice hung up.

So Skip was on vacation. But where? This sent Blossom into another of her high-flying obsessions. Her desire to know was making her crazy. Was he with his wife? Did they get back together? She couldn't even eat, thinking the worst, which in some ways, she guessed, was a good thing. The only thing that made her feel slightly better was swimming. And that she did to the extreme. She never seemed to tire of going back and forth, back and forth, ever so slowly, ever so measured, like a pendulum winding down, marking time, becoming lost in the rhythm of her own breathing. She was light in the water, light in her being.

She never felt that the person she presented to the world on the outside truly represented the person hidden away on the inside. It was as if she were two different people: the one the world saw and the person that she really and truly was. Wasn't it Robert Redford who had said the same thing about himself? He was beautiful on the outside, and clearly, Blossom was not. But perhaps it was similar in this way. Maybe she was interesting or even pretty on the inside, the part no one could see. That's what Robert Redford must have meant.

No one could get past his good looks to know who he truly was, and no one could get past Blossom's obesity to see who lay hidden beneath all those Krispy Kremes and sadness. She thought Robert Redford was misrepresented just like herself. Well not just like. *If truth be told, I'd rather be beautiful and have to prove I'm talented and smart than be fat and have to prove that I'm even worth talking to. It's so unjust.* At the end of the day, Blossom believed Robert Redford had it over her in so many numberless ways. Yes, he was talented and smart, and handsome to boot, but face it, he would have been revered even if he were a moron. Why were looks so important? *I say let's bring back the Rubenesque woman. Abundant, voluptuous, more to love. Yeah, what happened to her? Probably some eighteenth-century version of the South Beach Diet.* And so she dealt with life's inequities by taking her nightly constitutional in the pool and immersing herself into the only place she felt safe.

Water became her metamorphosis. Slowly but surely, a tiny transformation began to take place. It was not by design; she simply felt so wonderful in the water—so light—that she stayed in longer and longer. She hadn't felt this good in years. In fact, she had last felt this way well over a hundred pounds ago. Weightless and free.

CHAPTER 21

$\mathcal{B}$LOSSOM CONTINUED TO TRY to distract herself during the long days of Skip's absence. She began going to the movies, where she could escape for hours on end, forgetting her situation, forgetting it was still daytime outside, and even forgetting about Skip. But as soon as the movie was over, reality hit like a backwash of

Windex. Everything became window-clear, and to avoid going out into the light she would be off again to another movie. Once she watched *Casablanca* five times in a row.

She would silently mouth the words through each scene and always cry at the end. *Don't get on the plane, Ingrid, DON'T GET ON THE PLANE!*

Most of the movies she went to were retro. Old-time black-and-white movies or big extravaganzas like *Gone With the Wind.* She knew so much about what went on behind the scenes while making the movie, and about the actors themselves, she couldn't help but feel involved, a part of it. For instance, she knew Clark Gable didn't want to play Rhett Butler and never made much of an effort to perfect a southern accent. Further, he didn't like pictures where he had to put on a costume. But Blossom's favorite fun fact about Gable was that Warner Brothers rejected him because of his big, floppy ears.

During the time Skip was gone, she spent every afternoon at the movies, testing her memory for trivia. *The Old Maid* was playing at a little theater in Sherman Oaks, and Blossom made a special trip out there to see Bette Davis. She felt an odd kinship with Davis. The star had been taunted mercilessly by Howard Hughes; he constantly referred to Davis as an ugly duckling. But she overcame those cruel and undermining insults by creating unforgettable characters. Where she lacked glamour and that certain feminine charisma, she created an on-screen persona that made her immortal. And Blossom knew that. While most saw Davis as the ultimate spinster, Blossom saw her as a survivor. *We could have been friends, Bette,* Blossom thought as she sat in the lonely dark. *We could have been good friends.*

At long last Skip was back. Blossom sat under her usual tree, one eye on *People* magazine, the other surreptitiously following his shadow across the lawn.

"Hey, Blossom," he said, looking wonderful and relaxed, as if he had just got in from paradise that morning.

"Hey, yourself." Blossom was exuberant. "Where have you been?"

"Vegas, Sonoma, San Diego."

"Wow. World traveler."

"Had a couple of weeks coming to me. Jeannie and I spent some time together, and then I did some world traveling on my own . . . visiting friends."

Jeannie?

"Was it great?" Blossom asked. But that's not what she wanted to know at all. She wanted to know if he and Jeannie were back together.

"Yeah. It was nice. But all good things must come to an end. Back to work."

She wished he felt differently. And still she was dying to ask him a million questions. But it was so damn inappropriate to grill him when he'd been back less than five minutes. Perhaps she could plan another lunch. Information was more easily given up over champagne.

"Oh, by the way, Blossom, I haven't forgotten about your picture. But you've probably found someone else to help you with it by now."

"No, not at all. I forgot about it myself." *Yeah, sure, and there's central air-conditioning in hell.*

"How's Wednesday for you?"

"Wednesday's perfect."

"Great. Enjoy the afternoon, then." And she watched him walk away, thinking he looked like someone who could walk on water.

"How does that look?" Skip asked.

The picture was finally hung and Blossom stood back surveying its evenness.

"Perfect, Skip." As was everything about him.

"Well that only took three weeks." He laughed.

"Have you had lunch? I've got a ton of food here." Blossom struggled to sound casual as she issued this offhanded invitation, as if she weren't desperate for Skip to join her.

"Sure, why not?"

Joy.

She laid out the breads and cold cuts, condiments, and chardonnay.

Food had helped them slide into easy chatter once; maybe it would again.

"So how are you and Jeannie doing?" Blossom asked, fearful of the answer.

"Okay . . . You know . . . we had an interesting time together. The truth is, I love her so damn much, but sometimes I just don't know if we can work this thing out. I'm trying, but she's just not receptive to it. I think maybe I should just back off. Give her a chance to come looking for me. At least that's what I hope she'll do."

"It's funny how that works sometimes," Blossom replied. While her own experience was limited, she understood human nature. Not always her own, but others'. Pain had given her the inside track on how that worked.

"People don't want what they can have, but they'll fall on their sword for something that's out of reach, beyond them, the very thing they can't have." *And you're looking at her!*

"Yeah," Skip said, as though she had come over to him and put a light on above his head. "Why is that?"

"I'm not sure. Could be, she needs to walk away for a while just to look back and see just how good the thing is that she's got."

"Thanks, Blossom . . . Yeah, that'd be nice." But Skip said it in such a low voice, she wondered if he believed it. "What about you, Blossom? You ever been in love?" He paused. "If you don't mind my asking?"

Blossom was surprised by the question. She didn't think he would ask her something that personal. She didn't think he'd even be mildly interested. But she was glad. He was genuine about it, and it made her see his kindness.

"Yes, I was in love. Three times. The first was to a boy in high school; his name was T. J."—her voice lowered—"short for Trevor James. The second time was to a man named Tom. We had gone out for about six months. That's when my mother got sick. I ended up having to take care of her, and the relationship sort of fell apart." She didn't want to tell him about MaryAnn, about how he'd been snatched away from her like a beautiful brooch from a jewelry case when the saleswoman looks away. It was too long a story, and she didn't want to think about that now. Talking about it would just put MaryAnn back in the room with her, and MaryAnn was one of the reasons she had been happy to leave Gorham.

"And the third time?" Skip asked.

Blossom took a second before answering. She looked at him with a longing that could bring rain to the desert. She couldn't say "now"; she couldn't say "you." All she could do was stare and fumble for an alibi.

"You don't have to tell me," he said. He could see she felt awkward.

"I'd like to tell you," she said, and she would have, with every molecule of her existence. But she couldn't. Not yet.

"Yeah, some other time," he said.

Blossom shifted, trying to find a position to put her at ease, but comfort would not come by simply shifting in her seat. It was the conversation that had to shift. Away from love.

"So . . ." Blossom began, "what do you do for fun around here?"
Lame, Blossom, lame, lame, lame.

Skip could see her struggle and wanted just as much to move on and away from the *L* word.

"Let's see, fun," he said forcedly. "Well there are a lot of sights to take in. I mean, Hollywood and all. Have you gotten a chance to see anything yet?"

"No, not really."

"No? Haven't seen the La Brea Tar Pits or Universal Studios?"

"No."

"Really! How about the Farmers Market?"

"No, can't say I have."

"Well, you must have at least gone to Disneyland."

"Nope, haven't gotten around to that, either."

"You haven't gone to Disneyland? Blossom, I'm shocked! People come from all over the world, and you're a stone's throw from Anaheim. Jesus, I've been there at least fifteen, twenty times in my life. For crying out loud, it's *Disneyland,* Blossom!"

It was as if she had forgotten to take a very important step during the rites of childhood.

Blossom could barely visualize herself on a roller coaster, her tonnage swaying back and forth in the sharp turns.

"Jesus, Blossom, I'll take you there myself if I have to," Skip offered.

His eyes were big and happy, as if he were revisiting his own childhood and remembering something really wonderful.

Was this possible? The handsomest man she'd ever laid eyes on (Tom Selleck did not count, because she had never actually seen him in person) was offering to take her to Disneyland?

"No!" she protested, with about as much conviction as a lawyer refusing to take money for his services.

"Hell, yeah. Let's do it! Let's go. You'll love it."

And so, miraculously, Blossom had a date on Sunday to go to Disneyland and ride the roller coaster with Skip Loggins. It didn't get any stranger or any better than this. Wasn't it Marlene Dietrich who said she could watch Robert Redford filling out tax forms for hours on end? Yes, it was, and that's exactly how she felt. Yet at the same time, an odd camaraderie was clearly forming, lopsided as it was. For the first time in Blossom's life, what she was giving was not being refused, given back or pushed away. *This,* she thought, *is what empathy means; this is what friendship means. I'd almost forgotten.*

CHAPTER 22

$\mathcal{M}$AKLEY WAS GETTING TIRED of waiting for Kelly to arrange a meeting with his brother-in-law, so he decided to pay him a visit at the bank. He hoped it would serve as a sort of exclamation point to the fact that he didn't want to be jerked around—and cared less who knew or thought they knew that Kelly was mixed up in something bad. The time for protecting Kelly's tenuous reputation had passed.

All eyes were on Makley when he entered the bank and passed desk after desk filled with the redundant knickknacks of life in Gorham. Baby pictures taken at Sears, all with the same blue velvet backgrounds, candy dishes, a box made out of Popsicle sticks someone's granddaughter had created in art class.

A hush fell over the room. Tellers stopped their transactions, and customers turned and stared. Kelly saw Makley through the glass window that separated his office from everyone else. He closed the door quickly after Makley had gone in.

"Jesus, Makley, why'd ya have to come down here? It makes things look bad!"

"Look bad for who, Kelly?" Makley asked, eyes wide.

"Who? Me! Rumors are flying about that money. You know that. People think I had something to do with it. And then you walk in here! Jesus, Makley. Tact, where the hell's your tact?"

"Where the hell's my meeting you were supposed to set up with your brother-in-law?"

"I'm working on it. He's busy. In fact, I think he's even out of town."

"One way to find out. Give me his number, Kelly."

"What?" Kelly gasped, as if Makley were asking Kelly's wife for the number of his mistress.

"Give me the number of your brother-in-law, Kelly or I'll get a summons for it."

"Jesus, Makley, cut me some slack here. Do you know how much pressure I'm under? Believe me, I'm not particularly high on my brother-in-law's list right now. He just had two million bucks stolen under my watch. I mean, he's not even returning my calls right now. Frankly, I think the guy wants to see me dead."

"Only him?" Makley laughed.

"Yeah, very funny. Please, Makley, give me a couple of more days. If I can't get anywhere, the number is yours."

"What do you have to say to him that you don't want me to know?"

"Nothing, nothing. I just feel responsible for this mess, like I stole his money. Let me cool him down. The cash is on the up-and-up. I'm just in the shit house right now. And I haven't even begun to tell you what my relationship has become with my sister. She's not taking my calls, either. I'm begging you, Makley. Two days. That's all I need: two days."

"Two days. But that's it, Kelly. *Comprende?*"

"Yes, thanks, two days. Oh, and Makley, if you don't mind, let me come by your office. This little meeting, well, it doesn't look good, and now new rumors are gonna fly."

Makley stood up. "Two days, Kelly, or I'll move my desk into this bank."

CHAPTER 23

*B*LOSSOM BEGAN PUTTING miles of water behind her, and imperceptibly the fat began to burn off. She had lost twenty-five pounds, but Skip didn't seem to notice as he stepped aside and let her slide into the silver boxcar. It sped them into the pitch dark. There were screams, laughter, and pleas rising out of the blackness. Other than in the pool, Blossom had never felt so light. She felt she could reach out and catch stars in the palm of her hand. Whole universes fell behind her. She was a meteor shooting past new moons and Milky Ways toward heaven. She was falling like a star into life. And like a star that burns its brightest before going out, so was Blossom. She was heading fast and furiously somewhere to be happy, if only for a minute, before she died.

"Like it?" The ride was over. Blossom's cheeks were flushed.

"Like it? I loved it."

Skip was pleased. "I knew it. I knew you would. Don't ask me why; I just did."

"What about the ride we passed on the way over?"

It was a flume; they would both be drenched before it was over.

"No," Skip teased. He couldn't believe Blossom had it in her.

"Yes!"

"No."

"Yes!"

"Yes?"

"Yes!!!"

And they were off, cascading into the resurgent back splashes of cool, undulating whirlpools. From one end of the park to the other, Blossom and Skip, two unlikely comrades, moved with one mission: to have fun. And they did. It was late when they finally arrived back at Blossom's apartment. Skip walked her to the door.

"Wanna come in?" Blossom asked. There had been nothing awkward about it at first, but just the fact that Skip was saying good night at the door made him suddenly feel a little uncomfortable.

"No, I gotta get. Hey, it was fun, Blossom," he said, turning on his heels. "Thanks."

"No, thank you, Skip. Guess I'll see you tomorrow, then."

"I'll be there, lurking in the bushes."

She laughed and closed the door. But she was far from sleep when she looked into the mirrors surrounding her foyer. She was utterly happy and had completely forgotten that she was dying, had forgotten that she was fat, had forgotten that she still had that ridiculous Mickey Mouse hat on her head. She stood there laughing, thinking, *Yes, life is good. . . . I think I'll have some more.*

It was Saturday, and Skip would not be at the pool. Weekends were eternal for Blossom. She dreaded Fridays with an anxiety that began as early as Wednesday night and settled into an awful countdown by Thursday morning. All she could do was wait for Monday, when she would at long last see him again. She never stopped picturing him, remembering the different clothes he'd worn to work, what time he got there, what time he left. She contemplated his body as if it were a cure. She obsessed about his cerulean blue eyes. Eyes that were so effortlessly blue, you might find such color on a rare plate . . . or out at sea.

His lips were full and his nose slightly crooked, won years ago in a schoolyard fight. She would lie in bed dreaming that her arms were around him, whispering she loved him, confiding that he made her happy. Her imagination tossed and turned for hours, as if it were trying to break a fever.

As long as Skip was within smiling distance, Blossom felt she could live forever.

At two o'clock on Saturday afternoon, still dragging about in her cotton nighty and fluffy bunny slippers, Blossom had a flash thought. She dressed quickly and drove into Beverly Hills. She was on a quest. She wanted to buy Skip a present, a special, out-of-the-ordinary present. And the reason would be . . . would be . . . *because he took me to Disneyland, and it's a token of my appreciation for showing me something I wouldn't have gotten to see otherwise . . . yes, exactly. And for hanging the picture—yeah, there's that, too . . . and because . . . because . . .* because she loved him, but in no way could she present that as the reason.

She wandered around the store for a few minutes, unsure of what she was looking for. Suddenly, from behind a glass case, she spotted none other than Gene Hackman. Again? Gene Hackman, twice. Once more she deliberated going over to him, telling him what a fine actor he was and how much handsomer he was in person. But shyness overcame her, and she looked away trying to concentrate on her mission at hand.

A gold sport Rolex caught her eye. *That's Skip! It's so masculine, and waterproof. A perfect pool watch. He'll love it. The one he's wearing is all old and chewed up.*

Gene Hackman stood only a few feet away. She got up her nerve.

"Do you like this? I mean, as a present . . . Would it be something that someone would like to get?"

There, she'd done it. Hackman looked down at the Rolex.

"Anyone in their right mind would like that as a present."

Blossom smiled. "I'll take it," she said as she stared at it through the locked glass case.

"Do you want to see it on?" asked the salesman.

"No, I can see it from here. It's perfect."

"It's fifteen thousand dollars."

"Do you gift-wrap?"

And, as matter-of-fact as that, the watch was hers. The watch was his.

"No. Absolutely not, Blossom." Skip was staring at the watch. It was not even nine o'clock yet. She had been waiting for him to arrive like you wait for Christmas morning.

"I can't take this."

"Why?"

"It's too much. It's just . . . too much."

"Money?"

"Money and otherwise."

"But it's my thank-you . . . for Disneyland and for hanging the print."

"Hanging the print? Jesus, Blossom, this thing costs a fortune. My hourly rates are a little more reasonable than that. Anyway, all jokes aside, I know what a Rolex costs, Blossom, and I just can't take it."

"But Gene Hackman saw it, too, and he said anyone would like a present like this. I mean, Gene Hackman approved of it."

"Gene Hackman?"

"Yeah, he was in the store, so I asked him."

"Well, in spite of Gene Hackman, I insist you take it back, Blossom."

"But I really want you to have it—the money means nothing to me."

"I just wouldn't feel comfortable accepting this. It's really beautiful, and I really appreciate it, but I can't. I can't."

"It's rude to give a gift back, Skip," she said, in hopes this last-ditch logic would give him an excuse to accept it.

"I'll just have to live with my rude self. . . . I'm sorry, Blossom. I know you meant well by it, and I'm flattered, but it wouldn't be right."

Ever so reluctantly Blossom took it back. She put it in the box and closed it. "Well, I wouldn't want you to feel uncomfortable. That would sort of defeat the purpose, wouldn't it?"

"Yeah."

"So I guess you'll have to content yourself with my good intentions."

"That I can do. Thank you. I'll take that."

He walked away while Blossom stood there, not sure what to do next. She didn't want to appear hurt. That would be a completely inappropriate response, but she was too embarrassed to sit at the pool now.

She thought about Fernando Lamas and Ethel Merman in *Happy Hunting*. The scene they were in called for a kiss. One night Lamas was angry at Merman for some unknown reason. He walked off the stage after the scene and wiped the kiss off his mouth. He said kissing Merman fell somewhere between kissing a fat uncle and a Sherman tank. Blossom felt as if she'd forced Skip to kiss a Sherman tank, and he just couldn't do it.

"So I guess I'll just return this," she called out to him, looking for an instant exit.

"Thanks, Blossom."

And Blossom turned toward the gate, holding back the tiniest tear. *Oh, Blossom, snap out of it. He's right. It's too much, too much. Just like me. Too damn much.*

CHAPTER 24

$\mathscr{B}$LOSSOM DROVE AROUND for hours, practically turning pavement to butter before finally returning to the apartment at around nine. Why was she so sad? she wondered. It was just a watch. But it was more than a watch. She had given it to him out of a feeling of love, and it was as if in refusing it, he had given her love back.

She could reason it out, knew logically it made no sense to feel so crazy about it. Skip didn't love her. He liked her. And that was wonderful all by itself. But because Blossom craved love so badly, she couldn't seem to appreciate the gift he gave so freely. The gift of friendship.

Later that night she put on her bathing suit and walked down into the dark garden. By now, even the pool lights had been turned off. She dropped her towel behind her like an afterthought and slipped into the cold water.

She felt like a satellite given up to the sky, alone in her own awful orbit, surrounded by a jangling isolation. She floated for what seemed like an endless amount of time, looking for some tiny pinpoint in the black heavens to call home. But there were only clouds. An anonymous sky offered no comfort at all as to why she was there or why, one day, she would not be. And so she swam, back and forth, back and forth, woefully heaving her body from one end of the pool to the other, disappearing beneath her own heartbeat.

And as she swam, thoughts began to break like bubbles around her. *Words* . . . Back and forth, back and forth she swam. *Images* . . . She had something special and couldn't see it . . . *fragments* . . . until she almost ruined it. It all came into focus. Back and forth, back and forth, everything was becoming clear, unknotted, good again . . . *in spite of what I almost did* . . . and the clouds of clay that had sealed the sky shut thinned out and now shone like a deep field, glinting with mica and midnight.

She continued to swim until a certain lightness began returning to her body. Skip could see someone special hidden under all this ballast.

Back and forth, back and forth she swam, shedding the weight of whole loaves of bread. Back and forth, back and forth, she swam, purging the excesses of her life and leaving behind so much bread and sadness. Blossom, who had been buried for what seemed no less than a thousand years, yearned to get out and live and laugh and love. Yes, love. And so she swam. And swam. And swam. The water felt like a baptism to her. And she would swim all the way to Jerusalem if she had to, to discover who it was that was in there.

CHAPTER 25

*K*ELLY GOT AN UNEXPECTED reprieve from Makley, who had gone back to New Orleans. Someone had called asking if there was reward money regarding Charlotte, and even though the person refused to leave a name, and even though this inquiry didn't mean anything necessarily, Makley wanted to get back there and begin showing Charlotte's photograph around again. And so he did. A gut feeling told him there still might be something to learn there.

Mrs. Sippi was crowded when Makley walked in and made his way over to the bar.

"What'll it be?" Henri asked the stranger.

"Scotch, please, straight up."

Makley picked up a swizzle and wound it through his fingers like a string of worry beads. Henri brought him his drink.

"You get a lot of tourists in here?"

"A fair amount," Henri said.

"A friend of mine recommended this bar."

"Dat a fact."

"Yup." Makley brought out Charlotte's picture and showed it to Henri. "Recognize her?"

Henri recognized Charlotte right away: the lady who'd given him the biggest tip he'd ever seen in his life, the biggest tip he ever would see. The woman who had afforded him not only that brand-new fishing rod but a secondhand bass boat to go with it. He smiled. Then he looked at Makley, and a rush of mistrust flooded his basic instincts like an ill wind.

"Nope. Don't recognize her none."

"You smiled."

"She funny-lookin'." Henri felt bad disrespecting Charlotte by saying that. Especially when she had been so generous. But he was backpedaling now. He knew he had smiled, and was scrambling for an alibi. "Why you's wanna know if I seen her anyways?"

"She's been missing. I'm trying to find her."

"Dat all?"

"Isn't that enough?"

"I s'pose. How is you her friend?"

"I just know her . . . we go back a few years."

Henri could smell the lie like strong Stilton wafting from the doors of a cheese shop. But Makley could smell a lie, too.

"How come you're asking so many questions if you never seen her before?" Makley asked.

"Idle chatter's all. Da bartender's curse." A few seconds passed, and Henri's curiosity was still primed. "If she come in, ya wants me to give her da message?"

Makley grinned. He knew damn well Henri had seen her. He just wasn't sure if he had seen her a few minutes ago or last night or last week. "No message. I want to surprise her." He finished his drink and tossed down some cash. He knew more now than he had an hour ago, and was certain he was on the right track. Someone would recognize her picture and tell him something. It was just a matter of time. As he got up to leave, he thought he heard Henri say something. Could have sworn he heard him say something.

So he turned back. "S'cuse me?"

"Have a pleasant stay in da Big Easy."

"Thank you." But that wasn't it. It was something else. Something about tipping . . . or someone . . . being . . . a . . . better tipper . . . ? Was that it? Naaaa.

CHAPTER 26

$\mathcal{B}$LOSSOM LOOKED THROUGH the curtain and saw Skip adjusting a sprinkler. Sprinklers. They brought back such nice childhood memories of rainbows bowing back in the sun and turning the wet air red and purple and green. And then there was the ice-cream truck that would spread the thinnest tintinnabulation of cheap silvery bells throughout the neighborhood. How everyone would rush from their childhood obsessions of hopscotch and jump rope and freeze tag to the only thing on God's earth that could bring them unconditional happiness: a Hoodsie Cup. *That was when MaryAnn and I were small, when we were still friends.*

Happy. This is how Blossom felt watching Skip drag the sprinkler across the lawn. He waved, pulling her into the present. She waved back and moved away from the window. And then her eye caught a letter someone had slipped under the door. How odd. Who knew she lived here? Maybe it was from Skip. Maybe it was an apology for refusing the watch.

To Banjo and Moxie
R.S.V.P. only

It was engraved. She opened it.

Banjo and Moxie
are cordially invited to attend Jigsy and Pip's annual gala
on Saturday, the 9th of November at 4pm.
Casual dress is requested.
Mrs. Dolly Feingold, apt. 3B

Banjo and Moxie? Jigsy and Pip? How strange was this? Blossom tumbled into one of her titanic tutus and headed down to the pool with the invitation. Besides genuinely not knowing what the hell it meant, it was a good way to talk to Skip and defuse any strain that might have settled about the watch.

"Hey," Blossom yelled, "look what I got." She walked toward Skip, extending the letter. He read it.

"Do you have any idea what this might be about?" asked Blossom.

"Mrs. Feingold has two dogs: a bulldog and some big old French dog. I forget the name of the breed. Anyway, she throws this birthday party for them every year and invites all the dogs in the neighborhood to attend. I hear it's pretty wild, ya know, dogs dressed up in basic black and pearls."

"Really? Is that what she means by casual dress?"

"Yeah, last year I heard four male dogs ripped some female dog's satin dress right off her. It was a real scandal."

"So who are Banjo and Moxie?"

"Oh, they used to live in your apartment. Two Yorkshires. She probably thinks they still live there. Want me to say something?"

"Definitely not. I may never have another excuse to meet Mrs. Feingold. I'm going. Even if I have to rent a dog."

"Take my dog; Mrs. Feingold won't know."

"Yours?" *More information.*

"He's a mutt, but he might fit in. He's got a great personality, and I promise he won't gang-rape any of her guests. He's been fixed."

"I can borrow him?"

"Sure. Jeannie's dropping him off here today. She kept him for me when I went off alone on my part of the vacation. I'm finally getting him back. It's a custody battle," Skip laughed.

A custody battle? I didn't even know Skip had a dog. She's dropping him off here? Jesus, I'm not ready to meet his wife. No way. "So what time is she coming, Skip?"

"I think about three. I asked her to keep him till five, but she has to get to some audition. It'll be fine; he's cool. He'll just lay down under a tree."

Who cares what he'll do? I'm not even thinking about the dog. "Good."

"When's the party?"

"What party?" Blossom asked. She had put the invitation so far behind her, the party might as well have come and gone.

"Oh, the party, yes," she said, remembering, "Saturday . . . at four p.m."

"So you can have him if you want. I'll bring him over." Skip paused. He had a semiserious look on his face. "Unfortunately, he doesn't really have anything to wear. He's not that kind of dog."

"Don't worry about it, Skip," Blossom said; the worry in her voice and eyes had nothing to do with doggie attire. "I'll find something. He won't be underdressed. By the way, what's his name?"

"Valentine. Jeannie gave him to me last Valentine's Day. I just call him Vinny, though. It's less embarrassing on walks."

Valentine? Just kill me now. "Valentine. Great."

"So you'll meet them at three? Vinny and Jeannie."

"Wonderful. Looking forward to it." *Like a pencil in my eye.* "See you then," she said, disappearing upstairs.

CHAPTER 27

*B*LOSSOM MADE SURE TO STAY away the whole day to avoid bumping into Jeannie, but when she pulled into her parking space, she was horrified to see Skip standing there with Valentine and Jeannie. *Jesus Christ. She was supposed to drop him off two hours ago. Back up, just back up.* But she couldn't. Skip was waving to her, and Jeannie was staring.

"Hey, Blossom," Skip said as Blossom approached. Happily. Dreadfully. She felt as if she was fake-laughing. Something she swore she'd never do again.

"I'd like you to meet my wife. Jeannie, Blossom . . . Blossom, Jeannie . . ."

My God, she's beautiful.

"Nice to meet you," Blossom said, extending her hand. She wanted to die right there.

How could I have ever thought, for a second, for even a nanosecond, that someone like Skip could ever like me. Look at her. She's a long-stemmed rose, and I'm . . . I'm . . . I'm . . . a shrub!

"Same," Jeannie said. She was exactly as Blossom had imagined: five-eleven, lanky, blonde, her features as fine as smooth, white butter. "So, I hear you're taking Valentine to a formal?" *She's probably thinking I'm asking her dog 'cause I can't get a date.*

"Yeah, a dog party," Blossom said, smiling on. *God, how long do I have to keep this grin on my face? A dog party. I might as well put* bowwow *on my forehead.*

"A dog party. How quaint. Anyway . . ." she said, handing the leash over to Skip, "I gotta go; I'm late." And she dashed off, her long hair trailing behind like a silk scarf, her long legs taking forever to pull up into her BMW.

This is a nightmare. "Nice meeting you," Blossom lied. Jeannie said nothing.

Jeannie waved and took off.

"I thought you said she was coming at three."

"I did. Her audition got all changed around. That's Jeannie for you. You never know. So this is Vinny. Vinny . . . this is Blossom." Vinny was a black and white mixture of border collie and who knows what. He wagged his tail, obviously glad to be here. It wouldn't matter if Blossom were the queen of England or the duchess of York or just Blossom. Vinny was happy to meet her. This, she thought, is why animals are so wonderful. You could be anyone, even yourself, and they're still happy to see you. She gave him a scratch behind the ears.

"Vinny, how you doing, you silly boy?"

"I think he likes you, Blossom."

"Yeah? Well, I like him, too." She hesitated before asking one more time about borrowing Vinny for the party. She wanted to make sure she wasn't imposing. "So it's still okay to take him for a couple of hours, Skip?"

"Yeah, no problem. Saturday, right?" Skip confirmed, turning to leave. "Four o'clock?"

"Yes. Thanks, Skip. I really appreciate it."

"No problem."

And as Skip led Vinny down the path, she couldn't help herself; she just couldn't help it. She had to ask him one more question: "Oh, by the way, what was Jeannie auditioning for today?" *Deodorant, dental floss, hemorrhoidal suppositories?*

"I don't know," he called back. "I think it was for some skin cream or perfume. She does mostly fashion and beauty."

"Oh, that's nice," Blossom lied, watching Skip turn the corner. *You just had to ask, didn't you?*

CHAPTER 28

*W*ELCOME, WELCOME, COME IN."

"This is Vinny, Mrs. Feingold. I'm Blossom McBeal. We live where Banjo and Moxie used to live. I hope it's okay if Vinny comes to your party this year."

"Absolutely. Hello, Vinny, very nice to meet you. Do come in." Mrs. Feingold answered the door with a fake boa around her neck, sporting an ivory cigarette holder. Oversized butterfly glasses, trimmed in rhinestone, framed her face. Her hair was dyed fashionably blond and very done up, very Zsa Zsa. It was a pleasant and young-looking face for someone who was eighty-two years old. Eighty-two! It was really hard to believe. Mrs. Feingold didn't look a day over seventy.

"I brought rawhide," Blossom said, offering up the plate.

"How very thoughtful. Chi Chi and Lou Lou will love these. Chi Chi and Lou Lou are Rona Rosenberg's shar-peis. They're mad for rawhide."

Blossom looked around. Mrs. Feingold's apartment was elegantly decorated with beautiful paintings, period antiques, and Persian rugs. And displayed in the center on the dining room mantel was a replica of a fifty-foot Hinckley, finely appointed and exquisite.

Fresh roses were everywhere, roses that were so deep and velvety, they looked like opera curtains. If someone were to see the apartment without Mrs. Feingold in it, this dog party would truly be a puzzle. But there she was, standing between two large ceramic dogs that flagged her entryway and invited everyone in with a flair.

"You must meet Sputnik and Eloise, and, of course, Suzuki Beane. Over there, in the corner playing hard to get, is Lizzy, with that insistent pit bull Chopper, and out on the veranda, my very own Jigsy and Pip. And there's Louisa Parker's Chihuahua. He's got quite the bark. He looks like a soprano, but he barks like an alto. And want to be let in on another little secret?"

"Sure," Blossom said.

"Louisa's husband, Mr. Parker, thinks he was a dog in the time of William the Great."

Blossom laughed. "Let's hope for Mrs. Parker's sake he wasn't a Chihuahua."

Both women laughed now. Everyone here was a bit cuckoo, Blossom thought. Mrs. Feingold continued with her introductions, but not of the owners—they were quite secondary. Only the dogs got the honors.

"There's Max and Milou and Scout. Over there is Mochachina, River, Dottie and Spottie. Buddy, Blue, Emma, Peaches, Chelsea Fleemarket—because that's were she was found, poor dear—and over there is Casey, Winston, Travis, Tess, and Ted Koppel."

"Ted Koppel?"

"Mrs. Sorrenson loves Ted Koppel. She's watched him every night for twenty years. She was so worried that after the hostage crisis ended back in nineteen-eighty he'd be taken off the air. But he wasn't, and she's been loyal to him ever since. Hence the name."

"Ahhhh." Definitely cuckoo, no doubt about it.

Mrs. Feingold's apartment was so thick with dogs and hair, Blossom worried that someone's throat would close. The TV room played *Lady and the Tramp* while the TV in the bedroom played *Best in Show*. Human food and drinks were set up in the kitchen, while doggie treats were set up all over the place. Blossom caught sight of a table where dozens of gifts were piled neatly.

"Oh, my God, I didn't bring you a gift," she gasped, realizing her rudeness.

"My dear, you brought yourself and your handsome young dog. That's quite enough."

As the afternoon drew on, Blossom felt sure she'd landed in some strange parallel universe. It was as if a petting zoo had collided with a weird variation of performance art in Mrs. Feingold's apartment. After an hour, Blossom found herself in the kitchen with Mrs. Feingold.

"So these parties are somewhat unusual, Mrs. Feingold. How did you even think to do a dog party?"

"When my husband died, I was very lonely, so I decided to get a dog for company. I didn't get one right away, though. I waited for about two years. I think those two years were the hardest in my entire life. I never thought a dog would make any difference. I didn't think anything would. Hell, I wasn't even a dog person. But bringing a dog into the house was like bringing in life. It just made me happy. Their little tails wagging when you came home, jumping into your lap when you watched TV. That's, of course, when Pip was smaller. Now he'd break my lap. Slowly but surely I began to find my smile again. And part of that was because of a dog. Can you believe it?"

"I can totally believe it. In fact, I've heard of people even living longer because of their pets. I've never had one"—*Jasper was too long ago to count*—"but I've always thought about it."

"What about Vinny?"

Blossom had slipped. "Oh, yes, Vinny, of course." She didn't want Mrs. Feingold to think she was crashing her party under false pretenses, so she continued her charade. "Vinny's my first dog."

"Well, he's a good one. Maybe he can go to the park with Jigsy and Pip sometime."

"Ahhh . . . yeah . . . that sounds nice." What was she going to say? No, never? Blossom struggled to change the subject. "Why'd you get two dogs, Mrs. Feingold?"

"I got them from a shelter. Jigsy had only a day left before they were going to put him down, and I couldn't bear to take one without the other."

"That is such a nice story, Mrs. Feingold. What kind of dog is Jigsy?"

"A French briard. It was his ears that got to me. Every time he perks them up, it looks like he's trying to get Radio Free Europe."

Blossom laughed.

"Sometimes we just need rescuing, Blossom. The way I see it is, they rescued me as much as I rescued them. So I give them this little birthday party to celebrate another year of . . . of . . . just being here and being happy . . . happy and alive. It's just as much a party for me, too, being here for one more year and being happy. Does that make any sense to you?"

"More than you can imagine."

Blossom was pleasantly surprised by Mrs. Feingold's openness. She felt as if she had known her before this, perhaps in some other life.

Mrs. Feingold stood with some sort of delectable doggie casserole in her hands. "Well, my dear, can't leave the guests waiting."

Blossom gently touched Mrs. Feingold's arm. "I liked your story. Thank you for telling me."

"Oh, you're welcome, Blossom, dear. I have dozens. You must come over and let me chew your ear off."

With that, she swept out of the kitchen like a French chef, holding what looked like a swan carved out of Alpo.

When it was time for Blossom to leave, she gathered up her charge. Mrs. Feingold escorted her to the door.

"Perhaps next Sunday, if you don't find yourselves too busy, you can bring Vinny over and we can have a visit."

Oh, Jesus. I'm gonna have to borrow Skip's dog again.

"Well, I'd love to, Mrs. Feingold, but I'm afraid that's Vinny's day at the groomer's. I leave him there for hours. You know, nails, shampoo, massage."

"Oh, yes, absolutely. Well, then, perhaps you'd like to come by yourself for some brandy."

This was unexpected. Besides Skip's invitation to Disneyland, Blossom hadn't been invited anywhere in a long time. It felt very nice.

"Brandy? Yes, that would be fine. I love brandy." *What are you talking about? You've never had brandy in your life.* "Thank you for asking."

"Well, thank you for coming. This year was so much better than last."

"Yeah, I heard."

"You did?"

"Well, only a little bit. Something about . . ." She was trying to find a nice word for what happened.

"Gang rape. That's the word you're searching for. It was awful. Fortunately, Bruno had a prior engagement this year. Poor Eloise."

Blossom looked over at Eloise. She didn't look as if she was having such a great time. It occurred to her that Eloise was probably very disappointed Bruno did not show up this year.

"So I'll see you on Sunday, Blossom?" Mrs. Feingold asked as she slowly closed her door. Dogs were trying to get out.

"Uhhh, yes, Sunday . . . Sunday will be fine. Thank you." And Blossom walked away thinking how nice it was that Mrs. Feingold had extended herself. People in Gorham would never say, "Hey, you must come over this weekend," or, "Keep Tuesday night free for dinner." It was a different mentality completely.

Clearly, something had changed. Something was different. She was different. Blossom felt free, freer than she'd ever felt. She felt free to live. And it seemed so damn ironic to her that death had been the thing to give her this gift.

It was seven o'clock when Blossom returned Vinny. Skip was sitting on the swing by the pool, reading a paper. "Sorry it's so late, Skip, but Vinny was the first dog to leave."

"No problem. I got here only fifteen minutes ago myself." He looked at his watch.

"I hope I didn't keep you from anything."

"Not at all," Skip answered. "I was just going to grab a bite."

"Oh, well . . . ahhh . . . okay, then . . . thank you again," she said, handing him Vinny's leash. There was something awkward and apologetic in her voice. Skip sensed it. It had the ring of someone who looks around at others who have somewhere to go after a party, and it was clear to him that Blossom had nowhere to go.

"Have you eaten, Blossom?"

"Oh, I . . ." she mumbled. There she was again. Unable to make complete sentences with Skip.

"Would you like to get something to eat? It's dinnertime anyway," he said, "and I want to hear all about the party. There's a great place on Sunset. Café Med. They've got an outdoor space where Vinny can lay down. And good Italian food that's reasonably priced."

"Thanks, Skip. I'd love to. But I insist, this is my treat. A thank-you for borrowing Vinny."

"That sounds perfect." She could feel Skip's kindness like an embrace. How was he able to do that, understand her loneliness in an instant? And then reach out. Skip. There was so much to fall in love with. How could Jeannie even question what she had with him? She thought about how lucky some women are with the gifts they are given. Jeannie was thin and beautiful and had someone like Skip to love her. Probably many men had loved Jeannie and would love her. Jeannie had so much that she could throw things away and still have a lot left over. *What would that feel like?* Blossom could only imagine. Suddenly she felt jealousy rising in her like a green hatred.

She bit the inside of her cheek to feel something stronger than her loathing. She didn't want to be jealous or angry or sad. She had been given what she had been given, and it was time to find the good in it.

Skip and Blossom settled at a table beneath a yellow beer umbrella. Vinny settled, too, cooling his belly against the shaded sidewalk. No one even knew he was there.

"So he wasn't underdressed?" Skip inquired, looking at Vinny's red bandanna handsomely tied around his neck.

"Absolutely not. There were two or three dogs that had nothing on. We hid our eyes in shame," Blossom teased back. "And that patch over Vinny's eye is very distinctive. I told everyone he was the Van Heusen man."

"Know what you want?" he asked Blossom.

"Ahhhh . . ." *Get something thin. Don't go stuffing cheeseburgers into your mouth like Jughead.* "The shrimp salad looks good. You?"

"The pizza, I guess. Very unexciting."

"Hey, Skip," two voices called out from beyond the sidewalk. A man and a woman approached. He was tall and handsome and muscular, and she looked like Jeannie's clone. This city was relentless in spitting out beautiful people.

"Hey," Skip said back. "What are you doing here?" He turned to Blossom. "Blossom, this is Jeff and Summer Cross. Jeff . . . Summer, this is a friend of mine, Blossom McBeal." *Summer. Who's named "Summer"? She sounds like a bottle of room spray.*

"Hello," Blossom said.

"What are you up to?" Summer asked, looking at Blossom with a sideways glance that said *judgment.*

"Just getting something to eat. And you? I thought you were skiing or sailing or doing something exotic."

"We just got back," Jeff confirmed. "But you're right. We were at Summer's family house back east in Connecticut for a couple of weeks, and from there went to Zermatt."

"You must stop over, Skip," Summer chimed in ebulliently. "We've relandscaped the back forty when we were away. It's absolutely fabulous now."

God. She's Joan Collins in a Dallas *rerun.*

"Yeah, the pool has fountains, for Christ's sake," Jeff laughed. Summer laughed. Skip laughed, too. Blossom didn't laugh.

"Hey, you get the ten-year reunion notice?" Jeff inquired, as though he'd just remembered why they'd bumped into each other after all.

"Yeah."

"You gonna go?"

"No . . . I'm too busy, and to tell you the truth, I'm just not that interested right now. Got other things on my mind."

"How are you and Jeannie, by the way?"

Very nice. Very considerate. It's like I'm not even here. I hate Summer.

"All right . . . still working it out. Saw her a couple of days ago. She's good."

A look of sympathy crossed Summer's face like a passing cloud. Blossom looked down toward Vinny, anxious for a place to rest her eyes.

"Well, Skipper," Summer continued, changing the subject, "gotta run. Tag said if I came over right now, he would give me an emergency haircut. He's such a queen, but I love him, and he's got me over a barrel. Look at this," she said, pointing to her perfectly coiffed do. "Call us some time," she chirped, turning toward the street with Jeff in tow.

All Blossom could think about was Yul Brynner's comment: "Girls have an unfair advantage over men. If they can't get what they want by being smart, they get what they want by being dumb." That was Summer to a tee.

"Call," Jeff yelled back, "and if I decide to go to the reunion, I'll give you a full report on what all those dot-com dropouts are doing now. Take care, Bud." And he was off, a beat behind the scurry of his wonderfully wispy wife.

"Friends from college," Skip explained before Blossom had a chance to ask. "At least Jeff was. We were at Yale together. Both of us ended up coming out here when we graduated. He was coming home to go into his father's business. I was going to law school . . . which I did before I quit the fancy job it got me and took the job at the pool."

All this was news to Blossom. Her view of Skip was changing like a Rubik's Cube. He was suddenly all new angles.

"You were a lawyer?"

"For about six years. An entertainment lawyer, but I hated it. I didn't like 'making the deals'—negotiating with people, who, in my mind, were oilier than the stains my pickup leaves on the asphalt. It just wasn't my thing."

An entertainment lawyer. Blossom was dying to ask who he'd met, if he ever had any dealings with Tom Selleck. But she knew this wasn't the time, not after he'd said he hated it.

"So you quit?"

"Yeah, I quit. And it was kind of funny how I actually got the pool job. I saw the ad in the paper and stopped by Mr. Birnbaum's office. Sidney Birnbaum. He manages many properties like this. Well, when he saw my résumé, he nearly fell on the floor. 'Why do you want this job again?' he asked me.

"So I told him I was tired of entertainment law, that I was looking to do something that would use my hands, my back—something where I could be outside and breathe the air. And he said, 'You're willing to give up a six-figure job just to breathe the air? And it's not even air. It's smog.'"

Skip smiled. "'Well, it's not that simple,' I told him. 'But in short, yes.' This utterly perplexed Mr. Birnbaum. He said my qualifications were ridiculous, overkill. He said it would be like shooting a fly with a shotgun. But then he figured I might be an asset. Maybe I could help him with his books or legal matters, if they came up.

"He said what concerned him was that I was going to get tired of using my hands and breathing the air and leave him high and dry. He didn't want to have to start trying again to find someone new to fill the position. So I reassured him I'd be here for a while—not forever, but a while.

"After that, I started immediately. But the funniest thing happened when I was leaving his office. He stopped me one last time with the question of the hour. 'Just let me get this straight,' he said. 'You couldn't find yourself for four hundred thousand dollars a year plus bonuses?'

"'In a nutshell, no,' I said, and he said, 'That's the word I'd use.'

"I left the office smiling, knowing exactly how confusing all this must have been to him. Hell, it leaves me confused at times, too."

"Wow," Blossom said, barely able to grasp the breadth of Skip's story. "You must have really wanted out."

"I did. But the strange thing is, I never thought I'd be doing the lawyer thing for that long. My heart just wasn't in it. This pool thing was suppose to be strictly transitional. And it is, I suppose. But the transition is taking longer than I thought. Certainly longer than Jeannie thought. Jeannie's pissed that I'm not doing something that, quote, 'taps into my true potential, makes money, and isn't embarrassing.' She married a lawyer, not a pool guy. This pool thing was perfect. A simple managerial job, where I could be outside. I needed a respite, a little time, someplace simple to clear my head and genuinely decide what I really wanted to do. Figure out my future."

"Find your destiny," Blossom interjected.

"So to speak," Skip continued. "Jeff's destiny was set in stone. Wealthy family and all—he always knew he'd be back here. In spite of our different backgrounds, we were good friends in college."

"What was so different?"

"Well, for one, I was what you'd call a Southie. I came from South Boston, blue-collar territory. My education was possible because of grants and scholarships and whatever I had worked for and whatever my father had put aside for me. Jeff's education was possible because Jeff's father gave Yale enough money to build a science center.

"My dad and my grandfather all came from a background of hard workers who had to put their backs into it. Construction. I remember going to the sites they were working on when I was a kid and being absolutely awed by the buildings they were putting up."

"What stopped you from going into that business?"

"At the time, my father said, 'Over my dead body.' He'd worked hard all his life so that he could see me go off to a good school. Yale for him was like getting knighted by the queen. My grades were good, my SATs were good, so when I was accepted, I simply followed his wishes. The road of least resistance, as I look at it now. On one level I could see his logic—'local boy makes good'—but on the other hand, the route I took didn't make me happy. And law school made me even more unhappy. And then practicing law made me miserable. My fate seemed to continually tumble into the wrong place, and I couldn't redirect it."

"And your dad?"

"Oh, he was happy all right. I was the big success in the family, in the neighborhood, in the universe for chrissakes."

"So now what?"

"Now I'm trying to figure it out. Something I should have done when I was eighteen. But who knows what they want when they're eighteen? Did you?"

Yeah, I wanted to be a game show contestant and marry Tom Selleck.

"No idea."

"So that's my story, and I'm stickin' to it."

Blossom was letting it all sink in. "I had no idea," was all she could mutter with so many variables going through her head.

"Yeah, well, there was no reason you would. I don't like talking about it much. I feel like a guy in a Dominick Dunne novel. The one who had so much going for him and then suddenly can't quite find himself. It's even too cliché for me. Sometimes I feel my life is like bad summer reading . . . and worse, that Jeannie might be right: I should just bite the bullet and go back to being a lawyer. But then . . . I know there's something out there I was destined to do."

"I really believe that everyone has a destiny, Skip. Sometimes we find it when all other routes have been closed to us. When we don't have a choice. That's when we forge a new route. Sometimes we get so squeezed down from the pressure of life, the world just collapses in, and when that happens, all that pressure has nowhere to go but out."

"BANG," Skip said, "and that's how the universe was created."

Blossom smiled. "I know from my own experience that when everything feels like it's tightening around me, something bursts— like a frozen pipe. But when it bursts—and believe me, it does—the first thing you feel is relief."

Blossom recalled how horrible she felt when she'd gotten the news she was dying, and then how good she felt when she took some action—illegal though it was. She couldn't tell Skip the details, but she could tell him it was the start to something much better.

"Sometimes when life backs you against the wall, you've gotta pull the wall down."

"What happened to you?" Skip asked. It was a question in waiting. "You know . . . when you pulled the wall down?"

Blossom closed her eyes. She couldn't tell Skip about her prognosis or how she had stolen money from a bank and left town, or how she had taken on someone else's identity. She couldn't tell him how, for the first time, she was beginning to feel alive. She couldn't tell him any of that. But there were other tiny revelations that had been born from her actions. Maybe she could talk about them. And so she began.

"I had a friend," she confided. "Her name was MaryAnn."

CHAPTER 29

*B*LOSSOM SLIPPED INTO the blinking water and began her laps with the precision of a palace guard marching back and forth on sentry duty. Her arms sliced across the pool like sharp blades, and the rhythm brought her back to childhood, of teeter-totters and trampolines, of MaryAnn and herself sitting on the same swing, each of them pumping hard with tiny knee-socked legs. That was back when Blossom was Charlotte Clapp.

"Throw your head back so you can see the world upside down," exclaimed Charlotte.

"I'm afraid to," said MaryAnn.

"Don't worry. I'll hold you."

And up they went, so high that the swing chain went slack before grabbing itself and becoming taut again.

They put on their own talent shows in the finished basements where together they mouthed the words to "Soldier Boy" and pretended they were waiting for their boyfriends to return from the war. They nursed wounded birds caught by Charlotte's cat and held continual vigil over each shoebox. They sat together and watched *Magnum, PI* reruns, swooning over Tom Selleck. They learned how to make cinnamon toast in Mrs. Paley's home economics class, which was, Mrs. Paley said, the first important step in preparing them for marriage. And while they weren't particularly interested in marriage at that point, they most definitely preferred the cinnamon toast to the paste they'd eat in art class. The paste always sent them to the infirmary.

They would sign up for skating lessons at the local ice rink and practice their three turns and waltz jumps together. They would buy their matching sequined skirts and silvery capes and slide across the kitchen floor for hours, getting ready for their Olympic debut. They would meet the boys of summer at the roller rink and spend half their time at the snack bar waiting for these infallible champions to extinguish their thirst and then slyly corral them into the kissing corner. They would steal eggs from the refrigerator to throw against rocks up in the woods. Charlotte still pondered what motivated this rebellious phase.

More than twenty years of confidences and friendship, many of them standing in the chill September air, waiting for the bus to take them to their first day of school.

But after school, freedom rang like the bells of Saint Mary's, and they would run through the red double doors at three o'clock sharp and into life again.

They'd laugh down the high winter hill behind the Mobil station until Saturday slipped into Sunday, always finding their way to warmth in the form of hot chocolate and cider donuts at the 7-Eleven. There were so many years of tumbling into autumn and hiding themselves for hours under these colorful heaps of happiness. A time so faraway now, it was long lost like those fallen leaves that had blown away with the transient winds of childhood. To this day Charlotte could not smell the cold fires of late October without thinking of MaryAnn and endings. Endings. After all this time, Charlotte had not reconciled hers with MaryAnn.

Their friendship disintegrated in their senior year over a boy named T. J.—Trevor James. Young, handsome Trevor James. Charlotte was thin and pretty and barely had a sense of who she was and what she looked like, but Trevor James knew what she looked like, and liked what he saw.

They began dating, or at least, a relationship as close to dating as it could be for someone who was only sixteen and whose entire life experience was defined by the boundaries of Gorham, New Hampshire. Dating meant acting silly, French-kissing, even going as far as third base. While this was tame for the rest of the world, it was considered quite risque to the girls of Gorham. Charlotte had shared her secrets with MaryAnn, but as the months went by, MaryAnn still didn't have a boyfriend, and Charlotte stopped talking about T. J. as much. She felt bad that her friend hadn't had a steady boyfriend yet, and didn't want her to feel left out. In fact, it was around then that all three of them started spending time together in a group. This was Charlotte's quiet way of taking care of her best friend. And she'd thought MaryAnn was happy. MaryAnn never said anything to make her feel otherwise.

But there was an 'otherwise.' MaryAnn secretly harbored amorous feelings for T. J. She had been attracted to him for months. But MaryAnn had never kept a secret from Charlotte in her life. How on earth was Charlotte supposed to know all this? How could she have had an inkling how upset MaryAnn would be about Charlotte going to the prom with T. J.? She assumed MaryAnn would find a date—there were dozens of boys looking for dates of their own. Poor MaryAnn had lied and claimed she opted to work at the punch table when, in fact, she had not been asked to the prom at all. If only she had told Charlotte the truth, Charlotte wouldn't have gone to that stupid prom, either. They could have all protested together, ordered pizza, and rented movies that night instead. That would have been more fun anyway.

But instead, MaryAnn watched Trevor James slow-dance with Charlotte across the floor all night under the pink and blue streamers she'd spent all day putting up.

The three had planned to drive home together at the end of the evening, but by eleven-thirty MaryAnn was gone. Still, Charlotte didn't have a clue. She simply suspected that MaryAnn had gotten a ride from someone else. Until the next morning.

When she answered the knock on the front door, there stood MaryAnn.

"Hey, what happened to you last night?"

"I couldn't stay. I had to . . ." And MaryAnn began crying inconsolable tears.

"What? Tell me," Charlotte insisted. "Did someone . . . ?" She was afraid to say the word. Someone must have died, the way MaryAnn was weeping.

"Do you love T. J.?" MaryAnn finally blurted out.

Charlotte was taken aback by the question. What did this have to do with anything?

"Do I love T. J.?"

"Yes."

"I . . . I like him. Do I love him? 'Love' is a strong word. I like him."

"I love him, Charlotte," MaryAnn said in a low, confessional tone.

"You what?" Charlotte was shocked. "You love Trevor James? What are you talking about?"

"I love him, Charlotte. I have . . . for a long time."

"MaryAnn, you never said a word to me about any feelings you had toward him. When did this happen? Why didn't you ever say anything to me?"

"I couldn't. You were going out with him. What could I say? 'I love him, Charlotte . . . stop seeing him'?"

"Well, something. Jesus, MaryAnn, I had no idea. You and I are best friends. Why didn't you ever say anything to me?"

"I wanted to tell you, but I didn't know how. T. J. used to talk to me, smile and joke with me. At first I thought he liked me, but then I realized he was doing it to get to you. He couldn't get your attention, so he got mine, and through me he got you."

"That's not true."

"Yes, it is."

"Jesus. Does T. J. even know how you feel, MaryAnn?"

"No, but it doesn't matter. He likes you now."

Charlotte was completely flabbergasted at this moment. She went back and forth, agonizing over whether she should say something. She cared for T. J. a great deal. And yes, maybe she did love him. But how could she admit that at this moment with her best friend in tears? She'd seen so many girls forsake longstanding friendships when they met a boy. Hadn't she and MaryAnn promised never to do that? But Charlotte had such strong feelings for him. A paper valentine, that's how her heart felt, a paper valentine about to be torn down the middle. She stared at MaryAnn, who now sat looking at Charlotte as if Charlotte held the keys to her eternal personal happiness. How could she let her best friend down? But then, she would have to let go of a relationship she didn't want to end. This was awful. But, hard as it was, she knew what she had to do. Finally, she looked MaryAnn in the eye and said, "I'd like to say something to him, if it's all right with you."

"He won't be mad?"

"I don't think so. We're friends . . . mostly," Charlotte lied.

"Really, Charlotte? I wondered about that. 'Cause you don't really talk about him as much as you used to."

Jesus, Charlotte thought, *my whole plan blew up right in my face.* She wanted to scream, "BECAUSE I DIDN'T WANT TO HURT YOUR FEELINGS! BECAUSE I HAD A BOYFRIEND AND YOU HAD NO ONE! BECAUSE, BECAUSE, BECAUSE," but she held her tongue.

"So, what are you going to say?"

What am *I going to say?* "I don't exactly know yet. I need to give it a think."

"And this doesn't upset you . . . to do this?"

Yes, it breaks my heart. But you're my best friend, MaryAnn.

"I like T. J. He's a great guy, but . . . but I'm not in love," she said stumbling, searching for that line in the sand that separates "like" from "love." And then it was clear. That moment of confrontation forced her to define her feelings. Yes, she loved MaryAnn, but she loved T. J. as well. She dreaded the conversation she imagined having with T. J. She told herself that friendships last longer than boys. How would she feel if she had been the one without the boyfriend? MaryAnn had never been kissed, and it was true that Charlotte had many boys in school vying for her attention. But still, what if the tables were turned and T. J. dumped her? She would be miserable. Her thoughts were interrupted by MaryAnn, who seemed at that moment to be clairvoyant.

"Won't he be upset? He might be in love with you."

"I don't know, MaryAnn; he's never said those exact words to me." This was true, and Charlotte had never said those exact words to him, either, but her feelings were as close to love as she'd ever had. She was nearly positive he felt it, too. Sometimes the unspoken is more clearly heard than a thousand words.

"I'll talk to him," she said softly, in a voice so low only a dog might hear it.

"Thanks, Charlotte, you're a great friend."

And they hugged once more, securing their friendship with the belief that this sisterhood would always be thicker than water.

"What?" T. J. had asked, stunned. "She loves me?"

"Yes."

"Well, shit, Charlotte, what do you want me to do?"

"I want you to go out with her."

"Go out with her? What about us?" T. J. was clearly stricken with this unwelcome news. Oh, God, this was about to backfire. Charlotte could feel her mistake about to erupt like hot lava pouring into a wound she'd just opened up.

Charlotte didn't want to give him all the insane reasons. It was hard enough without going into it all. She struggled to find words.

"We can be friends," she muttered. Jesus, there was that awful phrase no one ever wanted to hear, the "we can be friends" phrase. T. J. looked crushed.

"Friends?"

"Yes, I mean we are friends, and we'll continue to be friends, only differently."

"I don't want to be your friend. I thought this was something more than that, Charlotte." He paused. "Isn't it something more to you?"

She didn't say anything. She was grasping for words, vowels, consonants. Nothing came. She was sorry she had said anything now. She wanted to take it back, but it was all too late.

"Shit, Charlotte," T. J. said. He couldn't even look her in the eye. He was embarrassed for feeling so much when she obviously hadn't felt the same. If only he knew. If only. She had flashed a red cape in

front of an angry bull. Then suddenly, he blurted out the only word
he could muster. "Fine," he said, but it wasn't fine. It was as if she
had put her hand down his throat and brought his heart up with it.
He was hurt. His anger and sadness mixed like two dangerous
chemicals that proved explosive when stirred together, and she stood
away from him, afraid to apologize or take it back. And he stood
away and said, "You'll be sorry. You'll see." She was already.

"T. J., wait, I'm sorry, I am. Please, wait . . . T. J.?"

But it was over. He disappeared out of sight, leaving Charlotte
feeling as if all the air had been sucked out of the room. How could
she have done this? She had only wanted to do the right thing, and
now everyone was miserable.

And then, to the amazement of all who knew T. J. and Charlotte,
T. J. began dating MaryAnn the following day. Everything suddenly
became awkward and strained for Charlotte. T. J. would never look
her straight in the eye when they were all together. But MaryAnn
seemed oblivious and happy. She built her days and nights around
this new and flourishing relationship. She saw her future surrounded
by children and PTA meetings and family holidays on Lake Win-
nipesaukee. Mrs. Trevor James, MaryAnn James, Mrs. MaryAnn
James. She would write it out on napkins and note cards and immediately throw them away for her silliness, though once Trevor saw it
and Charlotte thought she saw him cringe.

It was a year later, practically to the day, when everything went
terribly wrong. T. J. had told MaryAnn he wanted to talk to her. She
was excited. He'd put the evening aside especially. He never did
that. He was going to propose; she was sure he was going to propose.

But it wasn't that at all. He had other news to deliver to her that
night, awful news, the worst kind of news someone could hear. The
truth was, he told her, that he couldn't pretend anymore and that he
was still in love with Charlotte. That try as he might, he had never
stopped being in love with her, and he was going back to ask if they
could make a go of it again.

MaryAnn sat as still as a stump. She could not believe what she
was hearing. This was supposed to be her proposal night. Instead, it
felt as if a denial of clemency had come down from the governor. Let

the execution proceed. He might as well have taken the kitchen knife and run it through poor MaryAnn's heart.

When T. J. stood to go, she stood, too, grabbing his arms, his waist, begging and pleading with him not to go, to stay, to talk, to figure it out with her. But his mind was made up, and he said he was sorry, but he had to do this and he knew it was hard and he was sure in time that things would be okay, and he was sorry and he was so sorry and he was so very, very sorry. He left her in a slump, weeping in the kitchen.

Charlotte was home when T. J. knocked on her door. She was surprised to see him alone and asked where MaryAnn was. He wanted to sit down. He was acting oddly. He was drunk. He held a glass of whiskey and ice in his hand from wherever he had just been. She had never seen him drunk before.

"Charlotte," he began, "I want to talk about something that happened between us, something that happened a long time ago now." His words were slightly slurred. Charlotte could smell the Jim Beam lifting off him like a heavy mist. "Something that hurt me more then you can imagine." He paused before continuing. Charlotte was nervous. Where was MaryAnn?

He told her how hurt he had felt when she told him that they were not going to go out anymore, that MaryAnn loved him. He was angry, and he had left the relationship angry. He had thought, by going out with MaryAnn, Charlotte would be jealous. He had purposely paraded around, generously bestowing his new affections on MaryAnn to show Charlotte how awful it felt to be rebuffed. But it had all backfired. And now he had hurt everyone, including himself, with this stupid charade. He wanted to come back. Wanted to try again. Wanted Charlotte to try again.

Charlotte could not believe what she was hearing. She'd missed him so, yet had tried her best to move on. But she couldn't really move on in her head, and she failed completely in her heart.

"Just tell me you'll think about it," said T. J.

"T. J., I . . . I . . ." The truth began spilling out as if a watering can had been knocked on its side. "It was the worst mistake I could have made. There hasn't been a day that's gone by that I didn't wish

I could reverse the whole thing. I thought my friendship with MaryAnn wouldn't have survived if I continued going out with you. But I had it all wrong. If it was a true friendship, it would have." She began to cry.

T. J. threw his arms around her, held her, and cried, too. "I love you, Charlotte. I always have."

"God, this is awful."

"Awful?"

"Awful and wonderful, all at the same time. I mean, there's another person involved here. A person who loves you very much, thinks she's going to marry you. A person who happens to be my best friend. You have to tell her, T. J. It's the right thing to do."

"I did, Charlotte. I told her I still had feelings for you."

"Oh, God, but she has no idea I still have feelings for you. It makes it so much worse. Poor MaryAnn. Think of how she'll feel— I'm about to break my best friend's heart."

"I think I already did that, Charlotte."

"You broke it in two. I'm going to break it into pieces. Jesus, maybe we shouldn't do this, T. J."

"And what will that do? Make three people unhappy instead of one, and keep two from following their hearts? No. We did that already."

"You're right, it's just . . ." MaryAnn had told Charlotte that T. J. was going to propose to her that night. She had said she could feel it in her bones that tonight was the night. This conversation was going to be so horrible.

"Please, T. J., please find her and bring her over here. I think we should all talk this out together."

"Okay. That sounds like the right thing to do," he said, sounding unconvinced that there was any right thing to do. They embraced once again before he left, leaving his half-drunk whiskey on her kitchen table. Charlotte started to cry again as the door swung behind him. Her grief was physical. This was all her fault—she should have been honest with MaryAnn from the start, but she'd wanted so to protect their friendship. Now it seemed she'd destroyed it.

It was less than an hour later when she got that awful call from MaryAnn. The call that would change everything. The call that would fill her with guilt and untold secrets for the rest of her life. She listened to MaryAnn, who seemed light-years away from her. She listened standing powerless in the middle of her kitchen floor, all the while staring at T. J.'s drink, wet where his lips had kissed the rim, the ice cubes still unmelted in his glass.

CHAPTER 30

*S*KIP DREW THE POOL NET across the top of the water as Blossom watched from her shady corner. He wore only his work boots and shorts; his blue T-shirt lay on the grass. His proletariat tan gleamed in the noonday sun. He was beautiful.

Had he noticed that Blossom had lost twenty more pounds? How could he have noticed? How could anyone notice a thing under blankets large enough to cast up over Alaska and keep Nome warm? But Mrs. Feingold had noticed. They'd had tea just yesterday, and Mrs. Feingold had remarked that Blossom looked as if she'd lost weight.

"Twenty more pounds, Mrs. Feingold."

"Are you on a diet, my dear?"

"No, not really. The strange thing is, I hadn't planned to lose the weight. It just sort of started happening. I began swimming, and it started coming off. It's funny—you kill yourself on diets and nothing happens. Then you don't care, don't really think about it"—*because you're dying and what difference does it make?*—"and then *boom,* the pounds start coming off. The swimming makes me happy right now, and I seem to be losing weight from it. Crazy."

"And that has to make you feel better. I mean physically. And when you feel better physically that just opens you up to so much more."

It did make her feel better. Every pound she lost brought her closer to someone who was dying to get out. Someone who had remained hidden for years under the weight of guilt and loss and having given up. Here she was in the last year of her life, finding a love she had never expected.

The kind of love Skip offered was not romantic love but something else: something lighter, light as a feather. And now Blossom, discovering new and uncharted feelings, began to feel as light as a feather, too.

CHAPTER 31

$\mathcal{M}$AKLEY WAS STILL IN NEW ORLEANS, trying to find something more concrete than a hunch to help him. He had posted pictures, talked to every shopkeeper in the quarter, and at one point became frustrated enough actually to succumb and go to a fortune teller. It was not the same psychic Blossom had visited, but it was a reputable one according to the word on the street. Makley showed Ivan Borislavski the photograph.

"A very large woman," he said.

No shit, Makley thought, *a regular visionary.*

"She's here."

Now, this got Makley's attention.

"She's in the room," Ivan continued.

This bit of bullshit rocketed Makley back into his original cynicism.

"Yeah?" he asked. "Where? I don't see her."

"Shhhhhh. You will make her spirit weary of your presence. There is something not right between the two of you. She does not want to see you. She is running away from you."

"Well, then, I guess she's alive?"

The fortune teller paused. "It is strange, but there is a confusion here."

"About her being alive?"

"Yes, she walks a fine line between life and death. She is in a cemetery looking for a place to lie down."

"Well, is she alive or not?"

"I have never had such an unusual reading, but she is both dead and alive."

Oh, that's really helpful, Makley thought. "Well, where should I be spending most of my time looking? In grocery stores or cemeteries?"

"You make a joke, but it is not funny. This is a soul torn asunder. And I cannot tell you where she is, for she does not know where she is herself."

"Great. What do I owe you?"

"Nothing. I cannot accept money for such a reading."

Makley was taken aback. He thought all these mumbo jumbo voodoo wackos would take a buck from the blind when they weren't looking. "You're kidding—not a cent?"

"No, no money. I cannot tell you anything that feels sure. Your friend is floating; every night I feel her floating, but I don't know where. She is between worlds, and if you find her, it will no longer be who you are looking for."

Whatever that means, thought Makley.

"Okay, well, thanks, Kreskin, you've been a big help."

Makley's next step was checking and rechecking different hotels, motels, and B and Bs. He had already crossed many off his list from his previous trip. He made his way down Royal Street and finally arrived at the Cornstalk Hotel. Mr. Garnier was behind the desk in the reception area when he entered.

"We're all full until next week," he told Chief Makley.

"Don't need a room. Just need to ask you a couple of questions." This was always suspect in New Orleans. In Garnier's experience, "a couple of questions" always led to a dead body somewhere. Makley pulled out his police ID and flashed it too quickly to give Mr. Garnier a chance to see that it was from out of state. He followed up with a picture of Charlotte.

"Seen her?"

Mr. Garnier hesitated, then said, "Yes." Monosyllabic answers were better than blathering on. He'd learned that much.

"When?"

"Oh, about two months ago, I guess."

"Where?"

"Here. She stayed here."

"For how long?"

"I'd have to look back at the guest registry, but I guess it was somewhere around two weeks."

"Was she alone?"

"Yes."

"How did she pay?"

"Cash, I remember that. Cash on the barrel."

Makley smiled. "Can I see the registry?"

Sure enough, Charlotte Clapp had been in New Orleans, reaping the benefits of what Makley was sure was the two million dollars in stolen money. She had paid the hotel in cash. And there was her signature in black and white.

"Did she happen to say where she was going when she signed out?"

Mr. Garnier's wife had now come in and was catching up with the conversation.

"He's looking for a woman who stayed here back some two months or so ago."

Mrs. Garnier looked at the picture. It was not hard not to recognize Charlotte. She was ever memorable in her girth.

"Oh, yes, yes . . . I remember her. Very nice lady. As a matter of fact . . ."

Mr. Garnier shot his wife a look that said, *not too much informa-tion.* But her mind was on other things. She was remembering something.

"Yes?" Makley asked hopefully.

"When I changed her room, I found a book she'd left behind. It's still here in the lost-and-found. I figured she'd call for it, and I would mail it to her. But she never did call."

"Could you get it for me?" Makley asked.

"Yes, of course." Mrs. Garnier disappeared into the back room. You could hear her rummaging through a box.

"Ahhh, here it is!" she yelled victoriously, as if she'd found the missing piece to a puzzle. She handed the book to Makley: *Where to Stay and Where to Play in Hollywood, California.*

"Ah-ha," Makley said, taking it from Mrs. Garnier.

"Did she say anything to you about going to California?"

"No," Mr. Garnier said, his wife nodding in agreement. "We really barely spoke to her. She was in and out of her own accord mostly."

"I'm going to keep this, if you don't mind," Makley said, holding on to the book.

"Yes, yes, keep it," Mr. Garnier said, anxious to get Makley moving.

"What'd she do?" Mrs. Garnier asked. Mr. Garnier was annoyed. Too much information.

"She went over on her credit line," he said as he was leaving.

"That doesn't sound so bad," Mrs. Garnier said. "I do that all the time."

"Yeah, and how many times have I told you to stop buying from every catalog you get? Maybe now you'll listen."

Oops, Mr. Garnier thought, *she got me so mad, I said too much.*

Back at his hotel, Makley called the station.

"Well, she's alive."

"Really?" Officer Hobbs asked. "I'll be."

"Yup. Got a confirmation from a hotel that she stayed at. It was the eye-witness account I was hoping for."

"What now?"

"She left a book behind in her room. Something about Hollywood, California. I'm wondering if she ever spoke to any of her friends or colleagues about wanting to go there. I think we should get them in again and start asking some more questions."

"All right, I'm on it. Where did I put that initial list?" Makley could hear him shuffling through papers, opening drawers, moving chairs.

"Has Kelly said anything further about the money or setting up a meeting with his brother-in-law?"

"No, not yet. But I heard he got his lawyer involved."

"That a fact," Makley said. "Ya know, it occurs to me that we don't know the brother-in-law's name. All we call him is the brother-in-law. Find out what the hell his name is, Hobbs, would you?"

"On it, Chief," and Makley heard Hobbs both writing and reiterating his task at hand.

"Find . . . out . . . name . . . of . . ."

Makley couldn't stand it anymore. "Hobbs, listen . . . I'm gonna nose around here a bit more and probably book myself a flight to L.A. tomorrow."

"No shit." Hobbs was excited.

"Calm down. It's not a vacation. I'll call you when I'm settled somewhere. Do me a favor. Call the FBI and tell them what's going on. Okay?"

"Yeah, sure, boss."

"And check those lists of friends carefully. We don't want to leave anybody out."

"Okay, Chief. Okay . . . Oh, here it is. I found the list."

"Good. Don't read it to me; just get started on it. See if Charlotte ever talked to anyone about going to Hollywood. If she knows anyone there, etcetera, etcetera."

"Yeah, no problem. Right away, Chief."

"I'll call you tomorrow. And, Hobbs, this isn't *Dirty Harry*. Stay professional, will you?"

Hobbs hastily replaced the gun he'd taken from his holster and had been spinning on his trigger finger throughout their conversation. How could Makley have known that? Christ, he must have heard it, Hobbs thought, feeling like an idiot as he remembered the time he accidentally shot Mrs. Tretherow in the foot by showing off this particular maneuver. If only he'd remembered that damn safety. He now found himself hiding whenever he saw her limping out of the bank or the 7-Eleven. The local headlines didn't help: OFFICER HOBBS SHOOTS NINETY-YEAR-OLD WIDOW IN FOOT. She was no ninety, Hobbs sulked, but all that was beside the point.

"You hear me, Hobbs?" Makley asked again.

"Of course, Chief, professional. All the way."

After hanging up, Hobbs made his first call.

"Hello. May I speak with Mrs. MaryAnn Barzini, please?"

CHAPTER 32

$\mathscr{C}$OME ON, BLOSSOM, dear, we'll be late." Mrs. Feingold was pacing back and forth in Blossom's living room. She was dragging Blossom to a day spa. "You must do these things for yourself once in a while. They make a world of difference to your psyche."

"My psyche's fine, Mrs. Feingold."

"Oh, phooey. I can see your psyche's in need of a salt scrub. And anyway, you deserve a little pampering. We all do."

"But this is too much."

"Can't someone just give you something, Blossom?"

Mrs. Feingold's question sideswiped her. Why couldn't she accept a gift? Maybe Mrs. Feingold was right. Maybe she should just accept this invitation graciously. It was okay for someone to give her something. She was deserving of a gift. In fact, it was nice.

After the aromatherapy and the facial and the massage, Mrs. Feingold insisted Blossom have Franz do her eyebrows. He was a master at facial hair, and Mrs. Feingold said Blossom was in desperate need of a shape.

"Now, just keep your eyes closed." *Rip.* The wax tore across the bottom of her lower brow, forming the beginning of an arch. "Yes, already I see a difference. Much better." Franz took out tweezers and began, with surgical precision, removing all the extraneous top hairs.: "*Wunderbar. Wunderbar.*" Blossom only hoped that meant good. "When we are done, you may look." *Rip. Tweeze. Rip. Tweeze.* Twenty painful minutes on each brow, and Blossom was ready for her unveiling.

"How do you like it?" Mrs. Feingold was examining her with all the pride of a doting mother. But when Blossom was finally able to look in the mirror, she was horrified. Her eyebrows looked like Cruella DeVil's. Her expression hovered between anger and amazement, and she couldn't seem to wipe the look off her face. It had been irrevocably embedded. The arch was so high, trucks could pass under it.

"I . . . I . . ."

"That's okay, darling, no need to thank me. The expression on your face says it all." Franz was as clueless as he was talentless.

"I think it looks good, Blossom. Fresh. What do you think?"

"I look so . . . surprised."

"It opens your face right up, darling," Franz continued, as if to justify his colossal mistake.

"When will they grow back?" Blossom asked nervously.

"Oh, don't worry about that, darling," Franz said. "It won't be for a while, and you come right back to me when they do. I can maintain this shape forever."

When they left, Blossom insisted on stopping at the Beverly

Center. There was no way she was going to walk around looking like the Joker. Especially in front of Skip. She would buy herself a pair of sunglasses the size of satellite dishes before assuming her position back at the pool.

"What's with the glasses, Blossom?" Skip asked, looking down at her on the chaise. *Damn.* There was a fifty-fifty chance Skip would have just ignored these ridiculous glasses that resembled Frisbees or dinner plates. She had a million excuses to give him, but she just didn't feel like lying. It would be weeks before her eyebrows grew back. *Just confess the whole stupid thing.* She took them off.

He looked at her and couldn't quite figure out what was wrong. Like when a man shaves his mustache—you can tell something is different, but what, is a mystery. And then he saw it. Someone had shaped her eyebrows to look like one of those bridges that pull up to let tall ships through.

"Oh, my God." And he started to laugh, but immediately felt terrible for doing so. He covered his mouth and tried to stop. And he did. For a second. And then he started all over again. Blossom could have sat there, mad. But the truth was, it was sort of funny. Not hysterical—after all, she had to live with those eyebrows. But funny enough to make her laugh, too.

"I'm sorry, Blossom."

"Hey, what can you do? Mrs. Feingold had this big idea that I'd enjoy a makeover. For the next couple of months it's going to look like I'm leaning forward in a strong wind or about to start a race."

"You just look so . . ."

"Surprised?"

"Yeah."

"Angry?"

"Kinda."

"Amazed?"

"That, too."

"I know, I can't seem to get that expression off my face."

"I'll ask Jeannie who she goes to. I'm sure she knows someone who can help you."

No, not Jeannie. I'd rather go through life looking like this. "Thanks, Skip."

"She'll be over later."

Oh, joy. Why? "She's coming here?"

"No. Over to the house. It's my birthday on Thursday, and she says she bought me something two months ago and she wants to give it to me."

"Hey, happy birthday!"

"Thanks."

"How old will you be?"

"Thirty-five, Blossom—an old man."

Blossom laughed. "What are you doing to celebrate?"

"Nothing. Jeannie's giving me the present and taking off. She says she has plans. Should have figured. I might take off Thursday and go to the beach. No plans past that, though."

"Well, if you'll allow me, I would love to make you dinner. No one should have nothing to do on their birthday."

"You don't have to trouble yourself, Blossom."

"Trouble? It's no trouble at all. It'll be fun. Pick a night. If you're really not doing anything on your birthday night, then we can do it on Thursday."

"Okay. Thursday's great. What can I bring?"

"Yourself."

"Good, then."

"Yes. Good."

Skip took Thursday off. Blossom imagined him at the beach. *Mmmm.* Her first order of business that morning was buying him a birthday present. She wanted to make sure it was appropriate this time—something that he would be glad to have and not feel he had to return because of its price or its meaning.

There was a store on Brighton Way she had passed numerous

times and always wanted an excuse to go in. This was the perfect excuse. Roth & Co. had a fine selection of art and antiques, mostly from the nineteenth and early twentieth centuries. Blossom had never seen such beautiful things. It was as if she were walking through a museum, only here you got to buy the pieces. She made several turns around the shop, but nothing jumped out at her. Except Gene Hackman. There he was again, buying something and waiting to have it wrapped. How could Gene Hackman appear again? In fact, she'd never seen any other actor in Hollywood. She contemplated going over to him. Would he remember her? *Hello, Gene, it's so nice to see you again. I see we shop at all the same stores. Perhaps we could have coffee some time and compare purchases . . . Oh, Blossom, I don't think so.*

While she was lost in thought, he left. Oh, well. At last, a fine mahogany box with the initials *S. L.* inlaid in twenty-four-carat gold caught her eye. Now, what were the odds of that? Coming across a box with Skip's initials on them.

The salesperson walked over when he saw her interest. "This box," he began, "dates back to the 1850s. We surmise it was someone's personal cache. It has a secret drawer that slides out right here at the bottom." The man held up the box and pulled out the drawer. Blossom was delighted.

"What was that used for?" she asked.

"We're not sure, exactly. However, the secret compartment is quite large, so we guessed it might have been used to hide several secret love letters or perhaps some ill-gotten gains. It's always more fun to imagine the most wicked possibilities. It is quite curious, isn't it?"

"I love it. It's going to be a present. How much is it?"

"The price is . . . is . . ." The clerk looked for it on the back and inside but didn't see one. He opened the secret compartment to its full length. "Oh, here it is, hidden in the back. How appropriate." He laughed. "Two thousand dollars."

"Fine," Blossom said, "perfect." Skip would have no idea what she paid.

"Would you like me to wrap it?"

"No, thank you."

The secret drawer gave her a thought. She would hide a love note in there. Something that revealed her truest feelings for him. Then one day, when he was fumbling around, he would simply come upon it. She was sure she'd be long gone by then anyway. Perfect.

Next, she went to the market and bought all manner of goodies for the evening's festivities. In her downtime at the pool, she had learned recipes recommended by famous actresses who had served them only on special occasions. Recipes fit for a king . . . or an Oscar winner. *Maybe even Tom Selleck.*

To begin, she would make miniature chévre tarts, which called for mild chévre cheese, sweet butter, whipping-cream, eggs, cayenne to taste, and scallions, none of which she had in the house. Next she would serve cream of watercress soup, so she would need potatoes and nutmeg and heavy cream and, of course, watercress. She was pretty sure she had the shallots and chicken stock.

She was, however undecided about what to do for the main course. Fruit-stuffed Cornish game hens or pheasant with leek-and-pecan stuffing? Meryl Streep had great success with the hen, while Marisa Tomei swore by the pheasant. Finally, after sifting through six cookbooks, she decided: veal chops with sherry and lemon marmalade. There were no small bones involved, so no one would have to know the Heimlich maneuver.

She would make a simple salad with a raspberry vinaigrette dressing and ginger candied carrots. For dessert she would have birthday cake, of course. And champagne. What was a birthday without a birthday cake and a champagne toast?

Blossom spent the whole day preparing for this gastronomic delight. She set the table with fine linen, flowers, and candles. She put on Tony Bennett, the CD that had "Fly Me to the Moon" and "Falling in Love with Love." Then, thinking the candles were too much, too romantic, she opted to remove them.

Blossom put on a pretty dark-blue-and-yellow kimono and just a drop of vanilla perfume behind her ears. Then she wiped it off, deciding she'd smell too much like a cookie. Seven-thirty—that was the time they'd agreed upon. The clock clicked into place like the tumbler on a lock. She felt nervous.

Now, don't go getting the jitters, Blossom. This is just a friendly birthday dinner for a friend. Nothing more.

At 7:45 Blossom was peeking out the window. It was not unlike Skip to be late. Sometimes he'd show up a half hour late for work. Blossom contented herself by remembering that and by putting on some more music.

At eight o'clock she was rearranging the table setting, refolding napkins, refilling water glasses.

At 8:15 she was back in the kitchen, trying to reestimate the cook time on the various dishes.

By eight-thirty she was worried. He hadn't even called to say he'd be late. She paced back and forth from the living room to the kitchen, trying to keep things warm without ruining them.

At nine o'clock she was sitting by herself at the table, looking at the beautiful bouquet of flowers she had bought for the occasion. She got up and slowly began to remove the place settings. It was clear: He wasn't coming. He just wasn't coming.

She put the food away and threw out the cake. It was too hard to look at.

She waited until eleven before getting into her bathing suit and going down to the pool. The night was as black as the ace of spades. She was glad to be able to submerge her entire body in the water. That way she wouldn't feel the tears running down her cheeks. What was she thinking anyway? Her attraction was too great. She would only be hurt by continually setting herself up. This was the truth. This was how things were.

It was painfully clear that she would not find that special kind of love before she died, and that was that. Perhaps this awful fact would make the dying okay. What was life without love anyway? Just a series of meaningless events that filled the space of our lives with noise and distraction. It was time to face it. Time to face living alone and dying alone.

A sadness too great to hold spilled over Blossom, and it would not wash away when she dove beneath the black waters, nor did it dissipate into the night air when she resurfaced. It stayed there, like an anchor attached to her heart, pulling her down, ever downward into darkness.

CHAPTER 33

*S*KIP KNOCKED ON BLOSSOM'S DOOR in the morning. She did not answer. He knocked again. When there was still no answer, he just assumed she had gone out. He had no idea she was inside, sitting quietly.

"You see Blossom, Mrs. Feingold?" Skip asked. Mrs. Feingold walked toward the pool as if she were dodging land mines and hot coals. She didn't swim; she just got wet from time to time, tapping water on her arms and chest. She told Blossom this was her way of doing laps and called it "the Jewish crawl." Tap, tap, tap, and that was it. She would dry off the same way and go back inside.

"Not yet. But I will later. I have some tickets for her." Tap, tap, tap. "I double-booked for Saturday and thought Blossom would like them. By the way, did you see her new look?"

"Her new look?"

"It was my idea to do that with her eyebrows. She looks like Greta Garbo now, don't you think?"

"Oh, yeah . . . the eyebrows . . . very nice, Mrs. Feingold. Well, if you see her, can you tell her I'm looking for her?"

"Oh, yes, Skip. I'm dropping off the tickets before she takes Vinny to the groomer."

Takes Vinny to the groomer? This thoroughly confused Skip. He had no idea Mrs. Feingold was still laboring under the notion that Vinny was Blossom's dog. Oh, well, he'd ask Blossom what she meant later, when he saw her.

When Mrs. Feingold knocked, Blossom peeked through the peephole, then opened the door. Her shades were still drawn, which was not like her at all. The shafts of light that usually streamed through the rooms, warming the corners and the rugs, dusting the flowers, making them look as if they were wearing halos, were not there. Today the apartment was sealed as tight as an envelope.

"What's going on, Blossom?"

"What do you mean?"

"It's a beautiful day, and you've got this place closed up like a fallout shelter."

"Do I?"

"Yes, you do. Let's open some of these curtains." She walked over toward the window.

"Don't."

Mrs. Feingold stopped. "Okay." She came back into the living room. She could see sorrow in Blossom's eyes. An awkward silence passed between them until Mrs. Feingold broke the quiet. "Want to talk about it?"

"I've done something unbelievably stupid."

"My dear, I'm older than you. I've had many more opportunities to do unbelievably stupid things in my life. What could you have possibly done that I haven't done already?"

"It's not important."

"Well, important or not, I'm here if you want to talk about it with me."

"I don't even know you that well, Mrs. Feingold. Hell, I'm still calling you Mrs. Feingold. I don't even know your first name."

"Deneichia, darling."

"Deneni . . . Deneichi . . . think I'll stick with Mrs. Feingold."

"People call me Dolly, honey, to get around it."

"Dolly."

"Yes. So call me Dolly and tell me what's going on."

Tears were forming ever so slightly in the corners of Blossom's eyes. She could barely get her mouth around the words. She wasn't even sure of what she wanted to say. No one had ever asked her to express feelings like this.

"Everything's a mess, Mrs. Feingold—Dolly." She took another breath as if getting ready to take a deep plunge underwater. "The thing is . . . well . . . I'm in love with someone."

"So? That doesn't sound stupid."

"Someone who doesn't share the same feelings I have for him. He's in love, too, with his wife."

"Oh, Blossom, dear."

"They're separated. But he wants her back. He loves her and wants everything to be the way it used to be. I, of course, being the horrible person that I am, want it to fail miserably so that I can have a chance. But you know what the irony is, Mrs. Fein—Dolly? Even if that happened, I wouldn't have a chance with him. Even if he weren't married, even if I were the only woman within a three-thousand-mile radius, he still wouldn't be interested in me."

"How do you know this?"

"I just do. And what's worse, this was my last chance for love."

"Why do you say that?"

"It just is."

"That's ridiculous, Blossom. We always have opportunities to invite love into our lives. You have everything you need to have love; you just don't know it, honey. Now, I'm not sure about your friend who is married. It sounds like he has other things to work out that have nothing to do with you. But that doesn't mean you have to be tied up in knots, hoping, waiting. That's just disappointment preparing for its big entrance. You have to do something else."

"Like what?"

"Sometimes when a situation is at its worst, it can bring out the best in us. When Mr. Feingold died, my life stopped. My happiness had always been tied up with him, with everything that was outside myself. His death forced me to look in another direction. It forced me to look inside myself. And you know what I found?"

Blossom was trying to close down the sadness. Her throat hurt from suppressing the tears. "What?"

"Love, dear. Underneath the fear, the loneliness, the betrayal of being left behind, the insecurity of facing life on my own, I found love."

"How?"

"Through understanding. At my very lowest, just when I believed unhappiness would eat me alive, I surrendered. I didn't suddenly become happy all at once; it took time. But I grew through the pain, grew to a place where I finally found understanding, and through understanding I found peace."

"But someone you loved had died. My situation is completely different from yours."

"The situation isn't exactly the same, but the process is similar. Love is love, Blossom. It's a universal truth. You say you love someone who doesn't love you, and this is making you sad. Accept the sadness. Give yourself time to be sad. I did, and you know what happened? One day I was sad for a little less time than I had been the day before. And the next day I was sad for a little less time than that. And slowly the emptiness began to shift. Hell, it practically took an earthquake to shake me up, but I finally felt it. I was never good with subtlety."

Blossom smiled a little. Something of what that old bartender had said back in New Orleans reverberated in her. *Sadness is okay. You have to have sadness to truly know happiness. Then, when you get it, it's all that much sweeter, like honey from a rock. Yeah, that's what he said. Like honey from a rock.*

Dolly continued: "But let me tell you something, darling, sadness no longer tore me apart or made me so afraid. I knew I could get through it because I had accepted something. Something that helped me. And it wasn't the phone calls from friends who felt obliged, or the sleeping pills, or the endless glasses of brandy, or the noise of the TV, which distracted me from the pain. I had myself. I accepted myself. That's when it began to be okay. And this is where it is the same, Blossom. Are you catching my drift, or am I gonna have to bring in the June Taylor dancers?"

"I'm catching your drift."

"Good, 'cause most of those dancers are dead." Blossom smiled again. "My husband's death took so much, but it didn't take what was essential for me to live. For a while I thought I died with him, but after a few months I was still here. Yet I was still feeling terrible.

I couldn't go through life feeling this bad anymore. I had to come to my own rescue." Blossom realized at that moment that talking was as much a catharsis for Dolly as it was for her.

"Life hands us lessons, and my lesson was to face this awful situation and grow from it, Blossom. I thought love had been taken away from me, but it hadn't been. I was still the same person who had loved Mr. Feingold and my old aunts and my cousins and my friends. I still had love inside of me, and I still had it to give. Some people spend their whole life searching for love, Blossom. And the thing of it is, it's right there, inside of themselves. If you can find that inside yourself, then you will find the source of your happiness. Believe me, I went through a lot of tsuris, not to mention therapy with Dr. Yagozoski, to come to this realization. I hope I can spare you that."

"Doctor who?"

"My shrink. I know his name reads like an eye chart. But he came highly recommended. He helped that famous actress who was found in the bushes."

"Oh, yeah, I know the one. But, Dolly, what happens if I never find that special love, that one true love that every person has a right to know in their lifetime? The love that loves you back?"

"Find the love inside of yourself, Blossom, and the rest will follow. I promise you this with every inch of my being. I know this much is true, and I've got the scars to prove it."

Blossom walked over to the window and peered out through a separation in the fabric. She saw Skip carrying a large potted plant across the lawn.

"I don't even know if I have that kind of love inside myself."

"You do, my dear. Everyone does."

Blossom sighed under her breath. If only Dolly knew the whole story.

"You must think I'm foolish. It's not even like I have a relationship with this man, and yet I can feel so devastated."

"You do in your heart. And sometimes unrequited love can be more painful than actually having the relationship. I bet his wife is not in the same kind of pain as you are, and yet she's had the relationship. Love stinks sometimes."

Blossom got that. She understood it with excruciating precision. "Thanks, Dolly." She looked at Dolly with utter reverence. Here was a woman who had been through so much and was still here to tell the story. Dolly was like a well so deep that if one were to drop a coin into it, it would be a long time before they heard the splash. Yes, Blossom thought, her soul is as old as Stonehenge. She wished she could have the opportunity to grow into a woman like that.

Dolly interrupted her thoughts: "Oh, Blossom, dear, I almost forgot why I came over. Here are the tickets to that Tony Bennett concert I mentioned. They should be good seats."

"Tony Bennett?" Blossom exclaimed. She couldn't believe her ears. "You never said it was a Tony Bennett concert."

"I didn't? Do you like him?"

"Like him? Like him? I love him. I have every CD he's ever made."

"The only drawback is that you may have plans. It falls on Thanksgiving," Dolly said, "and that's the reason I can't go. I promised my niece I would spend it with her family this year. She's not really my niece. She's more of an honorary niece, someone who I've known since birth."

Blossom had forgotten all about the holidays. Here in L.A. the weather didn't get cold, the leaves didn't change color, and it just didn't feel like Thanksgiving to Blossom at all. In fact, she was grateful to have plans that day.

"Thanksgiving is perfect, Dolly. There is no one I'd more like to spend it with than Tony Bennett."

"So you see, my dear, things are already looking up. A few minutes ago I was ready to force you to watch those motivational tapes, all one hundred and thirty-six hours of them."

"You're kidding."

"Yes, I'm kidding. There are actually two hundred and thirty-six hours of them."

Charlotte found her laugh. "Tony Bennett. I've waited all my life to see Tony Bennett."

"And now it's happening. You see?" she said as she turned to leave. "And so will love."

CHAPTER 34

*T*HAT EVENING BLOSSOM slipped back into the pool, becoming lost again in her own lush liquid world. She lay on her back, looking up into the ineffable darkness, listening for answers. But there were only stars. Watery spears of light shooting across the night sky.

She wished she could pitch a tent among the stars and wait for God. That way she'd be even closer to hearing the answers when He finally whispered them in her ear.

Each star was beautiful tonight, blinking down at her from nowhere at all. A fistful of fire opals, white gold, a whole sky salted with silver, randomly shaken onto a vast black silk swath.

Back and forth, back and forth, she began her nightly routine, her breath breaking like white noise around her ears.

At first all she could think about was Tony Bennett. But the rhythm of her strokes brought her around to other thoughts. How many months did she have left? she wondered. It took eight months before her mother showed any symptoms of cancer. She was fine, and then one day she was not. Blossom presumed the same fate awaited her. She'd be fine until she woke up one morning, and it would be obvious. It would be over.

But for now she was still alive. She was still waking up every morning as a member of the living world. Was this how she wanted it to be when she left Gorham? Was this how she envisioned the last year of her life? Mooning after someone who could not reciprocate in the same way? No, this was not what she had wanted. What she wanted was simple. To love and to be loved. To come to Hollywood, a place she had heard so much about, a place she believed that dreams could come true, and to find her destiny. Was that too much to ask? Clearly, it was.

Why do I want love so much? Is it because I don't want to be alone in the end? She struggled to stay honest with herself. She believed it was more than that, but she also believed it was okay that love serve as a buffer against loneliness. *Isn't this true for people who are not dying? Isn't this an unsaid truth for most of the men and women we pass on the street every day? The women who are buying Cheerios at the grocery store, the men who are fixing their ties at a stoplight, looking at their watches, late for a meeting? People don't want to live alone, and they certainly don't want to die alone.* Yes, it was true.

Perhaps, she thought, she could look for love elsewhere. After all, the world was filled with people. Skip was not the only man on earth. But then again, there were her feelings. How could she just turn off her feelings?

This question was so familiar. Why? She swam, back and forth, back and forth and then it finally came to her. Of course, it was difficult to remember. She had tried so hard to forget. She'd experienced those very feelings with T. J. Just thinking about him brought the horror of that evening. It was a moment that would remain fixed in time. As if the hands of the church clock had frozen because of some chance cold snap, hands that stayed locked in the final stroke of their last bitter seconds. All one could hear, now and forever, were the hollow groans of loss blowing through the bell towers above the town.

And Charlotte remembered, "Go find her, T. J." The words still echoed in Blossom's ears like a judge's gavel bringing down the final sentence. If she could only take them back. The guilt was overwhelming. How could she have let her own feelings dominate everything? How could she have told him to go and find MaryAnn? After he'd hurt MaryAnn so, she'd never agree to come back to Charlotte's with him. Better to join him over there. She had rushed over to MaryAnn's house, but no one had been there. Where could they be? She decided to leave a note: *Out looking for you. Will go home after. Please, please, call me there as soon as you get this.*

She drove past the school, the 7-Eleven, the Mobil station; she drove past T. J.'s house, the police station, the post office, then finally decided this was futile and went home. They could at least reach her there. Barely an hour had passed when the phone rang.

"MaryAnn, I'm so glad to hear from you, I—"

But MaryAnn cut her off. "Charlotte, I'm at the hospital."

Oh, my God. What happened? Did she hurt herself?

"Are you okay? I'm coming over right now."

"No, don't."

MaryAnn was sobbing. "But, MaryAnn, I—"

"Charlotte, it's T. J. . . . T. J. . . . He's dead. He was drunk. He drove straight into a tree on Lowell Street." There was silence, and then MaryAnn continued.

"Did he go to your house, Charlotte?"

Oh, God, he was at my house. How could I have told him to leave when he was drunk?

"Was he at your house?" MaryAnn asked again.

"Yes, he was."

"Was he drunk?"

"Yes, it seemed as if he'd been drinking a lot." *And I let him go. I let him drive that way.* Charlotte bit her lip till it bled. "I'm coming over to the hospital. I don't want you to be alone."

"No, don't."

"Why?"

"I don't want you to."

"MaryAnn, please . . ."

"No, don't. I have to go with his parents to ID the body now. I don't want you here."

"Oh, please, MaryAnn, please don't be alone right now."

"I'm not alone. I'm with the person I'm supposed to be with."

Everything changed after that. MaryAnn withdrew from the friendship. Charlotte felt terrible. If she hadn't told T. J. how she felt, maybe he'd still be alive. Maybe she and MaryAnn would still be friends. Maybe God was punishing her. She would never tell MaryAnn the truth—it would only hurt her, and there was nothing to be gained by her having such knowledge now. No, Charlotte would have to carry her grief over losing T. J. privately. Everyone felt so bad for MaryAnn; no one guessed the anguish Charlotte suffered. But guilt began to outweigh anguish, especially because it was clear that MaryAnn blamed her for T. J.'s feelings and his death. Charlotte blamed herself even more. *If only*, she'd think. *If only, if only, if only* . . .

Seducing Tom away from her had been MaryAnn's way of getting even, and Charlotte had no choice but to painfully accept the situation. Perhaps there was a part of Charlotte that felt undeserving, guilty. *Yes, this is right; why should I have Tom? MaryAnn deserves his love more than I do.*

But this was years ago, and the guilt was still there, nipping at her heels, like tiny fish that swim in the shadow of the shark, nibbling incessantly at its skin no matter where it goes. Guilt had become a symbiotic relationship for her.

But wasn't it her turn now? Hadn't she paid her dues, learned enough lessons? Why was it that there were so many hard lessons to learn in life, in love? Why, she wondered, couldn't it all be as easy as floating on your back and looking at the stars?

CHAPTER 35

*E*IGHT-THIRTY IN THE MORNING would have found Blossom at her desk a year ago, but now it was early for her, so early she was roused from a deep sleep. What had woken her? A knock at the door, followed by "Blossom, you in there?"

Jesus. She flew through the closet, looking for anything to throw on. A wrinkled caftan fell to the floor, and she grabbed it up and shimmied into it. It was bigger than she'd remembered. And it simply wouldn't adjust to fit quite right. But she had no time to think about that now. She had to answer the door.

She took a quick glance through the peephole as if visually bracing herself, and there he was, looking handsome as ever even through this unflattering lens.

"Skip!"

"Blossom. Hi. You're finally home. I tried to find you yesterday. You were nowhere in sight. Listen, I'm so sorry about the other night. Can I come in?"

"Yes, by all means, come in. Would you like a cup of coffee?"

"No, no thanks. I can't stay, but I just wanted to apologize and tell you what happened."

Blossom didn't say a word. An apology was appropriate, and she took it. And she was curious about what happened, so she didn't stop him.

"Jeannie came over . . . to give me the present."

Right, right. Must have been some present.

"We got to talking. I thought she was just going to stay until I opened it. But she ended up staying longer."

The night?

"She said she was glad we had this time together, because she had wanted to get together for a while now, but with her schedule and mine . . ."

Jesus, Skip, just say it already. You and she are back together. It was a wonderful night. You never expected it. You're so sorry that you couldn't even manage to call me, but the evening just slipped away.

"So anyway, we got to talking, and she asked me if I was happy. She asked how I was doing with the separation. I told her okay, but that I really missed her, missed being with her, waking up with her, going to sleep with her. She was quiet. I suddenly got the feeling that I had given her the wrong answer. My instinct was right," Skip laughed wryly. Blossom looked on, surprised, unsure, waiting for him to continue. "She said she was sorry that was how I felt, because she had met someone. Someone she liked . . . a lot."

"Oh, Skip . . ."

"I asked her if she was in love, and she didn't say anything. So I asked her again and she said maybe."

"Oh, Skip, I'm so sorry." It was strange, but no part of Blossom felt happy. Her heart broke for him at that moment. She knew what it felt like to be told no, to be told it would not work out, to be told by the person you needed and loved that they didn't feel the same way about you. She remembered when Tom Barzini told her the very same thing. And, of course, when she told T. J., even though it had been a god-awful, irretrievable lie in that case.

"So I asked her if it was over, if our marriage was completely over now, and she said she didn't know. She said she needed more time to see where her feelings were taking her, and she didn't want to say anything absolute yet, but that she thought it was important that I know. She didn't want to keep secrets from me. We never did that with each other, and she didn't want to start now."

"Oh, Skip, it must have been a nightmare for you."

"It was, Blossom. We ended up talking until three in the morning. We cried; we held each other. I had this awful feeling that it was the end. I'm sorry that I didn't call. I know you must have gone to a lot of trouble."

"No, don't worry. There are always opportunities to have dinner." She paused before continuing. "Maybe it's not over, Skip. Maybe this is just something she has to do before coming full circle." *Is this me? God, I sound so magnanimous. More normal than I ever have, even to myself.*

"Part of me would like to think so, Blossom, but there was something about it that just didn't have that feeling. And if we did get back together, could I ever really trust that Jeannie would not want to split again? I'm feeling so many different things, I don't know what I really think. I do know if she called me up right now and said she'd made a mistake and wanted to work on it, I would be there in a heartbeat. I do know that."

"Maybe she will."

"She won't. You know, I've tried to break down in my own head what it is I love about Jeannie. She's completely rejected me, yet I still love her."

"Sometimes you're even more attracted to what you can't have. It's human nature." *Ain't that the truth.*

"Yeah, that's true. But there's something else. Something I can't put my finger on. When we got married, it was so wonderful. It seemed there were no major difficulties to overcome."

"This is your first bump in the road?"

"Yeah. And it hurts me to think she can't stick it out with me. When I was a lawyer, even an unhappy lawyer, she could hang in there. Now that I'm doing this pool thing, faraway is not faraway enough for her."

Blossom didn't know what to say, but fortunately, she didn't have to. Skip wasn't finished.

"And the thing that has me somewhat baffled is, what does that say about me, that I could be in love with someone who's that superficial?"

Blossom understood Skip and could see why he had believed Jeannie was without flaws. At first sight of Jeannie, Blossom thought the same thing. But when Skip found flaws, flaws that were so glaring they blinded him, it made him feel he was incapable of making good judgments.

"Well, this is yet another reason to work at the pool. It's not just the job thing I need to figure out. I need to ask myself some serious questions. Who'd have ever thought a pool job would be this hard?" Skip laughed ruefully.

"You'll get there, Skip."

"Lord, I hope you're right."

They sat quietly for a few minutes, Blossom struggling to produce some solution for her friend. Dolly had been so good at it. What would she say if she were here?

She would be coming up with a hundred explanations of why things happen, and two hundred ways to make Skip feel better. She longed to call Dolly over and point to Skip and say, "Tell him, Dolly; tell him all the good stuff you always say to me. Tell him how marriage takes many turns, how some people just grow differently. Tell him that stepping off a moving train is scary at first, but the good news is that if somehow he can manage to jump off, then he can begin living again, because in making that leap of faith, he'll arrive at a much better place than where he was when he began."

So Blossom tried to say what Dolly would say.

"You know when a train is going very fast and you decide to jump off . . ."

Jesus, Blossom, you sound like you're suggesting suicide!

"But it's okay because you won't get hurt in the fall."

"What?" Skip asked, looking utterly perplexed.

"Oh, nothing. I'm trying to say something but it's not coming out right. Oh, Skip, I want to say something to you, do something. What can I do?"

"Nothing, Blossom, there's really nothing you can do."

"Listen . . ." She reached down as far as she could. "Mrs. Feingold—Dolly—gave me tickets to a Tony Bennett concert for Saturday. Why don't you take them? Take a friend and forget about everything for the night."

"Oh, Blossom, that's really nice of you. But I don't know . . . my head isn't really in a place . . . Can I tell you tomorrow?"

"Yeah, sure. It's no big deal." *Do this. It's a good thing to do. Don't make it about you. Let him take whoever he wants.*

"Thanks." Skip turned to go.

"Skip, one more thing . . ." Blossom reached for his present. It looked perfectly wrapped in beautiful gold paper embossed with muted blue flowers and tied with a silver string.

"Oh, Blossom," Skip said. He looked embarrassed. "I wish you hadn't."

"It's not much, really. Just a little something."

"It doesn't look that little to me."

"It's just a token, that's all."

"Why don't I leave it here and open it some other time in front of you?"

"No, take it. Open it later—it'll be a little diversion on a gloomy day."

Skip left with the box and the tiniest smile, which made her feel good. It surprised her to realize she did not covet anything else from him. It also surprised her that she was willing to part with her Tony Bennett tickets.

Something was changing within her, like a fault line moving ever so subtly to align itself with the rest of the earth. She didn't want anything, wasn't receiving anything, and yet felt compensated, happy. What was this tiny truth she was experiencing? What strange reality? And then it came to her, just like that. It was, simply and solely, *acceptance.*

CHAPTER 36

I'M GONNA TAKE YOU UP on those tickets, Blossom, if it's still okay."

Blossom was excited. Seeing her favorite singer of all time with Skip—what could be better?

"Fantastic!"

"Yeah, I mentioned it to a friend of mine, and she was thrilled beyond belief. I had no idea what a fan she was. Apparently, he has a big following."

Blossom's heart sank. She had forgotten she had given him both tickets. Somehow, the way he had said it, she thought . . . she thought . . .

"Oh, no, he has a very big following." Her voice softened. "I'm quite a fan myself."

"Did you want to keep them?"

"No, absolutely not. I can't make it actually. I have a date."

"You do? Good for you. Who's the lucky guy?"

Oh shit. "Bill . . . Bill Bailey." *Bill Bailey? What am I, an idiot?*

"Bill Bailey? Like the song?"

"Yeah, I know, he hates when people bring that up." *A nervous, stupid idiot.*

"Well, I won't break into song when I meet him."

Meet him?

"You sure you don't want to keep these tickets for your date?"

"No, we're going to Morton's for a big Thanksgiving dinner. He has a lot of friends in show business. We'll be eating with them. Hold on a second and let me get them for you."

Blossom went into the bedroom to get the tickets. *Bill Bailey? Morton's? A lot of friends in show business? Why didn't I just tell him I was going out with Brad Pitt or Steven Spielberg or Elvis? Jesus, Blossom.* "Here they are," she said, handing them over. She watched him pocket both tickets as if he were taking the only transport papers that could get her out of Casablanca.

"Thanks, Blossom. I'll give you a full report. He's the one that sings that song about leaving your heart in San Francisco, right?"

"Right." That was all Skip knew about Tony Bennett? He'd won Tonys and Grammys; he was Frank Sinatra's favorite singer, for God's sake!

"Have a great time," she said, passing over the keys to the kingdom. *I'm just gonna go inside and kill myself now.*

Blossom sat there thinking about the tickets. She was truly happy to have done something nice for Skip. She was. But she wanted to see that concert, too. And then it came to her. Why couldn't she go to the concert? There was no reason she couldn't call up the box office and get a ticket for herself. After all, Bill Bailey wouldn't be that upset that she wouldn't be able to attend his Thanksgiving soiree at Morton's. So she picked up the phone and called.

She made sure her seats were miles away from Skip's. The Hollywood Bowl was way too big ever to bump into someone you knew. Perfect. Everyone would get to see Tony Bennett.

Blossom put on a chiffony black muumuu with a belt that gathered up most of the overly abundant fabric. It was her only muumuu that could pass for a fancy dress if she accessorized it. She finished the look with six strands of long, fat pearls. Her hair was up, her makeup on, her eyebrows growing in nicely. It was crowded at the

Hollywood Bowl, just as she had suspected. Thousands of people poured in, mumbling, laughing.

She found her seat way up in the stands. Nosebleed seats. She didn't care—she was lucky to have even gotten a ticket. Most people had purchased them weeks ago. She peered through her binoculars to assess the stage. Not too bad. She would be able to see him quite well when he came out. She held the program tight in her hands. Maybe she could even get his autograph later.

The lights went down, the audience hushed, and the announcer began:

"And now, ladies and gentlemen, the man of the hour, the man you've been waiting for, the only man whose artistry and talent get better year after year, please help me welcome to the stage this evening, the one and only Tony Bennett!"

The crowd went wild. People stood up and cheered and clapped and yelled, and in a moment the elation was broken with "Come Fly with Me" and "I Wanna Be Around." Blossom was ecstatic. She hadn't felt this happy since . . . since forever. The music filled her up like chocolate. It was sweet and rich and satisfying, and how she wanted more. "It's the Good Life," "Day and Night," "Two for the Road." She held her binoculars tight to her eyes, afraid of missing a single note. The audience loved it to. She scanned it to see that hundreds had come with the same zeal she had. And then he sang "Smile," and she smiled as she slowly drew the binoculars over the crowd, smiled, smiled, smil—and then she froze.

There was Skip. Third row, center. Who was he with? A woman? Yes. Who? She couldn't quite see her. She was half turned, leaning forward. *"Smile though your heart is aching; smile, even though it's breaking . . ."* She was blonde. Was his arm around her? Yes. Was it Jeannie? Tony Bennett kept on singing: *". . . That's the time you must keep on trying; smile; what's the use of crying?"* It wasn't Jeannie. It was someone else. Someone just as pretty. Someone who was not Blossom. *". . . You'll find life is still worthwhile, if you'll just smile . . ."*

Oh, God. Don't go there. Listen to the music. Love the music just as you did one minute ago. Look at the stage and listen to the beautiful music. "If you just smile."

But she couldn't. She excused herself down a long row of annoyed people and hurried out of the Hollywood Bowl, all the while hearing Tony Bennett's distant voice rise over the walls, singing, *". . . If you just smile . . ."* She got in her car and drove home.

The pool lay in front of her like an interlude that separated deliverance from devastation. She eased herself in gratefully.

Back and forth, back and forth she swam, stretching out along the pool's full length. The water felt so good washing over her as she left the last hours behind her in their wake. One arm over the other, she swam. Oxygen infused every pore, drenched every atom of her being. And with the unnumbered refrain of each round, she began to breathe again. Deep breaths. Cool, energizing breaths, as invigorating as an open window in winter.

How could she have left the concert? She had waited her whole life to see Tony Bennett. It was love that drove her to the concert; it was jealousy that drove her away. Jealousy. If she had stayed with that feeling of love, she would never have left; she would have remained and listened to the music, embracing the moment.

Skip was handsome and kind, and she was drawn to him with a powerful magnetism, with that XYZ of attraction, the hard-wiring of love.

But he shouldn't be the only reason to feel alive . . . and suddenly, from the mute bottom waters, she found her smile; from the lipless dark that had swallowed her whole came an unexpected surge of hope. She was healing. She was letting go. And promise poured over her like a christening. It was all right. It was all right. And it was going to be all right.

CHAPTER 37

*A*s the pounds came off, so did the awful weight of despair that Blossom had been carrying around with her for so long. Even her obsession with Skip began to fade like a dream that loses its detail by the afternoon. And this particular afternoon found Blossom sitting at an outdoor café on Rodeo Drive, enjoying a double espresso and reading L.A.'s second-most-read magazine, a publication that informed people with money about what to do in Los Angeles. She had vowed to expand her interests beyond the pool—beyond Skip—so here she was, at a chic café, trying to look as though she belonged there.

From out of the glossy pages leaped a painting that demanded her attention. It was an aqua pool, with refracted light breaking across the page. It was cool, inviting. It was where Blossom had enjoyed the best hours of her recent life. Who painted this? Where could she see it? She read on:

David Hockney. Gallery of Contemporary Art.
David Hockney will be speaking at 2 p.m. Sunday afternoon.

It was already Sunday afternoon, and Blossom had only twenty minutes to get over there. *David Hockney. He's good. I wonder if he's done any more of these pools. This would look nice in the living room. I wonder how much he'd charge for something like this?*

Blossom entered the gallery and made her way over to the exhibit and the area where he would be speaking. She couldn't remember the last time she'd been in a gallery. Had she ever been in a gallery? She had gone down to Boston one Saturday to see the aquarium, but then, that was not exactly a gallery. Maybe fish enthusiasts might consider it a fish gallery, but Blossom doubted it.

Everyone sat hushed in a semicircle. Blossom took her place toward the end of the row. The room was awash in pools. Blue pools, green pools, pools with people, pools with diving boards, pools without diving boards, pools cut with sunlight—lots of sunlight, a tiny bit of sunlight, no sunlight at all.

She was happy being surrounded by so much water. It was as if the secret life she had created were splashing around her at high tide. Back and forth, back and forth her eyes darted, lost in their own laps.

And then David Hockney came out. Blossom began to applaud, but no one else joined in, so she stopped immediately. The distraction didn't seem to faze the artist, and he began to talk about his pools. Blossom listened with the concentration of a Buddhist. Nothing could sway her attention from the way he portrayed his pools. It was as if she were back in the voiceless water, making her midnight rounds.

And as she sat worlds apart from the others, she felt that Hockney was speaking only to her. Describing, illustrating, elucidating—it was all directed toward Blossom.

"So are there any questions?" he asked finally.

Those were the words that broke the trance.

"No? Well, please feel free to walk around and enjoy the paintings. Thank you for coming."

"Excuse me?" Blossom said, her hand raised.

"Yes?"

"How much is the painting behind you?"

Supercilious laughter tittered throughout the room.

Was that a stupid question?

"I actually have no idea how the gallery finally priced this. But I would be very happy if you bought it."

See? He'd be happy if I bought it! It wasn't a stupid question.

"If you'd like, I would be more than glad to find out for you."

"Yes, that would be very nice. Thank you."

The group got up slowly and started fanning out among the pools.

"I enjoyed your lecture very much," Blossom said. "I swim every night, and I've really come to love the pool in our complex. When I saw your ad in *L.A.* magazine, I had to come and see if you had more pictures of pools. They're really, really nice, Mr. Hockney."

"My ad?"

"Yeah, you know, the ad that showed the pool picture."

"Oh," Hockney laughed. "Thank you . . ."

"Blossom."

"Blossom. Oh, there's the curator now. Let's ask what this dicey little pool painting is fetching," he said. "Paul, the painting hanging on the back wall—what exactly is the price on that?"

"Is this for madam?"

"No, it's for me," Blossom said.

Hockney laughed again. The curator remained humorless. "I'll check." He sniffed out of the room, his nose pointing toward the ceiling.

"Are you a collector?" Hockney asked Blossom.

"No. I just like your pools."

"I'm flattered."

It was at this point Blossom noticed the hearing aid Hockney had in each ear. It was curious to her, yet she didn't perceive it as a handicap. On the contrary, she truly believed this helped him hear the music of his art more clearly. It must have, because every painting sang to her, invited her to wade in, to lay back into the deep, dazzling color of the blues. The blues. It was more than a mood or music. It was the cool smell of a minty sky that fills the air with a sharp, glacial clarity. It was a bowl of beach glass, smooth, rounded, and glazed with a tint of turquoise or a hint of aqua. It was an old cup, a broken shard softened by the sea. It was an endless, cloudless canvas painted with such hope and heart, it became imminently clear to Blossom that this artist, this gifted, beautiful man had made love . . . come out of the blue.

The curator was coming back with a piece of paper in hand.

"That painting, *Pool Number Fifteen,* is six hundred thousand dollars."

"Oh," Blossom said, disappointed, "that's more than I was hoping."

"We do have a slightly smaller painting actually," the curator explained, "still using the pulp paper method. . . . I believe that's going for one hundred thousand, perhaps one hundred fifty thousand dollars. Would you like to see it?"

"Very much."

"Yes, well, it's not out on the floor, but we do have it in the office. If you don't mind coming this way, Miss . . ."

"McBeal. Blossom McBeal."

"I'm heading that way," Hockney said. "I'll walk with you."

Blossom grinned when she saw the painting. It was wonderful. It didn't have the yellow diving board, but again the blues were mesmerizing, a crackling current of color.

"This piece is one hundred twenty-five thousand dollars."

A little more then she ought. But Blossom could not take her eyes from it. "I'll take it. It's absolutely beautiful." *An early Christmas present to myself. Why not? This is my last Christmas. I deserve something this special.*

Hockney smiled. "Good, then." And he shook Blossom's hand. "And I'm glad it's going to someone who likes it so much. Blossom, it's been a pleasure."

"Thank you. Perhaps when it's hung, you'd like to come over and see it."

The curator shot a look at Hockney.

"That's a nice invitation, and if I am still in the area, I would be happy to."

"Oh, you don't live here?"

"Yes, I live here, but I spend a lot of my time traveling back to England. But if an opportunity arises that extends my stay here, I will let Paul know."

Paul cleared his throat. "Yes, by all means."

"Again," Hockney said, looking at Blossom, "a pleasure." And he left.

Blossom had to pay with cash, of course, and she announced that she had to go home to get it. The curator smirked, then covered his rude behavior by explaining that he'd never dealt in cash like this before. Blossom knew he doubted that she'd return, but who cared what he thought? It was the painting she was bringing home, not him.

She returned later that afternoon with a brown grocery bag, the only thing she had available to carry that much money in. Her handbag was far too small, and her suitcases far too big. Paul gasped when he saw she'd returned, and gasped again when she emptied the cash on his desk.

"Go ahead, count it," Blossom said.

"Ummm, I'm sure it's all here." He thumbed the dozens and dozens of packages of fives, tens, twenties, and fifties. "Let me just secure this for you," he said, lifting the painting and preparing to box it.

"No, that's okay. I'll just take it as is."

"You'll just take it? As is? Without protective wrapping?"

"Sure. My car is just outside. No problem."

Paul stared at Blossom, then reluctantly handed her the Hockney. "Careful."

"Yeah, I will be. Oh, and thank you for all your trouble. I really appreciate it."

"Perhaps you'd like to get on our mailing list for future shows?"

"That's really nice, but I think I'm kind of in a pool phase right now."

"I'm sure there will be other shows coming up that might suit your interests." The allure of cash always triumphed in the end, Blossom thought.

"Well, okay. I'll write my name and number down. Call me if you get more blue paintings in. My living room is blue."

"Picasso had a blue period, so I'll certainly keep you informed."

"Good. Guess I'll just take this, then, and be getting along."

Paul watched Blossom disappear with the Hockney painting casually swinging under her arm. This gave him immediate heartburn, and he hurriedly retreated into his office, desperately searching for nothing less then a wheelbarrow of antacids. And if those didn't work he always had Valium to fall back on.

CHAPTER 38

*D*OLLY, COME OVER AND LOOK at my new painting," Blossom said. When she hung up the phone, she went immediately to the window and called out, "Skip, come up and look at my new painting." Skip arrived first.

"Thank you for those tickets, Blossom. They were amazing. Do you know where we sat?"

Yes, I know exactly where you sat. "Where?"

"Third row, center. It couldn't have been more perfect."

Yes, the whole evening was like that for me, too. "Oh, good."‘

"And, Blossom . . ."

"Yes?"

"Your present, the box, it's so nice. Thank you."

"What are you going to keep in it?"

"I don't know. Right now it's just out on my coffee table."

"Well, it seemed to be you, with your initials and everything. By the way, I've been meaning to ask you, is Skip your real name?"

"Actually, no. My dad is Dennis Loggins, and I'm Dennis Loggins Jr., so somehow I got the nickname Skip."

"Oh, well, still, S. L. seems like you."

"Without a doubt. I wouldn't have any other initials on it. I'm Skip, just like you're Blossom."

Blossom smiled. *Not exactly.*

Finally, Dolly arrived, and Blossom was all excited about presenting her newest magnum opus. She corralled both her guests into the living room.

"Ta-da," Blossom said, pointing toward the Hockney that now replaced the print Skip had hung. Both Skip and Dolly were taken aback.

"An original David Hockney?"

"Yes, how did you know?"

"I just know," Dolly said.

"It's wonderful, Blossom," Skip added, looking more closely at the pulpy paper.

"Don't you love it?"

"Yes, Blossom, I do, I love it," Skip said.

"It's not a copy, either. It's an original. I even met the artist. He was so nice."

"You did?" Both Dolly and Skip were doubly impressed. "He's quite famous, you know," Dolly said.

"Yes, I know. I mean, I know now. I didn't know before I bought it, but I know now."

"You just bought this painting like that?" Skip asked.

"Yup. Sometimes you just gotta go for it."

"Good for you, Blossom. It's a wonderful piece," he said. "Only someone like you could come home with a Hockney, just because." This made Blossom smile. "I'm sorry to rush out, but I left the water running downstairs so I gotta go—but thanks for calling me up and showing it to me. It's fantastic."

"Oh, you're welcome, you're welcome," Blossom said, still beaming. When Skip left, she turned to Dolly.

"I want to tell you something, Dolly," she said gravely. "If anything happens to me, I want you to take this painting. I want you to have it."

"Don't say that, Blossom! Nothing is going to happen to you."

"I know, but if it does, promise me you'll take the painting."

"Blossom!"

"No, Dolly, just promise me."

"If something happens to you?"

"Yes."

"But nothing's gonna happen to you."

"Dolly!"

"Okay, okay—if anything happens to you."

"If anything happens to me, what?"

"I'll take the painting."

"Good."

"Wanna glass of hemlock?"

They both laughed at Dolly's unexpected joke. "I can't believe I said that."

"Yes, you can," Blossom giggled.

"You seem to be feeling a little better, Blossom, honey. Are you?"

"I am, Dolly."

"You put that love thing into its right perspective?"

"I think I did. Something just sort of came to me the other night, and I started feeling better about it. My heart still goes pitter-patter when I see him, but at least it's not breaking."

"Exactly, honey. The thing about love, besides needing to have patience with it, is acceptance."

"Now, that was from a self-help book. Fess up."

"No, that was on Oprah's show." They laughed.

Blossom thought back to the other night, when she felt as if she were swimming toward her own deliverance, when a sudden strike of recognition helped her understand that love was bigger than Skip, that it did indeed have everything to do with acceptance and with herself.

She sighed. "We have so little time on this earth to get it right, and then again, there are times it feels as if some days won't end. Ever feel like that, Dolly?"

"When Mr. Feingold died, I felt like that every day. I had gotten so used to being sad, being happy felt strange. I even started feeling guilty if I felt happy; I thought I was disrespecting him. Sometimes sadness is a comfort: You carry it around like a blanket and let it keep you company. But as you find happiness, the blanket becomes heavier."

"I think I've done that. Like being fat—it kind of covers you up."

"Sadness can be a very seductive suitor. He calls on you every night; he wakes up with you every morning. You hold on, afraid to let go. At least it's something, you think."

"Dolly," Blossom asked quietly, "do you think you'll ever be with anyone else again?"

Dolly paused. "I don't want to say no, because I've worked too hard celebrating life's possibilities to ever say no. But it's difficult for me to imagine. Mr. Feingold was the love of my life." Her voice was as soft as ice cream.

"The love of your life. Wow. I would love to have a love of my life." Blossom took Dolly in with a new regard. She had lost the love of her life and survived. She might as well have climbed Mount Everest, for the enormous amount of strength it must have taken.

"Someday I'll tell you all the endlessly amazing things about him, but I'd need a day. Of course, he could be quite the pain in the ass at times, but he was a wonderful, wonderful man."

"What did he do?"

"Well, his family had money, so it allowed him to follow his bliss. He was a philanthropist, really, particularly for animal rights, saving endangered species, stopping big business from clearing wildlife refuges. I wanted him to spend all that money on people, patients who had heart problems. Millions of Jews have heart problems. His whole family had heart problems. Spend it there, I said. But he ignored me and set up funds for researchers to be able to continue their work in the field to save endangered species, animals I never heard of."

"Wow, Dolly, that's incredible. He has a legacy."

"He certainly does." Dolly loved to talk as much as Blossom loved to listen. Blossom was a perfect audience.

"I wish I could make a mark."

"You can, my dear."

"How? What can I do?"

"Something good every day."

"No, Dolly, that's not enough."

"It doesn't have to be big; it just has to be kind."

What kind of mark was that? Blossom wondered. Was that even

leaving a mark? She didn't think so. Now, Douglas Fairbanks Sr., he left a mark. He had a whole mountain range named after him. That's a legacy. *I'd settle for a park bench or a plaque or even a directional sign.* Blossom didn't want to contradict Dolly, who thought perhaps that she was leaving her mark by just being kind. Somehow, Blossom had forgotten that the real Blossom McBeal had left her mark by doing just that. Blossom McBeal had left behind love. She'd said it herself at Blossom's wake. But it didn't feel enough to her now. All she could think of was that in the end we'd all be laid out in uneven rows, where the wind and weather would eventually blow our names away. We'd all march into eternity without testimony, without signature. But someone like Mr. Feingold might be remembered. He might have an animal named after him. Feingold's marmot. Feingold's aardvark. Feingold's squirrel—a rare species found only in Guadeloupe.

Blossom looked far away again. Perhaps she was still in the underbrush of the jungles and mangroves with Mr. Feingold and his rare species, but Dolly could read Blossom's face.

"Blossom, living moment to moment and getting joy out of the smallest things can be enough. I believe it goes something like this: If you try to find happiness in the infinite, there's a good chance it won't happen. It's just too big. Small things hold wonder, and there is infinite wonder in a blade of grass. The same holds true for making your mark. It doesn't have to be some great, gigantic thing, a cure for cancer, world peace. Sure, that would be wonderful, but it doesn't have to be that. It can be simple kindness. I rescued Jigsy and Pip. Somehow, I made a little difference . . ." she paused. "Speaking of which, where's Vinny? He wasn't here last time I was over, either."

"Oh, Dolly, I have to confess something." Blossom didn't mince words. She just told Dolly the way it was. "Vinny isn't my dog."

"He's not?"

"No, he's Skip's. When I got your invitation, I wanted to come to the party, but I didn't have a dog. Skip gave me Vinny to make it legal."

Dolly laughed. "Silly. You could have come without a dog. I would have let you in."

"I was going to tell you at some point, but the opportunity never seemed to present itself. Yup, I crashed your party with a mongrel."

"Well, I'm glad you did. It's why we're sitting here right now. And who would listen to me go on and on as I do? Jigsy and Pip have heard it all—twice. If they could, they would gag and bind me. Fortunately, I picked animals that don't have opposable thumbs."

"How about a cup of tea, Dolly?"

"Yes, that would be lovely."

"With a shot of brandy?" Blossom had bought this expressly for Dolly's visits.

"Absolutely."

"I'll just be a minute," she said, disappearing into the kitchen. Dolly rose and moved toward the Hockney painting to look at it again. It was inspiring.

"I almost forgot to ask, how was the concert?"

Blossom was suddenly grateful Skip wasn't still in the room.

"It was fantastic, Dolly. I can't thank you enough for those tickets."

"Who did you end up going with?"

"Just myself." The old feeling grabbed Blossom around the throat. She wished that when she said "myself," she could feel as happy as Dolly did. Maybe one day . . . maybe one day.

CHAPTER 39

$\mathcal{M}$AKLEY HAD BEEN BACK AND FORTH to L.A. twice, trying to put the pieces together, but the jigsaw puzzle never quite formed a whole picture. On a hunch from MaryAnn Barzini, he set out one more time, hoping to make some new inroads.

He was becoming a regular at a cheap little motel on the east end of Sunset. Once again he began posting pictures and contacting the local authorities. They gave him the names of some local FBI agents who were ready to help him.

Charlotte's friends in Gorham had seemed reluctant to cooperate with the police. Whether it was an old and abiding respect for their friendship or just that good old Yankee tight-lipped sensibility, nothing much was emerging in the way of clues. But when Hobbs called MaryAnn for the second time, it seemed she remembered more than she had at first, and was quite happy to share.

"Do I have news for you," Officer Hobbs began when he called Makley. "First of all, MaryAnn Barzini was full of information. They used to be best friends. It seems they always talked about going to California, to find what they figured was everything they ever wanted. It all started when they were young, watching reruns of *Magnum, PI.*"

"Didn't they film that in Hawaii?"

"I have no idea. But if that's true, they missed their mark by a few thousand miles. Anyway, they both loved this guy Tom Selleck, and he kind of became their Hollywood idol, and they'd always talk about what it would be like to go and meet him."

"Go on."

"MaryAnn said at one time they both planned to vacation out there together, but she ended up getting married, and their lives went different ways."

"Anything else?"

"She said they were going to live in Hollywood and make money by becoming game-show contestants. Basically, their big goal was to meet Tom Selleck."

"How old were they, Hobbs?"

"Thirteen, fourteen." Makley was relieved to hear they weren't thirty. "But she said they even talked about it in high school, and MaryAnn had gotten some brochures on Hollywood and began trying to figure out where they would live once they got out there.

She said they'd even saved fifteen hundred dollars. It was all going to happen after they graduated from high school."

"So what happened?"

"So far as I can make out, a friend of MaryAnn's got killed in a car accident, and it kind of took the wind out of their sails. They both got a job in the bank, and MaryAnn married someone shortly after that."

"Did any of her other friends have anything to say?" asked Makley.

"Only that Charlotte was a very caring sort of person. She always put others first, always tried to make things better for other people. But they all said they never thought she would do something like rob a bank and take off. They said she was quiet—shy, even—that she changed after high school. Maybe it had something to do with her mother dying. She'd once been livelier, funnier, wanted to see the world, but after high school she became more withdrawn, gained a ton of weight. They all said they were particularly surprised when questions came up about Charlotte actually pulling off a stunt like this. Someone said we'd be better off dredging the river, 'cause we were more likely to find her there than in Hollywood."

"Did you ask them what happened after high school to make her change like that?"

"No."

"It might be a good question. I'm shooting with blanks out here."

"Maybe I'll get that MaryAnn Barzini in again. She's the most forthcoming with information so far."

"Good."

"What are you going to do?"

"I'm gonna nose around a bit again. Check with more Realtors. If she always wanted to live here, chances are, she bought a place. She couldn't rent—they'd want references. She could buy, though, and buy outright. No one would say no to that much cash. I've got a whole list of agents to contact. If you need me, I'm at the same place as last time, the Buena Vista Motel on Sunset. Oh, by the way, how's Kelly doing?"

"Acting cool, but I can see the feathers spilling out of his mouth. It's very hard to swallow a canary and not be obvious."

This made Makley laugh. "That's funny, Hobbs."

"Hey, I can be funny, even charming sometimes."

"Yeah, a regular Cary Grant."

"John Wayne, boss, John Wayne."

"Okay, Duke, call me when you have any more news."

"For what it's worth," he continued, "she had a lot of people who liked her here. Said she had a real kind heart."

"Oh, okay, I'll be really nice to her when I find her," Makley said sarcastically. The deputy heard it in his voice. Makley hadn't talked to all those people who had something nice to say. It annoyed him some. His response was one he thought Makley had coming.

"*If* you find her."

When they hung up, Hobbs looked at Charlotte's picture on his desk with a bit of wistfulness. He knew Makley, and he knew that whatever it took, Makley would find the elusive, ever unpredictable, ever generous Charlotte Clapp. Damn.

CHAPTER 40

*D*ECEMBER CAME IN WITH A WHISPER, nothing like the winters of New England. And as the days passed, Blossom's face began regaining the definition it once had. The plumpness that gathered around her jowls was slowly shrinking away, and the fine line of her prettiness was emerging. The same was true of her body. Her waist seemed to be finding its way to her middle. And yet, toward the end of December, she was still hiding beneath the big, floppy ponchos, unready to expose any part of her new femininity. It was nearly impossible for her to begin to let go of her fat mentality, she had hidden beneath it for so long. And the truth was, she had miles to go and many other things to put in order and settle.

As she figured it, she had several months left to live. Christmas was only a couple of days away, but it wasn't Christmas that was on her mind. The idea of wanting to leave a mark in this world resonated heavily with her. The real Blossom McBeal had left a mark, which was why this Blossom had been so attracted to her. Blossom McBeal had truly lived through her kindness, and she finally began to see Dolly's point more clearly: It was through her kindness that she was remembered.

But the real Blossom's kindness was spread over a lifetime. A few months of kindness is like putting a dollar into a homeless person's canister. Not much.

No, simple kindness just wasn't enough. She wished she had enough money left to make some large donation to cancer or diabetes or Greenpeace. Then someone would certainly remember her for her unsurpassed generosity. Her money, however, was dwindling. Between the apartment, the Hockney painting, and just day-to-day living, she figured she only had about six hundred thousand left. Of course, she'd have to put some money aside for her funeral arrangements. A plot, a stone, a fund to keep her area mowed.

God, what did she want on her stone? She hadn't even thought about that. And who would preside at the end? Would anyone say anything about the fact that she had lived? Maybe Dolly would give her a nice eulogy. Maybe Skip would go, too. This was too depressing even to think about. Right now, all Blossom wanted to think about was leaving her mark and understanding why she had been on this earth, why she had lived and breathed and loved and lost. She was desperate to make sense out of the whole thing before it was too late.

Every day she woke up struggling to figure out what it was she could do in the time she had left. For the first time since Dr. Jennings had given her the news, she was afraid. She saw the sands spilling through the hourglass just as Dorothy did in *The Wizard of Oz* when the bad witch told her she would die when the sand ran out. For the entire month of December, she found herself searching more than ever.

She found a church and went there every day. She sat there, with light streaming in through the stained-glass windows, quietly talking to the statue of Jesus. But he did not call her in. She read chapters of the Bible and conferred with members of the clergy. But this, too, seemed to be a pragmatic and ungratifying route. She left more disillusioned than when she went in.

She began reading Scriptures from the Old Testament: *For I, the Lord your God, hold your right hand; it is I who say to you, "Do not fear, I will help you."*

However, Isaiah did not help her, either, so she turned to Hindu prayer, Buddhist sutras, *The Bhagavad Gita,* and *The Tibetan Book of the Dead.* And still no answers came.

She stayed up all night watching Worship TV, and listened to the benign music that played over each clichéd scene of nature. She waited for the righteous poetry to impose itself over every waterfall, a field of flowers, a sleeping cat, and still she felt no closer to her salvation. She could have been looking at one of the many Gorham calendars given away free with a gas purchase.

Unable to sleep, she twisted and turned night after night, scared that everything she had ever wanted was beyond her reach. She would never have the love she desired in this lifetime, would never leave any kind of legacy. She would die alone. She turned to prayer in the dark of her room, whispering up into the airless night. Silence. She did not sense the calm presence of something greater offering her hope; she did not hear celestial messages coming to relieve her fear that held her in its grip. Her inability to envision her future in any positive way was utterly undermined by the present moment. The final reality was that she was trapped in Hollywood, California, the land where dreams do not come true.

Everything she ever wanted was beyond her reach, and the words that Dolly had spoken so eloquently seemed meaningless now. She had allowed herself a few moments of hope, but the feeling did not stick.

She gathered her suitcases filled with the remaining money and dragged them down to the car. What had she been thinking?

Hollywood, land of dreams. Whose dreams? How crazy was I to think everyone was happy here? Movie stars roaming the streets, Tom Selleck sitting next to me at Barney's Beanery.

How are you, Blossom?

Fine, Tom, how are you?

Just great, thanks for asking. Oh, you must stop by the set. I'm making a sequel to Magnum, PI.

Wonderful. I'll be there this afternoon.

We'll grab a bite after.

Perfect, Tom . . .

Am I crazy? What kind of whacked-out fantasy was that in Gorham? What did I think? People just make friends with their favorite stars? Who said dreams come true here anyway?

Blossom put her bags into the trunk and drove out into the still of the night. She passed under plastic reindeer hanging over the streets, swinging in the wind as if they, too, were trying to fly as far away from Hollywood, California, as she was. She passed houses lined with Christmas lights that looked like nothing more than hard candy to her, the type of candy a woman might have stuck to the back of her skirt as she rises from her seat and exits the train. Christmas in California. Fake snow, fake trees, fake everything. Blossom didn't want this to be the final image of her last Christmas on earth, so she drove. Toward what, she had no idea.

She was driving for about two hours when she saw a sign: *I-15 Barstow, Las Vegas.* Las Vegas! That was it! Yes, she would go to Las Vegas and win money, and then, like Mr. Feingold, she'd leave it to a worthy cause.

This was fate, kismet. These were the good-luck gods, calling her to her destiny. She did not see the irony in spending her last Christmas in Las Vegas. No matter. She believed she was meant to be on this road at five in the morning. She was meant to see that sign and go to Vegas. She was meant to gamble her money in order to win more for the greater good. Yes, Blossom would leave her legacy after all.

It was daybreak when she checked into the Golden Nugget, but people still sat at the tables, bleary-eyed and rumpled, acting as if they'd just arrived. Gamblers who'd been going at it all night were still in their losing positions.

Blossom got a suite with a bedroom overlooking the pool. It was the most beautiful pool she'd ever seen. But she wasn't here to swim. No, she was here to cash in, to make her money, to make her mark. She grabbed her first fistful of thousands from her suitcase, stuffing them into her bag, her pockets, her bra, until she was literally weighted down with her entire net worth.

As she wandered through the casino, she had no idea how to begin, so she simply asked someone. An obese man with a camera hanging around his neck and wearing ugly shorts explained to her that she needed to buy chips. It was his sixteenth time in Las Vegas, and frankly, he told her, he just couldn't see going anywhere else on his vacation. He worked for the phone company, and they even had their annual conventions here. Blossom listened politely, but the whole story gave her the heebie-jeebies. It reminded her of Gorham in some indefinable way, and she was happy when he looked at his watch and gasped that he was late for the bus that would take him to King Tut's tomb.

She got a bucket of chips and walked from room to room, trying to figure out what to do next. Baccarat, roulette, craps, poker, and blackjack all seemed out of her league. She didn't know the first thing about any of these games. So she decided to start off with the slots. She certainly knew how to pull a lever, and when she gained more confidence, she would move on to one of the tables.

The slots called for bills or coins. She had the bills, and so she began.

As beginner's luck would have it, Blossom thrived at the slots. Every fifteen or twenty minutes, a fistful of coins would fall her way. One hundred dollars, two hundred fifty dollars. Yes, this was how she'd imagined it going. But faster than this. At this rate it would take two years to make any real cash. But she persevered, losing a little, making a little. By lunch she was up by five hundred dollars. Not exactly high-rolling.

That's when she decided to wander. She knew that people played for high stakes. She'd seen a whole special on it on cable. She just had to find the room, the table, and the kind of game that promised high wins.

Her attention was drawn to a croupier who was spinning a red-and-black wheel. Around and around it went, until the ball settled into a slot with a satisfying click. Some chips were taken off the table with a stick; some people would jump up and down and spread out more chips on different numbers. It intrigued her, and she watched it for hours. Someone had walked away with fifty thousand dollars, someone with two hundred thirty-six thousand. Most walked away with nothing, but Blossom was not interested in them. They were not even registering in her mind. She only watched the winners.

At nine o'clock that evening, she was ready to put her first bet down on the table. She knew enough to play the game now. An intensity of excitement burned in her belly, the likes of which she'd never known. Some strange thirst was dying to be quenched. The gambling bug had bitten.

"Okay, ladies and gentlemen, place your bets."

Her first foray into the game was a straight bet. She put several chips on one number. The wheel spun. She waited anxiously, as if life itself were the wager. And the ball skipped, *click, click click,* over the wheel, finally settling on a number. Hers. She screamed with delight. This was going to be a breeze. And now the sweet addiction began pumping its slow drip into her system. Nothing could stop her now. She was indestructible, bulletproof.

She went for inside bets, split bets, trio bets, corner bets, five-number bets, six-number bets, and still she continued to win. Success wafted around her like the sweet smell of honey, and the bees continued to gather.

Every one loves a winner.

Three hours she played, three hours until she was up so high, the manager came over to witness the carnival.

"Okay," Blossom said, "I feel lucky. I really feel lucky. I want to wager everything." Everything was a million dollars. A silence swept the room.

"I'm gonna wager it all . . . on a straight-up bet. If I win, the house pays me thirty-five to one."

The crowd gasped. This was just insanity now, but delicious, exciting, the very reason they were all there—to simulate the rush of the forbidden, take a bite out of that apple in Eden, push the limits of this excruciating madness to its inevitable end. The croupier leaned over to the manager to make sure this bet did not exceed the house limit. It did not, and Blossom was good to go.

The dealer placed a token on top of her chips, indicating the value of her play. A complete hush settled over the room. She moved her chips onto the red seven. It was as if she were alone, with only the wheel, her chips, and the dealer in her vision. A blur of knuckles and nail polish unleashed themselves from the rim of the table. All breathing ceased. No one even dared clear his throat. Slowly, moving at half the speed of life, the wheel began to spin. A million dollars all on a single number. Every dime she had won, every nickel she had left. *Red seven, red seven, come on, red seven.* The wheel turned; the ball bounced, jumped from one number to the next, in and out of the red seven, slowing, skipping, slowing, skipping, slowing, slowing, slowing . . . and then it stopped. Thirteen black. And everything was gone in an instant.

Disappointment echoed around the table. People meandered away, but Blossom just stood there, staring down as if there'd been some huge mistake. She'd been winning all night. What happened? She wanted to retake the shot. That was just a practice turn, like in bowling, when you get a couple of free rolls. But it wasn't a practice shot; it was the real thing, and it left Blossom standing there without a dime, without a prayer. She was aware and unaware all at the same time. She was numb. A man was talking to her, but she could barely hear him. He sounded muffled and faraway. It was the manager.

"We'll comp your meals and your room," he was saying, as if that were a consolation, but she could not move, frozen in her defeat.

"Are you okay?"

And she looked at him, through him, to the door, which she began walking toward.

"Can I get you a drink?"

But she continued walking out into the surreal world of glass and glitter, of bulbs and overblown boulevards. She wandered for hours past the Bellagio, the Mirage, past Harrah's and the Luxor, all the way down to the Mandalay. These casinos were long distances apart, but she wasn't conscious of logging the miles between them. Lost in the carnival-like madness of Elvis look-alikes, newlyweds, showgirls and call girls, lost in the glare of amusement rides, fake sphinxes, Eiffel Towers, and Venetian canals, she walked. And she walked and she walked and she walked, but had no sense of having moved at all.

She had lost all track of time. Maybe six months had passed in the last twenty-four hours, and she had died tonight and ended up here, in hell, in Las Vegas.

Suicide, that's all she could think of right now. It made perfect sense at the moment. No money, no prospects, no life span (which at this point she took as a positive). How would she do it? She wanted a clean, simple exit. All drama kept at a minimum. Pills. But where would she get the pills? And what on earth would she say in her suicide note.

Dear Dolly and Skip,
  I know you're wondering why I swallowed that poker chip that caused me to choke to death.

Dear Dolly and Skip,
  I'm sorry I hung myself from the grand ballroom chandelier, but it was the only one in the hotel I knew would hold me.

Dear Dolly and Skip,
  What a lousy place to take a vacation. If you're planning any sort of getaway, consult a travel agent first, but don't come here. This place sucks.

How she found herself seated at a second-string performance of Stanoslofsky's animals acts was a mystery. The stage was small, the cages cramped, the man with the whip, dwarfish and gray. Time and space had no reality. Things were just happening without any rhyme or reason. But she knew she must have met some awful fate to see such beautiful cats in such a bizarre place. Why weren't they in the forests, sleeping by a stream, or running free under an endlessly blue sky? Why were they here instead, jumping through hoops of fire? The whole world seemed like a distortion. She couldn't sit there any longer.

With excruciating fatigue she rose to leave, but the glare of the lights and the sound of the drum roll were utterly disorienting. She hadn't eaten or slept in two days, and when she stood, dizziness overcame her. The last thing she remembered was a man whose hands looked like lobster claws, waving for help. Blossom went down with a thud, straight onto the stage, as if she were throwing herself to the tigers.

CHAPTER 41

*A*RE YOU OKAY?"

"Where am I?"

"Back in your room . . . at the Golden Nugget. You passed out."

"I did?"

"Yes. The manager who helped you found your I.D. and room key in your bag. That's how he knew where you were staying. We brought you back here in one of the complimentary limos."

"How fancy! I'm sorry I missed it. And who are you?"

"The hotel doctor at the Golden Nugget. How do you feel now?"

"When did this happen?"

"About half an hour ago. When's the last time you slept?"

"I don't know." And then Blossom recalled what had happened. "I lost all my money. Every cent of it."

The doctor looked down. He had seen this before. He could offer no cure for having gone broke in Las Vegas.

"Where are you from?"

Where am I from? "I don't even know how to answer that."

"I suggest you sleep here tonight. Get a good night's sleep and go home in the morning. You'll be surprised how much better things can look in the morning."

"Yeah, right."

"The hotel can reach me if you have any more episodes." He stood to leave. "Do you have enough money to get home?"

Blossom looked away from him. How could she have gone from where she was to this? It was inconceivable.

"Here," he said, putting some money on the table. "This should be enough to get you to where you're going."

"I don't know where I'm going. I've lost everything. And not just the money. I've lost my mother, my father, my best friend, T. J., Tom . . . everything."

She began to cry, inconsolable tears, tears filled with the salt of a hundred wounds. Tears that looked like glass fell from her cheeks, breaking to the floor as if a chandelier had snapped from its anchor after years of hanging ever so tenuously.

"I am completely alone, and I just can't do it anymore. It's too painful." Blossom wept. "I want to go to sleep for a hundred years and wake up in another time and place. Can you do that, Doc? Is there anything in your bag that can do that for me?"

The doctor took her in with such empathy, it made him turn around and look in his bag. "This won't put you to sleep for a hundred years, but it will help you sleep now."

"What is it?

"A shot of Valium."

He rubbed her arm with alcohol and injected the tranquilizer.

"I am going to stay with you until you are asleep."

She lay back and closed her eyes. "Even whales have families . . ."

She was fading now, and her words became slurred. "And they sing to each other."

"It's going to be all right."

"I'm so sorry, so . . ." But she couldn't finish her sentence. She was swimming with whales somewhere in the middle of the sea.

She awoke in the evening, having slept nearly twenty hours straight. *Oh, my God, what did I do?* Blossom was trying to remember what she had said last night. She was bereft: she recalled that. But what did she say, and to whom? Regret grew in her heart and spread through her loins like a chill, as if someone were walking over her grave. All she could do was get up, shower, and leave. There was no reason to take her suitcases now. They were empty.

Blossom made her way back home. It was late when she got there, almost midnight when she walked down to the pool. How often it had soothed her, helped her to disentangle from the complicated strings that life had attached to it. It had been the place she could come to hold confusion at bay. But now all those hours in the water felt as if she'd only been swimming upstream. She was so tired.

She slipped in and pushed off, breaking the stillness in half. Back and forth, back and forth, she began her laps. Distant thunder rolled in from the valley, and rain started to fall. But she felt nothing. Hot tears fell from her eyes only to dissolve beneath the wash of the cold water. Sometimes, she thought, even the sky needed to have a good cry. *I've lost everything. Money, love, hope.*

Today someone will fall off a ladder and hit his head; today someone will realize the proverbial prediction of being hit by a bus; today all the little cells will continue their death march inside my body. So arbitrary, so inevitable. We live; we die . . . someone else is born. No matter how rich or famous a person is, it just doesn't matter. We all have our day to die. On the day Jason Robards died, someone was laughing at a joke; on the day Jack Lemmon died, someone was throwing a birthday party. On the day I die, Skip will be watering the lawn. Life is so unfair; it just goes on without you.

She plunged below the clear black surface, wishing the water would just close over her forever. Even her brain hurt, thinking about it all.

Dolly, you tell me I must love myself before I can love another. You tell me that sometimes when a situation is at its worst, it can bring out our best. You tell me that I can grow through my pain if I learn acceptance, especially of myself. But I can't, Dolly; I can't. I am trying to, but I can't. People need love; I need love. I'm all need and loneliness right now, Dolly. And you tell me that the one thing I need I can't have, just because I need it the most. There are too many lessons to learn, Dolly, and I just can't do it. I just can't do it.

She didn't remember exiting the pool and standing in the rain for hours. She didn't remember walking across the lawn and climbing the stairs with the new light breaking against the eastern sky. She didn't remember being dripping wet when she knocked on Dolly's door at five in the morning, crying under the enormous burden of sadness and secrets. And she didn't remember standing in the hall, holding on to the doorjamb, with an ache in her heart so great, it was as if it had been split by an ax.

"I have to talk to you, Dolly. I need to tell someone the truth."

Dolly took her in and put her to bed. The next day she would hear the entire story, unedited and untold to a single soul—until now.

CHAPTER 42

WHEN BLOSSOM OPENED HER EYES, she was in bed. But not hers. She looked around and saw that she was in Dolly's guest room, and the events of the nights before came rushing back. Dolly was there in a chair by the bed, smiling gently at her. "At last, Sleeping Beauty arises." And then Blossom spoke, emptying her heart, a heart she thought had nothing left in it to empty. She told Dolly every-thing. *Everything.*

"So just to review," Dolly said an hour and a half later, "you robbed a bank in which you had worked for fifteen years, left town, changed your name, and moved here. You did this because a doctor gave you one year to live, and you thought by moving to Hollywood you would find love and happiness before you died, because Holly-wood is the land of dreams. Is that about right?"

"In a nutshell." Blossom went on to tell Dolly about T. J., MaryAnn, Tom Barzini, and Skip. She opened up like a water tower struck by lightning, and a billion tears came down in one final deluge.

"Does that pretty much bring us up to the most recent Las Vegas debacle?"

Blossom nodded.

"Lord, Blossom, when you tell a story . . . you tell a story. Well, the first thing we need to do is to get a second opinion."

"On what?"

"Not your sanity. I know you're crazy. But your health is another matter altogether. We need to get you to a doctor and get a second opinion on your health."

"No way, Dolly. My mother had refused treatment, and she was doing okay. She really was. But then when she began doing worse, they talked her into chemo, and that's when it all fell apart. It's what killed her; I'm sure of it. I don't want to go like that. I want to go like this. Intact. The poison that kills the disease is worse than the cancer. No, no doctors, Dolly."

Dolly regarded Blossom. She looked so healthy, but maybe that was why she had lost all this weight. At least seventy-five pounds. And she looked so good with it off. But maybe it was the disease. Dolly wasn't finished trying to convince Blossom to get a second opinion; she was just finished for now. She would definitely get her to see a doctor, by hook or by crook; right now, however, she just wanted to get her up and flying right.

"We need a plan, Blossom."

"A plan?"

"Yes, you're a mess. You're a shade paler than milk. Look at you. Somebody call nine-one-one."

"Are you sure you want to give me this pep talk now?"

"Well," Dolly said, "you've got to sell your Hockney. I have a couple of connections. I know some dealers and some collectors. Hey, we might be able to get you an even better price than what you paid. You never know."

"That was supposed to be for you when I died."

"Well, you're very much alive, and that painting's worth something."

"But that was my gift to you," she said in a sad, low voice.

"Make me a card instead—I'll be just as happy."

"Dolly?"

"What?"

"You're not freaked out that I'm a fugitive from the law?"

"No, not at all. I'm far more 'freaked out,' as you say, that you won't get a second opinion from a good doctor out here." She paused. "Let's concentrate, Blossom; what we need is structure."

"Structure?"

"Yes. You just can't go lollygagging about every day, looking at Skip with big, sad eyes and doing nothing. In a couple of days, when you're feeling better, you'll come with me. I have something in mind."

"What?"

"Don't you be worrying about what. You'll see."

"Dolly, how is it that . . . that you always know what to do? I feel so clueless right now. Yet you seem to understand things that . . . that . . ." She couldn't finish her thought. Couldn't quite find the words and connect them to what was going on inside her. Even words were alien at the moment.

"Therapy, Zoloft. And remember, Blossom, I was out of it for two years. I don't think anyone could have been as sad or lonely as I was during that time. Oh, I'm sure that's not true, but that's how it felt. I'm just remembering what it was like, and I'm offering you a couple of shortcuts to help find your way out of it. Unfortunately, there's no getting around it: People have to work for their happiness.

We go into battle every day, and we have to work to be happy. It just isn't handed over to us, as much as we wish it was. I know. It stinks."

It was the first time Blossom thought destiny wasn't just "what happens"; destiny was what you made happen. Ingrid Bergman didn't have to get on that plane. That was her choice.

"All I'm doing is giving you a couple of tips before you go into battle."

"But all I wanted to do was leave a legacy before I died; that's all."

"Love is a legacy, Blossom. Love is how we stay alive after we die."

Blossom got up and walked toward Dolly. Her arms were open. She hugged her as if she were the last person on earth. Somehow, Dolly's words always felt like a salve on her sadness.

"Dolly, why are you so kind? I mean, to me. Why are you . . . ?"

"Well, besides the fact that I love you, honey, you're like the daughter I never had. Mr. Feingold and I tried and tried, and then we found out we couldn't have children. That was a sad day. I wanted a little girl more than anything in the world. And because I'm an only child, I didn't have a shot at even being an aunt. If I had had a daughter . . . I would be happy if she was just like you."

"Why? I'm one shade paler than milk."

"Because you've got guts. And I admire that. You're not content to settle for what scraps life throws you. You want more. You remind me of myself in that way."

"And did you live happily ever after?"

"Who lives happily ever after all the time? But I was lucky enough to figure out, at some point in all the pain, what was important to take away from it."

Blossom was still embracing Dolly. She didn't want to let go. "And all this time I was looking for love, it was right here."

"It's much closer than that. You see, Blossom, darling, it's not in front of you; it's not in back of you; it's not sleeping beside you; no, it's much closer than you ever imagined."

"Where?" Blossom asked, perplexed.

"It's right here." And Dolly touched Blossom's heart.

Blossom stayed with Dolly for a couple more days and slept

through New Year's. On January first, Dolly opened Blossom's door quietly and tiptoed in with a cup of coffee.

"Blossom, darling, wake up. I have something really good to tell you."

Blossom opened one eye and peered up at Dolly. "You do? What?"

"It's a new year. You can get up and start over again."

CHAPTER 43

*T*HE FOLLOWING DAY, Blossom awoke in her own apartment. She forced herself up and into the shower. She looked in the mirror and drew her hands over her face. She had never looked so tired. *Who was it who said of Peter O'toole that he was walking around to save on funeral expenses? God, that's me!*

After dressing, she nursed her coffee by the window. There was Skip, cutting the lawn. Suddenly, she saw Jeannie enter the gate. He noticed her come in as well and turned off the mower. Blossom gazed at her like an owl studying a mouse. What was she doing here? She watched Jeannie hand Skip an envelope and stand there talking for several minutes.

How do you do it, Jeannie?

How do I do what?

Stay so happy, never have a bad day?

I don't know; I just don't let things get to me.

Have you ever been depressed?

No.

Do you have any idea what that would feel like?

Not really.

What about love, Jeannie?

What about it?

Love just comes your way like that?

Yup.

Ever wonder what it's all about, Jeannie?

What what's all about?

Life?

No, not really.

Do you ever think about death, about what kind of impression you want to leave behind in this world?

No.

So you're just happy, no worries, no questions, no sleepless nights?

Pretty much. Isn't everyone? Aren't you?

Me? Hell, life is just a bowl of cherries.

A knock on the door woke her from the conversation she was having with herself.

"Be right there," she yelled, and pulled herself away from the window. It was Dolly, with Jigsy and Pip.

"Ready?"

"Yeah. Am I dressed okay?"

"Perfect."

Blossom was wearing a plain beige A-line dress that was too big for her. But it was all she had. Everything else in her closet was even bigger.

"So you still won't tell me where we're going?"

"Nope. You'll see. We'll be there in twenty minutes."

They took Dolly's car and headed off with the two dogs. Finally, Dolly took a right into the Cedars-Sinai Medical Center parking lot.

"Dolly!" Blossom was surprised and upset.

"What?"

"I told you I didn't want a second opinion. What are you doing?"

"I'm doing what I do every Monday and Thursday. Bringing Jigsy and Pip to therapy."

"What? You have your dogs in therapy?"

"Jigsy and Pip aren't just your ordinary, happy-go-lucky everyday dogs, Blossom. They're certified."

"They seem okay to me, Dolly. Aren't you going a little overboard with this therapy thing?"

"Not certifiable, certified. They got certified to be therapy dogs. They go through the hospital, into the different wards, and help the patients. You can't believe how much joy they bring these people. A lot of these patients haven't gotten out of here for weeks. Some are in critical care; some will go home; some won't. When I bring the dogs in, it's like bringing in a friend with only good news. They light up, young and old alike. The hospital started this program six years ago, but we've only been doing it for about eight months."

"I had to go through therapy training as well with Jigsy and Pip, to make sure we all knew how to act around the patients, the equipment. We're a team in there."

"Why did you want me to come?"

"Because I want you to see just how good something like this can make you feel."

Blossom followed Dolly into the hospital, with Jigsy and Pip in tow. Everyone was happy to see them.

"Blossom, I'd like you to meet Alison and Liz."

"Nice to meet you, Blossom." Liz and Alison worked in reception.

"Blossom came to escort us on our rounds today."

"Oh, okay. Let me get you a pass, Blossom," Liz said, writing her name on a small paper tag.

Blossom, Dolly, Jigsy, and Pip went up to the children's floor first. The children were in their individual rooms, sleeping, watching TV, getting checked by roving doctors, sitting with their families. When Jigsy and Pip entered, the mood changed immediately. It was as if a light came on in a dark room. They would go directly over to the kids for licks and pats.

Some of the kids were too weak to sit up, but even they managed a smile when Jigsy and Pip began their rounds. A small girl named Heather occupied the last room on the children's floor. Dolly and Blossom quietly walked in.

"Hi, Heather. Are you up for a visit from Jigsy and Pip today?"

Heather nodded. She was thin and pale, and the dark rings under her eyes were accentuated by the unfortunate baldness she had to endure.

"What's your name?" she asked Blossom. "You're new."

"Blossom."

"That's so pretty."

"Thank you."

"When I was home last time, we planted a garden."

"What did you plant?" Blossom asked.

"We planted pansies, tulips, and daffodils. My sister told me the daffodils will come up year after year."

"She's right. I planted daffodils once, and they bloomed for years."

"They blossomed!" Heather giggled.

"That they did," Blossom said, smiling back.

"I don't think I'll see them blossom again," Heather said softly. Her candor startled Blossom. She lifted Jigsy's paws up so Heather could pat him.

"My sister says that I don't have to worry about missing the daffodils. She said they grow in heaven."

"I bet they do. I bet there are roses and daisies and irises and hyacinths."

"I told my sister when the daffodils come up in the garden next year, then she'll know I'm saying hi."

Blossom turned away; she didn't want Heather so see the tears in her eyes. But it was unnecessary; the uncanny sixth sense both children and animals possess had already alerted Heather to Blossom's sadness.

"I'm not afraid, Blossom. You know why?"

A little girl who's dying, trying to make me feel better. Get a grip, Blossom.

Blossom put her hand on Heather's legs. "Why?"

"Because I once had a dog like Jigsy. Not exactly like Jigsy. He was a golden retriever named Otis. Well, one day Otis didn't feel good. He was getting older, and the doctor said it was better not to operate. He said it would be too hard on Otis. So Otis lived with us for another month, but then poor Otis couldn't walk anymore, so my parents took him to the doctor. He didn't come home that afternoon, and when I asked where he was, my dad told me Otis was happy. He had gone to heaven and he wasn't in pain anymore. I know when I go to heaven, Otis will be waiting for me. So I'm not afraid. You know who told me Otis would be there?"

"Who?" Blossom asked.

"Jigsy and Pip told me."

"Well, they're very smart dogs. If any two dogs know this, I know Jigsy and Pip would."

"Yeah, I think so, too." Heather closed her eyes, clearly exhausted.

"I think we should go now," Dolly said.

"All right." Blossom rose, stroking the last feathery wisps of Heather's hair.

"Would you mind if I visited you again with Jigsy and Pip?"

Heather smiled and whispered her approval. Blossom and Dolly walked out, the two dogs padding quietly behind.

"So what do you think?" Dolly asked Blossom.

"Daffodils are out of season."

"So?"

"So I think I have to scour the county until I find daffodils to bring to Heather on Thursday."

As they were descending the stairs, Dr. Cohen was just going up.

"Oh, Blossom, I want you to meet the smartest doctor in this whole hospital: Dr. Cohen, a heart man. Dr. Cohen, this is my friend Blossom McBeal."

"Very nice to meet you," he said—friendly, accessible, not like so many other doctors Blossom had met. But the thing that surprised Blossom the most was Dr. Cohen's age. He had to be in his mid-seventies yet was spry, youthful, and working.

"So you up visiting the kids, Dolly?"

"You betcha."

"Looks like Pip is putting on a little weight around the middle. You're not sneaking him kippers and bagels again?"

"Me? Never!"

"Well, gotta go. Rounds."

"See you on Thursday, Dr. Cohen."

"Oh," he said, looking down at Dolly's feet, "nice shoes."

"Why, thank you, Dr. Cohen."

Dolly was blushing. "He was the chief cardiologist. Now that he's older, he wanted to step down, work less. But he's so brilliant, the hospital asked him to stay on. Can you imagine? Isn't he nice?"

Blossom looked at Dolly. "Very nice. Dolly, you're blushing!"

"I am not."

"You are, too. You're red as a beet."

"A hot flash."

"Sure, and pigs fly."

CHAPTER 44

$\mathscr{B}$LOSSOM COULD NOT STOP THINKING about her experience at the hospital. The poignant memories replayed painfully on her heart and mind. She wanted to do something other then feel sorry for the children sleeping in their wards, waiting for salvation. Money didn't seem right—she didn't really have enough to make a difference anyway, and it wouldn't have mattered to the kids. Jigsy and Pip were a tangible happiness, and that's what she wanted to effect. Something that would make them smile.

Money was like opening an envelope at Christmas from an uncle you'd barely even met. The real joy came in a box with bright paper you could tear open to find that doll, or train, or something special you just couldn't live without, that had been picked out just for you. But what could she do for the children that would please them like that?

A visitor. Someone who would come every week with a grab bag of toys and tricks. But not a clown. Clowns were creepy, macabre even, with their painted grins and overbearing antics. And certainly not a mime. Blossom believed mimes should be banned. They were the worst aberration of the human condition there could possibly be. When she saw them on the street, she wanted to tip them off their invisible tightropes. And then there were those stupid boxes they were always trying to get out of. Why? What the hell was with that? No, they were even creepier than clowns.

Then it came to her. Something that would bring magic and music to the children: a wizard. But this would be no ordinary wizard, with a pointed hat and a cape full of stars. This wizard would not only pull rabbits from silk scarves and levitate nurses; this wizard would use a wand to put wonderful spells on everyone. This wizard would spread gold fairy dust over the antiseptic sheets and listen to all the wishes the children kept secret. This wizard would be Wednesday's cure. This wizard would be . . . Blossom.

And so Blossom went to work calling every costume company listed in the Los Angeles phone book. She found Costume Creators in Sherman Oaks and drove right over. By two o'clock she had found herself a wizard.

She slipped into her new blue satin cape and a silver body suit. It was topped off with a pointed hat embroidered with constellations and stars, while a gold bell jangled at the top. She painted her face white and, following the "How to Look Like a Wizard" instruction booklet, added long gold, glittery wings that she painted from the corners of her brows. She applied both gold and silver to her lips to offset the sparkle in her eyes.

She named herself Snow because she decided she would always leave snow globes behind for the children. It was something they could shake and make wishes on. She bought globes, each with a wizard inside, from a distributor on Melrose. Written on the snowy bottom was the word *Luck* in silver glitter, yet every time a child would shake it, it would form another word, like *Hope* or *Joy* or *Bliss*. How on earth did it do this? Anything was possible in this town, especially when it came to illusion.

Blossom was anxious to get out and try her new wizardry on the kids. She entered the hospital looking no less than mythological. All the grown-ups oohed and aahed, and Dr. Cohen didn't even recognize her.

She entered the children's ward, and all their little mouths opened in an ovation of ovals. They could hardly contain their excitement at the prospect that a wizard would pay them a visit.

Heather was awake and cooling her thirst with some ice chips and apple juice when Blossom walked in.

"How are you, my beautiful little angel?" the wizard asked.

"You're a wizard!" Heather exclaimed as if she were looking at Santa himself.

"Are you enjoying your apple juice?"

"Do you want some?" Heather asked, extending her paper cup. Her sweetness nearly broke Blossom's heart, and threatened to liquefy her painted grin.

"Oh, no," Blossom explained, "I only drink from mountain streams and sometimes rain barrels."

"What do you eat?" Heather asked, mesmerized.

"I only eat flowers and four-leaf clovers and sometimes new grass that comes in during the spring."

"Can you make magic?"

"Yes, I can."

"Can you make me better?" Heather asked in a small, breakable voice.

Blossom hadn't been prepared for that. She didn't know why; of course these children would want a wizard to perform the hardest miracle of all: life.

"Perhaps I can do some things to make you feel better," Blossom said, a knot tightening in her throat. *Jesus, Blossom, wizards don't cry.* But the fact was, she could make Heather feel better. At least for a little while.

She opened the inside of her satin cape, which was lined with what looked like hundreds of pockets. From the mysterious pockets she took out bottles of all shapes and sizes, each crowned with a gold top and an engraved inscription explaining what the potion did. But the bottles looked empty.

"There's nothing in them," Heather observed without guile.

"Oh, yes, there is," Blossom insisted.

"What?"

She arranged the bottles neatly on the table.

"There's joy, happiness, harmony, enchantment, bliss, pleasure, hope, vivacity, laughter, exuberance, cheer, playfulness, high spirits, dreams that come true, acceptance, exultations, spring, whimsy, relief, deliverance, comfort, well-being, faith, fearlessness, optimism, great expectations, courage, luck, and pluck. But I'm always working on more."

"How do they work?" Heather asked, utterly fascinated by the array of vials lined up on her table. They looked like ancient perfume bottles washed down from the Nile or the River Jordan. They looked as if they'd only been used by Egyptian goddesses.

"Well, you choose one that you hope will come true or help you in some way or help someone else. Each one has its own aroma: vanilla, raspberry, lemon, cherry, apple, peppermint, butterscotch, fresh grass, roses, cacao, huckleberry, tangerine, juniper, lilac, pine, honeysuckle, lavender, seaweed, and garlic."

"Garlic?"

"Oh, yes. That could be my favorite. The smell of garlic has an all-encompassing sense of well-being. In fact, that's what you smell when you open comfort."

"Can I try one?" Heather pleaded.

"But of course. What's your pleasure?"

She studied the bottles on the table. They all had something wonderful to offer, but she picked one that had caught her fancy as the wizard was reading them off. She picked up the bottle that read *Dreams that come true.*

"Now what do I do?"

"Simply open the top and breathe it all in, like you would pine or warm cookies on a snowy day. There are some potions where you can even smell blue skies or bubbling brooks or daisy chains worn by the invisible forest fairies. Things you never thought could have a perfume to them, do. Have you ever smelled a white fluffy cloud?"

"No."

"Now, clouds smell like pink cotton candy. How about the moon?"

"Never."

"Ahhh, the moon, that smells like peppermint. And joy smells like lavender and happiness like ginger snaps and rainbows like M and Ms. So are you ready to open your bottle?"

Heather carefully uncorked the top of her bottle and leaned forward. Although the bottle had appeared empty, a foggy plume escaped the flask, forming a curl of cold air. It had the distinct smell of roses caught in their first frost. Both sweet and cool.

"There was nothing in there a minute ago, and when I opened it, something came out. What was it?"

"It was your heart's desire."

"Will it come true?" she asked.

"I will hope and pray it does, my beautiful angel. I will hope and pray it does."

"Could you visit me again?" Heather asked hesitantly.

"My goodness, yes."

Blossom smiled at Heather as she made her way to the door.

"What's your name?" Heather asked.

"Snow, my dear, just like the snow globe I left on your table."

Heather looked over and found the globe, a glorious globe with nothing less than a wizard whirling her wand inside. She shook it and looked back up to show Blossom, but just like snow, she had melted and simply disappeared.

CHAPTER 45

*A*FTER A FEW WEEKS, the pink began to come back into Blossom's cheeks. She was going to the hospital every Tuesday and

Thursday with Dolly and every Wednesday as the wizard. Her out-look began to change, too. You could see it in her step, her eyes, her general demeanor.

She sold the Hockney for even money, a hundred twenty-five thousand, and was able to live quite comfortably for the moment. She worried that Hockney would call on a whim to see it, but Dolly assuaged her concerns. "He's back in England, dear, working on a canvas the size of an IMAX movie screen. He won't return until it's done, and you know how long that could take. Ever paint a room?"

Blossom could not believe how good she was feeling, and took stock of how much control the mind plays over the body. She even thought she might have put the disease in remission. How could she feel this well and still be sick? Surely it was the perfect example of mind over matter. She traded in her reading on death and dying for think-healthy, be-healthy books. *Attitude, it's all about the attitude.*

The other thing she began doing was taking in the sights. After all, she'd barely seen anything since she'd arrived in California, the land of dreams. Except, of course, Gene Hackman.

She walked through the open-air Farmers Market, simply absorbing the mood and spice of it. So many different foods were out on display, as well as kitsch souvenir stands brimming with Los Angeles key chains and all sorts of junky Hollywood paraphernalia. She took in Grauman's Chinese Theatre and meandered down the Walk of Fame to see if her hands or feet fit any of the various stars. The closest match was Joan Crawford's, which she found immensely depressing. She'd rather have matched Trigger's.

She toured Paramount Studios, which was a personal thrill, never having been so close to her longtime passion. She knew every story, every detail of the famed histories that hovered like secrets around every corner—the best of which, she recalled, was Fred Astaire, who took his screen test here. They said of him, "He can't act, can't sing, is balding, and can dance a little." This made her laugh.

She wished MGM still had a studio she could meander through. That was where so many of the big stars made their names—people like Judy Garland, Spencer Tracy, Greta Garbo, Clark Gable, Gene Kelly, and Elizabeth Taylor. She imagined the ghosts floating through those abandoned lots, revealing all the gossip, the affairs, the transgressions that had taken place on these mystic grounds.

She had so much cinematic history stored in her brain. What on earth would she do with such useless information now? So what if Bing Crosby had an ermine-covered toilet? Did it matter that Buster Keaton was drunk when he married his second wife and didn't even know he'd done it?

On and on the trivia crissed and crossed Blossom's brain. She had saved every scrap of fact and fiction about Hollywood, and now it all seemed like so many useless pieces of paper that better served as kindling. A whole life of gathering information that was as unimportant as week-old newspaper left on a bench at the train station.

Blossom made her sojourn to the new Getty Center, perched high on a hill. It was beautiful up here, traversed with courtyards, fountains, and gardens. *And to think I might have missed this. Someone would ask, "How was Hollywood, Blossom? What did you see?" And I was inches away from just being able to say, "A pool."*

However, Hollywood was all about stars, and Blossom yearned to see one celebrity, just one, other than Gene Hackman. So in a last-ditch effort she took the Warner Brothers tour. The tour was chock-full of executives, carpenters, prop assistants, production staff, and tourists, but absolutely no stars.

Still, it was exciting finally to see everything she and MaryAnn had only read about or seen on TV. At long last she was here, in the middle of it all (middle—the word had found new meaning), and she was sure she was at least close to someone famous, but who they were and where they were would remain a mystery.

She drove through Malibu, skirting the homes of the rich and famous, though most of them were obstructed by walls and garages. She couldn't for the life of her figure out what was so great about Malibu. The homes were close to the road and, from what she saw, not very attractive. She had to give full credit to the East Coast on this one. They had it all over Malibu for beauty.

She rose early one weekend morning and took in the famed Pasadena Flea Market, where she was able to find twelve silver charms in the shape of roses. These would be perfect for the secret present she was preparing for Dolly, especially since there was never a day that Dolly did not make sure to have fresh roses in her house, happily, gratefully carrying on a tradition.

She rented a bike and followed the stretch of sand for miles down Venice's boardwalk.

She lost herself in the hillside curves of Mulholland Drive, riding the crest of the Santa Monica Mountains. She stopped several times just to take in the views. This was the most spectacular road she had ever been on.

What if she had missed all this? What was she thinking? Now she had done something. Now she had her own stories to tell, if only for a short time.

CHAPTER 46

*B*LOSSOM HAD NOT SEEN SKIP in a few weeks. She was still swimming at night, but always long after Skip had gone home. She'd lost fifteen more pounds and looked like a different woman from the one who had arrived in Hollywood. Dolly insisted they go out and buy Blossom some new clothes. She was literally lost beneath the fabrics of her shifts and caftans. Blossom reluctantly agreed, and together they headed to the Beverly Center.

She tried on dresses she never imagined getting into. At five feet four she found she could even fit into some size eights. It was a revelation, looking in the mirror and seeing a shapely, pretty woman looking back.

"That's your color, Blossom."

Blossom looked down at the bright orange skirt and matching blouse. She thought she looked like a crossing guard or a Popsicle. And, after all, Dolly had thought she looked good after she had her eyebrows done. So she tried on another skirt and blouse. An apple green skirt with a washed-out peach top. Yes, that looked much better. She even tucked it in at the waist, which she hadn't dared do in years.

"Not too terrible, Dolly." Dolly laughed. Blossom had such a self-effacing way of giving herself a compliment. In fact, as Dolly thought about it, Blossom had never given herself a compliment. It was as if she didn't dare.

"You look wonderful, Blossom; yes, you do! Now it's time to buy you a new bathing suit. You have to be floating in your old one."

It was true. Lately, Blossom felt as if she were swimming in an empty potato sack. She even had to pin the back when she swam, so that it would stay on. And so it was off to the dreaded bathing suit section. Even as a size eight Blossom was still self-conscious.

"Honey," Dolly said, "even if you weighed sixty pounds soaking wet, you'd still hate buying bathing suits. There's not a woman I know who likes this part. So just relax and pick out your favorite colors."

Blossom just sort of flew through the racks and grabbed what looked reasonable.

"Now how about going all out? How about a haircut?"

Blossom was hesitant. Visions of Franz, the eyebrow man, danced in her head.

"Who did you have in mind?"

"The hairdresser of the stars," Dolly said.

Phyllis Diller is a star; Sinead O'Connor is a star; Eddie from Frasier *is a star.*

"Who goes there?"

"Everyone."

What the hell? Take a chance. Hold on to a mirror. If something's happening you don't like, grab the scissors and stab the hairdresser to death.

"Okay," Blossom agreed, and off they went.

The salon was lovely. Tea and sandwiches were being served, while several other employees asked you every fifteen minutes if there was anything else they could do for you.

Blossom was led to her chair. "I think," a young woman said in an English accent, "you should cut about six inches off. You have beautiful hair, but there's just too much of it and it weighs you down. You're not big enough to carry it all."

Not big enough to carry it all? Had Blossom heard right? She turned around to make sure the hair dresser wasn't talking to someone else behind her. She wasn't. So short of kissing this woman, Blossom simply threw caution to the wind and said, "Do what you think is best." She could have shaved the NBC peacock onto her scalp after that comment.

"And the other thing I think would work quite well with your coloring," she continued, "is some gold highlights to frame your face. What do you think?"

Blossom cocked her head and studied what she had to work with.

"All right, what kind of look were you thinking of?"

The hairdresser pulled a picture out of *Glamour.* It was a shoulder cut that was light and easy, suiting someone like Meg Ryan.

"I love it. But will it look like that on me?"

"Better."

And so it began: the tin foil, the washing, the drying, the cutting. After five hours it was over. Blossom looked in the mirror and did something she hadn't done in a long time when she looked in the mirror. She smiled. But this was no ordinary smile. This was the smile of acceptance.

"I love it," she said.

Dolly was pleased as could be. "You look beautiful, Blossom. I don't know why we didn't do this sooner."

"It suits you," said the hairdresser. And it did. Even at six hundred dollars. It was the first time in eons that Blossom had held her head up when she left a shop. *Watch out, baby . . . coming through, coming through.*

When she arrived back home, she saw Skip, dragging a wheelbarrow across the lawn. He looked up, then down, then up again. He was startled to see it was Blossom. He simply had not recognized her.

"Well, Lordy, Lordy, Lordy, look at you."

Blossom's face reddened. Skip could still do that to her.

"You look absolutely radiant, Blossom."

"Thank you, Skip." She felt awkward, anxious to change the subject, move the attention away from herself. "So how are you doing anyway? I haven't talked to you in so long, it seems."

"Oh, fine, fine," Skip said in a not-so-fine way.

"I saw Jeannie here; it must have been three or four weeks ago now. How's that going?"

"She served me with divorce papers."

Blossom was shocked. She really hadn't expected to hear that. So that was what had been in that envelope. "Oh, Skip, I'm so sorry. Are you okay?"

"I'm sad, but you know what, Blossom? In some ways it's better. I mean, if this is the way it's going to be, then so be it already. I was hanging in there, waiting, wishing for another ending, but at least this way I can start getting on with my life. That's the line I keep telling myself anyway. Sometimes the day drags on so long, I feel like a week has passed—and it's only one o'clock."

Blossom was well acquainted with that awful sense of interminableness. It wasn't too long ago when she'd experienced the endlessness of days.

"Hey, why don't we have dinner this week? We haven't gotten together in a while. We deserve a catch-up." She felt so easy in suggesting it, it even took her by surprise. But she truly meant it. Her heart was becoming full, just as Dolly had predicted. Blossom was happy for the first time in weeks.

"I'd love that, Blossom. When's good for you?"

"Anytime, really, Skip. You say."

"Tomorrow night?"

"Tomorrow night it is. Oh, wait, damn, I completely forgot, I have a dinner party." Someone from the hospital had invited Dolly and Blossom to a benefit dinner party. "The night after? I know I'm definitely free then."

"The night after is great."

"Perfect." She couldn't believe she was the one who couldn't make it for dinner with Skip, but she had said yes to this other invitation already. A tiny part of her felt good she could say that to him. Two months ago she would have managed to be with him come hell or high water. But Blossom didn't want to disappoint Dolly. Her friend had expressed some excitement about seeing Dr. Cohen in a more social situation, and this made Blossom happy. Dolly, too, was returning to the living, in ways she perhaps wasn't aware of.

When Blossom turned to leave, Skip called to her again.

"Hey, Blossom," he yelled as she was halfway up the steps.

"Yeah?"

"You look good, really, really good."

"I feel good," she said as she headed upstairs, all grin now. She looked over the railing. "Thanks, Skip." He smiled. She smiled back. *Cha cha cha.*

CHAPTER 47

*B*LOSSOM *WAS* FEELING GOOD, but still, in the back of her mind, she was counting the minutes. She made a list of things she wanted to do before she died. Her mother's last words rang in her ears: "At the end of our lives, all we have are our memories or our regrets." Blossom wanted no regrets.

THINGS I WANT TO DO BEFORE I DIE

1. Take a hot-air balloon ride
2. Wear a bathing suit at high noon
3. Meet Tom Selleck
4. Do something wonderful for Dolly
5. Go sailing
6. Meet Tom Selleck
7. Sing a song out loud for everyone to hear
8. Tell Skip my feelings for him

She read over her list and realized she had written *Meet Tom Selleck* twice, and laughed. What would she say to him anyway? *Tom, I just wanted to tell you I've enjoyed all your TV shows and movies. Especially* Magnum, PI. *I wish you could have gotten out of your contract at Universal and been cast in* Raiders of the Lost Ark. *You would have been great in that. And never forget, you were really their first choice. . . . Yeah, right; you're an idiot, Blossom. It's a good thing that people can't read other people's minds, 'cause then everyone would know you're an idiot.*

She crossed Tom Selleck's name off her list and thought that finally, finally, she was over that girlhood obsession. Then she looked over the list one more time.

All this can be done. I can do this.

She put on her bathing suit and took her nightly constitutional down at the pool. A cool and invigorating whirl of water undulated around her as she sank to her shoulders. The stars hung like Christmas lights on black cords. Jupiter was brighter than usual, and Venus, her elusively perfect self. Light reflected in the pool like silver coins tossed into a fountain. But the light would sift through Blossom's fingers when she tried to capture it. *Ahhh, just like love,* she thought.

She had to pull herself away from the sky to begin her laps. The stars could have held her in their gravitational orbit all night.

Back and forth she swam, thinking about all the things she had to be grateful for. Dolly was one of them, the kindest person she had ever met. And how strange the timing of their meeting was. It was as if some mystical deity had been watching over her and decided, *This would be a good time to help Blossom out. Send in Dolly.* She was so grateful to whatever gods had prevailed to bless her with this friendship.

She was grateful to Jigsy and Pip and the people at the hospital, especially the children, who, through the acceptance of their own life lessons, had truly taught Blossom what it meant to accept.

She was grateful for having met Skip. No, it wasn't romantic love, but it was special all the same.

She was grateful for these past several months. She was in the last sips of spring and still had summer to look forward to, and maybe, if she was lucky, a bit of September. That would bring her to a year.

She was grateful for Henri, the old bartender back in New Orleans, who was right in telling her we have to take the sad with the happy, that sorrow is a gift, yes a gift and by going through it we get to happiness . . . like honey from a rock.

Finally, she was grateful for these long watery evenings when she could stretch out beneath the moon and sense the acceptance of a whole world embracing her. The stars didn't laugh at her; the clouds didn't turn away; the rain didn't refuse to caress her. She was grateful for all the warm, wonderful nights that strengthened her, gathered her up, and held her without judgment. She was grateful for the chance to be herself in her final days.

Blossom was still changing, even as time was descending. It felt as if an apple press were squeezing out the last of its juices. She reveled in the reward, which was every last sweet drop life had to offer.

And she believed. While she was still here, life was limitless. She was believing in herself and, for the first time, witnessing the successes of that belief. Her own happiness. It was so simple. It stunned her. Dolly once told her we have everything we need to love inside ourselves. Why hadn't she seen this sooner? Had it always been there? It seemed impossible that it could have been there the whole time. With all she'd gone through, how could happiness and love have been quietly waiting in the wings, waiting to be discovered? But every cell alive in her being was recalling the feeling so vividly that it must have been there all along.

All she needed to do was believe. Not with her eyes but with her heart. And there it was, as matter-of-fact as it was unexplainable: just the way people believe in something beyond themselves. A simple faith. Like . . . like when you're in Wyoming and you swear that you can smell the ocean.

CHAPTER 48

*T*WO NIGHTS LATER Skip showed up at Blossom's apartment around seven. She had mentioned she would put something together for dinner, but when he arrived, nothing was prepared.

"So listen," she said in a conspiratorial tone, "I have a more interesting idea . . . I think."

Skip sank into her plush couch and stretched his long legs out onto her coffee table. He looked good. You could see his strong muscles even under his khaki pants—this position pulled the fabric taut. All Blossom could think about were those fireman calendars back in Gorham that had raised so much money for the volunteer fire department.

Concentrate, Blossom, concentrate.

"So this is the thing, Skip. I made a list of all the things I want to do before I die."

Skip seemed taken aback by Blossom's announcement, so she hurried on.

"And one of the things on my list is to sing a Tony Bennett song live and in person, like in front of a whole audience. Now generally, I would never dare to do anything like this. I would find a million excuses. I'd be too afraid, too self-conscious, etcetera, etcetera, and believe me, I am afraid and self-conscious; however, the thing is, what if I went through the rest of my life being this way? Well, then I'd never do anything. I'd just die without experiencing the best that life has to offer, and then, there I'd be, on my deathbed, looking up at the cracks in the ceiling and thinking, 'Hell, I didn't do anything I wanted. I didn't sing that Tony Bennett song in public, and now it's too late; now it's over and now I can't' . . . so I thought tonight we could go to a karaoke bar."

Skip looked at her, wide-eyed and speechless.

"Well?" she said, as if she'd been waiting hours for a response.

"Why did you make this list?"

"Because there are things I want to do—like singing, for instance."

"Carpe diem."

"What?"

"Seize the day."

"Exactly. So what do you say?"

"I say absolutely."

"Now, when we get there, don't push me. I'll have a drink . . . or two, to relax a little bit. Hum in my seat to get warmed up, maybe have another drink, hum some more, and then—"

Skip interrupted, "And then you'll fall off your stool and I'll carry you out as you sing 'Show Me the Way to Go Home.'"

"No. Then I'll see. Okay?"

"Okay, let's go," he said, smiling.

They arrived at Mr. Chokee's karaoke bar on Eighteenth and Vine. It was seedy, both inside and out. The room was dark, and Blossom was grateful. She could hide in the shadows or, even better, face the wall when she sang. They took a seat at the bar, and Skip ordered a beer. Blossom ordered a martini.

"Nervous?"

"I am a little nervous, but now that you just asked me that, I'm much more nervous."

"Sorry."

"Can you see it in my eyes? Do I look like I'm meeting Hannibal Lecter for dinner?"

"A bit. Don't worry. You'll do fine. Once you get up there, you'll . . ."

Blossom was staring at Skip with an expression that said, "Don't push me." He got it.

"Hey, that's if you even go up. We can always come back. No pressure."

The drinks came, and she relaxed back onto her stool, consuming her Stoli as if it were ginger ale.

"Can I see the karaoke book, please?"

The bartender handed it to her, and she flipped to the right section. Tony Bennett had several songs under his name. Good, she had some choices. Someone was already up at the microphone, bellowing out "Girls Just Wanna Have Fun." It was a rather incongruous visual because the woman had to be in her seventies.

Oh, God, I hope I don't come across like that.

Blossom stared at her as if she were witnessing dementia in its first stages.

On the other hand, she's up there, isn't she? She's up there singing her heart out. Yes, she is.

"Can I have another?" Blossom asked the bartender, pointing to her glass.

"Blossom!"

"It's okay, Skip. I don't even feel it. I'm bulletproof tonight. I think that when the adrenaline is running this high, it's hard for anything to penetrate the fear."

"Yeah, but after you sing, you'll collapse in a heap."

"I just hope I can get to that point."

"Why are you torturing yourself? Just because you put something on a list doesn't mean you have to do it."

"I hear you, but it's bigger than that. It has to do with taking control of your fear instead of letting your fears take control of you. I know it all sounds like a self-help book, but I can't tell you how long I've done that. And I'm just sick of it. You know that saying, 'Sometimes you get the bear; sometimes the bear gets you'? Well, the bear always gets me, so tonight I wanna get the bear."

Now someone else was up there, singing "YMCA," arm gestures and all. Blossom was feeling better about her musical credibility as one shameless customer after another got up as if they were Aretha Franklin or, more torturous, Wayne Newton.

"These guys suck, Blossom. You have nothing to worry about.

Jesus, even if you had strep throat you'd be better than this. Hell, I could sing better than this."

Blossom thought she was better than these other fearless patrons, but still her nerves rattled like loose hangers in an empty closet. Performance anxiety. *Jack Benny had performance anxiety, too. He threw up every time he had to perform.* By her fourth martini her nerves were steadied.

"I'm ready," she said, sliding off the stool.

"You okay?"

"Yeah, I'm fine. *No problema.* How do I look?"

"Like a torch singer. A pro. Move over, Barbra."

Blossom straightened her blouse and made her way to the mike. She was thinking, *It ain't over till the fat lady sings,* although the description was no longer apt.

"I'd like to sing 'Fly Me to the Moon.'"

The young man cued the song.

"What's your name?"

"Charlotte," Blossom said by mistake, not even realizing it.

"Ladies and gentlemen, let's welcome Charlotte to the stage tonight to sing 'Fly Me to the Moon.'"

The intro played a few notes to ease her into the song, and then she began. Her voice rang out like pure water pouring over smooth white stones. It was light and lyrical and lovely. One by one, everyone turned toward her. Her phrasing was intimate and sure. It was as if she'd sung this song a thousand times before, and she may have, with all the times she'd sung it to herself. Even the bartender stood still, polishing a single glass and watching her.

In just three minutes she had transformed both herself and the people in the bar. And when she had finished, the room exploded with applause. They asked for more, but Blossom was grateful for her moment and anxious to get back to her seat. She had done it! She had honest-to-God done it! And she could do it again; of that she was sure. But most important, she had broken through that invisible wall of terror that surrounded her, and lived to tell the tale.

"You were great," Skip said as he pulled the chair out for her.

"Incredible. I didn't know you could sing like that. You're like a well-kept secret. You're amazing."

Blossom was blushing. "Thank you, Skip, thank you. I did it. I got up there and I did it." Skip took her hands and squeezed them.

"You did, and you were spectacular."

People were coming over and saying as much, too. Blossom beamed in her victory. It was like getting an A on a final exam.

"Well, I guess we can go now."

"You don't want to stay and sing another song?"

"No. Why ruin a perfect moment? Maybe some other night. I know I can do even better than I did tonight."

They got up to leave.

"Blossom, I just have one question for you. When the guy asked your name, why did you say Charlotte?"

She couldn't recall even saying it. She found herself scrambling for an answer.

"I didn't want anyone to know who I was, just in case I was terrible. So I said Charlotte. Don't you think I look like a Charlotte?" She was playing with fate.

"Truth is, I don't think you look like Charlotte or even a Blossom, for that matter," he said, studying her face.

"Really?" Blossom squirmed. While she had never quite felt like a Charlotte, she knew damn well she wasn't a Blossom, either.

"Let me think about it," said Skip. "There is a name that suits you, and I'm close to it, but it's not quite formed yet. I'll tell you when it's all right there. But there is a name that belongs to you. And just you."

Blossom wondered what that was. She wondered if Skip would truly one day remember this conversation and actually tell her the name that was uniquely hers.

"Don't forget, will you, Skip?"

"Oh, I won't. Don't worry about that. All things have their time."

CHAPTER 49

*B*LOSSOM SAT AT THE POOL, her eyes closed to the sun, when Skip cast a shadow over her face. She opened her eyes.

"So what else is on your list?" he asked.

"What?ª

"Your 'to do' list?"

It was a question from out of the blue, and Blossom had to focus. What was on the list?

"Take a hot-air balloon ride, go sailing . . ."

"Sail, as in a sailboat?"

"Yup."

"Well, I can help you with that."

"You can?"

"I've been sailing all my life. Used to take a sailboat out on the Charles River back in Boston. We can rent a boat down at Marina del Rey and go out."

"Really?" Blossom was excited. She had always wanted to sail, but the opportunity had never presented itself. And in the past she never would have gone anyway. Now she could cross two things off her list.

"Would you like that?"

"Yes, I would love that, Skip."

"Good, I'll pick you up on Saturday, then, at eight-thirty. Sound good?"

"Sounds great."

She sat there thinking about the ocean and the wind, thinking about the white sails breathing in and out. She could almost hear the clanking of metal against metal and taste the salt. In all of this, she wasn't even imagining Skip. Her mind was on the moment, on the sea. For the first time, Skip had moved from her direct line of vision to someplace else. Someplace better. And now she could finally see the full view.

The day was bright as snow. Skip helped Blossom into the boat with a casual competence, while Vinny just jumped in and found his spot. Skip raised the sails, hauled the lines, impressing her with his nonchalant manner. She watched him, enjoying the authority with which he moved about the boat in his cutoffs and faded denim shirt. She was still too self-conscious to wear a bathing suit so she opted for baggy white linen pants and an oversized blouse.

Marina del Rey was like a parking lot of boats. She wondered how they'd find their way back to the slip, but Skip seemed to have it all under control. In a matter of minutes they'd cleared the harbor and were riding the vast expanse of the Pacific. The Palisades, loomed like ancient animals grazing along the shore, their round backs leaning out toward the sea as if to drink from it.

Blossom couldn't take it all in fast enough. Light and weightless, moving effortlessly over the water, it reminded her of swimming. They slid over the silver Pacific, completely free.

"What are you thinking?" Skip asked, breaking the silence.

"I'm thinking that life is good."

He winked, but Blossom's eyes were closed.

The next hour passed in silence. There was so much transient beauty to absorb. Finally, Blossom turned to Skip and asked the same question he had asked her.

"What are you thinking about?"

"Soul mates," Skip answered.

She was surprised. "Soul mates?"

"Yeah, soul mates, divorce, Jeannie, you."

"Go on," Blossom said, curious.

"I was thinking about Jeannie and how I was so taken by her beauty, the way she commanded the attention of a room, her charms.

I really thought it was going to last forever. It amazes me now that I was so off the mark with it. Even if she came back now, I wouldn't want her."

Blossom was shocked to hear this admission. "Why?" she asked.

"She was never in my corner. You and Jeannie are complete opposites. Jeannie has no staying power. Depth, the ability to love on the most fundamental level, just wasn't there. She proved it. What I find incredible is that I didn't see it sooner."

"You were in love."

"I was seduced," Skip said. "And Jeannie was seduced. We seduced each other because we thought we could give one another what we both so badly wanted. It came out of a place of need, of lacking. Not from a place of abundance or, more importantly, real love. Then the weirdest thought crossed my mind the other night. What if I was badly burned or something really awful happened to me? I know that's sort of catastrophic thinking on my part, but it led me to wonder: Would Jeannie have stuck it out? Even if I were still a lawyer? No. I hate to admit that, but it's true. Jeannie was more interested in pretense, rather than essence. Do you follow me, Blossom?"

"Yes, I do."

"It's not what I want anymore. Working at the pool gave me space to think about a lot of things. Jeannie just pushed it a little further. I wasn't ready at the time, but now I'm glad it happened."

"Really?"

"Really. Remember, a long time ago we were talking and I said there was something I needed to figure out about myself as much as I needed to figure it out about my job?"

"Yeah, I remember. I remember your saying that you never thought a pool job would be this hard."

"Well, I did figure out a thing or two. First, about my marriage. Jeannie thought she was getting a real catch: Yale grad, lawyer, money. But I thought I was getting a real catch, too. Growing up poor in South Boston was a big contrast to L.A. I had gotten myself a trophy wife with Jeannie. And our mutual superficial needs were confused with love."

"I'm sure there was love, Skip," Blossom consoled.

"Not the kind I want. Maybe at the time . . . maybe I did want a beautiful woman, a pretty face, and that's what I got. But that's all I got. I've changed."

"You have. I've seen it," Blossom admitted.

"Both Jeannie and I thought we were getting something good for all the wrong reasons. It couldn't have lasted. We wouldn't have wanted it to. So now I've thought long and hard about it, about what I want in my next relationship."

"And what's that?"

"At the end of the day, you have to love your partner, not for what you can get from them, but what you have by being together. Someone you can cry and laugh with, someone who accepts your foibles and loves you in spite of them, someone you can show your soft underbelly to, and they don't perceive it as a weakness."

"That's exactly what I want."

"I know." He paused and then continued. "I'm glad I had what time I did with Jeannie. I learned a lot about myself."

"It's great to finally get it. At least that's how I've experienced the last few months," Blossom added.

"And you know what else, Blossom? You know what I've finally been able to see?"

"What?"

"I am going to tell you, but I don't want you to say a word after I'm finished. Promise?"

"Promise."

"I have seen a spirit and a generosity that is unmatched. Someone who is beautiful, both inside and out. Someone who is genuine, and loving, and unequaled, in every way possible. It's you, Blossom. I have seen you for who you are, and I am so, so . . ."

He leaned in to kiss her. Blossom's whole body tingled in readiness, but suddenly, out of nowhere, the wind kicked up and the boat lurched, so that Skip had to turn and quickly change his tack. She was but an inch away—a quarter inch, really—from consummating a desire she'd had from the moment she'd first seen Skip, a dream she had long since let go. The boat was sailing steadily now, but an awkwardness had passed over them like a dark cloud eclipsing the sun. How Blossom wished the wind had held its breath for just a moment longer.

"I guess we should head back in," Skip said, trying to navigate toward normal. "What do you think?"

"I think we should follow the currents all the way to the horizon."

"Then what?" Skip asked.

"Then we fall off the edge of earth."

"And then?"

"Well, then we become part of what happens to everyone who falls off the edge of the earth."

"What do we become?"

"Free, Skip. We become free."

"We are free."

"Not quite."

"No? What will make you free?"

"When I can tell you that, well, then I'll be truly free."

Skip tacked and headed out again toward the western horizon.

"Where are we going?" she asked.

"Like you said—let's follow the currents to the horizon."

Blossom smiled. *Sometimes we need to go to the ends of the earth to find our answers.*

CHAPTER 50

*T*HE NEXT MORNING, Blossom woke up with a terrible headache. *Oh, God, here it comes.* Time had been on her side, but she'd known eventually it would catch up. This was the beginning. She took two aspirin and went back to bed. By noon her headache was gone.

She was becoming more and more impressed with her own personal power, her capacity to wish the disease away. If she beat it, she would spread the word like gospel. She imagined herself up at the pulpit, yelling to her followers to throw their crutches away, while all the time a 1-800 number blinked at the bottom of the screen. The image gave her the willies. Maybe she'd just work on healing herself.

Dolly came over with some soup—vichyssoise, with freshly chopped dill sprinkled on top. She coaxed Blossom out of bed and into the living room.

Blossom sipped it and an odd look crossed over her face.

"What is it?" Dolly asked.

Blossom, not wanting to be rude, simply said, "Nothing."

"What?" Dolly asked again. She knew Blossom well enough to know a look when she saw one. And this was a look.

"The soup . . . it's cold. That's all."

Dolly laughed. "It's supposed to be cold. It's vichyssoise, darling."

"Oh," Blossom blushed.

"So?" Dolly asked.

"So what?"

"Are you ready for that second opinion yet?" Dolly was a pitbull when it came to follow-through.

"No. I am doing perfectly well without any doctors intervening."

"Yeah? Was that before you called me this morning to inform me that you had only twenty minutes left to live?"

"I panicked."

"No," Dolly said sarcastically.

"I think I can beat this thing on my own."

"Number one, you don't even know what thing this is that you're talking about, and number two, western medicine has been known to do a few positive things, Blossom. It's not such a crazy idea."

"No, it's not, but I want to wait."

Dolly sighed.

"Except for that awful headache this morning, I've been feeling good, really good. I've even wondered about the possibility of beating this thing and living. What if I live? I've made all my short-term plans for death, but I've made no long-term plans for living."

"Yeah, that would really screw things up."

"I'm serious, Dolly."

"You will do the exact same thing as you've been doing. Live your life 'as if' because it's rich and wonderful right now. I believe dying helps people live well. It helps you see what's important. The truth is, we're all going to die someday, so we should treat every day 'as if.' My husband's death did that for me at first. Now my own mortality does it."

"It's so funny you should say that, Dolly. I've thought that myself. When I initially heard my diagnosis, it was the first time I was motivated to act. For fifteen years I was eating bonbons and watching *Magnum, PI* reruns. Suddenly, I saw my own end and decided to change everything. I decided to live for the moment because the moment was all I had."

"And that's how we should live. We won't be here forever, so we must laugh and love as much as we can now. Especially love." Dolly paused. "So how's Skip?"

"Good. We went sailing a couple of days ago."

"Oh, yeah?"

"Yup."

"Are you still mad for him?"

"Coming back from Las Vegas forced a shift in me. I got scared. I let go of things that weren't helping me be okay. And one of those things was this crazy desire for Skip. Let's just say I'm not as Adele H. about him anymore."

Dolly laughed.

"And that's allowing us to develop this really nice friendship. The other thing, call it obsession or crush or whatever, isn't lurking in the corner waiting to pounce. Our relationship just *is* now."

Dolly hadn't heard Blossom sound so self-possessed since she'd returned from Nevada. She could see her friend growing more confident. She took her hand.

"That's good. That's so good."

"Dolly, you know all those books you have in your library?"

"Yes. They were Mr. Feingold's. Now they sit around and collect dust mostly."

"I was just wondering if I could borrow a few. I'd like to expand my reading list beyond *People*. I've never really read poetry or some of those other authors you have in there. I've heard of them but never read them."

"Oh, sure, darling, take whatever you like. Better somebody read them than they just sit around for posterity. Mr. Feingold would have liked someone reading his books."

"Thanks, Dolly. I'll take a few today, if that's okay."

"Perfectly."

"Oh, by the way, you know what Skip and I are doing on Saturday?"

"What?"

"Hot-air ballooning. Wanna come?"

"Uhhhh . . ."

"Oh, come on, Dolly. It'll be fun. Please come."

"You better check with Skip and make sure it's okay with him first."

"It's fine. Just come. Please, Dolly?"

"What the heck," she said, "it's good to have your head in the clouds once in a while, I suppose."

CHAPTER 51

ℳAKLEY HAD BEEN BACK AND FORTH from Gorham to L.A. so many times, he earned a free trip with his miles. He was now leaving California once again after coming up empty. No one had called him about the pictures he'd plastered on telephone poles and left on windshields. His calls to Realtors resulted in dead ends, and many did not even return his calls. Frustrated, he flew back to New Hampshire to talk to some of Charlotte's friends and acquaintances.

His personal investment in apprehending Charlotte had become
more than the two million dollars she had stolen. Hell, the money
didn't even belong to the bank. No, it was emotional with Makley
now. How could a 250-pound woman, a simple, small-time bank
manager with no worldly experience, have eluded his grasp? His
father had always figured it out. His father would have figured this
out already, no doubt. Makley would, too. After all, he was his
father's son, was he not? He reviewed the notes he had accumulated
over the past several months, and studied them judiciously:

Sally Adams Baxter—Enjoyed Charlotte quite a bit. Especially
during the Christmas drive. Charlotte would make sure every needy
child had a toy. Even if she had to take money from her own pocket,
which she did on several occasions.

Jean Anderson—Charlotte is kind, warm, and giving. Helped
find my kids summer jobs. Even let Sam work at the bank between
semesters at college.

Lynn Robinson—Charlotte helped stuff envelopes to reelect
Josh Connelly.

Mary Alice Babson—Charlotte helped run the food drive for the
coalition for the homeless. Walked from door to door collecting
canned goods.

Connie Pardee—There isn't a nicer person in Gorham, or New
Hampshire for that matter. Just stop looking for her already. If she's
alive, let her be, for God's sakes. (This interview was stopped
because Mrs. Pardee was getting more and more agitated with
Officer Hobbs.)

Stan and Happy Turner—She shoveled us out from two bliz-
zards. And brought over food and firewood for our stove.

Evie Schwarz—Charlotte brought my dog to the vet when I couldn't bear to put him down. It had to be done. There was no one more gentle I would have entrusted him with. I couldn't go in—I had to sit in the car. She stayed with me till eleven that night.

Grace Poole—Very nice.

Jane Clay Marchhill—She loaned my cousin money after he got out of jail when no one else would. I just want to say Cal didn't try to kill his wife. The gun misfired in the kitchen.
   *Makley, just a note about this interview. Cal Vincent Clay runs a gun shop in Claremont. Something to watch.

Dottie Spencer—Charlotte brought food over when I broke my leg on the icy steps. And stayed to make me dinner on many occasions.

Lisa Bilfuco (known among her friends as Lisa Bifocals as she was vision impaired)—Charlotte always took me to the eye doctor when I needed drops, and waited to drive me home. She's the only person who didn't call me Bifocals, which I appreciated. I know who my friends are. I'm not blind!

Ellie Leger—Doesn't know Charlotte well, but said she seemed very nice. She knows people that know her, and they like her.

Cassie Winthrop—Charlotte has the bank sponsor the 10-mile walk to raise money for Cystic Fibrosis. She walked herself every year even though it's hard on her being a very large woman.

Ellie Leger—A lovely woman that Charlotte was. Always to be counted on and brought the best manicotti to every Auxiliary meeting. We miss her. We also miss her manicotti.

Honey Withrop—Charlotte had such a great sense of humor. She always said if I had married Sophia Bea's husband my name would

be Honey Bea. She said it would have been worth it just for the
name alone.

MaryAnn Barzini—See separate notebook.

Makley put the notes away.

Hobbs's regard for Charlotte had deepened. He wished he had
known her before she was placed on the FBI's most-wanted list.
Makley warned Hobbs not to go soft on him. "She's still a felon."

"Allegedly," Hobbs reminded Makley.

"Let's call MaryAnn Barzini one more time."

"Again?" Hobbs asked.

"Yeah, she's our best shot. Maybe there's some question we
haven't asked. Maybe there's some detail she forgot to share."

"I don't know, Chief. She's practically given us her blood type."

"Yeah, well, then get her blood type, but call her in."

"And ask her what?"

"I don't know." Makley was agitated. "Ask her if Charlotte had
any hobbies, if she was superstitious, if she ever had a secret lover."

"I've asked those questions, Chief."

"Well, ask them again."

"Okay. Okay."

"Anymore news on Kelly?"

"Jeez, I almost forgot to tell you, being all wrapped up with Charlotte. I got a call this morning. It seems the FBI has tracked Kelly's
brother-in-law to a ring of gamblers that have been laundering
money. The suspicion is that Kelly has let him keep his stash in the
bank every now and then until he could move it."

"Unbelievable. I knew something was rotten in Denmark when
we had two million in this bank. Where do we get off with that kind
of cash? Certainly not from the 7-Eleven, not from the Ladies' Auxiliary bake sales, not from the food mart over at the Cash & Carry. I
can just see it now," Makley laughed, and his voice went up into a
high pitch, "Oh, Ms. Turner, could you deposit eight hundred thousand for me today? You can't believe how many chickens we sold
this week. Heck, we have back orders on rotisserie chickens till

2008. Women are fighting to get the last chicken. It's gotten ugly down here at the Cash & Carry. We may have to get backup, bring in the heavy artillery, particularly for the poultry section." He laughed again, even harder.

"Now the Banking Commission is placing a temporary halt to all of Kelly's doings as president till this mess is cleaned up," Hobbs continued. "He might be doing jail time."

"Ouch. He must be madder than a junkyard dog."

"He's mad, all right."

"Well, we'll have to see what they turn up. Meanwhile, call the Barzinis again. Maybe there's some stone left unturned. MaryAnn worked at the bank. Find out what she knows."

And so Hobbs called the Barzinis again.

"Mrs. Barzini? This is Officer Hobbs from the Gorham Police Department. I'm sorry to bother you again. I just need to ask you a few more questions regarding Charlotte Clapp."

He leaned back in his leatherette chair, poised to take more notes. MaryAnn was always ready to talk about Charlotte Clapp and never seemed to run out of things to say.

CHAPTER 52

$\mathcal{A}$T THE LAST MINUTE, Skip had to cancel the balloon trip. He had been all set to go, but something had come up.

"That's okay," Dolly said, "I have some errands to run anyway."

"What do you mean?" Blossom exclaimed, "Oh, no. We're going, Dolly."

"But wasn't the whole idea to go with Skip?"

"No, the whole idea was to go hot-air ballooning. And I'm as happy to do it with you as I was to do it with all three of us."

Dolly could see more clearly than ever that Blossom's obsession had truly changed into something far more realistic. But she was still curious, and tested Blossom's resolve.

"Are you sure, Blossom? I mean, you would certainly have more fun with Skip than with this old fart."

"First of all, you're not exactly what I'd call an old fart, Dolly, and second, yes, I'm sure. It would have been wonderful to have Skip come along, but I feel worse for him than I do for us. Look what he's going to miss!"

"You could have made it for a different time."

"Nah, I was already psyched. I think he was a little disappointed, though."

That confirmed it: Her friend had truly blossomed. And for a split second, Dolly could actually envision Skip and Blossom together.

Two hours north of Los Angeles they passed a sign: *Hot Air Balloon Rides, one mile.* When they arrived, their balloon was just being filled with propane. It was strange to see these enormous swaths of silver cloth lying on the ground like a great gray elephant trying to stand up. The pilot asked if they wished to help, and both volunteered like excited schoolchildren.

Holding the edges of the balloon, they could see its lungs taking in more life. They laughed as this playful monster tugged them first one way, then another, until the balloon finally lifted up off the ground and swelled like a glorious chef's hat above their heads.

"Ready, ladies?" the pilot asked.

At that moment a pickup came careening down the dirt road toward their launch pad. It skidded to a halt, and Skip came charging out, armed with champagne and glasses.

Something occurred to Blossom at that moment: When Skip had canceled, she had told him she'd be going anyway. And now here he was, after all. Was this that little dance of intimacy that men and women do? She certainly hadn't done it on purpose, but she found it quite amusing that he had shown up. Did he sense that it didn't seem to matter to her? Men!

"I postponed the business I needed to deal with regarding the damn divorce. When I thought about missing this, I said to myself, 'What, are you crazy?' So here I am."

Dolly was delighted, while Blossom simply smiled and made room for Skip as he slipped over the edge of the basket.

"Expecting anyone else?" the pilot inquired.

"Nope. Up, up, and away," Dolly declared.

"Wait, wait," Skip insisted, pulling out a camera. "I have to get a shot of this." And so he took a picture of Dolly and Blossom, standing in the basket rosy cheeked and ready like a couple of perfectly picked apples.

They went, higher and higher, until they were floating over the ragged hills and plains of Antelope Valley. Skip broke out the champagne and poured it into each glass. Blossom watched the bubbles float up in a giggle of effervescence. She felt a rush of clarity and happiness.

"Look!" Skip said, pointing to a bicycle race below. Wending its way along the road was a long kaleidoscope of color. The riders were dressed in bright neon blues and roaring reds, hot yellows, and fiery oranges. They lit the course as if throwing sparks off the backs of their wheels. The happy balloonists watched as hundreds made their way toward an underpass only to disappear beneath the belly of the bridge. From up in the sky, Blossom thought they looked like so many marbles spilling into a child's dark jar.

"What do you think?" the pilot asked.

"It's amazing. And you know what else is amazing? I have a fear of flying."

"You do?" all inquired, surprised by Blossom's confession.

"Wow! It took some gazumbas to try this," Skip said.

"Maybe, but I had to. It was on my list."

Blossom settled back to revel in this new sensation, which was truly glorious but strangely familiar. It felt like . . . like . . . And suddenly, she knew: She felt as if she were swimming in the endlessly blue sky that lay before her like a celestial pool. Back and forth they went, back and forth. It was as close to heaven as Blossom had ever felt.

CHAPTER 53

*T*HE WATER WAS WARMER than usual when Blossom lowered herself into it and began her nightly meditation. She wondered when she would know it was time to say good-bye. Every time she didn't feel well, she worried it was the beginning of the small breakdowns her body would begin to suffer. All terminal illnesses started with a first twinge of something. Hadn't her mother's? *Stay positive* was the mantra she tried to reiterate in her head. Stay with the hope of beating it. *Because I can, because I can, because I can . . .*

Whom would she be leaving behind? Not only Skip and Dolly, but all the others . . . People and places flashed like electric memories, reconnecting her to the past. The townspeople of Gorham might have said good-bye to her months ago, but she hadn't said her final good-byes to anyone yet in her own mind.

MaryAnn, standing at the altar with Tom, making her vows under the flowery canopy. There had been three hundred people fanning themselves on that hot, sunny June afternoon, to witness their nuptials. And during it all, Charlotte's heart was breaking into tiny pieces like a fragile porcelain plate dropped without care to the floor. She held her own, repressed the tears, flashed the obligatory smiles, as if she'd built a dam around herself.

Now, under the pull of the moon, she drew hard with every stroke, forgiving them both. She forgave MaryAnn for Tom, and she forgave Tom for his own betrayals. She needed to forgive them as much as she needed to forgive herself. She had conjured up so much anger toward them for so long, it exhausted her. The amount of energy she had expended could light up whole cities.

She had to forgive in order to go on. If she didn't, she would die with anger and regret. And that was far too high a price to pay. She relinquished both MaryAnn and Tom from the hurt that bound her to them, and whispered a long-awaited good-bye with every new breath she took. And in the close and tender night, she recited a little eulogy to the friendship they once had:

Go now, MaryAnn. I cannot bear to be held down by the sadness anymore. We were once good friends, you and I. I choose to remember only our youth, our age of innocence. I forgive you for what happened and, by doing so, free myself from anger. I am tired of anger. So very, very tired, so I'm letting go, MaryAnn, letting go and making more room for love.

She apologized for stealing the money, which she knew was wrong. It had been a moment when the lines between reality and fantasy blurred, when sanity and craziness merged. She did it, and now in the waters that seemed to cleanse her conscience, she forgave herself. She forgave herself for that fateful night with Trevor James. She wished she could turn back time and have it all end differently, but the simple act of forgiveness removed the armor that had been welded to her body for years. She became more buoyant as she forgave.

It was nearing the end of Blossom's season. She had fooled death, kept it from nipping at her heels so she could finish her unfinished business. But she wouldn't kid herself. Hadn't her mother thought she could beat it? And when she couldn't, she had pumped herself full of false hope in the form of chemo. Blossom would not do that. But at least she had time to forgive. At least she had time to do the most important thing of all before the end came. She had time to love.

As she made her way from one end of the pool to the other, a comforting resignation filled her entire being. It wasn't fatigue or giving up or inevitability; it was a feeling of coming home, of belonging somewhere, of finally having a place in the heart.

She swam for several more hours and did not tire. It was as if her own well-being kept company with her, lap after lap. How on earth, she wondered, could she remain so invigorated, so alive? Back and forth, back and forth she swam, cradled in the watery arms of the happy night, rocked to and fro in some hypnotic and infinite rhythm. And still she did not tire.

When she finally lifted herself out of the pool and lay down on the cold grass, she understood. It was love that brought her here. Love that brought her the gift to forgive. How could she have tired? How do you tire of love?

The next morning Blossom relaxed in the garden, reading poetry. Hidden under her big-brimmed straw hat, its silk tie blowing back in the breeze, she was surrounded by books: Theodore Roethke, Philip Levine, Maya Angelou, John Berryman, Graham Greene, John O'Hara, Ralph Waldo Emerson. She looked like something out of a Merchant Ivory film. The air was cool and silver, and the petaled tongues of the roses were drunk with morning dew.

Wrapped in a towel, she leaned back and closed her eyes, thinking about nothing at all. It was so nice to be able to do that from time to time. She must have fallen asleep, because when she awoke, the sun had shifted in the sky. She didn't even realize Skip was late for work until he showed up at noon.

"Hey."

"Hey, yourself. Are you just arriving?"

"Yeah. I had an appointment. Guess what?"

"What?

"I think I figured out what I'm going to do with my life."

"That's all?" She laughed. "Tell me."

"Well, remember a long time ago, when we first met, I told you my dad and my grandfather were in construction?"

"Yes, I remember."

"My fondest memory of my childhood was going with my father to the various sites and watching them move these giant blocks around like Legos. It seemed, out of nothing, something wonderful was emerging."

Blossom listened intently.

"Did you know my grandfather helped build the new Pru and the Boston Public Library?"

"No."

"And he worked on some other very impressive buildings. I real-

ized that's what truly interests me: architecture, construction, creating something wonderful where there once was nothing. Hell, it's
why I'm on the Protection and Betterment Committee in Venice.
Venice is always going through some sort of structural change. It
was so obvious, Blossom. It was right in front of my face for years
and years. I don't know why I didn't see it."

Blossom thought about how Skip had viewed Jeannie. How
something could be right in front of your eyes but you don't see it.
And then she thought about herself. How many times had she done
the same thing?

"So, I met with some old friends from Yale who have this very
successful architecture firm. I've decided to go back to school and
study architecture, Blossom. And you know what?" Skip continued
excitedly. "I called my dad last night and told him. I had no idea
what his reaction was going to be."

"What did he say?"

"He cried; he said if my grandfather were still alive, he'd be as
proud as my dad felt at that moment. And you know what else he
said, which completely hit me from left of center?"

"What?"

"He said, 'I never saw you doing that lawyer thing anyway.' God,
I had to laugh."

Blossom laughed, too. "I'm so happy for you, Skip."

"And this firm has offices all over the U.S. and Europe. It might
give me a chance to start fresh, get away from California, Jeannie,
all the stuff that's happened to me this year. I gotta tell you,
Blossom, I feel like I've had heavy iron chains unlocked from my
ankles."

"Destiny, Skip. This is your destiny. I am so happy for you."
Blossom was tempted to tell him right then and there to look at the
note she had tucked away in the secret compartment of the box. But
she worried it was too soon.

"When would you go?" she asked, barely able to contain her envy.

"I don't know. I have to apply to a couple of schools first. But that
being said, I guess I would shoot for August. Either way, staying or
going, August seems like a good time. It sets you up for September.

No matter where I decide to go, I'd have time to find an apartment, get straightened out for fall enrollment. The firm is willing to pay me as I learn, sort of like an internship of sorts. It's not a lot, but it's enough to survive."

She could clearly sense his new buoyancy. He floated just like Saturday's balloon, light and happy and ready to take to the sky. August. It was July. That gave them a little time.

"Let's celebrate!" Skip exclaimed.

"Absolutely."

"Tonight I'll take you out."

"Perfect."

He turned, making his way to the garden shed.

"You see, Skip, everyone has a destiny, and you have found yours."

"I just might have, Blossom. I just might have."

Blossom picked up the book she'd been reading before she fell asleep. There was a poem that had accompanied her well into her dreams, and was still with her when she woke up, hovering just above her conversation with Skip. It reverberated with such a sense of truth. Caught in the inevitable passing of time, I must find my fate by not being afraid to find it. In short, "I learn by going where I have to go."

She had indeed felt her fate by overcoming the many fears that ran her down so many days and nights, and she had learned by going wherever her new life took her. She pondered this notion over and over till the small black letters of the poem floated off the page like birds lifting off a wire to begin their migration. Some birds would fly over four thousand miles to go where they had to go. *We learn by going where we have to go. Me, Dolly, Skip, even the migrating birds. They, too, must find their way home season after season. Yes, if we're lucky, we learn, and if we're brave, we go.*

CHAPTER 54

*B*onjour," Skip said to the maître d'.

"*Bonjour. Comment allez-vous ce soir?*"

"*Bien, merci. J'ai demandé une table prés de la fenetre. Est-elle libre?*"

"*Absolument. Suivez-moi.*"

Skip could speak French? Why not? He was always so understated about his accomplishments. What else could he do that she had no idea about yet? Probably everything.

Blossom loved hearing him speak French. She didn't know what he was saying, but it didn't matter. Everything sounded better in French. You could tell someone to go to hell, and it would still sound wonderful.

"Madame." The maître d' held out Blossom's chair. She sat down.

"Monsieur." And Skip was seated.

"*Je vais appeler le garcon. Bon appetit.*"

"*Merci.*"

"Wow, Skip, you speak so beautifully. Just like Maurice Chevalier."

"You flatter me. I had to learn a language in order to graduate from college. I had to work hard at it. Some people have a knack for it. Not me. And you?"

"Pig latin, that's my second language. Ipslay oopslay." They both laughed.

Blossom looked lovely. The pretty ivory dress with a low-slung neck flattered her figure. A simple diamond solitaire rested in the hollow of her throat. While she still felt shy about showing off her shape, she had dared just this once to wear a more revealing dress, which Dolly swore looked fabulous. Her hair was gently pinned up, with a few tendrils falling around her face. The candlelight fell on her soft pink skin, making her look almost ethereal in the mahogany dark.

"You look lovely," Skip said.

Blossom blushed. "Thank you. You do, too. I've never seen you all dolled up in a suit before. It makes you look very . . . handsome." *Sexy.*

"Really? I'm so not used to it. It makes me feel like I have an appointment with an arrogant agent. Working days."

"Oh, no, it's perfect." Here was a perfect segue to ask Skip all about his former clientele, but she didn't care anymore. Funny.

"I also like your necklace, Blossom—simple, yet very elegant. Did you just get it?"

"No. It was the one thing my mother left to me when she died. It had belonged to my great-great-grandma. My mother kept it in her jewelry box. She never wore it—I didn't even know she had it. She gave it to me on her deathbed, literally. It's a solitaire, but as I watched her suffer, it filled a void of emotions crying inside me; I couldn't help thinking of this diamond as a solid tear."

"You have such a way of turning something ordinary into poetry, like straw into gold. Who have I met as special as you, Blossom?"

"Oh, many, I'm sure."

"Not true."

Skip picked up the wine list. "Red or white?"

"White, I think."

"Good. A nice Pouilly Montrachet."

"But of course," she giggled.

He gave the wine steward their choice and settled back.

"So, you must be excited, Skip."

"I'm happy. I'm finally moving forward toward something I have a genuine interest in. I feel so much better about this than I did about becoming a lawyer. As I told you, it was easy for me, so I took the road most traveled."

"Do you regret it?"

"Regret? No. That's a dead-end emotion. Every decision we make has its place. There's always something to get out of it. If I stayed in law, if I had stayed with Jeannie, I would have had a job and a marriage I wasn't comfortable in. I can just hear the clinking of silver now during dinner, in lieu of conversation. A country house with all my business partners visiting for the weekend and Jeannie entertaining up a storm. Putting chocolate shavings on the tiramisu. Or better, instructing the cook to. Jesus, she'd have loved that. I would have been discussing cases, stocks, the new Beemer just off the block, billings, and how Bucky J. Worthington managed to sneak in those Cuban cigars during his last trip. As you would say, 'Just kill me now.'"

They both laughed. "How do you know I say that?" Blossom asked.

"I know."

"I have some regrets," Blossom quietly admitted.

"Like what?"

"Like, I waited until this year to take my life by the horns and go after what I wanted."

"But you're doing it now."

"Yes," Blossom said, thinking how late she'd come to it and how little time she had.

The wine steward came over and showed Skip the bottle. He nodded. The steward opened it and poured a small amount into Skip's glass. With his eyes closed, he swirled the cold, gold elixir and then took a sip. Again he nodded, and the steward filled both glasses.

"I propose a toast," Skip said.

Blossom lifted her glass to his.

"No regrets," he said.

She smiled. "No regrets," and they clicked the crystal together like tiny silver cymbals, sealing it with a sip.

Their hands brushed as they were toasting; Blossom blushed at the mere feel of it. The tiny touch was nothing, yet it held the impact of an embrace for her. She pulled away, taking a generous sip of wine in an effort to soothe her nerves. Then she searched for conversation to distract Skip from her obvious embarrassment.

"Does Jeannie know you're leaving?"

"Yes."

"How does she feel about it?"

"She's anxious to get our paperwork squared away regarding the divorce before I leave."

"Sentimental, isn't she?"

Skip smiled.

"I have to look at it like this. When it was good, it was very, very good, and when it was bad . . ." He shrugged, unwilling to finish the thought. "No regrets," he said again.

"You know, 'no regrets' is a good philosophy if you can do it. Sometimes it's just too hard to move on. Sometimes you carry the pain or the loss around with you like excess luggage."

"It sounds like you know something about that."

"I do, but I've worked hard this year to put that in back of me. And for the most part, I have. As you say, no regrets."

They brought their glasses together again.

"Are you happy now?"

"Happy? That's a funny word. I'm smarter, freer, more accepting. And that makes me happy. But I could still be happier."

"How?"

Blossom didn't want to say she longed for intimacy, love with a significant other before she died, the very same thing she had wanted so many months ago. It seemed odd to say this to Skip. She didn't want him to feel it was directed toward him, didn't want to do anything to make this wonderful dinner become awkward.

"How?" she repeated, stalling, searching for an appropriate answer. At this point the waiter came over.

Thank God.

"Our specials this evening are *blah, blah, blah.* Blossom wasn't listening. She was thinking about her answer. She still believed it was okay for her to desire this connection. She didn't want love to save her, but to add to what was already good. It had taken her many months and hard lessons to find her center. She didn't want pity. Just to love a man and have a man love her. This was nothing to apologize for or feel weak or needy about. It just was. And that was fine. In fact, it was as it should be. Men and women needed each other. Of that she was sure.

"Blossom?"

"I'm sorry, what?"

"May I make a suggestion this evening?" She suddenly got uneasy. Was he reading her mind? What possible suggestion was he about to make? *Oh, God.* "Sure. What's your suggestion?"

"Escalopes de Bar aux huitres."

Jesus, thank you, God. "Yes, that sounds wonderful." She paused. "It's not frogs' legs, is it?"

"No, not at all."

Good. It'd be like eating leftovers from science class.

"Rabbit?" she asked fearfully.

"No, it's striped bass. You'll love it."

"Good." *Because frogs' legs would be a breeze compared to the Easter bunny.*

He handed the waiter the menus.

"So, are you seeing anyone?"

"Me?" Blossom giggled to cover her nervousness. "No."

"You laugh."

"A little."

"Why?"

"I don't know."

"Have you looked at yourself lately?"

Blossom blushed.

"I'm serious. Have you?"

"No—yes . . . I don't know."

"You're transformed. And it's not just the weight you've lost. Of course, that's an obvious change, but it's other things, Blossom. You've just . . . I don't know, emerged."

"Thank you, Skip." She paused. "Skip?"

"Yes?"

"Will you promise me something?"

"Yeah, sure. What?"

"This might sound like a strange request, but it would mean a lot to me."

"Sure, anything. What?"

"When you go to . . . wherever you end up . . ."

"Stay in touch?" he interrupted.

"No. When you go, will you take the present I gave you?"

"The box?"

"Yes."

"Of course. I was going to take it anyway."

"Good. Just something to remember me by."

"You think I'm going to forget you?"

"No, but it would make me happy if you had it with you."

"No worries. I'll definitely bring that with me, Blossom."

"Good, good."

"You will come and visit, won't you?"

"Yes, of course," Blossom lied. She wanted this evening to be perfect.

"Anyway, let's not talk about endings tonight. There's a whole month left. You still have your list?"

"Absolutely."

"What else is on it?"

But at that moment she was distracted by the sight of Gene Hackman being escorted past them, to his table. She sat there open-mouthed.

"What?" Skip asked, looking around. "Gene Hackman? Is that who you're looking at?"

"Skip, this is unbelievable. Ever since I came to Hollywood, I've only seen one celebrity. Gene Hackman. This is my fifth or sixth time seeing Gene Hackman. You know what I think?"

"What?"

"I think there are only a handful of actors in Hollywood, and they all play Gene Hackman."

Skip laughed. "It's true. He does do a lot of movies. Maybe too many for one man. I bet he's eating somewhere else at this very moment."

"You kid. I'm telling you, he's been cloned."

Gene Hackman looked over toward Blossom's table. She looked down, afraid of being caught gawking. Skip gave him a little wave.

"Skip," Blossom whispered.

"What?"

"Don't wave."

"Why?"

"'Cause he'll think we're stalkers. One of those weird fans that breaks into your house, goes through your underwear drawer, tries on your red panties, and waits until the owner comes home to kill him."

"Jesus, Blossom, where on earth do you come up with these things?"

"Movies."

Skip started to make ridiculous faces at the table where Hackman was sitting. He stuck out his tongue, crossed his eyes, scrunched his face.

"Jesus, Skip, what are you doing?"

Skip laughed again. "Look."

Blossom turned slowly, self-consciously. He wasn't there. He had gone to the men's room. *Thank God.*

"So, where were we? Oh, yes, I was asking you what else was on that list of yours."

"Oh, I don't know," Blossom said coyly.

"Any biggies? I don't want to be left out of any biggies."

Oh, if only Skip knew. Her last and most important wish, desire, whatever she called it, was to tell Skip how she felt about him. She blushed again.

"There is a biggie! What is it?"

"Nothing."

"Tell me."

"I can't."

"Why?"

"Because I can't, Skip."

"I won't tell anyone. I swear."

"I can't."

"Okay. Don't tell me." He paused, then continued, "Can I guess?"

"No."

"Oooo, it's killing me. Can you tell me another time?"

"Yes."

Skip was surprised. He was sure Blossom would say no, tell him to stop asking.

"Yes? Well, that's progress. When?"

"I don't know."

"Well, give me an idea."

"When do you leave for your new job?"

"I don't know. I'm thinking around August fifteenth. I can start looking for work and for an apartment. School would begin in September some time. So I guess around August fifteenth."

"Then I'll tell you August fourteenth."

"But you're going to tell me?"

"Yes."

"Goody. I love secrets. So what did I say to get you to change your mind and tell me?"

Blossom leaned in close to Skip, her mother's last words pounding in her heart.

"Because I want no regrets."

CHAPTER 55

*B*LOSSOM LOOKED FOR WRAPPING PAPER. She had worked on finding just the right present for Dolly for so long, and was thrilled that she had come up with something. It had been hard; Dolly was already rich in books and paintings and friends, rich in money and collections and antiques. What did she need? Nothing. What could she use more of? That was easy. She had taught Blossom what everyone could use more of: love. So she slowly put her gift together with love in mind.

She wrapped it up carefully in bright red foil, crowning it with a glossy gold bow, and headed to Dolly's, where her friend was expecting her for breakfast. Jigsy and Pip greeted her at the door.

"Hello, sweeties," she said, scratching them both behind the ears while opening and knocking on the door at the same time.

"Well, hello, yourself," Dolly greeted Blossom, just behind the dogs.

"I'm starved," Blossom announced.

"You look it. What are you weighing in at these days?"

"One hundred and twenty-five."

"That's incredible. You could do a Subway commercial."

"A Subway commercial?"

"Yeah, remember that guy Jack, or John, or whatever his name was? Anyway, he was a whale and then he started eating Subway sandwiches—I think he ate roast beef subs for a year—and lost, like, two hundred and forty-five pounds. Now he's the spokesperson for Subway."

"Darn. All those endorsement opportunities, and they've slipped through my fingers. Anyway, I'd have to do mine for aqua pool paint or chlorine additives."

"Well, come in and have some lox and bagels, and we'll think of another way to make millions. Of course," she continued, "we could always make money the old-fashioned way. We could steal it."

"Dolly, no one's supposed to know that. Shhhh."

"Your secret's safe with me."

They walked into Dolly's dining area. She always felt as if she were visiting the queen when she came over to Dolly's apartment. Her walls were covered with tapestries and paintings. A long marble table supported an old pristine silver set bookended by Victorian candlesticks. As usual, the rooms were filled with fresh roses. Roses everywhere, relinquishing their scents, but not their secrets.

"Tell me, Dolly, why is it that you always have roses and no other flowers? Is it because that was Mr. Feingold's favorite flower?"

"Well, that's part of it, darling, but there's more to it than that. I think that a rose is the most perfect gift God gave us. Can you imagine that this beautiful color and shape and fragrance emerges from nothing at all? It just one day appears out of the earth to make you happy."

"They are beautiful."

"I'll tell you a little story that I believe sums up the rose. There is a place in Spain—Barcelona—that runs a poetry contest. For the poem that is selected for third place, the writer is given a silver rose; the second prize is a gold rose; but the first prize, the prize for the very best poem of all, is a real rose."

Blossom sat silent for a moment. "Dolly, that's the most wonderful story I've ever heard. I will never look at roses the same way again."

"And isn't this the year you've stopped to smell them?"

Both women giggled. "That it is."

"You seem in an especially good mood today, Dolly."

Dolly blushed.

"Okay, tell me, I know there's something," Blossom teased.

"Well, there is something," Dolly confided.

"What?" Blossom was bursting with curiosity.

"Dr. Cohen asked me to dinner."

"No!"

"Yes!"

"Are you going?"

"Well, I was nervous to say yes at first. And then, of course, I began thinking of Mr. Feingold. But I thought, he would have wanted me to do this."

"So . . . ?"

"So . . . I said yes."

Blossom jumped up and did what looked like the happy dance around the dining room table. "Dolly has a boyfriend; Dolly has a boyfriend."

"Hush, Blossom," she said, embarrassed. "I do not. I have a dinner engagement."

"Dolly, I couldn't be happier for you. You deserve this more than anyone I know."

"It's just dinner."

"Sure, and pigs fly," Blossom said, reiterating the same phrase she had used when Dolly first downplayed her crush on Dr. Cohen. "Well, the timing couldn't be better. It just so happens that I have a present for you, Dolly—something you might want to wear on your date."

Blossom pulled the gift out of her bag.

"Well, well, well, to what do I owe this pleasure?"

"Truth is, I've been wanting to get you a present for a long time, but I had to wait until I found just the right treasures. Do you mind if we open it after breakfast?"

"I have to wait till after breakfast?"

"Well, I don't want to get too sidetracked. . . . I have to ask you something, Dolly. A special favor."

"Ask away, darling, but pass the capers."

"I bought a plot at the Westwood Village Memorial Park and Mortuary. Marilyn Monroe is buried there in the corridor of memories, number twenty-four."

"Oh, goody. I can visit both of you. Really, Blossom, must you be so morbid before coffee?"

"I have to think about this."

"What you need to think about, Blossom, is getting another opinion from a good doctor."

"Dolly!"

"What?"

"I need to make sure that someone gets me to it when I die. Someone has to know who I am and where I'm going. I need you to do that. I hate to ask you, but I don't have anyone else to ask."

"On one condition."

"What?"

"I will do whatever you want if you do something for me: Get a second opinion."

"Why? Dr. Jennings said it point-blank. I had a year to live."

"If you don't make this deal with me, then you're gonna be ripening in your apartment for weeks. And then whoever finds you won't know what to do. Cremate you, perhaps? Then you'll end up inside an empty Ronzoni tomato sauce jar. Ever see those jars? Not roomy. And worse, I knew a guy who used to tap his cigar ashes into his boyfriend's urn."

"Jesus, that's horrible. Whatever possessed him to do something that awful?"

"He wanted their mutual friends to think Otto was even fatter than they remembered. So, I'm just saying Blossom, you can face that dreary scenario or you can finally see a doctor."

"Okay, okay already. I'll see a doctor."

"Don't you find it odd that the closer you get to D-day, the better you look and feel?"

"I've been meditating."

"Oh, please, Blossom. I'm making an appointment today."

"Wait, Dolly, make it for August sixteenth."

"Why?"

"Because Skip will be gone by then. I just want to say good-bye without having to think about this other stuff. I want to enjoy this time."

Dolly hesitated and finally acquiesced. "Okay. I'm not happy, but okay. . . . Are you coming to the hospital with us today?"

"Absolutely. I'll come over at one-thirty so we can go together. But first, I have one more request."

"You know the house limit. Only one request a day if it has to do with burials or cremations, and two if it's something normal like 'watch the dogs for me this afternoon,' or 'pick up a couple of chickens at the market if you're going that way.'"

"Come on, Dolly, I'm serious."

"Me, too! . . . Okay, what?"

Blossom handed Dolly a bag full of cash. "Now, when I die, I want you to hire a new wizard to continue visiting the children. You can pay whoever it is with this. I don't want those kids left high and dry. Can you do this, Dolly?"

"Jesus, Blossom, you are getting weirder and weirder." Dolly pushed the money back.

"Take it!" Blossom insisted.

"You want me to do this for you?" Dolly threatened.

"Okay, okay," Blossom said, retrieving the money. "Thank you." She reached over to squeeze Dolly's hand.

"You're welcome. Now can I open my present?"

Dolly opened it up with abandon. Out came the most beautiful charm bracelet she had ever seen. But this was no ordinary charm bracelet. This bracelet was thick with charms that had special meaning to Dolly only. Two sterling silver dogs—a bulldog and a French briard—a little silver invitation to a dog party; Dolly's initials in white gold; a heart with *Love* inscribed on it; a tiny bottle of brandy; a replica of her husband's boat, the one that Dolly and Mr. Feingold had spent so many hours on; and finally, a dozen tiny sterling silver roses.

Dolly was speechless. Tears filled her eyes as she tried to talk. Nothing came out. Blossom broke the silence.

"You taught me all about this, Dolly. I am only returning a gift that you have given to me many, many times. So thank you."

Dolly got up and hugged Blossom, trying to clear the knot in her throat. "I don't know what to say, and you know that's very unusual for me. I will hold this gift close to my heart. Will you put it on me now?"

Blossom attached the clasp, and Dolly jingled it down to her wrist.

"Perfect," she said. "Absolutely perfect. I'll think of you every time I wear it, which means I'll think of you often."

And then she hugged Blossom with all the intensity of a life well lived. Dolly wasn't eighty-two; Dolly was ageless.

CHAPTER 56

*T*HERE WAS A LIGHT DRIZZLE in the air as Blossom walked down to the water. The evening looked blurred behind its wet veil. She was tired tonight. She sat at the edge of the pool for a few minutes before going in. As she stared at the water, a thought worked its way into the front of her mind: *Some men die with their music still in them.*

She'd read these words recently, although she couldn't remember where. She'd read so many books lately. It could have been in one that told her how to live, or one that told her how to die, or how to beat the odds, or how to understand God, or how to meditate yourself to wellness. Perhaps it came from one of Mr. Feingold's borrowed books. Wherever she read it, the sentence had stayed with her.

It was the saddest thing she'd ever read. But hadn't this year been all about finding her music? Yes, it had. If she had stayed in Gorham, she would have died with her music still in her. No matter what, that was no longer true. She wished she had longer to live so that she could make more music. But at least she had gotten to sing, and at least she had been heard. Life could always be more and better. That was simply life.

She slid into the water and began. Back and forth. Back and forth, swimming with the grace of a ray, fanning out her arms with a wide undulating ease. She could feel the hair on her shoulders, the straps along her back, the water rushing through her fingers. Everything had a heightened awareness this evening, as if another unseen layer had been peeled back and exposed the raw skin of her new perceptions. The water felt good, like a salve, but then, it always did.

Back and forth, back and forth she went, like a tireless wave curling toward two opposite shores. She thought about how we are here for only the blink of an eye and then gone, and how we try to make sense out of that, out of all of that. Not just she, but everyone.

And how poets and painters try to crystallize that reality into something immortal so that they might be able to live forever in some way. And perhaps they do. But not really, Blossom thought.

We are here, we do our thing, and then it's over. That's how Blossom understood the idea of love. Love was poetry in its purest form. It existed when it did, and there was nothing that could match its truth, its mystifying magnetism, its unequaled emotion. Love was a perfectly written sentence without using language, an exquisite blend of music without using sound, an unparalleled array of visual harmony without using color. You created it, and it was there to have and to hold without your ever actually being able to see it. It just was.

The pool lights shut off automatically at midnight, but Blossom continued swimming. The drizzle had subsided and pulled its curtain back to reveal a clear night sky. She floated on her back, finding the seven sisters, the Big Dipper, Venus.

A sudden swish in the grass startled her, and she dipped down low in the water. She could make out a pair of work boots trudging across the wet lawn. Whoever it was, was walking toward her, deliberately but slowly, trying to find his way in the dark. It wasn't until he was at the pool that Blossom could see who it was.

"Skip!"

He jumped.

"Jesus, Blossom, you scared the hell out of me! What are you doing in the pool so late?"

"I like to swim at night. What are you doing here so late?"

"I was getting my tools out of the shed. I was working on something and I didn't have the right tools at home, so I had to stop. Then I couldn't sleep, so I thought I'd come over and get the stuff I needed."

Blossom rose out of the pool and wrapped her body in a towel. Skip had finally seen her in a bathing suit. She was grateful it was night, but in Blossom's mind this was still a personal milestone.

"Do you want to come in for coffee or anything?"

"No, it's late. I think I'll just pick up what I need. So this is when you swim?"

"Yeah, I really like it. It's quiet, and the pool is just sort of . . . healing. It clears my head. I go back and forth . . . get lost in my thoughts."

Skip looked at the sky. "And you get to see stars. It's so dark here. I hardly ever see stars where I am. Once in a while, but generally there are too many lights on."

"Yeah, I get to see stars. But you know what? I think I honestly prefer the morning sky to the nighttime sky."

"Why?"

Blossom walked with Skip toward the shed. "Because the night-time sky is all about yesterday. The light that you're seeing from the stars happened millions of years ago. Looking at the night sky is like looking at the past. But the morning sky, on the other hand, is right now. It is in the present and holds the hope of a brand-new day and so many new opportunities—to live, to be happy." *To love.*

"Hmmm, I never thought about it like that. C'mon, I'll walk you to your door."

They cut across the damp grass toward the gate and made their way up the circular staircase. The lights were off in Dolly's apart-ment, but not because she was asleep. It was because she wasn't home, and Blossom wanted to share this wonderful secret with Skip.

"Dolly is seeing someone."

"What?" Skip asked. He had no context for the comment and was completely confused.

"Yeah, she has a boyfriend."

"You're kidding."

"No, I'm not. I'm so happy for her."

"Who is he?"

"A doctor from the hospital she volunteers at. At first he invited her to dinner, and then *bam,* just like that, he had invited her to his house in Palm Springs. That's where she is now."

"Wow. And a doctor, no less." Skip smiled.

"Or as Dolly puts it, 'a heart man.' "

"A heart man. That has a certain parallelism to it." Now both of them smiled.

"Oh, by the way, Skip, about the stars . . ." Blossom said, returning to their original conversation. "One thing remains true about them."

"And what's that?"

"We can still wish upon them." And with that she said good night and closed her door. Skip wished she had stayed there for just a moment longer. A twinge of something having slipped away crossed over him like an unexpected chill. She, on the other hand, resisted the urge to look through the peephole and watch him leave.

If she had, she would have seen him standing there for a long, long time.

CHAPTER 57

$\mathscr{B}$LOSSOM SAT ON THE CHAISE LONGUE by the pool, in her bathing suit. Skip was mowing the lawn on the far side of the courtyard. The sun shone down on her like a spotlight, but she was unconcerned. Another milestone. The motor coughed off, and Blossom looked up to see Jeannie opening the gate, holding a large envelope. Blossom watched her, and she watched Skip watching Jeannie, saw the deep breath he took as she approached. It occurred to Blossom that Jeannie never came through those gates without holding some sort of large envelope.

She heard Jeannie say something to Skip about needing his signature, and she heard Skip say something about having a pen in the shed. Jeannie followed him, and they were in the shed for about twenty minutes. Blossom assumed he was carefully reading the final papers she'd brought, and that his lawyerly training would make him review everything twice before dotting every *i* and crossing every *t*. Finally, they emerged. Blossom lifted her book quicky, as if she were thoroughly engrossed, but they were walking her way. *Oh, God. You never get a break, Blossom. Never.*

"Jeannie," Skip said, "you remember Blossom."

Jeannie looked Blossom up and down—the sort of look a cheerleader might give the quarterback's pretty girlfriend. All judgment.

"No, I don't believe we have met."

Blossom stood up. "Oh, yes, we have. Several months ago, Jeannie. Right here, as a matter of fact."

Jeannie studied Blossom. "I'm sorry, but I don't remember."

"Sure you do," Skip said. "Blossom borrowed Vinny for a party. Remember?"

Jeannie gasped. If she had tried to hide that moment of recognition, she'd failed miserably. All she could muster was "Oh, yeah, right, right." Then she pulled herself together. "Your hair is shorter."

Blossom stood up and extended her hand. Jeannie was beautiful—of that Blossom was sure—but she was beautiful in a distant way. Jeannie was like a flower in spring during a cold snap, a flower that becomes sealed inside a very thin veil of ice, frozen, cold in its inaccessible beauty. You cannot smell the flower or touch its fragile petals. The sheerest sheet of ice separated Jeannie from the world, and her beauty was eclipsed by it in some way. If Blossom looked different to Jeannie from when they had first met, Jeannie looked *much* different to Blossom.

"It was nice meeting you again," she said confidently, picking up her book and towel, turning toward the stairs. Jeannie's eyes followed Blossom until she disappeared.

"That's the same woman I met? The same woman who borrowed Vinny?"

"Yup."

"What happened to her? She dropped a whole other person."

"Yeah, she looks great, doesn't she?"

"She looks okay."

"Oh, Jeannie, loosen up. It doesn't take anything away from you to say she looks great."

"She could be more toned."

"Meow."

"So is this who's putting you in a better mood lately?"

"How do you know I'm in a better mood lately?"

"We still have mutual friends, Skip."

Skip was walking Jeannie toward the gate. "Well, yes, she's helped make this transition a little more palatable. And yes, I enjoy Blossom's company. What do you care? You're with Felix now."

"Fallon, Skip—his name is Fallon."

"I knew it was an F word—I mean name." Skip smiled.

"Cute, Skip." Jeannie took the envelope. "I'll send you a copy of all this stuff."

"So I guess this is sort of *it*. Guess this wraps up things between us."

"I guess it does."

There was an awkward pause. Skip shifted from one foot to the other.

"Good luck, Jeannie."

"Yeah, you, too."

Jeannie turned and walked toward her car. Skip watched the past seven years of his life disappear in front of his eyes. How could it be? Two people can hold each other for seven years, ten years, twenty years, laugh and cry with each other, love each other through the best and worst of times and then, one morning, one of them wakes up and has absolutely nothing to say to the other. This thought stayed with him as Jeannie headed down the street, turned the corner, and drove out of his life forever.

CHAPTER 58

*M*AKLEY WAS IN HIS OFFICE going through unpaid traffic violations when the phone rang.

"Mr. Makley?" asked an unfamiliar female voice.

"Yes?"

"My name is Sandra Lockley. I'm calling from L.A. Actually, from Beverly Hills."

Makley sat up in his chair.

"Yes?"

"I work in realty here. Sandra Lockley Fine Homes and Realty. I returned last week from maternity leave, and I was going through some old messages; the woman I had hired to fill in for me while I was gone obviously didn't give me all my calls. I've been going through them one by one, and I just got to yours. So I'm just getting back to you now."

Makley sat up in his chair. "I'm glad you called. What can I do for you?"

"Your message said you were looking for a large woman who might have purchased a home in the past year. Your description of the woman fits someone I did sell a house to, and she was from New Hampshire, as I recall. But the name you gave doesn't fit. You said it was someone named Charlotte Clapp?"

"Yes, that's right."

"Well, the woman I sold the house to, her name was Blossom McBeal."

"Blossom McBeal?"

"Yes."

It could be a different woman. Then again, it would be quite a coincidence. Charlotte could have changed her name.

"The reason I remember her so clearly, and the reason why I'm calling, is because she paid in cash."

"Cash?"

"Anyway, I thought it odd. It was mostly in small bills: tens, twenties. It took us an entire day to count it. You don't forget something like that."

"How much was the house?"

"A million dollars."

Bingo! Makley knew he was close. "Can you give me the address?"

"Under one condition."

"What's that?"

"I'd like my name to be kept out of this. If she should be arrested for something she did, I don't want her to know how you found her."

"That isn't a problem, Ms. Lockley. I give you my word your name will not be mentioned."

Sandra Lockley gave Makley the address.

"I really appreciate your calling. If this is indeed Charlotte Clapp, then you've helped bring a situation to its rightful end."

"I don't want to know anything about it, Mr. Makley. I'm glad to have helped, but when I hang up, I hope we'll never have to speak to each other again."

"I understand, Ms. Lockley."

"Good."

"Thank you for calling."

"You're welcome. Good-bye, Mr. Makley."

And she hung up. Makley sat there looking at the address as if it were a winning lottery ticket. So Charlotte Clapp was now Blossom McBeal. Well, well, well. He called information in Hollywood and asked for her number. There was a Blossom McBeal listed at the same address that Ms. Lockley had provided. A moment later Officer Hobbs walked through the door.

"I'm going to L.A. again," Makley announced.

"On another one of MaryAnn Barzini's wild-goose chases?"

"Nope. We got a lead to beat all leads. Seems our little Charlotte Clapp has been living the high life in Hollywood, California, under the name of Blossom McBeal."

Officer Hobbs stepped back. It almost looked as if he were using the wall to hold himself up.

"You're kidding!"

"I'd say there's a ninety-nine-point-nine percent chance that we just might have our girl."

"This is unbelievable."

"That it is."

"When do you leave?"

"Tomorrow. Keep this under wraps. I don't want the whole town buzzing. Gossip spreads like an epidemic in Gorham. I don't need the Ladies' Auxiliary calling up here and asking a million questions."

"Right."

Makley got up. "I gotta get to the bank before it closes. Do some last-minute errands before I leave. I'll see you in an hour."

And he left, with a strut in his walk that said he was having a good day. A very good day.

Officer Hobbs was still leaning against the wall, thinking.

"Damn," he said softly. After all the good things he had learned about Charlotte, this was the one he hoped would get away.

CHAPTER 59

*B*LOSSOM CARRIED HER BOOM BOX down to the pool. She wanted to swim to music tonight.

Tony Bennett's voice hovered over the water like a light mist as she stepped into her netherworld. "Old Devil Moon," "It Has to Be You," and "Body and Soul" drifted like wispy, low-lying clouds over the pool, caressing her. She fell back on the music as if soft pillows were catching her in their embrace.

Back and forth, back and forth she went with dolphin ease. The lights flicked off at midnight, as they had so many times before, and Blossom lay on her back drinking in the night sky like a dark, sweet liqueur and thinking about Skip. Was he leaving this week? Next week? Then, as if desire had conjured up his very presence, Skip appeared at the edge of the pool like an apparition. She blinked to make sure she was actually seeing him.

"Skip?"

"Hi."

"What are you doing here? Getting more tools?"

"Uhhh, yeah," he lied, kneeling down by the edge of the pool, drawing his hand through the water and feeling the warm-cold silk of it.

"Guess you leave soon, Skip." She just couldn't help saying it. That reality was as present as they were, as present as the grass he stood on or the sky above them. But it was a starless sky tonight, and suddenly the feeling of being lost in a lush, liquid world dissipated, becoming bowls of blackness and a barren feeling of loss.

"Yes, I leave soon." He paused, then tried to change the subject. "But more importantly, you still haven't told me what the last thing on your list is. You said you'd tell me before I left."

"True, I haven't. But I will. There is something I would like to tell you. Something I've tried to tell you a hundred times before, but the words never came out. It's not on the list, but it's important."

"Okay."

"There is no right time to tell someone this. This isn't a right time, either. But the truth is, there will never be a right time. The thing is . . . it's a sort of strange thing to tell you, Skip, but the fact is . . . I'm kinda sick."

"What does that mean?"

"Well it means that several months ago I was given a year to live, and my year is almost up."

"What are you talking about, Blossom?"

"And I need you to know this so when you go away, you won't wonder why you haven't heard from me. You will always be in my heart, Skip; I just won't be here. Here like this."

She went on to tell Skip exactly what Dr. Jennings had told her and how she had decided, in the last stretch of her life, to change everything. She did not confess any of the other strange and incalculable circumstances of her life. She did not tell him she had robbed a bank or changed her name or had fallen hopelessly in love with him. She did, however, tell him what she believed to be true. She was dying and most likely had less than a month left.

Skip listened with eyes wide, as if he had inadvertently got tied into a party line that was none of his affair and was unable to hang up although he desperately wanted to.

"This can't be right."

"It is, Skip."

"I don't understand."

"There's nothing to understand. It just is."

"I don't believe you. I refuse to believe you, Blossom."

Blossom was quiet. She finally broke the black, inscrutable silence. "That's okay."

Skip stood up slowly and stared at Blossom in the pool. She

seemed so far away from him, as if he were running toward her in a
dream, but she only continued to move farther, ever farther away.
No, this wasn't true, this wasn't right. No, no, no, no, no, no, no . . .

Still with his gaze fixed upon her, he began unbuttoning his shirt.
Blossom watched as he loosened every button, one by one. He took off
his watch and undid his belt. He removed his shoes, slipped off his
khakis, and tossed them onto the grass. Finally, he stood naked in front
of her. He was perfect, like one of those Parisian statues in the center
of a fountain. Blossom did not say a word. He entered the water like a
secret, a leaf floating down from a tree and landing effortlessly on the
surface. His strong, masculine body moved toward her with purpose
and tenderness. He reached for her, only a sheer curtain of water sepa-
rating their bodies. He slid the straps of her bathing suit off her shoulders and pulled them down to her waist. Now even the water between
them disappeared. He brought her in close, her breasts warm against
his chest, his hands around her back. Tenderly he lifted her face in the
half-moonlight that hung like a candle behind the clouds and kissed
her cheek, her eyes, her lips. Blossom's eyes closed, defenseless against
the utter pleasure of his touch. Was this a dream? If it was, she didn't
want to wake up. She wanted to stay folded in the sweetness of the
unexpected "now" of it, experiencing the pure distillation of every
feeling she'd ever had for him.

He slipped off her suit and carried her down to the shallow end of
the pool. He laid her back along the top step and gently lay on top
of her. He opened her legs and, in the pearl black darkness, found
his way to the center of her being, the very core of her existence.
Then he rocked her back and forth, like the movement of water
finding its way to the shore. She held on to his neck as to a lifeline,
taking in every sweet and excruciating plunge. A distant chorus of
music drifted in and out of Blossom's brain. "The Good Life" played
on, somewhere in the middle distance of the moment.

And Skip kissed her neck and whispered something, though she
couldn't quite hear it. She only felt the strange shape of words
against her ear.

Small, undulating movements came quicker now. She was so hot,
she thought the water might start boiling around her at any moment.

And then, in the slippery wet underworld of wonder and dream, they released themselves utterly and completely to each other. Everything that was far away became tactile and immediate. Everything that "was" or "had been" changed in a second. They held on to each other as if they were the lone survivors of a shipwreck in some nameless ocean.

"Let's go upstairs," Skip whispered.

"In a minute," Blossom answered, not wanting to let go of this exquisite moment.

"Okay. . . . Do you remember a while back when I didn't know what name fit you exactly? And I told you when it came to me I would tell you?"

"Yes, I remember it well."

"Well, it's finally come to me."

"Tell me."

"Your first name should be Lila."

"Lila?"

"Yes, because Lila means 'night,' and your last name should be Nata because Nata means 'swimmer.' Night Swimmer—that's what your name should be, Blossom, because that's who you are."

"I love you, Skip."

"I love you, too, my beautiful night swimmer."

He finally lifted her out of the pool, wrapped a towel around her and then around himself, and carried her upstairs to bed, where they tumbled under the white waves of sheets and down until morning.

CHAPTER 60

KIP AND BLOSSOM SLEPT, two lovers tied together in a single knot of bliss. A sudden knock at the door woke them both. Blossom looked at the clock. It wasn't yet six. She rose, threw on her robe, and walked, half awake, to the foyer. She opened the door to three people standing before her like Publishers Clearing House representatives.

Makley thought he might have the wrong person. In no way did this woman standing before him resemble the Charlotte Clapp in her pictures, the Charlotte Clapp who had made an indelible impression on him for months.

"Charlotte Clapp?" Makley asked tenuously.

Charlotte saw Makley and knew. He didn't need to say another word.

"Yes."

"We have a warrant for your arrest, originating in the district of New Hampshire, authorizing us to arrest you for a charge of bank larceny."

Skip had gotten up by this point and was standing beside her, listening to the charge.

"What?" he asked, incredulously. "There must be some mistake," he continued.

"No," Charlotte said, turning to Skip. "I'm afraid there's not."

He stood there, staring blankly, too stunned to move from his spot.

"We'll wait here, Charlotte. Please get dressed," Makley said.

"Who is Charlotte?" Skip asked, confused.

Charlotte walked past Skip, who turned and followed her mutely back into her bedroom.

"I can't tell you everything right now, Skip. It's too long a story. Ask Dolly. She knows the whole thing."

Skip watched Blossom hurriedly dress and gather some things up from her bureau. As she began to walk out, she turned to him one last time.

"Thank you for the most unforgettable night of my life, Skip. I was able to complete my list . . . more than complete it. So now you know. Now you know what the long-withheld secret remaining on my list was. It was to love you."

She stood on tiptoes and kissed him. "And I do love you," she said, as easily as if she were telling him a wonderful dream she'd had.

Two local FBI agents—one male and one female—and Makley all piled into a police car and headed to the federal courthouse, with Blossom in the back, staring forlornly out the window as Makley read her Miranda rights.

"How did you find me?"

"It took quite a while, Charlotte. We just pieced it together bit by bit."

"What happens now?"

"Well," Makley continued, "you'll be arraigned in a California federal court and formally charged with bank larceny in New Hampshire. And depending upon whether you want to contest identity, you'll either stay here and have a hearing, or agree to go back to New Hampshire, and plead guilty or be tried."

"I'm guilty. I'm the one. I stole the money. I'm not going to put up any fuss about it. I don't need a lawyer. Especially since I'll probably be dead in a month anyway."

"What?" the male FBI agent asked, turning toward Charlotte. "Are you planning to commit suicide?"

"No. I was given a year to live, and that was just about a year ago, so I'd say my time is almost up here."

Makley cringed. Jesus! Charlotte was still laboring under the belief that she was going to die. Of course she was—no one had told her otherwise.

"Charlotte," Makley said, adjusting his whole body toward her so that he could see her face. This was not news you delivered while looking away.

"Yes?"

"Your doctor was Jennings, as I recall. Is this correct?"

"Yes, sir."

"It seems he made a very large and serious mistake."

"How do you mean?"

"When you went in for your routine physical, somehow, someway, your chart got mixed up with another woman's, whose name was, coincidentally, Charlotte Clapp as well. She was from Durham, New Hampshire. It was this other Charlotte Clapp who was actually dying. Not you. So in fact, you're okay . . . you're going to live."

Charlotte sat flabbergasted in the backseat. "I'm what?"

"Going to live," Makley said again. "We thought you might have actually gone over with your car after hearing such awful news. We combed the river for months."

This couldn't be right. She'd robbed the bank because she believed she was going to die, and now she was going to live? Was this some sort of cosmic joke the gods were playing on her? Was this . . . destiny?

"Dr. Jennings tried to call you immediately when he was informed about this awful mix-up. He told me he rang you at four in the morning but there was no answer. We thought the worst."

No, Makley. This *is the worst.*

"That's impossible. I . . . I didn't plan on this. I mean, I was feeling better and I thought maybe my good attitude was helping me beat it, but I never thought I'd actually live. Now what am I going to do?"

"Go to jail," the mean-spirited FBI agent said, lashing out, her claws exacting their strike. "So are we still guilty?"

Charlotte didn't say anything. She had fifteen minutes to decide what she would say as they made their way to the police station.

A year. A whole year had gone by, and every day of it she had believed she was dying. How odd. How this had changed everything for her. If she had known the truth, she probably wouldn't have left the safety of Gorham, and her lackluster life there. She'd probably still be sitting at her desk in the bank with some states calendar over her head, drinking coffee from an employee-of-the-month cup. *No regrets.* Yes, this is what Skip had said, what her mother said, and she knew they were right. She ruminated about something that Dolly had told her on more than one occasion. *Dying helps people live well.* It was so true, truer than she could ever have imagined. But now she was going to live, and she didn't have a clue what to do about it.

She stood in front of the judge at the federal court and was formally charged with bank larceny. When the judge asked her if she wanted a hearing to contest her identity, it seemed like an obvious choice.

"No, Your Honor," was all Charlotte said.

"Well, Ms. Clapp, since there seems to be no contest here, I am submitting an order that you be taken back to New Hampshire, where you will be formally arraigned and charged with this crime. However, for the time being, I am going to hold you here without bail until you can be moved."

Makley, along with the two agents, escorted Charlotte down to a cell, where she would change her clothes, be fingerprinted, and pose for a mug shot.

"Can I see it?" Charlotte asked after it was taken.

"Sure," Makley said, and showed her the picture.

"Not bad," Charlotte gloated, her confidence returning by degrees. She just looked so good these days. Even if there was a number across her chest . . .

There were other people in different cells around her. She had never seen an actual jail cell before, especially not from the inside. It was nothing short of bizarre.

"I'll come by tomorrow, Charlotte, just to see how you're doing," Makley promised.

Makley was nice, Charlotte thought. Nicer than that female FBI agent, certainly.

"Bring a cake with a file in it," she joked. The situation called for humor or hysteria.

"Is there any money left, Charlotte?" Makley asked before turning to leave.

"No. It's pretty much all gone now. How many consecutive lifetimes do I get for that?"

"Don't know . . . Try and get some sleep."

"Why? Will this all look brighter in the morning?"

Makley smiled as he turned to leave, but Charlotte had one more question.

"What did Jennings say about all this?"

"Jennings? Jennings could barely speak. He no longer practices in Gorham. In fact, we wondered if he was practicing at all. Before he left, he said something about becoming a golf pro. Probably figured he couldn't kill anyone with a putter."

"Don't be so sure," Charlotte said. "Young, single, handsome Dr. Jennings. What a putz."

Makley tried to hold back his laughter, but he couldn't; he just couldn't. And as he left, Charlotte could hear a trail of titters.

Suddenly, she was alone, looking through the bars of her new world at another woman locked up in a cell across from hers.

"What are you in here for?" Charlotte asked.

"Murder. But I didn't do it. And you?"

"Trying to live my life as well as I possibly could. But I got caught."

"Did you do it?"

"Yes, I can happily say I did."

CHAPTER 61

*C*HARLOTTE HAD BEEN IN CUSTODY for three days, and three times Dolly and Skip tried to visit with her, but they had not been allowed in. She appealed to Makley to let her friends visit. He explained that he didn't make the rules here, but promised he would see what he could do.

"At least tell Skip I'm not dying, Makley."

"All right. I'll make sure to get to him and let him know."

"Not that it matters anymore, but I want him to know something of the truth."

"I promise you, Charlotte, I'll let him know."

Charlotte was asleep when a familiar voice called out to her from the freedom beyond. It was Dolly.

"Oh, my God, they let you in."

"Yes, darling. I pulled some strings. But they won't let me stay long."

The guard opened the door, and Dolly entered, arms outstretched. It was a much-needed hug, and Charlotte devoured the affection.

"Is Skip okay?"

"Yes. You know he's come every day. He is so worried, honey. He had to do something about closing or selling his house. I can't remember exactly what he had to do, but he's coming over directly after. You'll see him."

"God, what must he think? First I tell him I'm dying; then I'm not. Then I'm arrested for robbery. Then he finds out I'm not Blossom McBeal from New Orleans but Charlotte Clapp from Gorham, New Hampshire. I can't believe he'd even want to see me."

"He fell in love with you. You," Dolly said again, pointing to her heart. "The real you. It's not about anything but that. That's who he's come to know, and he knows he's not wrong about what he feels and what he sees in you. However, about the dying . . . I told you to get a second opinion."

Charlotte sighed. "Don't even go there. Luckily, they removed everything I can use to hang myself. But you know what the best part is, Dolly? I mean about Skip?"

"What?"

"He didn't see me as the enormous bridesmaid in the purple chiffon dress. He didn't see me as fat or ugly, Dolly. I was pretty and interesting and kind. I was funny and loving. I was someone, Dolly, and he saw that I was someone."

"You *are* someone. This was the year you set out to find her. And you did. And I did. And he did."

"And now it's over."

"Do you know what they have planned for you?"

"I go back to New Hampshire to stand trial."

Dolly shook her head. "We've got to do something. Somehow, we'll get you through this."

"Thank you, Dolly. You know, I think I feel better already. So tell me, how are we going to do this?"

"I have no idea, darling."

Charlotte looked at her as if she had just taken back the keys to the kingdom. Dolly saw her expression and punctuated her plan with a final positive. "*Yet,* darling, I have no idea *yet.* But we will; I know we will."

The guard appeared at the cell door like an evil stepsister. "Time's up."

"But I just got here," Dolly argued.

"And now you have to go," the guard croaked sarcastically. Dolly gave Charlotte a mournful look.

"I'm sorry, honey, but I'll be back." She exited the cell, looking back at her joyless friend.

"Dolly," Charlotte piped up, "I almost forgot. How's Dr. Cohen?"

"Fine," Dolly said, not wanting to make it seem as if life was good for everyone else beyond the bars. But Charlotte knew better.

"Oh, come on, Dolly. Just fine?"

"Okay. Wonderful." And they parted company with smiles upon both their faces.

Dolly had left before Skip arrived, and the guard would not let him in. Charlotte's allotted time for having visitors was over. Charlotte was in anguish.

"Please. Just let him in for a minute. Thirty seconds. Please."

But her words fell on deaf ears. Skip was somewhere upstairs less than a hundred feet away, but he might as well have been on the moon for the terrible feeling it gave her not to be able to see him.

If only she hadn't opened the door that morning. If only she had stayed in bed with him and made love again. If only she had had some prior warning so they could have slipped away in the night. If only, if only, if only . . . She wanted to explain everything. It didn't matter that he already knew, that Dolly had told him. She wanted to do it herself, to make him understand why she had done it. She needed to look him in the eye, take his hand in hers. She needed to kiss him. One night—they'd had only one night together. How could their joyous song end on such a sad note?

She lay back down on her small cot. Everything good was slipping away, as if the earth had slipped off its axis overnight. She would end up going back to New Hampshire without even seeing him. She would ask for the death penalty, she thought; it was easier than living with this loss.

She tried to think of other things to ease the pain of thinking about him. Like Tony Bennett songs. *Skip.* Like Jigsy and Pip. *Skip.* Like swimming at night in the rain. *Skip.* But with every distraction she could summon, her mind always seemed to wander back to the one thing that had made her richer than she'd ever thought possible. *Skip.*

The day had come to go back to Gorham, New Hampshire. Charlotte sat in her cell, waiting for Makley and the two FBI agents. Finally, they arrived.

"Time to go," Makley said. "The plane leaves in an hour." She still hadn't seen Skip. They refused to let him visit her.

"You can't take a felon on a plane," Charlotte said. "I saw *Midnight Run.* Robert DeNiro couldn't take Charles Grodin on a plane."

This made Makley laugh. "It's a special plane, Charlotte. A JPAT."

"A what?"

"A JPAT. Justice Prisoner and Alien Transportation System. It's a jet, a seven-forty-seven or seven-thirty-seven, depending, but it's used for transporting prisoners."

"You'll be in good company," the female FBI agent snarled. "There'll be about thirty other felons on the plane."

The harsh reality of that statement startled Charlotte. What she had done had suddenly hit home as it never had before. She was a criminal. She had committed a crime, a bad one. But she wasn't a criminal. Not really. She hadn't killed anyone for chrissakes. She had

just gone off to live the last year of her life somewhere new, somewhere different, somewhere exciting. And now what? Now she was
going to live, which was the worst possible news of all, because now
she would spend the rest of eternity in jail. What a cruel turn of
events, a hoax of the worst kind. A life sentence.

"Can I have a word with Mr. Makley?" Charlotte asked.

The female agent stood there, not moving.

"Privately?"

Makley and Charlotte stepped to the side. "I know this might
sound ridiculous in the light of things, Mr. Makley, but I'm scared
of flying. I've never been on a plane before."

"There's nothing to worry about. It's safer than driving."

"I know, I know . . . but nonetheless, I'm still freaked out."

"Don't worry. I'll sit next to you. You can hold my hand if you
need to."

All this was of little comfort to Charlotte, but it was clear she had
no choice in the matter.

She looked at what the policeman carried in his hands: shackles
and handcuffs. He'd brought shackles and handcuffs with him. He
gave them to the female agent to put on Charlotte.

"Is this really necessary?" Makley asked. It was, after all, just
Charlotte Clapp.

"Yes, it is," the agent hissed. "It's regulation."

How odd, how incongruous, Charlotte thought, walking down
the corridor in chains. All she could think of was that movie with
Sean Penn and Susan Sarandon. *Dead man walking; stand clear; dead
man walking . . .*

"I feel like Jacob Marley in these things."

"Who?" the mean agent asked.

"You know, Jacob Marley, the ghost of Christmas past."

The woman didn't say anything, and Charlotte figured she probably didn't know what Christmas was, either. *Joy to the world? Good-
will toward men? No? Halloween's probably your big holiday. You'll
probably be flying beside the plane on a broom.*

"Don't worry, Charlotte," Makely said, trying to comfort her. "It's
a short trip if the tailwinds are behind us."

"Dolly would suggest these chains don't work with what I'm wearing. Perhaps something simpler, something more understated, like a chain belt and a matching bracelet."

"Shhhhh," the female FBI agent warned.

"Is she coming with us?" Charlotte asked Makley.

"No. There'll be several female marshals on board."

"Pity," Charlotte mumbled sarcastically, "she's so much fun."

And so Charlotte scuffed her way out of the federal prison, clanking away, trying to remember everything good that had happened during the past year and humming to herself, "They Can't Take That Away from Me."

CHAPTER 62

$\mathcal{C}$HARLOTTE NEVER EXPECTED IT. No one did. And yet there they were, the crowds of women at the airport when she arrived, holding banners and flags welcoming her home. Short of a ticker-tape parade, she was greeted with all the celebrity of a quarterback who had single-handedly led his team to glory. Charlotte Clapp had become a local hero. But why? Because she had done what every woman in Gorham had wanted to do for years: escape the monotony, the dull, relentless throb of the ordinary, the terminal illness of the suburbs that offered nothing but Chef Boyardee and canned peas, corrugated carports and vinyl pools, decorative gnomes and cyclone fences.

Charlotte had done it. Realized something. Dared to pull down the proverbial wall of boredom, the wall that hermetically sealed in every woman living—or trying to—in Gorham.

Makley was shocked, as were the marshals. They entered the airport to an ovation of cheers and adulation.

The women were yelling, "You go, girl!" "Charlotte, you're our hero." "Charlotte, tell us all about Hollywood." Even the local paper had turned out to cover the story. She was front-page news. Placards were held up heralding Charlotte, while the headlines read, CHAR-LOTTE BREAKS THE BANK, and BETTER CHARLOTTE THAN A CHAR-LATAN.

And then the felons who trailed behind her began rattling their chains with abandon, celebrating what, they weren't sure, but it seemed at least something positive from one of their own.

"Balls out, baby." "Kick ass, Charlotte." "Shake that booty." "Fucking A."

"All right, all right," Makley yelled, trying to calm the crowd as they walked through. "Hobbs," he grumbled to himself. "I asked him to do one thing, one thing—keep his mouth shut—and he just couldn't do it."

Charlotte was escorted to a waiting van and whisked away to a federal court, which in this case also housed the jail that would serve as her home while she awaited sentencing.

She was immediately introduced to the lawyer who'd been appointed to the case. They would have a short time to get to know each other, and he would prepare a statement. The arraignment would be in two days, so there was little time to waste. The lawyer seemed nice enough, though a little untucked and harried: smudged glasses, a pocket protector, but smart-looking, as if he read lawyerly reviews for relaxation. Walter Bloomberg. Even the name sounded right to Charlotte. He was probably on the debate team and got good grades in school. She hoped Jewish lawyers were as good as Jewish doctors. It dawned on her that Jennings was clearly not Jewish—at least not practicing.

He made plans to meet with her in the morning to go over her case. Charlotte didn't quite understand what he was talking about, since she had planned to tell the truth, the whole truth, and nothing but the truth. But she would save all that for tomorrow. In the meantime, Makley escorted Charlotte downstairs to the cell where she was to be incarcerated.

It was all a blur as she walked with Makley to her new home: the night with Skip, jail, the plane ride, the strange welcome home she'd received. And then something occurred to her.

"Mr. Makley?"

"Yes?"

"I'm allowed one phone call, am I not? Every movie I've ever seen allows one phone call."

Makley paused. "That's right, Charlotte. You are allowed one phone call."

"Well, I'd like to make that now, if you don't mind."

Whom was she calling? Makley wondered as he led her down the corridor to find a phone. He spotted one in an empty office.

"Go ahead, Charlotte," he said, motioning to the phone. "Make your call."

Charlotte dialed the number. She did not need a phone book or information. It was a number that had been indelibly committed to her memory for a long time now. The phone rang. Once. Twice. And then a man answered.

"Hello?"

"Hello."

"Yes?"

"This is Charlotte, Tom. I'd like to speak to MaryAnn, please."

"Charlotte? Charlotte Clapp?"

"Yes."

"We thought you were dead."

"Well, Tom, I'm not. Nor, it seems, will I be, for years and for possibly decades. So is MaryAnn there?" she asked again.

"Yes, hold on, I'll get her."

There was a pause, and she could hear Tom calling to MaryAnn to pick up the bedroom phone. However, he did not have the time to warn her that it was Charlotte Clapp on the phone. Moreover, Tom and MaryAnn had been in Florida, on yet another in a series of Sea World vacations, so MaryAnn knew nothing of the recent buzz in town.

"Hello?"

"MaryAnn . . . this is your old friend Charlotte. Charlotte Clapp."

There was a scream on the other end, and a noise that sounded like a thud. MaryAnn had passed out and lay like a trout next to the receiver.

CHAPTER 63

*T*HE NEXT MORNING Charlotte met with her lawyer. She would be arraigned the following afternoon.

"I want to plead guilty as soon as possible, Mr. Bloomberg. In fact, if I could plead guilty today, that would be just fine with me."

"You can't plead guilty today."

"Why not?"

"You haven't been indicted yet. This is just an initial complaint."

"Whatever that means. All I know is, I'm sick of lying, and I just want to get it over with."

"Let me start by explaining a little bit about the procedure," Walter Bloomberg began. "I want you to understand every aspect of your decision, and I especially want you to understand the consequences of a guilty plea. You don't want to have to make more license plates than necessary." His stab at humor was fruitless. Charlotte stared at him as if he were the last man she would want to see naked on a nude beach. Bloomberg tightened his tie uncomfortably and said, "I'm sorry, just a bad attempt at humor to put you at ease. I never was any good at putting people at ease."

And Charlotte wasn't of a mind to cut him a break. "I think it's a bit ironic, Mr. Bloomberg, that the New Hampshire license plates rallying cry is 'Live Free or Die.' Don't you?"

Bloomberg was clearly flummoxed. He stumbled in his answer, "Yes, that does seem like an oxymoron, Miss Clapp."

"Yeah, well I'd like to meet the moron who thought of it."

"Perhaps we'll just continue with our business at hand." He paused, took a breath, and soldiered on.

"Is there any money left from the original two million?"

"No."

"None?"

"None."

"Well, that's not good."

"How about plea bargaining? I saw that once on *Perry Mason.*"

"In this sort of situation, Miss Clapp, there is no plea bargaining. We just have to sort of go with the facts."

"No plea bargaining? Why?"

"The crime you committed plays by different rules. While plea bargaining might affect what crime you plead guilty to, under the federal system, it doesn't affect your sentence. The federal courts use a point system, and it supercedes the plea-bargaining possibility."

"Great. So what kind of point system are you talking about?"

"It's a set of sentencing guidelines governed by chapter eighteen of the United States code."

"English, please."

"Well, being that it's bank larceny, we have to add up the points commensurate with your crime."

"How much time could I get if I'm found guilty?"

"That depends on a lot of factors, Miss Clapp. Two things govern your sentence, and these sentencing guidelines differ radically from person to person."

"Is the idea to get as many points as you can?" Charlotte asked.

"No. The idea is to get as few."

"Like golf?"

"Now, everyone accused of larceny starts out with six points."

"That's not too bad."

"But because you stole two million dollars, you get twenty-two more points."

"Oh, that's bad."

"And because it was *bank* larceny, we add two extra points."

Jesus, if I were bowling, I'd have a perfect score.

"Now, if we decide to go to trial, Miss Clapp . . ."

"Please, call me Charlotte; that personal touch will make me feel like I have a friend while walking to the electric chair."

"If we decide to go to trial, Charlotte, and we lose, we're looking at a sentence of anywhere from fifty-one to sixty-three months."

"What's that in years?"

"Four years and three months, maybe five years and three months. Now, if you plead guilty—and I'm not sure you should yet, but in the event you plead guilty—then the court drops three points off your total immediately. That brings your time down to anywhere from thirty-seven to forty-six months."

I see you three months and raise you two.

"And there's more good news. A lawyer can make a case for you. This is called a 'departure from the sentencing guidelines.' In other words, because of who you are, a decent human being who projects no threat to society, then there's no need to protect the public from you. That's also a positive."

This made Charlotte laugh. What possible danger did the women of Gorham propose? She had a vision of mugging citizens with turkey thermometers and knocking them unconscious with soup ladles.

"We also ask the judge to consider your work history. For fifteen years you were an upstanding citizen with absolutely no previous record. You held a good job, worked for charitable causes, and donated time and money to civic interests. When you committed the crime, you used no guns or lethal weapons. Further, the crime was not drug-related. Lastly, we will ask the judge to consider the motivating factors. You were completely upset, and with good reason. You had just received news that you were going to die. Wham! You go bonkers. You're in what we might call a 'fugue state.'"

"A what?"

"Diminished capacity. Unable to control your impulses. Aberrant behavior."

All Charlotte could think about was the movie *One Flew Over the Cuckoo's Nest.* She didn't want all Gorham thinking she was a Looney Tune now.

Watch out for Charlotte Clapp. She runs after bakery trucks for prune Danish and barks at garbage cans.

"Diminished capacity? Is this really necessary?"

"That alone could reduce your sentence to under three years, Charlotte."

"Oh, God, let me think about it."

"Yes, think about it. I also need to talk to the prosecutor and see what she knows. After I have learned all the facts, I'm better prepared in planning your case. You may be right in wanting to plead guilty, but I just want to make sure. The more informed we are, the better decision we can make."

"I didn't know the prosecutor was allowed to share information."

"Yes, it's common practice, and actually, we happen to be friends. We don't always agree, but Denise is pretty fair. You're a first-time felon. You made a mistake, which you have to pay for in one way or another. But you didn't murder someone; you're not a pedophile or a rapist. You haven't smuggled heroin in from Columbia and sold it to first-graders. There's a lot worse out there. Even the assistant U.S. attorney will see that. So are you ready to talk more specifically about the arraignment?"

"Jesus, I'm in judicial hell. I can't remember all this stuff Mr. Bloomberg. Can't we take a recess? They take recesses on *Law and Order*!"

Bloomberg looked at Charlotte sympathetically. It was a lot to absorb. He knew it, and he knew how she felt.

"You're right. Let's take a recess. The arraignment is tomorrow afternoon. I'll be back in the morning, and we can talk about it then."

"Thank you."

"I think it's going to be okay, Charlotte. You're a good client to have."

"Oh, I'm a dream. I just wish my parents were still alive to share in this wonderful moment with me."

Bloomberg laughed. "You're funny."

"How many points do they take off for that?"

CHAPTER 64

*I*T WAS LESS THAN AN HOUR LATER when Charlotte was called out again.

"Miss Clapp," the guard announced, "you have a visitor upstairs."

"I do?" she asked, surprised.

She followed the guard to a room divided by bulletproof glass and small enclaves, each with its own phone. She looked down the row and saw women talking with husbands, boyfriends, children, and weeping parents. Suddenly, her eye settled on a face she recognized. Her first visitor shocked her, but pleased her even more. There, on the other side of the partition, was MaryAnn Barzini. Charlotte sat down and stared: MaryAnn looked exactly as she had at Charlotte's going-away party: stiff, cool, and right. Slowly Charlotte began to talk. MaryAnn pointed to the phone. Charlotte nodded and picked it up.

"How are you, MaryAnn?"

"Fine, Charlotte. How are you?"

"Oh, all right, I guess."

"You got thin."

"That I did."

"You finally made it to Hollywood."

"Yup."

"Did you meet Tom Selleck?"

"No, never saw him once. I did see Gene Hackman."

"Was that exciting?"

"Every time."

"So you robbed the bank, Charlotte. You just took all that money and fled."

"Pretty much. I mean, it wasn't like I'd been thinking about it for months or even weeks. I just sort of snapped. You know the whole thing about how I thought I was dying?"

"Yeah, I heard about it on bingo night at the church from a waitress who works at Bickfords and is friends with Jennings's nurse . . . old nurse. As you may or may not know, Jennings no longer practices here, so his nurse is working at Bickfords until she can find other work. You know, nursing-type work. Meanwhile, she makes the pastry. And she's quite good. Especially her Boston creams."

Jesus, MaryAnn, I'm telling you how I thought I was dying and you're going on about the dessert tray in Bickfords.

"Anyway, that's how I heard it. So, what happened, Charlotte?"
Finally.

"There I was, thinking I was dying, when it dawned on me that I hadn't really lived, and I wanted to. I figured I had nothing to lose. And then the strangest thought occurred to me during that time."

"What?"

"Do you remember that ceramic frog that was stolen out of someone's yard one night? I think it was in New Hampshire or maybe in Massachusetts."

"What frog?" MaryAnn clearly had no idea where Charlotte was going with this. Had she gone mad?

"You know the one. It was all over the news. That decorative frog."

In an obvious attempt to placate her, MaryAnn smiled, "Right. *That* frog."

"It was on someone's lawn, and the next day it was gone."

Suddenly, MaryAnn *did* remember the frog. "Yes, I remember that frog, Charlotte!" She looked relieved, although still a bit wary.

"Well, whoever stole that frog took it all around the world with them and would take pictures of it in front of the Eiffel Tower, in front of the Kremlin, in front of Buckingham Palace. The robbers kept sending pictures back to the frog's owners, telling them their frog was having a great time seeing the world and they would one day return it, after it had experienced life to the fullest."

"Oh, yes, yes, and the owners made a plea to the robbers. They wanted their frog back. They had the matching frog. They wanted them reunited."

"Right. And then one day the frog did return. In a limo. And there was a big celebration."

"I remember," said MaryAnn, but she still couldn't imagine why they were talking about frogs.

"Well, I kept thinking about that ceramic frog. That frog had seen more of the world than I had. It had done more and seen more than me or anyone else in Gorham, for that matter."

"So?"

"How could a ceramic frog have more to say at the end of its life than me? I mean, if I couldn't have a better life than a ceramic frog, I'd say that's pretty damn pathetic."

"When you put it that way, it does seem somewhat depressing."

"Well, I'd say that frog and I are even."

"So you're even. But . . ." MaryAnn looked down, then looked up again directly into Charlotte's eyes in a confused and searching way. "But, Charlotte?"

"Yes?"

"Why did you call me?"

"I knew you'd wonder that."

"I have. I've scratched my head over it a hundred times. Honestly, I wasn't even sure if I'd come."

"Why did you?"

"Because . . ."

"Don't lie, MaryAnn. We've got nothing to lose anymore."

"Well, to be perfectly honest, I was just busting with curiosity."

"Okay."

"So why *did* you call me?"

"You know why? This past year has been an amazing one, MaryAnn. In so many ways. And I have to tell you, you were on my mind a lot of it."

"I was?"

"Yes, you were. I thought about our friendship when we were kids, about high school, about T. J., about Tom, about how things changed between us. I thought about how bad I felt for so many years and how I couldn't seem to move on from that feeling. I got fat and sad, and angrier with you. It just seethed under the surface, like the La Brea Tar Pits."

"Like what?"

"Oh, never mind. Anyway, I'm really glad you came today, because I've been wanting to tell you something."

MaryAnn braced herself. She was ready for Charlotte to take her down, tell her she was the most horrible person on earth and that she hated her now more than ever.

"Yes?" MaryAnn asked tentatively.

"You did what you did, good, bad, or indifferent. And so did I. But you know what, MaryAnn? It's okay. I want you to know that whatever happened—your marrying Tom, your silence and rejection after T. J., your general feeling for me—I forgive it all. I love you, MaryAnn, for the person you once were and who I believe is still in there somewhere, somewhere deep down. The same funny girl who played freeze tag with me after school, the same girl who cut her thumb so that we could be blood sisters way back when, the same girl who promised, no matter what happened in life, somehow, someway, we'd always remain friends. That's what I choose to remember, MaryAnn, and to celebrate. If I learned anything this year, it is that life is too short to do anything else. Not forgiving eats you alive."

MaryAnn sat looking at Charlotte, trying to process what she was hearing. After everything, Charlotte forgave her. Even as she sat in jail and awaited her uncertain future, she was forgiving the past and all its big and small injustices.

There was no denying it: On MaryAnn's part, there had been many. And she had hardened her heart to feel justified. But now, looking at Charlotte through the glass, something in her softened. She was undone, utterly unprepared for this. And she began to cry. It was as if she'd waited years for someone to say something first, but then, after a while, she'd become lost within her own bitterness, and that had become her life. Perhaps she'd even forgotten it could be any other way. But Charlotte hadn't, and today she reached right through the barrier that kept them separated, and hugged her with her heart.

"Charlotte?" MaryAnn whispered, her whole being changing with every word. "I don't know what to say. . . . I . . . I . . ."

Charlotte simply nodded her head yes and understood. She knew that words wouldn't have said it at that moment anyway.

"And now look at you. In jail. How could someone like you . . . ?"

"It's going to be okay."

"How?"

"Oh, I don't know. Christ, maybe it won't. But you know what?"

"What?"

"The most wonderful thing happened to me this year, MaryAnn. It almost puts this in perspective in some weird way."

"What happened?"

"I got something that I'd wanted all my life. The one thing that I never seemed to get, the one thing that slipped through my fingers, or got away, or somehow was never truly there in the first place."

"What?"

"I found love."

"You did?"

"Yes, I fell in love with a man who is kind and smart and good. And do you want to know what the best part about the whole thing is?"

"Yes. Tell me."

"He loves me."

MaryAnn looked at Charlotte with a mixture of happiness and envy. She had finally found it. The elusive, unexplainable luckiness of love.

"Who is he?"

"His name is Skip—well, that's really his nickname. But that's what everyone calls him. Skip."

"Skip's a nice name."

"Thinking about him is the only thing that helps get me through these days and nights. I just keep going over the wonderful times we had, and somehow I'm able to deal with it." She paused. "I wonder if I'll ever see him again."

MaryAnn's heart ached at that moment for her old friend. She wasn't even sure where it was coming from. Perhaps from the deep well of shared experiences and innocence, of an untouched time that even the hurt of past lives couldn't taint. She saw Charlotte in her sky blue snowsuit, sledding down that hill behind the 7-Eleven. She saw her twirling a silver baton and borrowing frosted lipsticks. She saw them both hiding together in Charlotte's bedroom, sharing the strange and mysterious secrets of how boys were different from girls. How faraway this all seemed now. And yet, a certain closeness prevailed between them, and MaryAnn wished she could make it better for Charlotte.

"Of course you'll see Skip again," she said, breaking free from memory. "There is no doubt about it. You will see him again, Charlotte, and don't think otherwise."

It was the first soft thing she'd said to her in years. And it felt so good, yet Charlotte's gaze still clearly indicated sadness.

And MaryAnn wanted to rescue her from it. "So what happens next, do you know?"

"My arraignment is tomorrow. My lawyer tells me that's when they set bail. It doesn't matter. I can't afford it anyway. We'll see."

"All right," a middle-aged, overweight guard barked, a guard who looked more like a man than a woman, sporting a slight mustache, "visiting hours are over. Say good-bye." *Jesus,* Charlotte thought, *do all guards go through the same training, the Mein Kampf obedience school for dogs? One thing was clear—they could all use an Epilight treatment.*

"Charlotte, can I come by tomorrow? Would that be okay?"

"Sure, just check outside about times and all."

"Charlotte?"

"Yes?"

"Do you mind if I come to the arraignment? Me and the other girls?"

"The other girls?"

"Yeah, everybody: the Ladies' Auxiliary, the Horticultural Club, the Church Society."

"They want to come?"

"Yes! They're all on your side with this."

Charlotte couldn't imagine why, but it felt good to know. "Sure. It'll be nice to have the support there."

"So we'll see you later, then. All right?"

"Yes, see you later, then."

And MaryAnn lifted her hand to the window, and Charlotte lifted hers, and their hands fit together, just as they used to.

CHAPTER 65

*T*HE NEXT MORNING, Charlotte's lawyer went through the proceedings with her in her cell.

"So you understand what's going to happen upstairs?"

"Yes."

"What?"

"The judge is going to explain in factual terms the reason for my arrest so I can understand the nature of the charge and know my constitutional rights."

"Excellent. Then you'll request a preliminary hearing, and the judge will give us a date to appear for it, which will be ten days from now."

"Right."

"By the way, the prosecutor informed me that the camera that hangs over the door at the bank wasn't working. Did you have something to do with that?"

"Absolutely not. In fact, I forgot all about the camera. It never worked. Had it been on, you would have seen me, but I swear I didn't touch it. You can check the maintenance records."

"I believe you, but besides that, we still have a pretty unconvincing case for innocence."

"This is what I've been trying to tell you."

"I know, but it's my job as your lawyer to be as informed as possible and make sure we do the right thing to get you a lesser sentence. So what I'm suggesting is that we simply go upstairs and ask for a preliminary examination. After he gives us the date, he'll set bail."

"Then what?"

"Then you go back to jail until bail is put up. Do you have a suretor?"

"A what?"

"Is there someone who can put up bail for you?"

"How much will it be?"

"I don't know."

"A lot?"

"It could be more than a hundred thousand dollars," said Bloomberg. He knew it could be more than that, but didn't have the heart to tell her.

"A hundred thousand dollars? Are you kidding?" She put her hands up to her face and covered her eyes. "I'm a lifer."

All she could think of was Skip. She would never see him again. She tried to comfort herself with the story of Patricia Arquette and Nicholas Cage. They dated for only three weeks and then didn't see each other for another eight years after that. But when they finally met again, the love was still there and they got married. *Maybe this could happen to me.* But they got divorced a few years later. *Jesus.*

"Be positive, Charlotte. You have a lot of good things going for you. And all of this is going to be taken into consideration."

"Okay," she said reluctantly while an old Joey Bishop joke kept running through her head: "Who am I going to believe, you or my eyes?"

CHAPTER 66

*T*HE JUDGE'S GAVEL CAME DOWN, and bail was set. The Gorham contingent sat quietly during most of the public hearing, except when the bail amount was announced.

"Two hundred thousand dollars?" Whispers and exclamations reverberated throughout the room. Charlotte sat back and looked at the wall. Clearly, she was going back to jail for a long, long time. As she was escorted from the court, the women cheered her on.

"It will all work out, Charlotte!" "Hang in there!" "We're on your side!"

"MaryAnn!" Charlotte yelled.

MaryAnn walked quickly over to Charlotte. "Could you do me a favor?"

"Yes, what? Anything."

"Call my friend Dolly. Tell her what's going on. She has no idea." MaryAnn grabbed a pen out of her bag. "What's her number?"

She scribbled it quickly on her hand as Charlotte was being escorted back to jail. "And tell her to call Skip," she yelled back.

As Charlotte disappeared through the doors of the damned, MaryAnn turned back to her brigade of believers. "We've got to do something, girls," she implored.

"Yeah!" someone else chimed in.

"We have to," another agreed.

"Right now."

"Yeah, right now."

And then a pause fell over the rally. No one had a clue what to do.

"We'll raise the bail," exclaimed Dottie Spencer.

"How on earth will we do that?" questioned Grace Poole.

"Shhh," MaryAnn said. "Go on, Dottie, let's hear your plan."

"It's two hundred thousand dollars, MaryAnn," Grace said again. "That's a lot of bake sales."

"Don't be so negative, " MaryAnn protested. "Maybe we can't do it on your rhubarb pies, but we can do this. Among all of us, we can raise this money."

"If only Edgar Halfpenny didn't go broke. He could have put up this money in no time flat," Grace said.

"He didn't go broke," MaryAnn reminded her. "He gave his money to charity."

"Same thing," Grace grumbled. "Why he did that, I'll never know."

"I think it was the Lord that told him to do it," Happy chimed in. "At least that's what I heard."

"I ask the Lord for money every day and get passed right over. The Lord could have given me some of that money. Edgar only lives two doors down, for heaven's sake. It's a pretty short commute, especially for the Lord."

"I think he gave it away because he saw others had more need for it than he did," Happy said.

"Well, whatever the reason, he did it, so let's not dwell on it."

"Stan and I have some money saved," Happy admitted. "Three thousand dollars. We can at least start it off."

"No, we don't have to go into our savings quite yet. Let's see what we can raise first," MaryAnn said. "Maybe Charlotte has some money left."

Everyone looked around at one another, weighing the possibility. A pall settled. They knew she didn't.

"And even if she doesn't have any money left, there's hundreds of us!" Addie Latham exclaimed. "If she can figure out how to get out of Gorham, we can certainly figure out how to get her out of jail."

Cheers prevailed again.

MaryAnn looked at her watch. "I'm going over right now and see if I can talk to Charlotte, ladies. She needs a pep talk. Let's meet at my house tonight at six-thirty. We'll make some kind of plan then."

"Tom won't mind?"

"Don't worry about Tom. See you tonight. Six-thirty sharp."

And so it was done. A plan was in the works. True, it had no clear idea or strategy or design, but what it lacked in direction was more than made up in enthusiasm and hope.

MaryAnn waited in the cubicle in the visiting room. Charlotte scuffed in, looking defeated. She picked up the phone.

"I called Dolly shortly after the arraignment, Charlotte."

"How is she?"

"Fine. She told me to tell you that Skip's fine, too." MaryAnn tried to sound upbeat. "He's doing everything he can to try and help. He's got some lawyer friends in Boston who are getting in touch with your lawyer."

"They're entertainment lawyers. What can they possibly do? Book me singing engagements in maximum-security prisons?" It was clear: Charlotte's depression had crossed the line into desperation, anxiety into anger.

"I'm sure he knows normal lawyers, Charlotte. He's not going to send up Don King to help you. And Dolly told me that Skip is planning to come here."

"Planning to come here? Oh, God, it would be so good to see him. I miss him; I really miss him. And how's Dolly, MaryAnn? Is she good?"

"She's worried."

"What did you tell her?"

"I told her you were doing as well as could be expected. I didn't mention the bail money. I wanted to talk to you about that. . . . So, Charlotte, how are you doing?" MaryAnn asked. It was a rhetorical question. She could see how Charlotte was simply by looking at her face; the sadness in her eyes traveled for miles, but painfully arrived back at its own end of the road.

"I'm never going to get out of here, and you know what the worst part is? The way I'll be remembered. It's exactly what happened to James Cagney. Did you know he was this really, really kind man?

That he was a good father and a faithful husband? Did you know he wrote poetry and painted? He even kept a garden, like me. Remember my garden? Tomatoes, corn, and geraniums? But is that what Mr. Cagney's remembered for? No. He's remembered as that sociopath in *The Public Enemy.* That's how I'm gonna be remembered now, too."

"That's not true, Charlotte. You'll be remembered as the only woman who was ever willing to take a chance in this godforsaken town. As someone who was loved and valued and who opened our eyes to what the heck life's all about. Living it fully and . . . and . . . with love. And there's not a soul who ever had one of your tomatoes who will ever forget how good it was! But I don't want to talk about how you're going to be remembered, because even as we speak, the girls are putting together a plan."

"They are?" Charlotte's eyes opened as wide as curtains, ready to let any hope of sun in.

"Yes, they are. The women of Gorham are going to raise the money for your bail."

"What . . . ? Why? How?"

"How? I'm not sure how. Somehow. That's all I know."

"I'm so touched by this, it's amazing, but honestly, MaryAnn, these women work hard for every dime they have. They can't do this. I don't want them to. I don't want you to. No, it's enough that you want to. Face it, I just have to pay the piper. Hopefully, Bloomberg will figure out a good deal for me." Charlotte looked down. MaryAnn tapped on the window with the phone.

"Don't you go sad on me, Charlotte. Don't you give up. There are too many women depending on you."

"Depending on me?"

"Yes. Happy Turner and Dottie Spencer. Sally Adams Baxter, Jane Root, Sophia Bea, Cassie Winthrop, me, to name just a few. All those women who were in court today? Well, they all want to get you out of here."

"Why?"

"Because you did it. You took a chance. You went to Hollywood; you lived; you fell in love. You did everything that we've only dreamed about. You can't give up on us now. We're not giving up on you."

Charlotte stared at MaryAnn through the streaky bulletproof barricade. She hadn't realized that she meant so much to these women. It gave her a newfound zeal. She was a hero of sorts. Charlotte Clapp, a person who was looked up to! How odd. How amazing.

"I won't give up, MaryAnn. I won't. Tell Cassie and Dottie and Happy and everyone else, I won't give up." If she could have marched to a John Philip Sousa tune, carrying a flag, and done a split jump at that very moment, she would have. Charlotte had made her mark. She had a legacy after all! And it was better than what money could buy. Better than a statue or a whole mountain range being named after you. It was love.

"Good," MaryAnn said, satisfied.

"By the way, MaryAnn, what happened to my house here in Gorham? Is it still there?" Charlotte asked, wondering if there was any money to be had there.

"The bank repossessed it."

"Oh, yes, of course."

"Don't worry. The Auxiliary is having a meeting tonight at my house. You don't know just how formidable we can be, Charlotte. We got that miniature golf course built, didn't we?"

"Yes, you did."

"We stopped that bookstore from selling that book with all those dirty pictures in it. Who was that by, again? Mapleleaf, Mapletree, Maple-syrup . . . something like that. I just remember the owner of the bookstore calling it art. Art! Ahhh. Remember that, Charlotte?"

"Yes, I certainly do." Although Charlotte had thought it was art, and still did.

"And who got permission to not only have those flowers planted on Middle Street every spring but got the town to pay for it, too?"

"The Ladies' Auxiliary."

"Damn straight. So this is just another challenge."

Charlotte smiled. It wasn't quite the same thing, but it was good enough. It had to be.

"Now you go and relax." MaryAnn paused. "Is that an appropriate thing to say?"

"Oh, sure. I got this great entertainment system with a built-in bar. Actually, several built-in bars. I haven't counted, but I will tonight when I run my spoon down them."

MaryAnn smiled. Charlotte's humor was still intact.

"It's not so bad. Just when I think I can't stand it another minute, I remember a Jackie Mason or Joan Rivers routine and realize how much worse it could be. I could have tickets to their show tonight. Laugh when you're under fire, MaryAnn. Dolly taught me that." She paused. "MaryAnn, why are you doing this for me? I mean, it's been so long since we've been friends, and you've just risen to the occasion like nothing I ever expected."

"I'll tell you why, Charlotte. I'll tell you exactly why."

And just when MaryAnn was about to tell her, that booming, gravelly voice of the guard came down like a sledgehammer.

"Wrap it up. The party's over."

"Charlotte, I've got to go. But I'll be back tomorrow, and I promise to tell you everything."

CHAPTER 67

WHEN MARYANN APPEARED in the visitors' booth the next day, she looked different. Less made up, less coiffed. It seemed she was letting her hair down in some way, and in fact, it was down, dropping gently just above her shoulders. She also looked more tired, as if their reunion had taken its toll the night before. She sat down and slouched toward the window. It looked as if she was leaning toward her confessor. Charlotte lifted the phone.

"Hi."

"Hi."

"We didn't get a chance to talk yesterday. And I had so much I wanted to tell you. I haven't stopped thinking about us since the first time we spoke. So now I think it's time for me to talk a little bit about what happened. I could hardly sleep last night, going over everything in my head again and again. The good times, the bad, what went wrong and why."

MaryAnn paused as if she had just come up for air and was about to dive down again.

"First of all, I think it's my turn to apologize."

Charlotte started to say something, but MaryAnn held her fingers to her lips.

"I've been thinking about this long and hard, Charlotte, so let me just get it out in one straight shot if I'm to get it out at all." Charlotte nodded and remained silent. "I shouldn't have held you responsible for T. J.'s death the way I did. I can see that, too late as it is, but I never should have done that. I was distraught. Out of my mind, really, and I needed someone to blame, so I blamed you."

"It's all right, MaryAnn."

"I swear, Charlotte, let me get this out. I've been practicing all night. You gotta let me get through it." Charlotte nodded. "So where was I? Oh, right. When I won Tom away from you, I felt triumph. Yes, I got the prize. But when I was actually married, actually in the marriage, it was awful, and I blamed you."

Charlotte was stunned by this bit of the confession. She always thought Tom and MaryAnn had a good marriage, a perfect marriage.

"I didn't blame Tom, and I didn't blame myself. How could I? I'd have to wake up every day and look in the mirror and take responsibility for the stupidest thing I'd ever done. And the reason I couldn't blame Tom was because as miserable as he made me, he was all I had. So he became exempt from everything. How can I explain it, Charlotte?

"It's like when a woman finds out her husband is having an affair with another woman. The other woman may not even know the man is married—maybe she was lied to, as well—but the wife hates the woman and forgives the husband. It's easier to hate someone outside the relationship. That way, for better or worse, the relationship can stay intact.

"It's too hard to continue living with a man you hate, so you hate the other woman. And to me that other woman was you. If you hadn't been dating him, I wouldn't have wanted him. I know it's completely irrational, but it's where I put my anger. It was easier to be mad at you, just as it was easier to be mad at you regarding T. J.

"But by the time the truth caught up with me, it was too late, too damn late. There was this awful moment when I could see everything more clearly than I ever had before. I could see who I should have blamed . . . every time I looked in the mirror.

"But I had to hang on to that anger, Charlotte. I'd already built a life around that anger, so to let it go would mean I'd have been living my whole life as a lie. It would mean the house I was living in was sadly and simply just a house of cards."

This sounded so similar to the way Skip felt about life with Jeannie. *How odd so many of us live our lives this way,* she thought.

MaryAnn took a deep and sorrowful breath, as if she were exhaling all the days and nights of her life.

"You were completely unselfish, and I . . . well, I got it all turned around, Charlotte. So I'm sorry. So very, very sorry."

Charlotte couldn't bear MaryAnn's thinking it was all her fault. It was time to confess the truth—even if it hurt, MaryAnn wouldn't have to shoulder all this guilt alone. Charlotte knew too well how hard that could be. So she began: "MaryAnn, I wasn't always unselfish, I—"

"I'm not through. Wish I were, but this, unfortunately, is a first in a series of long-overdue apologies."

"Why?"

"Because somewhere along the line, I turned into a really lousy person. In a word, Charlotte, a bitch. I was jealous. As simple as that. Jealous of you. You were thin and pretty and always seemed to have what I wanted. Especially in junior high, when kids begin noticing those things for the first time. It was painful watching you get picked for this and that while I just sort of sat on the sidelines, looking like everything was okay. It wasn't okay, and I was so damn envious. It was a feeling that never seemed to go away. Even as we got older, even when I should have outgrown these sorts of adolescent feelings, I didn't. I just got more jealous. Face it, Char, I wasn't the prettiest flower in the bunch, and I wasn't clever, and I wasn't . . . I just wasn't much."

"That's not true," insisted Charlotte. She couldn't believe the deluge of grief and self-effacement that was pouring out of MaryAnn.

"It's true. I was dull, not particularly fun, and certainly not interesting. In fact, I was rigid. It had to be just so. Like when you color, God forbid you go outside the lines. I could never go outside the lines."

Silently she acknowledged that there was this side to MaryAnn. But this was not the time to talk about it. This was the time to listen.

"So anyway, when I had a chance to be with Tom, I just went for it. I justified it in my own head by being convinced that you killed T. J. But we all killed T. J. Me, you, and T. J. himself. We all played a hand in his fate. And you know what else, Charlotte?"

"What?"

"I know you still loved him."

Charlotte was shocked. How could she possibly have known this?

"I know because I know you. I could see how you glanced at him when you thought no one was looking. And I saw the way T. J. still looked at you, as much as I wanted to deny it. And that was so hard for me to see, to accept. So I didn't accept it."

"I can imagine how hard that must have been, MaryAnn. But you still believed he was going to ask you to marry him? Why?"

"Did you ever want something so much you thought you could will it so?"

"More than you will ever know."

"Well, as crazy as it sounds, I honest to God thought I was going to get a proposal. I was marching to my own drummer, and I was clearly out of step with reality. So, that's why it felt so good to win Tom, someone you liked. I finally felt more worthy—or less unworthy, somehow. 'Wow,' I said, 'I'm getting Charlotte's boyfriend. I must be okay.'"

"Oh, MaryAnn, you don't have to do this."

"I do. I really do. So I figured now we were even. I got the prize. And now I have to tell you that I am as sorry as sorry can get, from the bottom of my heart. Nothing can make up for what I did, but please know how awful I feel for all the pain I must have caused you. And then to make you wear that stupid bridesmaid's dress at the wedding."

"Yeah, well, I'll give you that; that was pretty hideous."

Both women laughed, and it filled the room with relief.

"But I've got to tell you, Char."

"More?"

"Oh, yeah, this is the best part. This is the part where it all gets really good."

"What?"

"I had reservations even on my wedding day. I looked over at you and even envied you then. There hasn't been a day that's gone by that I haven't looked at Tom and thought I married the wrong man."

"MaryAnn!"

"It's just been one unhappy disaster after another. He's always unemployed. We are always at odds. I've lost respect for him, and once that's gone, it's all gone. God punished me. He trapped me in a loveless marriage."

That's why MaryAnn always said be careful what you wish for. It suddenly made sense.

"Why didn't you end it?"

"Because I got pregnant so fast. I felt guilty and scared leaving with a new baby. I was worried I didn't have enough money to do it on my own. I just kept saying that when Clare was old enough, I'd leave. And the most ironic thing? You had the nerve to leave. You even did that right. Well, not exactly right. I mean, robbing a bank is not exactly the ideal way to go, but you got out. So now that you've paved the way, I even think that maybe I'll finally have the nerve to leave the marriage now. Clare's old enough. I think she could handle it."

"I wouldn't hold myself up as your role model exactly, MaryAnn. You're talking to me in jail."

"Yeah, but you did something about your life. You didn't settle for something ordinary, something where you'd look back and say, 'So what?' This is what makes me so happy that you have Skip. You deserve him, Charlotte. And he sounds so wonderful."

"He is pretty wonderful. But look at this situation: He's there; I'm here. Who knows what's going to happen?"

"It's going to be okay. I don't know how, but all the ladies are putting their heads together. It can't end like this."

"Oh, yes, it can. Those are the nasty curve balls life throws you. It could end like this, MaryAnn."

"No. Somehow, you and Skip will end up together. If anyone deserves love, you do. It has to happen. It just wouldn't be fair."

"Fair?" Charlotte eked out a small laugh. "Fair. Life is not fair. It's interesting, unexpected, but not fair." She was thinking of Heather, of Timmy LeBlanc, of all the other children in the ward waiting for something good to happen—because children always had hope.

"But you have love, Charlotte. Don't underestimate that. Oh, God, when I think back, sometimes I wish I could experience this life again. You know, a do-over."

Charlotte knew exactly what MaryAnn meant. She had known when she stole the money and fled. She had to try life on rather than regret everything she might have missed. *No regrets.* Whatever life would be now for her, one thing was sure: She would never feel like she needed a do-over.

"How I ever ended up with Tom . . ." MaryAnn sighed. "Trust me, Charlotte, you didn't miss a thing. Didn't you ever wonder why I didn't talk about him?"

"I just figured you wanted to keep it private."

MaryAnn laughed. "Private? I was embarrassed. He hasn't been able to hold on to a job ever . . . in his life. I don't know why. He just has no drive, no get-up-and-go. Maybe because he knew he could always fall back on family money. When we were first married, he sold mattresses. Then he was a magician/juggler at children's birthday parties; after that, he was hired as a night guard down at the fish plant, but he kept falling asleep. But this next story takes the cake: He invented a nonskid wax for industrial floors so employees wouldn't slip on the job. We thought this would be our break, so we sank every dime we had into it, including Clare's college-fund money. It was going to be good. It was going to be the thing that finally got us out of debt and let us live like normal human beings. Except that six months later, this miracle floor wax started eating through the floors of every customer we had. Literally boring holes through their concrete. We had more lawsuits than Philip Morris. The only recourse was to declare bankruptcy.

"If I have to look at one more self-help book lying around the house, I'll go crazy. Everywhere you look, *Ten Steps to Success, Finding the Millionaire in You, Motivational Exercises in Climbing the Corporate Ladder.*"

"What happened to him? He seemed to have so much potential?"

"Who knows . . . who knows?"

"And his family, they couldn't help?"

"They helped here and there, but I didn't want to get mixed up with them. You know how I always dodged that conversation with you."

"Yes, I remember, but I never understood why exactly."

"Doesn't the name Barzini mean anything to you?"

"No."

"Well, it didn't mean anything to me, either, until after Tom and I were married. That's when the ghosts in the closet began machine-gunning themselves out with names like Guido Tetrazini and Harry the Hammer. Where normal relatives had jobs, most of Tom's were in the witness-protection program. I should have been suspicious at the wedding when I saw so many bodyguards hanging around. Tom is the grand-nephew of Anthony Barzini. Anthony Barzini was the most feared guy in Boston. I mean, we're talking loan-sharking, extorting, killing. When I found this out, I lost it. We had one Thanksgiving dinner with my family and his family. I needed two coat closets: one for the coats, the other for the Uzis. It was a nightmare, Charlotte. After that, I didn't want anything to do with them."

"I can't believe it. That's why Tom would never tell me anything about his family when I asked him. He'd always change the subject. Tom's family is straight out of *The Godfather*."

"Don't romanticize it, Charlotte. Remember when Clare was born? They sent all that furniture up from Jordan's? And when they came to see her? We had eleven limos lined up and down the street, complete with drivers-slash-henchmen."

"Yeah, we all thought that was odd, but we chalked it up to family coming in from out of town."

"Yeah, Sicily, by way of the North End. I was such a wreck the entire time they were here for Clare's christening. All I could see were tomorrow's headlines: 'MaryAnn Barzini has the whole gang over for the christening.' 'Uncle Anthony is made godfather.' 'MaryAnn says she couldn't refuse.'"

Charlotte laughed.

"I told Tom that if he had anything to do with his family, baby or not, it was over. I was not going to be a moll, or whatever they call their women."

"You're right. God, look what happened to Diane Keaton. She ended up with nothing in *Godfather Two*. Not even her kids."

"Charlotte, no one knows about Tom's family, even to this day. You can't tell a soul. I still have to live in this town, godforsaken as it is."

"I won't. I promise."

"There were so many times I wished we were still close. I wanted to tell you, but I was too afraid. When we were really down on our luck, his family would help out, but I was desperate. My job at the bank alone couldn't keep us going. I had to start selling Mary Kay products in the evening to supplement my income at the bank. We finally had no choice but to take his family's help. It just killed me to do it, but we had no money. Nothing."

"But, MaryAnn, don't you go and visit some of his family in Florida every year? When you go to Sea World?"

"Those are *my* relatives, Charlotte. It's not that they're so normal either, but in comparison, they look like the Waltons, for Christ's sake. Anyway, they don't have two nickels to rub together. They live in a trailer community on my uncle's post office pension."

"You know, for a small town, there's a lot going on. Our very own *Peyton Place*."

"Well, it ain't Mayberry."

The women laughed.

"What does Tom do now?"

"Nothing. He's between jobs . . . Now, that's a laugh."

"Jesus, MaryAnn, I keep saying I'm sorry. I don't know what else to say. It's all so . . ."

"No, Char, I'm sorry. Sorry for everything. If I sat here all day, I couldn't begin to cover it all. So you see, my being able to help you helps me, too. It's not enough—I know that—but at least it's something. And I'm lucky to have this chance."

"A do-over?"

"Yeah, a do-over."

"As Dolly says, 'It's all blood under the bridge.' Speaking of which, would you call her again, MaryAnn? Tell her what's happening. Tell her to tell Skip thank you for getting his lawyer friends involved, and try to find out more specifically when he's going to come?"

"Of course I'll call. As soon as I leave here. So how about we cut our thumbs once more and become sisters. What do you say?"

"I'd say yes, but they confiscated all my sharp objects."

Again they laughed, and MaryAnn put her thumb to the window. Charlotte followed suit.

"Friends."

CHAPTER 68

*T*HE NEXT MORNING, the door opened to Charlotte's cell, and Walter Bloomberg sauntered in like an old friend.

"How are you, Charlotte?"

"Couldn't be better." The ache of defeat still ran like an undercurrent through her heart, and the false bravado was becoming ever more transparent.

Bloomberg sat down next to her on the cot and flapped wildly through his papers. They splashed to the floor in his effort to find the right one.

"The prosecutor called me today and said she'd presented the case to a grand jury and got an indictment."

"That doesn't sound very friendly."

"Don't worry, it's all routine. Instead of having a preliminary hearing, the judge will just arraign you on the indictment."

"What does that mean?"

"It means he'll explain to you what the charge is, and you'll be asked to plead guilty or not guilty."

"Today?"

Bloomberg looked at his notes. "No . . . on Tuesday."

"And what happens after I plead guilty?"

"Well, because you have no one to go your bail, you'll unfortunately have to go back to jail and await sentencing, Charlotte."

"You mean to tell me, even if I plead guilty, they'd still let me out if I had the money?"

"Yes. This is common in a federal case, particularly where there are no drugs involved. Why? Do you have someone to go the bail for you?"

"No, but it's always nice to know—I mean, if I ever find myself in this predicament again. So how long will it take until my sentencing?"

"Your sentencing could take anywhere from six to eight weeks."

"Six to eight weeks? Jesus, I'll go crazy in here."

"You hang tight, Charlotte, and we'll see what we can do."

Hang tight. Sure, I'd love to hang tight, but they confiscated my belt. And what does he mean, we'll see what we can do? Like we're roommates, except he gets to go home and watch Access Hollywood *tonight while I eat gruel.* Bloomberg stood up to leave.

"Well, if there was ever an end to Blossom season, this is it."

"What?" Bloomberg asked. She had said it so low, a dog couldn't have heard it.

"Never mind, Mr. Bloomberg."

"Call me Walter, Charlotte. The people I like call me Walter."

Charlotte watched him ascend the stairs and disappear.

"Good-bye, Walter," she said softly.

CHAPTER 69

$\mathcal{T}$HE GUARD WOKE CHARLOTTE. Sleeping had become her best defense.

"You have a visitor."

She got up and flattened her orange jumpsuit.

"Come with me," he said.

"Where to?"

"Going to another room today."

"Really?"

"Yeah, I think you'll like it. It's more open. No windows dividing you."

"And why is this? Rewarded for good behavior already?"

"Don't know. I don't ask. Just do as I'm told."

Charlotte entered a large room of the color 'infirmary green,' with various plastic chairs staggered around.

"Over here." MaryAnn waved. She was comfortably situated in a more or less private corner.

Charlotte pulled up an orange chair. It was hard to see where she began and the chair left off.

"A rec room. I must be moving up in the criminal system."

MaryAnn smiled. "Listen, I have some news for you. I spoke with Dolly."

"Tell me."

"She said Skip was definitely planning to come here."

"He's all that I can think about, and it drives me crazy, and yet it keeps me sane."

"I haven't gotten to the best part of my story yet, Charlotte."

"Yeah?"

"Well, I told Dolly the Ladies' Auxiliary was raising the money for your bail, and she said that was ridiculous. She said it would take too long, and she had the money. She wants to put up the bail. In fact, she insisted on it."

"No!"

"Yes!"

"She can't do that. It's too much."

"She said it was 'a spit in the bucket' for her. Those were her exact words: 'a spit in the bucket.'"

"God almighty. I'll never be able to repay her."

"She's not worried about that. She wants you out of here. It's already in the works. It has to do with putting a bond up or something like that. Your lawyer will explain it to you."

"This means I can just walk out of here?"

"That's what it means."

"When?"

"Whenever the money gets here."

"Oh, my God. That's fantastic. Then what?"

"You plead guilty or not guilty, as I understand it, and then the

judge decides something. I couldn't quite follow—it's all very complicated."

"I know. Bloomberg's going over it with me now. It's like he's
speaking in tongues." Charlotte paused. "But either way you look at
it, MaryAnn, I still have to do time; I still have to be punished for
what I did."

"But maybe it won't be so bad."

"I just don't think I'll survive in jail. I was in jail for thirty-four
years, living in Gorham. I spent a whole year being free. I finally figured out how to be free from sadness, from anger, from hurt, and
now I have to go back to jail?"

"It's not the same, Char. They can't jail your thoughts. You're still
the same person inside. The person you've become."

"I know, but I just don't think I can do it, MaryAnn. I'll be
blackmailed by some woman called Dutch, who'll promise to protect me if I meet her twice a week in the yard for sex and cigarettes."

"And you don't even smoke."

"Very funny."

"Charlotte, you've seen too many movies."

"I can't do it, MaryAnn. I'll go mad in jail. I'll kill myself. I'll die
from a broken heart. That can happen, you know. Didn't Satchmo
die two days after his wife? And didn't they bury him with his horn?
I thought that was the saddest thing I'd ever heard."

"I don't think it was Satchmo," MaryAnn said.

"Who cares? Who cares who it was?!" Charlotte yelled. "It was
somebody who played the damn horn. The point is, even if it's a
short sentence, it might as well be a million years, 'cause that's what
it will feel like without Skip."

MaryAnn took her hand and studied her face long and hard, as if
her intensity alone would beam them both out of there.

"There is another way," MaryAnn said quietly, leaning conspira-
torially toward Charlotte.

"There is?"

"Yes, there is. Let me just think about this for a minute before I
say it out loud. I want to make sure we can do it."

A minute passed. Charlotte stared at MaryAnn until she could no longer stand the tension. "Tell me already!"

"Shhhh. Okay. I'm going to tell you, but you can't tell a soul, not a soul. Not Dolly, not Skip, not the ladies, no one."

"Not Skip or Dolly?"

"No. At least not yet. Later, when it's over. Much later. The time has to be right."

"When what's over?"

"You are sworn to utter and complete silence for the moment. Even when it's over. Even after we've pulled it off, both Skip and Dolly have to wait. You can't make any calls. I'll handle that. They'll all be made from outside of my house. Can you do this, Charlotte?"

"Yes, yes, I can. I promise. I can do it." She paused. "Do what?"

"Because if Tom ever knew that anyone else knew what we were planning, he'd put a contract out on me. So after I get him to agree with me—which I will—Tom has to be sure this whole plan is on the Q.T. Got it?"

"Got it."

"You know about Tom. I told you about his family."

"Yes?"

"Besides the fact that they're total sleazebags, scum of the earth, unredeemable, unforgivable slime buckets in every way . . . they just may be able to help us."

"How?"

"We've never really asked them for a favor. A *big* favor. They've thrown some stupid jobs Tom's way so we could make a little money when things got tight, but they did it mostly for the baby. Tom's never been a bookie or a numbers runner or really 'in' on the family business, but he's blood, and they take that very seriously. It's a big deal to them in that family."

"Yeah?"

"I could ask him to ask one of his cousins or uncles or conciliators to fake a passport for you," MaryAnn whispered.

"Fake a passport?" Charlotte almost fell off her chair.

"Shush! Yeah. You get out of jail, and we get you out of here. That way you don't have to do any time."

"Jump bail?"

"Well, yeah, I guess that's what it's called."

"Jeez, MaryAnn, I have to think about this. I mean, that's against the law."

"And stealing two million dollars is just an oversight?"

"Good point."

"You could start a new life, just the way you were starting it in Hollywood. Except this time it will be forever."

"Can I mull this over? I'm not asking for a lot of time. Just one night."

"Of course. It's a big decision. But when you're mulling, remember this: You won't be in jail, Charlotte. You'll be free. Free as a bird."

"Free," Charlotte repeated it. She could taste it, like a cold glass of water on a long hot day. *And then all I need to do is fall off the ends of the earth.*

"And think about two other things while you're mulling: Where do you want to go, and what do you want your new name to be on your passport?"

"My new name?"

"Well, you can't exactly travel as a known felon on your passport. For God's sake, even I know that, Charlotte. I'm going to talk to Tom tonight. No commitments yet, so don't worry. It's all set in Jell-O right now. But if you decide to stay cooped up in jail and eat food that makes school lunches seem like fine cuisine, and wear stripes every day that do nothing for any woman's figure, and spend every afternoon on laundry duty with a woman whose first name is Frank but prefers that you call her Mommy, well, then, that's dandy. But if you decide to be free and smell the glorious air of a spring day and track down the man you've finally found love with, then you have to let me know. Because if that's the case, then I want to have your passport ready to go."

That was enough to convince Charlotte. She didn't need any more time to mull. It was mulled. MaryAnn had made her point. "I'll do it, MaryAnn; I'll do it. Set it up. I'm ready. In fact, I'm so ready, I'm late."

"Are you sure?"

"Yes."

"*Sure* sure, or half sure?"

"*Sure* sure."

"I don't think it's a bad idea to go to Italy, Charlotte. Tom has family there. If you ever needed help, well, at least you'd have a place to go."

How bizarre all of this was. Before California, Charlotte had never been out of Gorham, and now she was going to Italy. "All right," she agreed. Italy was as good a place as any.

"First class to Italy, Charlotte. First class all the way."

"This is just so . . . unbelievable."

"And what do you want your name to be—on the passport? You have to have a new identity."

Charlotte barely paused. "Lila . . . Lila Nata."

"Lila Nata? How'd you come up with that so quickly?"

"Because Lila means 'night,' and Nata means 'swimmer.' Night swimmer. Skip gave me that name."

"Oh . . ." but MaryAnn couldn't finish her sentence. Her voice was quivering ever so slightly.

"Now, don't go all sappy on me, MaryAnn."

"Okay." She took a deep breath and regrouped, but not without a twinge of wistfulness. "So tonight I tell Tom what we're planning and get him to help us."

"He won't mind?"

"After fifteen years of making me miserable, he owes me. It's a down payment."

Charlotte laughed.

"I think you may be rubbing off on me, Char. Next thing you know, I'll be smoking marijuana behind the Knights of Columbus clubhouse."

Now they both laughed, and MaryAnn stood to leave.

"I think of you as a little bird in a cage right now. And I'm gonna open that door. Somehow, it makes me feel oddly privileged to do it, too . . . and yet at the same time, there's some part of me that wants to cry. Strange."

Charlotte watched MaryAnn leave. That was exactly how she felt. Like a little bird in a cage. But MaryAnn was opening the door . . . of all people. And some part of that made Charlotte want to cry, too.

CHAPTER 70

"*W*ELL, WELL, WELL," Bloomberg said, approaching Charlotte's cell. "It appears you have a fairy godmother somewhere in this world."

"I do?" Charlotte flashed a smile.

"It would seem so. Someone is going to put up a bond for you to the tune of two hundred thousand dollars. A woman named Dolly Feingold in California, and, I come to find out, she's not even a relative."

"Yeah, well, I once watered her flowers and fed her cat when she went on vacation, and she's been eternally grateful to me ever since."

Both Bloomberg and Charlotte giggled as the guard let the lawyer into her cell.

"So what happens next, Walter?"

"There is a simple proceeding that takes place, which merely makes sure that the person signing for bail is legit. Your friend can post the money in California, and it then gets transferred into a New Hampshire court account."

"How long will that take?"

"You should be out of here by the end of the day."

"End of the day? That's incredible."

"Yup. Now, you have to remember that there are certain restrictions that come with your bail. You can't leave the jurisdiction of the state, and you have to be at the arraignment. Remember, we spoke about that? It's where you plead guilty or not guilty in front of the judge."

"Oh, yes, yes, I remember that." This was suddenly happening all too fast for Charlotte. When was her flight to Italy? Before or after she was supposed to plead guilty?

"When do I go in front of the judge?"

Walter scanned his page as quickly as an Evelyn Wood Speed Reader. Charlotte was impressed. *Now, here's a good Jeopardy contestant, all wasted on the law.* "You're set to go in front of the judge on Tuesday."

Today was Friday. She needed to speak to MaryAnn immediately. Tonight she would walk out of jail. She needed to speak to MaryAnn. Tonight she would finally be able to get in touch with Skip and Dolly. But where would she go? She needed to speak to MaryAnn. She needed to pull this crazy plan together in what seemed like only minutes. She needed to act natural, to stay calm and unassuming at all times. But more than anything, one thing was perfectly clear: She needed to speak to MaryAnn. She needed to speak to MaryAnn.

CHAPTER 71

$\mathcal{C}$HARLOTTE WAS SLEEPING when she heard someone clear his throat. For a moment she thought it was Skip, and roused quickly only to turn around and see that it was not Skip who stood just beyond the bars. It was Makley.

"Hello, Charlotte."

"Oh," Charlotte said, disappointed, "hello."

"May I talk with you for a few minutes?"

"Let me check my schedule."

Makley smiled, and the guard let him in.

"I'm visiting on official business. I thought maybe you could help us in clarifying what exactly went on with Kelly while he was president at the bank."

"I heard his little scam was uncovered."

"It was. But we still don't know the whole story. He won't talk. He has this high-powered lawyer now, as does his brother-in-law."

"Is he in jail?"

"Out on bail."

"You see? Where's the justice?"

"Well, I'm getting to that. If you can help us with whatever you know about Kelly, then maybe we can help you."

Maybe, there's always a maybe. "How?"

"The court will look very favorably on your cooperation, Charlotte."

The idea of nailing Kelly held great appeal for Charlotte. She hated him as much as the rest of Gorham did.

"You know, I'm getting out on bail today myself," Charlotte boasted.

"Yes, I know. Congratulations. However, bail is temporary; sentencing is another thing altogether. That's why I hope you can help us. In helping us, you help yourself."

Charlotte didn't know how much weight her information would carry, but she was willing to share what she knew. As much for herself as for the people of Gorham. They had a right to know. "I couldn't quite figure it out while I worked there," Charlotte began, "but in going over it again and again, I started to put two and two together in California."

"Go on," Makley urged.

"Well, I started thinking how odd it was that so many people were opening up bank accounts over the phone and sending in the applications rather than coming to the bank."

"Over the phone?"

"Yeah, it was a new initiative Kelly started. Sounded odd to me— who in Gorham didn't have time to make it into the bank? for some it was the monthly family outing—Anyway, all the paperwork seemed to be in order when I checked it. Funny thing was, Kelly insisted on taking care of these accounts. He'd approve them and personally open each account. I never really got to see all the information. Kelly kept a separate file in his office."

"How many accounts would you say you opened like this?"

"I don't know. I just remember seeing names on accounts that I didn't recognize, people who I'd never even seen in the bank," Charlotte said, squinting as if trying to visualize the files on each one. "What I found odd was, these accounts would be dormant, and then suddenly one or two of them would have a lot of activity. And I mean a *lot*. Hundreds of thousands of dollars were going in and coming out of them."

"Were you suspicious?"

"Yes, especially because it was only Kelly who was hovering over the activities of these accounts. He had no idea anyone had access to them. I only could get in because I had learned how in an advanced computer class the bank sent me to. Anyway, I watched Kelly become these folks' personal banker. But that's not a crime, is it?"

"No."

"That's what I thought, so I just watched and tried to figure it out. I didn't make waves; I needed the job. However, it bothered me. Even after I fled, it continued to bother me."

"So what did you conclude about this, if anything?"

"My theory? And mind you, Mr. Makley, it's only a theory, but I think Kelly was skimming from other people's accounts—real accounts—and putting them into illegal accounts, taking out whatever he could without raising eyebrows, and doing something with the money to make him more money."

"Yeah, but how much money does the average customer in Gorham have?" Makley wondered, as if he'd found some fatal flaw in Charlotte's logic.

"Well, when you think about it, there's about fifteen hundred accounts. There's Christmas funds, college funds, parents opening funds for their children. There's CD's, along with the checking and savings. Add it up. We had a surprisingly good bottom line to skim from, given the number of people, in spite of the fact we're not rich.

'We' being Gorham folks, except Halfpenny, whose accounts were never touched. I checked."

"And if you add all that up, you can see how it could come to something. I watched Christmas funds and college funds go up and down, and I think Kelly somehow deposited the original money he scammed back into our customers' accounts without them ever knowing it was missing. It all happened very fast. And with something like a retirement fund or a Christmas fund, you'd never check. Plus, Kelly would fool with account balances on the computer. I knew that, because in my night class, 'Computers and You,' they taught us to monitor irregularities in banking practices. I was good at it. It just sort of came naturally, and I got so I could figure out when these dormant accounts became flush with funds and went down again. Whatever he was doing, he and his brother-in-law, they were making money. And lots of it."

"We searched the banks files, and every person was accounted for. There were the correct balances, and we could find no absentee accounts opened," Makley said.

"Well, that doesn't surprise me. Once Kelly saw the red flags going up, he knew enough to destroy them."

"So we have nothing."

"Not exactly." Charlotte smiled. "I was certain something wasn't right. I just couldn't figure out what."

"And . . . ?"

"I thought maybe one day if I did figure it out, I might need copies of those accounts. See, like many people, I hated Kelly."

Makley's eyes widened. It was suddenly clear that Charlotte had something on Kelly that no one else had: evidence.

"So, before I left, I walked into Kelly's office and copied whatever accounts I knew about off his computer. Maybe not all of them, but enough of them. Copied the activity down to the penny of their last deposits and withdrawals. See, one of the specific questions I asked in class was, how do you gain access to the inaccessible?"

"Your teacher told you how to do that?"

"No, the sixteen-year-old boy who sat behind me."

"And you still have the copies of these accounts?"

"Yup."

"Where?"

"I put them someplace I thought they'd be safe. I mailed them to Washington, D.C., and had them copyrighted."

"You're kidding."

"No. After I got to California, I wrote away for the appropriate forms. I copyrighted them under poetry."

"Poetry?"

"Yeah, I kept thinking one day there might be poetic justice. Perhaps today's that day."

Makley laughed. "Perhaps it is. Can you give me the numbers that the account is registered under?"

"Got a pen?"

Charlotte had memorized the numbers; she knew them as well as she knew her own phone number.

"Thank you, Charlotte. Thank you very much."

As he was leaving, Charlotte called out to him one last time, "I just want you to know, Mr. Makley, that if I had figured out back then that Kelly was taking money out of people's accounts for his own gain, I would have stayed and made sure this was put right. I swear on my mother's grave, Mr. Makley. These people are my friends."

Makley looked back at Charlotte through the bars. "I know that." But just before he turned to go, he asked her one last question: "And if you had known then what you know now, would you have fled?"

"After everything I've been through?"

Makley nodded.

"Absolutely."

Makley shrugged his shoulders. "Huh," he said as he climbed the stairs.

He could not see the smile he left on Charlotte's face, nor could Charlotte see the smile she left on his.

CHAPTER 72

A GLITCH? What kind of glitch?"

Charlotte and MaryAnn sat in the cell, looking dumbfounded at Makley.

"The clerk that handles the bond transactions went home sick this morning before processing your bail."

"Then get him back here, and make him do it now," MaryAnn demanded.

"We can't. It's after five."

"Not in California."

"I'm sorry, there's just no one who can do it here."

"What does that mean?"

"It means, I'm afraid," he said, turning to Charlotte, "that you're going to have to spend the weekend here."

"Here? As in here, in this cell?"

"Yes, I'm sorry to tell you this."

"This is an outrage, a miscarriage of justice," MaryAnn protested.

"I know, but there's nothing I can do about it. You'll be out first thing Monday morning. I give you my word."

"In the meantime," Charlotte retorted. "I get to spend one more wonderful weekend here at the Ritz."

"Listen, I'm gonna go upstairs right now and make sure everything is in order for you on Monday. I promise you there'll be no mistakes then."

He left Charlotte holding her toothbrush. She really had nothing else to pack.

"Forget about it, Char. I've got good news for you anyway, and who knows? This may all end up for the better."

"Yeah, another night in the slammer can only mean I was born lucky."

"Tom can get the tickets and passport by tomorrow, Sunday at the latest. We can get you on a flight to Italy Monday night. At least now you won't be hanging around Gorham for two days having to answer a million questions. You could slip up and ruin everything. Try to relax. You'll be gone on Tuesday. Think about that."

"Tuesday! Jesus, that's the day I go before the judge."

"Well, you're going to be uncharacteristically late."

"MaryAnn, how will Dolly and Skip know what's going on? Please call Dolly; tell her to tell Skip that I'll be in Italy on Tuesday."

"I'll try, but I have to make all these phone calls away from my house. We have to be really careful now, Charlotte—really careful."

"What time do I leave Monday?"

"I don't know. I have to look at your ticket. It's at night some time."

"And what about my hotel? Did Tom or anyone set up a hotel for me?"

"It's all taken care of. I can't tell you where you're staying. Frankly, I don't even know. They won't tell me, either. But I know they'll give you enough money to cover yourself until you're settled. Tom's family has some connection over there in the exporting business. God knows what they export—body parts, probably. No matter, I'm supposed to give you the number. They can help you."

"I better write this down."

"No! Don't write anything down! The last thing we need is some guard or janitor discovering your travel plans under the mattress. Don't worry, we'll go through it all again on Monday."

"All right. You're right; I'm not thinking clearly."

"I'll pick you up Monday morning. In the meantime, I'll find a motel for you to stay in. We have to make it seem like you're settling in and waiting for your arraignment. It's better if you don't stay at my house, Charlotte; things could look suspicious. The cops may want to know if I knew anything about your plans."

"No, I should absolutely stay at a motel."

"Listen, I'm feeling really bad about something."

"What?"

"Tom and I promised Clare three months ago that we'd take her up to Niagara Falls for her birthday weekend. This is the weekend, and there's nothing I can do to get out of it. I feel awful."

"Why?"

"Because I won't be here to visit you in this dreary place. I'll be on some boat called *Maid of the Mist,* having a bad-hair day, I'm sure."

"Don't worry about it. It's fine. I'll be fine. You've done so much for me, MaryAnn. I don't know if I'll ever be able to thank you properly. I don't even know if I'll ever see you again. You realize, after I do this, I can never return home to the United States."

"I hadn't really thought of that. That's right. God, how do you feel about leaving here, knowing you can't return?"

Charlotte paused, thinking about all the things she wouldn't see again. "I'll miss the way the leaves turn color here, and the way the apple blossoms smell in May. I'll miss the way the snow covers the red barns in the farmers' fields. I'll miss all the ladies here who loved me. I'll miss Dolly and you, and God, I hope, I hope that Skip will find me. I can't even think about how much I would miss Skip. But you know, for all the people I've met and for all the sweet ladies of Gorham, I have a place to go when I feel the loss, the sadness and wonderful nostalgia of all that. I'll have a place that will bring back a happiness that's so special, so perfect, that when you feel it, it will almost hurt for all its sweetness."

"Where is this place, Charlotte?"

"My heart, MaryAnn—the place is in my heart."

MaryAnn got up and gave Charlotte a hug. She didn't want Charlotte to see the tears welling up in her eyes. So, holding tight, unwilling to unlock her embrace, she turned and whispered into Charlotte's ear, "I'll really try to sneak away from Tom to call Dolly tonight, Charlotte."

"And don't forget to tell her to tell Skip."

"Right."

"God, this almost feels like good-bye."

"No, this is just a run-through. The real one will be terrible. Listen, have a great weekend. See you Monday."

She turned to Charlotte one last time as she was leaving. "Oh, I almost forgot to mention, all the girls want to give you a getting-out-of-jail party. Haddie even made a cake complete with marzipan bars running top to bottom and a jail door that actually opens up. I saw it; it's really quite good. The door is made out of Lifesavers. Who'd have thought our own Haddie Bryce was nearly that clever? Anyway, it's all arranged for Monday at three in the afternoon, so don't make any plans."

Charlotte smiled. "I'll try to keep my calendar free. By the way, where will this gala event take place?"

"Bickfords," MaryAnn yelled back. Charlotte almost keeled over from laughing so hard. It was as good as she'd felt in days.

CHAPTER 73

$\mathcal{O}$N MONDAY MORNING, at last, Makley, Hobbs, a guard, and MaryAnn stood outside Charlotte's cell for the final time. The guard slipped the key into the hole and turned it as if he were cranking up an old Victrola. At least that was how it sounded to Charlotte. Like music to her ears. She stepped out and took in a big gulp of air.

"How does it feel?" MaryAnn asked.

"It feels great. Just great."

"Well, let's get out of here. I brought some clothes you can change into."

"Yeah, right upstairs there's a bathroom. Feel free to use it," Makley said, touching Charlotte ever so gently on the shoulder. "I just want to wish you good luck, Charlotte." Charlotte looked puzzled, even slightly worried. "On your arraignment and everything."

"Oh, right, right. Thanks," she said.

"Seems you got a lot of people rooting for you, and I just wanted to tell you that I'm one of them."

"Thanks, Mr. Makley."

"And that goes twice for me, Charlotte. Good luck with everything," Hobbs added. He was so goofy, Charlotte half expected him to say 'shucks' and kick the dirt. But the truth was, she would kind of miss Hobbs, too.

They ascended the stairs, and Charlotte went to change. She looked just fine in MaryAnn's paisley skirt and yellow blouse, in spite of the fact that they were too big on her. She emerged from the bathroom, and MaryAnn smiled. "You skinny mini," she said without the least bit of jealousy. And then they followed the long hallway out to freedom.

There, waiting on the steps, the walkways, and even the street, were hundreds of women with signs celebrating Charlotte's release. They waved Charlotte on as she and MaryAnn got into the car and drove off to the motel where she would stay until it was time to go.

"I wouldn't be surprised if those ladies mint a commemorative stamp in your honor, Charlotte," MaryAnn joked.

"So tell me, tell me," Charlotte said, quickly changing the subject. "What did Dolly say?"

"Charlotte, I must have called Dolly fifteen times, but she was never home."

"What?"

"She wasn't home. I didn't have Skip's number, and I remember Dolly saying something about his phone being turned off because he was moving."

"So neither of them know of my plans yet?"

"No. I even called Dolly this morning before coming over to the court, and there was still no answer."

"She must be with Dr. Cohen. He has a place in Palm Springs. They go there now."

"I'll keep calling her. If we don't get through by tonight, I'll try tomorrow. Maybe I can track down Dr. Cohen in Palm Springs."

"Yeah, there shouldn't be more than two hundred Dr. Cohens in Palm Springs."

"Well, at least I can let her know you're safe."

"And tell her to tell Skip, too."

"Of course. But it has to be done very discreetly. I have to keep making these calls from outside the house. We can't take the chance of having them traced back to my house. Ever."

"Yes, I know."

They drove silently to the motel for the rest of the trip. Clearly, Charlotte was anxious to get the news to Skip. Everything was happening so fast, and already it seemed that things were falling through the cracks. She hoped this wasn't an omen.

They finally arrived at the Pine Tree Motel. It was a broken-down building with twenty-three connecting units.

"Sorry, Char, the Days Inn was booked. Just think of it as a pickup place." They both laughed at the irony of that. "You know what I mean. Besides, it's not like you actually have to spend any quality time here."

The desk manager barely looked at them as he read his list of rules. "No partying, no drinking in the parking lot, no nonpaying guests, and no johns coming in and out all night," he muttered, as if that were going to ruin Charlotte's evening. "There's a pay phone in the parking lot and a soda machine at the end of the last unit. It's thirty-four dollars a night, paid in advance. Any funny business, you're out."

Charlotte looked at MaryAnn, thinking, *I don't care if the cops get suspicious; I'm going to your house.* But she handed him the cash, took the key, and left, the torn screen door hitting the jamb like a fist on a table.

"Wanna see my room?" she asked MaryAnn. "It's a rhetorical question. You're coming in with me."

The room was as unpleasant as the rest of the joint. A faded spread hid the stains on the bedcovers, and an orange linoleum floor creaked pitifully when stepped on.

"Oh, look, MaryAnn, a safety paper across the toilet. I feel like I'm in the admiral's suite."

"Come on, Charlotte, it's not even one night."

"Still, I'm a delicate flower," she joked.

The yellowed blinds were broken and would not go up. *Just as well.* The Formica table poised at the side of the bed sported a bouquet of plastic flowers. The only light in the room was a bare overhead bulb. The bathroom had a fluorescent light, which glared down ruthlessly, exposing every possible human flaw.

"If I didn't know better, MaryAnn, I'd say you were still mad at me." Both women laughed and collapsed onto the bed to go over the plans once more.

"You leave tonight after the party. The hotel is taken care of for an unset amount of time. A bank account is set up in your name, Lila Nata, at the Bank of, bank of . . . I can't remember. I'll give the information to the driver who picks you up tonight. There's not a lot of money in it, but it will see you through until you connect with Tom's family in the export business. They'll set you up doing something so you have money coming in. Joey, the guy taking you to the airport, will give you a couple of thousand just to have some pocket money. You can get it changed in Italy. You're on an eleven o'clock flight. That means you arrive in Rome at twelve noon the following day. A man will be waiting for you at the airport holding a cardboard sign with your name on it. He'll drive you to the hotel. You should get there around two after clearing customs and all."

"Do you have the passport and the tickets?"

"I'll give them to you later. The less time you have them, the better. As I said, Joey, one of Tom's uncles, is picking you up here at eight tonight to take you to Logan. He'll be driving a blue 1998 Ford Taurus."

"My God, this is better thought out than *Three Days of the Condor.*"

"And then, my dear, you will be on your way. Don't call for a while. If there is any suspicion that we had anything to do with your sudden disappearance, they could tap the lines, or worse, arrest us. Jesus, listen to me. I'm beginning to sound like a Barzini."

"Okay. I won't call right away."

"Really, Charlotte."

"I know, I know."

Unfortunately, so did everyone else who had tried to help Charlotte. It was unclear how the rumor started. An overheard conversation? Airline tickets peeking out of MaryAnn's pocketbook at the beauty salon? Charlotte talking in her sleep? However it started, gossip whetted the insatiable curiosities of the ladies of Gorham. But the rumor stayed tight within Charlotte's close family of admirers. The women didn't even tell MaryAnn they knew what they knew.

MaryAnn continued, "So, Charlotte, you know that if the cops make the connection, they'll be all over this. God willing, they won't put two and two together, and if they do, they'll think this isn't the kind of stuff the Barzini family gets involved with. Racketeering, big money, murder, but not something as small as hiding a local woman who screwed up. Hopefully, they'll think that the mob has nothing to gain by helping you and dismiss it as ridiculous."

"But how will I find out about Skip and Dolly?"

"I'll call you in Italy from a phone outside the house. I don't know when exactly. First I have to find out where you're staying. And I have to do that with great prudence. As for you, Char, don't make any calls, period."

"All right, I won't," Charlotte said.

"And no complaining about what your picture looks like on your passport. I remember the first license we ever got together, you were so unhappy with your picture, you made them do it over three times. They finally kicked us out."

"Hey, all that's changed. I accepted my mug shot without a moment's hesitation."

"Your maturity continues to astound me," MaryAnn teased. "And don't forget your name. When security asks, 'Lila, could you open your bag?' don't forget you're Lila."

"Right. I'm Lila. Lila Nata."

"Any questions?"

"Nope. None."

"Then why do you have that look on your face like something went down the wrong way?"

"I just wish Dolly and Skip knew what was going on."

"I'll try again tonight. Don't worry. We'll get in touch."

"So now what, MaryAnn?"

"Wanna take a ride around Gorham for old times' sake? Reminisce about all the places we used to get in trouble?"

"You were the one that got in trouble."

"Not me," MaryAnn insisted, putting on her coat. "You were the one that got caught kissing Jimmy Swenson in the locker room."

"Yeah, well, what about Mrs. Kleem? Remember when you put cleaning fluid in her perfume bottle?"

"Me? As I recall, that was you."

"Perhaps we both had a hand in it. God, what was it called again . . . ?"

"My Sin. Jesus, MaryAnn, how can you forget that?"

"I think I blocked it."

"Yeah, we got in big trouble for that little perfume prank."

"Oooo, big trouble," Charlotte recalled. "No *Magnum, PI,* no allowance, and no playing with you ever again."

"For me, too. What were our parents, crazy? As if they could make that stick?"

The two women giggled like young girls as they exited the room. They left a wake of light, lyrical laughter vanishing ever so sweetly behind them, as if no time had passed at all.

CHAPTER 74

*E*VERYONE WAS AT BICKFORDS. People from the bank, the Ladies' Auxiliary, the Horticulture Club, the DAR, the church bingo brigade, MaryAnn, Charlotte's old assistant Al, Edgar Halfpenny,

Hobbs, Makley, and even Bloomberg was there. Bickfords was jammed with friends and memories.

It struck Charlotte as somewhat ironic that here she was again, approximately a year later, having yet another going-away party at Bickfords. Of course, no one knew this except MaryAnn. Or so she thought. Here they were, the whole female contingent of Gorham gathered around, celebrating Charlotte's bravery and nerve and willingness to do the unthinkable: to break the barrier of boredom and try to grab that elusive ring of happiness. As scary as the proposition was, she had done it: Charlotte Clapp would not die with her music still in her.

Al made his way over. He was awkward and curious and hadn't a clue how to begin the conversation. So Charlotte made it easy.

"How's the job going, Al?"

"Good, Charlotte. They made me president, you know."

"I didn't know that. Kelly hated you."

"I know. That's what's so funny about it. He's in jail for helping his brother-in-law launder money, and I'm in his leather chair with the big window. It's killing him, I'm sure."

"So now *you* open and close the vault?"

"After you left, they changed the system. Everything's computerized now for security purposes."

Inappropriate as it was, this made Charlotte giggle.

"When I think about how many times Kelly bullied you and made you the fool . . . Maybe there is a God out there, Al, making sure things get evened up at the end. I guess they'd be called the 'getting even' gods! Yeah, that sounds about right."

Edgar Halfpenny came by to say hello.

"I missed you, Miss Clapp."

"Thank you, Edgar. I've always wanted to tell you, it was a nice thing you did, giving your money to the Timmy fund like that."

"You know, it was nothing. I didn't need it, and other people did. I just don't feel like I did anything that anyone else in this room wouldn't have done."

"Oh, Edgar, that's where you're wrong. You are one of the special ones. You won't be waiting in line when it's time to go to heaven."

"Good, because I hate lines."

Happy and Stan Turner interrupted Halfpenny by offering Charlotte a taste of the baloney roll-ups being served. Edgar excused
himself to get something to drink and went off grumbling about
there being a line at the punch bowl.

Charlotte continued meandering through the crowd, noticing the
new calendar posted over the cash register. (This year's theme was
Flowers of North America.) She noticed Ernie Amison next to the
bowl of mints, hoarding them with his fat, sausagelike fingers. And
then there were the deep-pink vinyl stools that spun endlessly at the
counter. And who could overlook the little tents propped up on
every table, heralding the early-bird special? Dinner, half price if
you eat it before lunch. Everything that once bothered Charotte only
made her smile tonight.

Was Bickfords different? Or had she changed that much? Was the
grief she had once held in her heart the oppression of a life not yet
lived? Had all that pain at long last been lifted?

She walked through the crowd of women wearing their early-
autumn-theme sweaters adorned with big orange pumpkins and
Indian corn. They must have gotten them together at B. J.'s and
wanted to show them off even though it was still September. All
these familiar faces . . . Some of the women had worked on the
checkout line of the 7-Eleven for over twenty years, some in the fish
plant, and some had never been out of New Hampshire—and all
Charlotte felt toward them was love.

The evening continued with heartfelt tributes and toasts made
with bad punch. It was a night she would remember forever. And at
the end of it, when she thanked everyone for coming, for their support, she added one last thought.

"Well, for those who were here last year, you may remember my
speech." Whispers ran like a current through the crowd.

"But I've had a year to work on a new one, and here it is. Everyone
has a journey in them. All we have to do is take that first step. That's
all I did. True, it was in a somewhat unorthodox way (*laughter*). Who
knows where it will all lead? But that's almost secondary. It's the
journey. It's all about the journey, because the journey is not about

waiting for life to take you someplace; it *is* life. And life at its give-and-take best is all about the love we give and take. So what I wish for you, my friends, my dear, sweet friends, is love. So much love that it can't help but spill over you until . . . until you're swimming in it."

Applause resounded, and Charlotte said her good-nights, moving through the pockets of people and making her way toward MaryAnn. MaryAnn put her arm around Charlotte's shoulder, and they strolled out into the parking lot together, collapsing into MaryAnn's car. She drove Charlotte back to the motel and parked in front of her unit.

"Well, this is the real good-bye, Charlotte."

MaryAnn leaned over and unlocked the glove compartment, handing Charlotte her new life.

"The man who picks you up at the airport in Italy will take you to wherever they've set you up. I'm sure it will be a nice place, something out of the way. Discreet."

"Did I ever tell you I'm petrified of flying?"

MaryAnn cracked up. "No. But then again, you've never been on a plane, to my knowledge."

"Unfortunately, I was on a plane, something called a JPAT, for prisoners. I threw up for five hours. Ever try that in shackles? Not fun."

"But this is first class, Charlotte. It's like being in a living room."

"It weighs a thousand tons. How do they get that into the air?"

"You're just one surprise after another, Charlotte."

"Don't try to comfort me or anything."

"Tonight, when Joey Buttabingbang picks you up, I'll tell him to give you some Halcion."

"What's that?"

"It's nothing bad; it'll just help you sleep on the plane."

"I'm not gonna see Jesus or anything with it?"

"Charlotte, I take it all the time when I can't sleep. You'll be fine. You'll wake up in Italy thinking you're still on the tarmac in Boston."

"Okay."

Then there was a silence, a sad silence that said it all.

"What can I say?" MaryAnn blurted out. "This sucks."

"Yeah, it really sucks."

"I know we'll see each other again."

"I know that, too."

"I called Dolly once more before I went to the party, but there was still no answer."

"Jesus! Maybe she and Dr. Cohen decided to stay in Palm Springs. Maybe they even got married!"

"Well, wherever she is, I'll track her down. If they are in Palm Springs, she'll eventually come home. Even just to get her mail."

"Yeah, that's right; she'd have to pick up her mail."

"So . . . I guess this is really good-bye, Charlotte." MaryAnn was desperate to keep this short. She didn't want to fall apart.

Charlotte lifted her thumb up to MaryAnn, and MaryAnn pressed hers against Charlotte's.

"Friends?" MaryAnn asked.

"Sisters," Charlotte answered.

"No tears, just well-wishes and good thoughts." Charlotte opened her door and got halfway out before turning back to MaryAnn and hugging her with all the rightful tightness of a friendship that had endured the thick and thin of twenty-eight years.

"Hey, need any money, like a couple of mil?" MaryAnn asked. And then they both broke into laughter, as though there were no funnier question on earth.

She closed the car door, waved, and did not move until MaryAnn's taillights faded into the distance.

She walked over to the pay phone in a desperate effort to reach Skip or Dolly one last time. She knew she wasn't supposed to, but she couldn't help it. It was stronger than she was. Skip's number was disconnected, and Dolly's rang incessantly, jangling like the endless throb of an awful toothache.

She walked back to her room, exhausted; she just wanted to close her eyes for a minute or two before she had to get ready to leave. These would be her last hours in the town she had tried so hard to get away from, and the irony was, she missed it already.

CHAPTER 75

*J*OEY WHATEVER-HIS-NAME-WAS banged loudly on her door. Charlotte had fallen so deeply asleep, he nearly had to wake her with a low-impact explosive. She felt as if she'd just closed her eyes.

"Jesus Christ, dey said you'd be ready. What da hell you doin' anyway?" he growled.

Charlotte gathered up her things as fast as she could and rushed out to his waiting '98 blue Ford Taurus.

She made the attempt to shake his hand, which he completely ignored. "Hi. I'm Charlotte Clapp."

"No ya not. Ya Lila Nata, and don't fah-get it."

You couldn't hear an "R" in his vocabulary if his life depended on it. It was as if his alphabet went N,O,P,Q, _ S,T.

"Do I have time to make a phone call?"

"No, get in."

So this was the way it would be all the way to the airport. Charlotte began to see MaryAnn's objections to her extended family a little more concretely. Joey didn't say a word the entire time; he just sucked on his cigar that seemed to be out more than it was lit, and kept adjusting the belt that traveled miles around his gut.

She took this time to think about the looks on the faces of the judge and Walter Bloomberg when she didn't show up for her arraignment. She wondered what the women would think, sitting like guests at a wedding awaiting their absentee bride. Would they be happy? Would they be disappointed? She might never know. She thought about Hobbs and Makley, and this made her laugh out loud.

"What?" Joey asked.

"Oh, nothing."

Joey grunted.

Finally, as the signs for Logan appeared and they traversed their way through the airport, Joey said his first complete sentence.

"Oh, shit, ya goin' to Innanational, ahn'tcha?"

"Yes."

"Fuck, I have ta make a loop. Dis Big Dig has evvyt'ing fucked up."

They finally arrived at Air Italia. Charlotte only had a carry-on.

"Well . . . thanks, Joey," she said uncomfortably, glad to be soon out of his company.

"Wait. Heah's da name of da hotel ya stayin' in, and heah's da Bahzinis' phone numba, and heah's da cash I'm suppose to give ya and da bank dat's got ya money unda ya name, *Lila.*"

His accent distorted the "Lila" so that she thought she'd never hear her new name normally again.

"Oh, 'n' one mo' t'ing, MaryAnn axed me to give ya deze." He pulled a bottle of pills out of his pocket. "Dey'll putcha out so ya ain't all jumpy on da plane. Dat's what she tol' me to tell ya."

Charlotte took the bottle of pills. "Thanks."

She walked into the terminal and turned around one last time to see if Joey No-"R" was still there. But he was gone.

CHAPTER 76

THE COURTROOM WAS FILLED with all of Charlotte's friends and fans. Her lawyer was there, waiting patiently; the judge came in and took his seat; MaryAnn was present clutching her purse; Makley and Hobbs stood in the back; Edgar Halfpenny sat front and center; and, of course, a barrage of reporters held their notepads at the ready throughout the room.

Five minutes passed from the time Charlotte was supposed to appear, and suddenly, the door opened. All heads turned; however, it was not Charlotte. It was a handsome man with blond hair and blue eyes you could see from clear across the room.

MaryAnn knew who this was from the moment he entered. Skip. How had he found out about the arraignment? What would she tell him? Skip was at long last here, and Charlotte wasn't. This would be hard. He squeezed into the room and stood in the back.

The crowd continued to sit quietly like shills at a funeral. But the ladies of Gorham knew full well that the casket was empty. Every now and then, someone would pass a furtive glance but then look down immediately if the person behind them looked back.

The minutes dragged by: 9:10 . . . 9:15 . . . 9:20 . . . The judge, Bloomberg, and the prosecutor looked baffled. MaryAnn was as calm as the eye of a storm. The minutes passed with excruciating anticipation. It was as if someone had wound a watch too tight and the spring finally had to snap. At 9:25 it did.

Judge Cavallo stood up. "It appears that Miss Clapp is not going to show up today, so what I propose to do is to—"

At that very moment the door of the courtroom sprang open. There, to everyone's shock, stood Charlotte Clapp, who was supposed to be gone hours ago—Charlotte Clapp, beneficiary of MaryAnn's grand plan gone somehow awry. MaryAnn looked pale as a ghost.

Cautiously Charlotte walked down the center aisle of the court, as if she were avoiding land mines that lay between her and the judge.

Bloomberg stood up as Charlotte approached. If eyes had the capability to drill holes through someone, Charlotte would have become a pasta colander under Bloomberg's gaze.

"Thank you for joining us today, Miss Clapp," the judge said, irritated beyond the pale. Then, turning to her lawyer, he asked if he was ready to begin.

"Yes, Your Honor," he replied, though he did not look entirely convinced.

"Where the hell were you?" Bloomberg hissed quietly so that only Charlotte could hear him. "I can't decide whether to defend you or strangle you!"

"I got caught in traffic."

"Gorham has no traffic!"

"Exactly. That's when I realized I was lost."

"We'll talk about this later," Bloomberg grumbled.

Charlotte's lawyer stood up before a room of fans that seemed to have had a spell of sad resignation cast over them. There was no way their heroine would avoid jail now. She had already sealed her fate by admitting guilt weeks ago. This was just due process now, merely a last opportunity to say good-bye.

"Your Honor," Bloomberg began, "I have informed Miss Clapp as to what will transpire here today."

"Miss Clapp," Judge Cavallo asked, "would you approach the bench?"

Charlotte stood up and walked toward the judge.

"Miss Clapp, for the bank robbery perpetrated on the Gorham Savings and Loan, in which you stole two million dollars, how do you plead?"

"Excuse me," Charlotte interrupted.

"Yes?" Judge Cavallo asked.

"I have something to say to the court first, if it's okay with you, sir."

"Okay? Why wouldn't it be okay? You come in a half hour late; then you want to have a little chat with the court. What next? Recess? I should explain to you now, Miss Clapp, that recess does not mean milk and cookies." The gallery giggled.

Bloomberg tried to sit Charlotte down, but her momentum could not be reversed.

"I know this is highly unusual, but I've been up all night thinking and rethinking about today, about this moment, and I really feel I need to get something off my chest."

"I don't exactly know what you mean, but court decorum became a moot point about a half hour ago, so by all means, take a load off your mind," Cavollo offered. Cavollo was clearly becoming more curious than annoyed. Even for him, Gorham could be a bit hum-drum. This was at least out of the ordinary, albeit, irregular.

Charlotte turned to the anxious crowd. It was standing room only. People were wedged into that courtroom tighter than acorns in a squirrel's cheeks.

"I know most of you," Charlotte began, looking around the room. "Not all of you well, but we've talked and shared, laughed and cried, endured and survived. On some level there is this unspoken connection we have, be it our town or some history we've had along the way. But it's a strong bond. You've showed me that in so many ways these last few weeks.

"I've committed an unspeakable act, robbing our bank of two million dollars, and all of you have stuck by me. I have to be honest. I was going to skip bail, leave town without a trace, flee the scene of the crime, and leave you all wondering what happened to Charlotte Clapp."

No one stirred. No one looked around. No one wanted to convey that they knew anything. They sat at attention with military precision. Even MaryAnn sat so still that it looked as if she would burst into a million pieces of confetti if someone simply tapped her on the shoulder.

"Skipping bail was the only way I could stay out of jail. But last night, when I should have been well on my way, something clicked. It was as though a stoplight went off in my head and leaving became a problem for me.

"I have to admit I was torn. On the one hand freedom awaited me; on the other . . . well, you know. But in thinking about it, I realized that it wasn't freedom that awaited me at all. I would have still been behind bars, except this time the bars would have been my own. I was running away from the people who believed in me, who supported me. How could I be free with that knowledge? I'd be more free being in jail, knowing I had done the right thing by everyone who stood by me.

"The closer I got to leaving, the less free I felt. After a year of growing, learning, coming into my own . . . how could I run away? Hell, I had just arrived!

"And so I want to thank you all for helping me do the right thing. Destiny? I don't know. But I do know this: I wouldn't change a thing. Not for all the money in the world."

Applause rang out through the court, and instead of hurling his gavel down, the judge just sat there, letting the room revel in what seemed more like a celebration than an arraignment. Even he could feel the strange joy. Finally, the clapping subsided and an eardrum-breaking silence spread over the court.

"Miss Clapp," the judge said, gathering his thoughts together, "thus far, this hasn't been your ordinary, everyday arraignment. So, since we have broken with judicial tradition already, I suggest either Mr. Bloomberg or our court-appointed prosecutor, Ms. Larson, say a few words now."

Bloomberg and Larson looked over at each other as if to say, "You first," "No, you first." Finally, Ms. Larson rose and faced the court.

"Okay. Well, as you may or may not know, our revered ex–bank president, Mr. Kelly, had been illegally harboring great deals of money over the years in Gorham Savings and Loan.

Boos and hisses rumbled amid the pews. The proceedings were becoming more like a boxing match than an arraignment. Cavallo's gavel came down.

"Order!" he yelled.

"It took a disgruntled employee, who was tired of receiving honeyed hams for Christmas, to come forward and bring this to our attention. But it was Charlotte Clapp who helped us fill in some of the details of Kelly's scam."

Again the court cheered, and again Cavallo struck his gavel down.

"That scam not only involved outside funds, but your money as well. Unbeknownst to the good people of Gorham, you were getting . . ."

A voice from the back called out: "Screwed!"

"Yes," the prosecutor agreed, "in a manner of speaking, you were getting screwed."

"Without any of the pleasure!" someone else yelled out. Laughter exploded. Cavallo did nothing: it was hopeless.

"And so, with the help of Ms. Clapp, we were able to gather a great deal of the information needed to track Kelly's actions to the penny and indict him on felony charges."

Everyone clapped, even Makley and Hobbs.

"Now, as a prosecutor, it is within my power to make certain decisions with regard to the prosecution of a defendant. And so, after deliberating, I have arrived at a conclusion." She turned to Charlotte. The only sound you could hear in the entire courtroom was a fly caught in the blinds.

"Ms. Clapp, because of your invaluable help in exposing the illegal escapades of both Kelly and his brother-in-law, it was decided by the government two days ago to drop all charges against you. Needless to say, I'm glad you opted to stay here."

"The bond is exonerated," the judge exclaimed. "The money posted is to be returned to the suretor, and the defendant is free to go." Judge Cavallo was relieved, as happy for Charlotte as he was to have an end to these unorthodox proceedings. He needed to go back to his chambers and have a well-earned drink.

Well, it was as if the governor had delivered a reprieve with less than a minute to go.

Applause, cheers, and downright jubilation could be heard a quarter mile from the courthouse.

Charlotte was free to go, free to walk out into the streets of Gorham without fear, without shame. And a town that was once anything but happy to her now felt like the happiest place on earth. These once ordinary streets were transformed as a host of hundreds escorted her into the new day.

"What took you so long?" MaryAnn asked when she was finally able to get close enough to Charlotte.

"You said yourself I would be uncharacteristically late, as I recall."

"That I did. You know, Charlotte, we should have a party, to celebrate. Let's all go over to Bickfords."

"MaryAnn," Charlotte said, her arm around her friend, "I don't know how else to say this, so I'll just say it: Fuck Bickfords!"

"Really? I thought you loved it."

Charlotte simply rolled her eyes. And as she did, she caught sight of nothing less than a miracle: Skip. He was standing at the bottom of the court steps, waiting for her.

"Oh, my God," she screamed, and rushed toward him, collapsing into his arms as if he were a life raft that had floated in. "When did you get here?"

"I got here this morning. I heard everything. I was in the back; that's as close as I could get to you until now."

Charlotte looked at Skip as if her heart would break with happiness.

"Sometimes the gods punish you when they answer your prayers, and sometimes they just answer your prayers," she said, drawing ever closer to Skip.

"Did I tell you today how proud I am of you, how lucky I feel, how much I love you? Because if I didn't, it was a grievous oversight."

"Oh, Skip, I love you, too, love you, love you, love you . . ."

The crowds were still surrounding their hometown queen. But Skip was anxious to be with Charlotte alone.

"Is there someplace we can go?" he asked.

There was really no place that Charlotte could think of. "Where are you staying?"

"A little hotel two towns over. Let's go there," Skip said.

"You have to tell me everything that's been going on with you, Skip. And I have to call Dolly. She won't believe this."

CHAPTER 77

*N*EVER RELEASING THEIR HOLD on each other, they entered the Comfort Inn and found their way to Skip's room. He waited until Charlotte had sat down on the bed.

"Charlotte, I have to tell you something."

"What?" Charlotte asked, so happy to be here, in this room, with Skip.

"There's no easy way to tell you this, so I'm just going to tell you." He sat down and put his arms around Charlotte. "Dolly . . ." He paused. "Dolly passed away last Wednesday, Charlotte. They think it was a stroke."

Charlotte sat there stunned. It was as if a knife had been driven through her heart. All joy disappeared.

"You're lying," she said, knowing Skip would never lie to her. However, it was not an accusation; it was a plea. She wanted him to retract the statement, say something else—anything else. But it was clear, he would not.

"Oh, my God," she cried, and the tears began to come like rain. "Oh, my God, my God, this can't be. How can this be?" She rocked back and forth, back and forth, but she could find no comfort within her own skin. Skip held her and just let her cry. She needed to.

"Shhhh, shhhh, shhhh," he said softly. "I'm so sorry, sweetie; you cry; you cry as long as you want."

"But she was fine, Skip," Charlotte wept. "She was going out to Palm Springs with Dr. Cohen; she was happy."

"She was. And that's something to feel grateful for. She was happy. She had no regrets."

"Did she have a funeral yet?"

"Yes, in the Jewish religion it happens quickly."

"So I can't even say good-bye to her properly."

"You'll never say good-bye to her."

"That's true. That's a nice way to put it." Charlotte paused. "But it's still not fair, Skip; it's not."

"No, it's not." He held her to his heart, wishing he could absorb all her sadness. But just as much as he couldn't bring Dolly back, he could not take Charlotte's sorrow away. Suddenly, something occurred to her.

"Jesus, what about Jigsy and Pip? Who has them?"

"We do. She states that she wanted you to have them. I brought them with me. Along with Vinny. They're all in a kennel."

"A kennel? Where?"

"Don't worry. I did my homework. There's a kennel in Andover, Massachusetts, that's more like a country club for dogs. I figured they'd be happier there—just until we can pick them up."

"They must be so confused. So sad."

"They're going to a loving home—ours. We just have to figure out where we're going to live. But we can get them as soon as you want."

"Tomorrow. I want to get them tomorrow."

Skip was not sure where they would all go, but he didn't care. They'd figure it out. Somehow, it would be all right. They would get them tomorrow.

"Perhaps it's not the time to even mention this, but there is one other thing," Skip said.

How could there be one other thing? There was nothing more to say. It had all been said.

"Dolly's lawyer called me. She wanted you to have this." Skip handed her a letter. It was a copy of part of Dolly's will. She had left Charlotte close to ten million dollars, which, as Charlotte came to find out, was only a fraction of what she had. She'd left money to the hospital for an ongoing wizard and therapy dogs to continue there, to the children's families who were in need of money to pay hospital costs, to the animal rescue shelter where she had gotten Jigsy and Pip, and to numerous other causes—including her husband's, which got the greatest share. Charlotte looked at the paper and could not understand it. It was unfathomable to her. She looked at Skip.

"Could you explain this to me? I . . . I . . ."

"She bequeathed this gift to you in her will, Charlotte. She wanted you to have this money."

"Why?"

"She loved you . . . like a daughter."

Charlotte lay back into the pillow and quivered with grief.

"I don't even want it. It seems so mercenary to have her money and not have her. Like we're going through the pockets of the dead."

"Maybe you can do something with the money. Something that Dolly would have loved. Something from your heart, Charlotte."

Charlotte stopped crying for the first time. She was thinking. Yes, she could do something Dolly would have liked. Something that would have made her happy. *No, something that* will *make her happy.*

She sat up and hugged Skip. "This is good; this is very good. I will do something with it that Dolly will love. Thank you, Skip, thank you."

She got up and threw some water on her face. The feel of it reminded her of the cool, renewing waters of her nightly swims. She remembered floating on her back and looking up at a sky dappled with diamonds. And now her friend, her beautiful friend, was lost somewhere among those stars . . . or, knowing Dolly, not lost at all but dancing among them.

She returned to the bed, and as she was lying back down, she caught sight of the box she had given Skip. There it was, sitting on top of the bureau. She could not believe Skip had carried it with him all the way to New Hampshire.

"The box, Skip. You brought it with you."

"Yes, of course I did. It was the only thing of you I had to hold on to."

"Bring it over here," she whispered.

He brought the box over to the bed.

"Did you know that there is something very special about this box?"

"Other than the fact that you gave it to me?"

"Yes," Charlotte said, sliding the invisible drawer open. Skip was seeing this tiny, well-kept secret for the first time.

"I had no idea that drawer was there. All this time and I never even saw it."

"Because it was made this way for a very special reason. Years ago, someone kept their letters, their love letters, in this box."

"Really?"

"Yes. And do you remember asking me what the very last thing on my wish list was? I told you I'd tell you one day. Well, I did tell you, ever so briefly, the day I was taken away. But earlier, much earlier, I had enclosed a little note to you. I didn't know if I'd ever get to tell you anything before I died, when I thought I was dying. So I wrote you a letter because, in your words, I wanted 'no regrets.'"

Skip was bewildered. He opened the letter and read it quietly to himself. It was everything she had felt for him, everything she wanted for him, everything she loved. And it was signed, *With no regrets, Blossom.* He walked over to her and laid her back on the bed just as he had that night in the pool. He drew his body around her so close, there were no state lines, no prison bars, nobody to separate them anymore. They were one.

Everything seemed so odd to Skip, as if a strange alchemy were dusting the world with a bit of sugar and magic. And he began to smile. And somehow, through the pain of loss, Charlotte was able to find the smallest bit of relief rising to the surface.

"My beautiful Blossom, my sweet Charlotte, my lovely, lovely Lila Nata. Lila Nata, Lila Nata, Lila Nata. You'll always be my night swimmer. Do you know that?"

"Yes, I know that now."

Skip paused. "How is this possible?" he asked softly.

"How is anything possible? You, me . . . love."

He took her in his arms.

"Love. I certainly went the long way 'round to find it," she said.

"If there's a short way to find it, show me the way," Skip murmured as lightly as a butterfly kiss against her cheek.

"I miss Dolly."

"Yes," said Skip. "I do too."

"She was always this bright bunch of balloons whenever she entered a room. Ever notice that? And now she's . . . she's just slipped away, just like those balloons, somehow lost from the hand that was holding them. If I could have been there, I would have held her so tight, she never would have been able to go."

"Sometimes we have no say over such things. And you know what? She's left a legacy with you. It's everything she always said. "Love is how we stay alive after we die."

Charlotte looked amazed Skip knew this. "Those were her exact words to me!"

Skip simply smiled.

"Why do you think it's so hard to come by, Skip? Love and all. So many times when I thought about life or thought about love, it kept eluding me over and over. I just couldn't seem to grasp it. I may as well have been trying to grasp the distance between stars."

"Maybe because there's not enough of it to go around . . . or maybe because most of us don't know how to get it . . . or maybe because when you finally, finally get it, it's all the sweeter for the wait."

"Like honey from a rock," she sighed, echoing the wisdom of an old bartender from New Orleans.

"Exactly," Skip agreed. "Like honey from a rock."

They wound themselves together and curled up into a single braid under the blankets. She was thinking about Dolly again, and then she was remembering what Henri told her: "You have to know sadness to know happiness. Sadness is a gift. You give it its due and then you move on. Without it, how can you really know the worth of being happy? But when you finally get it, it's as sweet as honey. That's what happiness is about. It's like getting honey, like getting honey from a rock."

"Honey from a rock," she repeated one more time, as if by just saying it she could suck all the sweetness out of that stone until it lay like a whisper on her lips. And then she kissed Skip, hoping he could taste it. And he could. And she, at long last, could, too.

EPILOGUE

$\mathscr{C}$HARLOTTE SETTLED BACK in the passenger seat, newspaper on her lap. Skip was driving her to Logan Airport, for a trip that would be her first time away from him since the arrest. She picked up the paper before her to read the latest column about her most recent escapades. The *Gorham Times*'s lone gossip columnist had revealed in detail every episode of Charlotte's year. It was, to say the least, the most exciting read the town had seen in years, but it still amazed Charlotte to see her name in print. Why? how? seemed to be her mantra. Nonetheless, this was the latest installment in her personal saga.

CHARLOTTE GOES TO HOLLYWOOD . . . AGAIN!

Sometimes dreams do come true, as proven by Charlotte Clapp. As our readers know, Ms. Clapp inherited ten million dollars from one Dolly Feingold, of West Hollywood, CA. Ms. Clapp took that money to build a much-needed medical center in Gorham, New Hampshire, and named it after its benefactor: The Dolly Feingold Medical Center. This came at a crucial time for Gorham, as the town no longer had a practicing physician.

Our Charlotte didn't give it all to charity, though—she had to save a little for the wedding. Dennis Loggins Jr. (better known as Skip) proposed to Charlotte Clapp eight months after their moving in together. The celebration was attended by everyone who had ever lived, passed through, or read about Gorham and its famous first lady. Judge Cavallo presided over the nuptials. Their three dogs, dressed in tails, were unlikely witnesses to the ceremony, while MaryAnn Barzini served as matron of honor. . . .

Charlotte stopped reading for a moment and laughed, recalling the unbearable purple chiffon dress MaryAnn had worn. It made her look like a puffed pastry. MaryAnn told Charlotte, in no uncertain terms, that wearing that dress made them finally and forever equal in the eyes of the "bridesmaid gods." Charlotte picked up the paper and continued reading:

> Mr. Loggins has taken a job at the very prestigious architectural firm of Bookman, Barkley and Birkbeck while simultaneously attending Harvard University's school of architecture.
>
> Ms. Clapp's story is now being made into a major motion picture. The production company has invited Charlotte to attend some of the filming in an effort to create some public relations buzz around the movie. She now goes to Hollywood, not as a fugitive but as somewhat of a celebrity herself. For Charlotte, it's a long overdue opportunity to meet some of the stars she had always wanted to meet.
>
> Finally, Ms. Clapp gave us an exclusive on another important story she announced just yesterday. It seems Skip and Charlotte are expecting their first baby, a girl! When asked if the happy couple had a name picked out, she said yes, but that would remain a secret between three people: her husband, herself and the angel on her shoulder.

The article ended there. Charlotte stared out the car window, thinking about all that had transpired and all that was about to. Here she was, her belly full of butterflies—not to mention a baby— her mind full of memories, going back to Hollywood. Except this time with first-class airline tickets and accommodations at the Four Seasons.

She was nervous as Skip approached Logan. Her fear of flying had not subsided with time. She had asked MaryAnn for some of the pills she had once given her when she was about to skip bail and flee to Italy. MaryAnn was glad to assist and assured Charlotte that they would not affect the baby but would only make Charlotte less anxious. She kissed Skip good-bye, very happy she'd be home in just a few days. Skip patted her belly.

"No muumuus, Skip. All my maternity clothes will come from Victoria's Secret, not the Curtain, Shade, and Drapery Outlet." They laughed, and she blew him a last kiss.

As Charlotte waited for her flight to be called, she took two sleeping pills. The stewardess had to help her into her seat, and she was fast asleep before the first round of mimosas was served.

She did not hear the hubbub of excitement surrounding her as she slipped deeper and deeper into unconsciousness. She did not hear the flight attendant's oohing and aahing over the gentleman who sat next to her. She had no idea whose shoulder she inadvertently snored on as they made their way to Hollywood, land of dreams.

Five hours later the stewardess was rousing Charlotte awake.

"We're here, Ms. Clapp. Time to get up."

Charlotte rose tentatively, like a diver who had gone down too deep and was now making her way slowly to the surface. She was mumbling something, but no one could quite figure out what. The steward brought over Charlotte's East Coast coat, unnecessary in the eighty-degree weather that awaited her. However, the attendant persevered, trying to negotiate Charlotte's arms into the sleeves.

"We do apologize for all the commotion and noise, Ms. Clapp."

"Noise?" The only noise Charlotte heard was a sublime lapping of waves coming ashore from the innermost recesses of her brain. "I didn't hear any noise."

"Oh, then you must have missed the whole thing."

"What whole thing?" Charlotte was clueless.

"Didn't you know who was sitting next to you?"

"Are you kidding? I didn't even know I was on a plane."

"Oh, what a shame. But maybe you're not even a fan, so it wouldn't matter anyhow."

Charlotte was mildly curious and still mildly confused. "Jesus, who was next to me?" she asked. She couldn't imagine whom she had missed.

"Tom Selleck. Tom Selleck sat right next to you for five hours. Every woman on the plane was dying."

"TOM SELLECK? TOM SELLECK SAT NEXT TO ME FOR FIVE HOURS?"

"Yup! Magnum, PI himself, and boy, if you think he looks good on TV, you should see him in person."

"TOM SELLECK?" Charlotte said again, as if she couldn't believe the words forming on the flight attendant's lips.

"Do you know how long I've waited to meet Tom Selleck? Just my whole life! And he sat next to me for five hours? I was unconscious for one of the most exciting five hours of my life?"

She got up and made her way to the exit, still a bit crooked in her balance. These must be the gods of brutal irony, she thought.

The captain tipped his hat as she crossed the threshold onto the Jetway.

"We hope you enjoyed your flight," he said amicably. Charlotte groaned.

The head flight attendant, standing at the exit, found that rather disconcerting. After all, Charlotte's name was starred. She was listed as a VIP under the name of a very important studio.

"Is there anything we missed that we can rectify on your next flight with us? If there is, please let us know. We'll make every effort to see that whatever you need is completely available to you."

She looked at the flight attendant as if he were the Creature from the Black Lagoon."

"Tom Selleck," she said emphatically. "Tom friggin' Selleck!"

And with that she deplaned.

Standing in the middle of Gate C with an arm full of flowers awaited none other than the only actor in Hollywood. Gene Hackman. Charlotte began to laugh uncontrollably. *How perfectly perfect,* she thought. *Gene Hackman welcoming me to Hollywood, no less.* Hackman walked over to Charlotte and extended his hand, presenting her with a dozen deep-red roses. Charlotte smiled as she brought them to her heart, thinking, *Ahhh, how fitting. Dolly's favorite.* Just then an odd feeling passed over her and she was prompted to look around the room. But what the eye could not see was achingly clear to the heart. The roses relinquished their exquisite scent as they had done a hundred times before and Charlotte knew. She just knew. These roses were from Dolly. She didn't know how they were but she absolutely knew that they were. And if she knew Dolly, Charlotte thought, *she delivered them herself.*

In memory of my dear friend Ric Wylie,
who remains alive in my heart and forever loved.
You are not gone . . . you've simply gone ahead.